A BALL IN
THE MUD

A football tale like no other

KEAGAN HERTZ

ISBN: 978-0-620-79880-8

Published by Gaudium Publishing, Johannesburg
aballinthemud@gmail.com

Layout and cover design by Kwarts Publishers
Printed in South Africa

*I have written this book in loving memory of my mother.
Thank you for all you did for those around you
throughout your life Jamecine Hertz.*

*There is never enough we can do to thank you for every-
thing you did for us during your time on this planet.*

*You touched many lives and you left us all
with so much gratitude in our hearts.*

Love you, Ma

*I am dedicating this book to her, as well as my father
and brother, Brett and Terrance Hertz; two people
who love the beautiful game just as much as I do.*

*You both mean the world to me. Thank you from the bottom of my
heart for your undying love and constant support for all that I do.*

You'll never walk alone, boys

PROLOGUE

There is joyful laughter and excited screaming emanating from a small, muddy soccer pitch in a vibrant township. Young children are kicking the ball wildly, their bare feet frantically making contact on the soft, muddy ground.

The hearts of a few elderly spectators watching the soccer are warm as they feel the happiness these children are feeling. They see the wide, blissful smiles on each of their tiny faces, the harmless cuts on their small knees and the sweat dripping off of their eager faces. These children have been running on this soccer pitch for the entire afternoon, making a loud noise and enjoying the intense match being played against one another.

Silence suddenly falls upon the pitch as a young boy is deliberately tripped from behind by another player. His face and hands land firmly in the mud. "Penalty!" is the undeniable chant from each of his team mates.

Every player on the pitch agrees it is a clear penalty. The dark-eyed young boy stands up, wiping his muddy hands on his black shorts and then wiping his muddy face with his red soccer shirt.

This mud on the pitch was created by an early afternoon thunderstorm over the Rustenburg area. There is a strong, warm breeze blowing the bright green leaves on the trees surrounding the pitch; it is an ordinary day on the wide and open South African plain, as the sun begins to set on a late summer's evening.

"Give it to me! I will take it!" is the plea from this young boy, who had been blatantly tripped in front of the oppositions goals. He desperately wants to score the penalty to win the game for his team.

He puts the ball down gently on the muddy surface and looks up, seeing an eleven-year-old goalkeeper without gloves standing between two wooden poles planted firmly in the mud. The gloveless goalkeeper is staring back at the young boy, clapping his hands loudly, trying to put him off; he senses the opportunity to become the hero of his team.

The young boy takes a few steps backwards, sinking his feet into the damp mud, the ball remaining motionless in front of him. He stops and looks up at the lively goalkeeper once more. The score is 9-9 and the game has come down to this one final, decisive penalty kick. Both teams had been evenly matched throughout the entire afternoon of soccer.

"You're going to miss it, TJ!" shouts Sihle, one of the best player's on the opposition's team.

TJ tries his best to ignore the comment from the desperate opponent. He runs at full pace towards the dirtied white and torn soccer ball. He makes contact with it and blasts it high and wide of the solid wooden poles. He immediately sinks his knees into the mud, clutching the top of his head as his team mates hurl complaints at him, letting him know how disappointed they are.

"You cost us the game, TJ!" shouts the thirteen-year-old captain of the team.

"Follow your dreams and fetch the ball!" shouts another player from the opposition.

Katlego, his best friend, grabs his arm gently and lifts him up off the ground. "Don't worry, TJ, it's okay" he says trying to comfort his disappointed friend.

As darkness slowly begins to descend upon the muddy pitch, TJ has just missed the chance to win the game for his team. There are no street lights to brighten the area when the sun disappears beyond the horizon. He reluctantly fetches the ball as the rest of the young children pick up their school bags on the side of the pitch and begin running home as fast as they can. This is to be sure that their mothers are not too angry that they are coming home so late but also, more importantly, to be sure they are safe and hidden from the harsh environment of the township at night.

TJ gives the tattered ball to an older player and then grabs his worn school bag off the ground.

"Are things better at home TJ?" asks Katlego, who knows his friend has been struggling with his father recently.

"It's not nice KT. I'm always fighting with my dad. I wish I could run away. I can't wait until we are professionals, so we can have lots of money and not live in this horrible place anymore."

"You just let us know and we'll run away with you. We can go be the best players in the world somewhere else together," says Nkosinathi, his other best friend.

"Yes! You know you can always count on us," says Katlego in agreement.

"Thank you. I'm so lucky to have you guys as my best friends," says TJ with a broad smile.

The three friends then put their arms around each other's shoulders and walk off the muddy pitch side by side.

"So, I will see you guys here tomorrow," says TJ. "I need to go home now or all the dinner will be eaten."

"It's the same at my house, TJ, but get home safe and I will see you tomorrow!" replies Katlego.

"See you tomorrow, guys," says Nkosinathi.

They sprint in different directions along the wet and sandy streets of the township, with no intention of slowing down or stopping. TJ has become accustomed to the stones on the damp unpaved sand road wedging into his feet as he runs.

There are many green trees within and around the township in sight. TJ barely notices them as he runs at full speed. It is late on a Friday afternoon and his father will be getting home soon; he needs to be sure he beats his father home or there will be no dinner for him.

Whilst reluctantly replaying the penalty miss over and over again in his head, he continues to sprint along a lively street of many adults all returning home from their days of hard labour.

I could have scored the winning goal for my team, he repeatedly thinks. He loves winning and he is deeply disappointed with himself for not being able to run home feeling happy.

He passes a small tin barber shop, an informal stall selling peculiar objects and then a tiny car wash business, where two young children are standing holding buckets and cloths in their hands, desperately hoping someone may still bring their car to be washed at this late hour.

He turns the corner of the street and slows down as he arrives home. He walks past the small patch of sand at the back of the house, ducking under some wet clothing hung across a long, thin wire attached to the house and the wall surrounding the property. He steps foot into the clean house, now protected from the outside world. As he walks into the dimly lit house, he greets his mother, Lerato, and then greets Bontle and Dineo, his older sisters.

"Is the electricity out again, Mama?" he asks, already knowing the answer.

She nods her head disappointingly at her son.

There are many nights lived without electricity where wood is used to cook, keep warm and used as a light. It is tougher in the winter months; the family's old, thin single blankets trying their best to keep them all as warm as possible.

TJ puts his school bag on his bed, which is resting on a few sturdy bricks, and then walks past a small bathroom the entire family shares, entering the bricked part of the house containing the dining room, kitchen and his parents' bed in the corner of the room.

He sits down and, feeling relieved, he begins eating his small dinner at the family's round tin table.

His father, known as Mr Sibeko, has not returned home yet and TJ is quietly hoping he is not drunk again. He believes his father to be a hard and serious man who becomes incredibly angry when he drinks alcohol.

He takes two bites of his brown bread and then the front door swings open. Mr Sibeko walks through the creaking wooden door; stumbling into the old brick walls and haggard furniture of the house. He slurs a few words and eventually manages to fall into a seat at the table with the rest of the family. His eyes are bloodshot and glassy as he slouches heavily in the chair. TJ can smell the alcohol's odour seeping off of him.

Mr Sibeko stares blankly at his family; nobody utters a word. He then lets out a deep sigh. "This world is not fair!" he bellows, looking around the table.

Everyone stops eating immediately to look at the grey-haired man in his dirty orange work overalls.

"Nobody cares about the human being next to them. You are just put on this earth to suffer for as long as possible and then you die! It's torture! And there is never enough money for us! I am doing everything I can! Everything! I just don't know what more I can do for you people!"

The family can barely hear him as the drunk man slurs each word he says.

TJ keeps his head down trying to avoid making eye contact with his resentful father. He picks off a small piece of brown bread with his hands, hoping to flee from the uncomfortable conversation.

Phokeng Sports Complex

Screaming and the loud shouting of coaches and supporters can be heard as a soccer field in Rustenburg is approached. There is the occasional sound of a referee's whistle and the emotional shouts of players giving each other instructions. There are certain noises a soccer field produces that make it a unique sound to the ears.

On this particular afternoon there is one team wearing pure white shirts and shorts playing against a team wearing black shirts and white shorts competing against one another in a closely-contested match.

The grass is dry, the sun is weak and there is a strong, cold wind blowing the ball in different directions when it is kicked in the air. The field being played on is in superb condition considering it is the beginning of winter.

There is a small crowd present as they watch the ball being moved around at an intense speed by the players. A skilful winger gets hold of the ball and he runs down the by-line on the right hand side of the field for the team in all white.

He takes on one man and gets past him.

He takes on another man and gets past him too.

Yet another defender approaches him, but this time he looks up and puts a curling cross into the box with his right foot. The ball curves in the air and finds the head of an onrushing striker who has sprinted almost fifty metres to keep up with the light-footed winger.

The average-sized striker jumps up and powerfully heads the ball into the goals, scoring the equalizing goal that makes the score line 1-1. His team mates rush to congratulate him as he smiles widely.

The game continues and the same winger for the team in all white is blatantly tripped in the box by the opposition. He earns a penalty for his team with ten minutes of the game remaining. The team in black and white swear viciously at the referee.

The striker, who scored the earlier goal, is the team's designated penalty taker. He puts the ball down on the penalty spot. He looks at the goalkeeper and runs towards the ball nervously. He makes solid contact with it but blasts it well over the top of the crossbar.

The small crowd around the field moan and jeer, his team mates are disappointed and the coach is yelling at him viciously from the touch line.

Shorty after the penalty miss, a midfielder from the team in black and white dives to win a free kick just outside the eighteen yard box. The midfielder steps up to take the free kick. He runs towards the ball and shoots powerfully. The ball beats the wall and curves in the air… and he scores to make it 2-1 to the team in black and white.

The final whistle is approaching as the skilful winger for the team in all white gets passed the ball. He is thirty yards out from goal and without hesitation he shoots powerfully. The ball takes flight. It dips, it dives, it curves and it beats the opposition goalkeeper's desperate leap. He scores an equalizing goal late on with a miraculous, long-distance strike to make the score line 2-2.

Not long after the goal the referee blows the final whistle. The skilful winger is the hero as he earns his team mates and supporters a deserved draw.

TJ, the determined striker from the team in all white, goes to congratulate the skilful winger, Francis, who was undoubtedly the team's man of the match.

"What an awesome goal, my boy, probably the goal of the season," he says enthusiastically to his team mate.

"Thanks, but how did you miss that penalty, TJ? You cost us this game, bra," replies Francis, disappointed that the team had not collected all three points from the game.

TJ cannot hide the shame on his face as they join the rest of the team in shaking the opposition's hands and applauding the small crowd that has come to watch the Rustenburg Rovers under-eighteen team perform.

Thulani Jabu Sibeko – TJ, as all his friends and family have nicknamed him – is a seventeen-year-old teenager living his dream. After years of playing soccer with his friends in the township and dreaming of playing for Rustenburg Rovers, the biggest club in the province, he feels honoured and privileged to be a part of this team. He is playing in their under-eighteen team and is on course to achieving his goal of playing in the club's reserve team next season.

Rustenburg Rovers first team play in the Premier Soccer League, the PSL, of South Africa and have just narrowly avoided relegation this season. They were promoted to the top division over fifteen seasons ago and have stayed in the PSL ever since. They do not compete with the top clubs in the country, although they surprisingly finished in second place a few years ago.

TJ and his team mates cool down and once they finish, he and his two best friends in the team begin walking towards the dressing room together. His one best friend, Zavi, is a central midfielder and the other is none other than Katlego, who has been side by side with TJ since they were children in the township. Katlego is a central defender and is also captain of the team. Having spent the last four years together in the academy, they make up the spine of the team, starting every game together.

Zavi is small and agile, sporting the nickname of 'Slow Poison' given to him because he is deadly with the ball at his feet but incredibly slow when he runs. He is short, but he has unique abilities, like being able to spin his passes and shots as well as the ability to do exciting flicks and back heels when he is in tight situations. He has a wonderful imagination on the pitch.

Katlego is tall and thin and is the resolute captain of the team. He is also known as 'The Great Wall' because nothing ever comes past him at the back. He is extremely brave and aggressive, but his greatest asset as a leader is his renowned communication skills. The coach, Mr Stevens, is a very defensive-minded coach and is a big fan of Katlego as he believes solidity at the back is the key to any team's success.

TJ's nickname is 'The Poacher' as most of the goals he scores are near the net; poaching on loose opportunities. His determination makes sure he is always in the right place at the right time to score the goals.

They are walking off the immaculate field at the excellent Phokeng Sports Complex in Rustenburg. The first team, reserve team and academy teams train and sometimes play matches at this wonderful facility. These same training facilities were used by teams during the 2010 FIFA World Cup.

The World Cup was a truly special time to be in the country. TJ went to the Royal Bafokeng stadium on two occasions with his cousin Marley. His cousin's wealthy family had organized tickets for the two soccer-loving children. Like so many people at the time, TJ could feel the difference in the country. He could feel the togetherness and common pride felt amongst South Africans as all issues, complaints and problems were put aside for a month of pure ecstasy and fascination with soccer.

TJ has never had a television so he did not know who the players were in the different national teams but he loved the amazing quality of soccer on show when he went to watch the world cup games. He has always loved going to the Royal Bafokeng stadium to watch Rustenburg Rovers play. When they do not have academy games on the weekend, he still loves going with Katlego to watch his local heroes play. They are thrilled to be wearing the same badge as their favourite stars. Being a part of the academy, the games are always free for them, but the stadium is never fully sold out. TJ enjoys watching the strikers of the team. He decided to become a striker when he joined the academy at thirteen years old and it remains his favourite and only position. He feels strikers have the best opportunity to win a game for their team and score important goals that bring joy to supporters and hero status to the player.

TJ, Zavi and Katlego continue walking towards the dressing room together.

"Sho, Zav's, you struggled today! Every time I looked up you were on the floor! Gravity was killing you, bra!" says Katlego in amusement.

"Yoh, bra, I know. Every time I touched the ball, there was a player there kicking and biting at my ankles!'

"Unlucky with the penalty miss, TJ", says Katlego looking at him. "It happens to the best of us, brother, so don't worry too much about it. It was great that you scored another awesome goal for us today. What a world class header!"

TJ sighs, remembering his woeful penalty miss.

"What happened with the penalty, bra? I've never ever seen you miss in training!" says Zavi, surprised his friend didn't keep his cool.

"I don't know. I was so nervous and I just kept telling myself 'don't miss, don't miss'. It's hard taking penalties in a match; I think it's the pressure. I have no idea how to handle it," responds TJ shaking his head, still disappointed with himself.

Katlego puts his arm around TJ's shoulder and replies, "Like I said, don't worry about it, brother. You've scored more than enough goals this season. The team needs you and, if you ask me, I think the club is definitely going to offer you a professional contract at the end of the year. I know you've been thinking about it. We've all been thinking about how awesome it would be to get that professional contract. I think the reserve team would be lucky to have us next year; you, me and Zav's."

"I don't know, KT. I mean, we have given everything this year, so hopefully you're right and they will want to put us in the reserve team after this season."

"Come on, TJ, think positively my boy, believe in yourself. The team will need you and us! It's okay to be arrogant sometimes," he replies, pulling his arm off of TJ's shoulder.

TJ smiles at the reassurance his captain has just given him and responds, "You're right. I should believe in myself more, but you know how I am. I don't like to get my hopes up too much but I do hope more than anything that we get offered those professional contracts. I'm trying my best not to worry about it, but we turn eighteen in a few months' time. I can't help but think about that moment we are called into the reserve team office to sign on the dotted line. Earning money from playing soccer is all I've ever dreamed about my entire life."

"That's the attitude, my boy! I can't believe how much you've improved since we started playing with you, TJ," says Zavi,. "I'm just saying, you were very average when I first met you but you are definitely a better player now, bra. You work harder than anybody I've ever seen. You try too hard sometimes – trying fancy things and stuff – but your work rate is on another level."

TJ is happy with the support shown by his friends.

"Thanks, Zav's. I don't want to get too carried away, but I have given my whole life to soccer. I just want to prove to everybody that, no matter where you come from or who you are, you have the ability to achieve your dreams."

His friends smile, feeling slightly inspired by how motivated he is to succeed.

They enter into their plain white dressing room and then sit in their usual spots next to one another on a brown bench that circles around the entire room. They sit patiently waiting for Mr Stevens, who will give his verdict on the game.

TJ has been sitting in this old fashioned dressing room for just over four years. Rustenburg Rovers have given him free accommodation and food at the training grounds since the age of fifteen. He stays at the academy during the week and goes home on weekends. He feels he repays their faith with the work he does on the field each week, never missing a game or training session and always working his hardest for the team. He finished school a year early at a home school close to the academy which most of the player's attend. His schooling ended six months ago so his only focus is soccer and a part-time job he has at a petrol station in a distant town. He is a bright boy, but an underachiever. He passed Matric but his marks were well below average and not good enough for a university entrance, not that he worries too much about it. He feels he does not need a university entrance to play soccer.

TJ takes the mud off his brand new red and white boots in the dressing room as Mr Stevens walks in, seeming extremely agitated, causing each player to stop whatever he is doing. He is wearing a blue Rustenburg Rovers cap and tracksuit; it looks as though he has not shaved or slept for a week.

Mr Stevens looks around the dressing room.

"Two-Two! Two-Two! It's not good enough! You looked like a bunch of clowns out there!" he begins shouting. Each player sits in silence, "We were one-nil down for most of the game and then we equalize and we think our job is done, like we were happy with drawing. I always tell you, a team is most vulnerable after scoring a goal and as soon as you scored the goal you switched off, thinking the job was done. You need to concentrate harder after scoring a goal!"

The team nod their heads, each player looking at the ground, hoping he deos not make eye contact with them.

Mr Stevens then looks at the defenders of the team and says, "In my day, if players were that soft, you would all have had broken ankles. Defending in football has gone to the dogs. Nobody wants to put a hard tackle in anymore. We need to be resilient! We need to be impenetrable! You are all so worried about playing beautiful football and doing fancy skills and things that you have forgotten the art of defending. I need defenders who are hungry for the ball! Resilient defenders who want the ball more than the opposition! If we keep a clean sheet, we cannot lose the game, simple. No one tracked their runners or took responsibility for their defensive job. None of you put in any blocks or made any interceptions today. You need to put your bodies on the line for the team. It's not just our defending; even the finishing today was abysmal. I could have given most of you a one on one with the goal line and you would have missed it!"

Mr Stevens continues his rant; each player just accepting the insults thrown at them.

"You are clueless!" "You can't pass!" "You were standing like a statue the entire game!" "Your movement was horrific!"

He looks at Zavi and says, "You were fighting with your feet and the ball the entire game. You need to relax! Your football brain just gave up on you today!"

He then looks at the team's timid goalkeeper, who had made a few mistakes during the game.

"Why are you even here?" he asks the unconfident teenager. "You need to command respect as a goalkeeper! Communicate with your team mates. I never heard you once. Command your area! You need a larger than life personality! You are too soft and you are getting bullied in the air. You read crosses very well but you get bumped off your feet too easily. Your shot-stopping and reflexes need work too. You could have saved those two goals if you had been working harder in training. So get into the gym more and bulk up. At least your kicking was okay today. The good news for us is that a goalkeeper uses his feet more than he uses his hands during a game so maybe there is hope for you."

TJ notices the goalkeeper's body language; it looks as though the words of Mr Stevens have broken his spirit. He puts his head down, not wanting to make eye contact with any of his judgmental team mates.

Staring at the despondent goalkeeper, Mr Stevens notices TJ. "And you," he says. "Missing penalties like that aren't getting you any closer to the reserve team."

TJ looks at the floor and begins to feel the terrible emotions he felt when he missed the penalty.

"We take that chance, we gain momentum and we win the game but instead we miss it and momentum switches to the opposition. Don't put your head down. You need to take responsibility for your mistakes."

"Yes, coach," he replies, lifting his head.

"I'm only hard on you boys to prepare you all for next year. There is no time for messing around in the reserve team! So I do not care if every single one of you hates me. At least then you will all have something in common."

The players nod their heads, understanding their coach's determination to help them improve. He is always angry, never satisfied with the performance of the team, and if a player makes a mistake he makes sure the guilty player knows it. The players are scared of making a mistake or losing a match because of his aggression and ruthlessness.

"Put your shirts in the yellow bag so the club can wash them. See you all at training on Monday," he says, bringing the aggressive shouting to an end.

TJ puts his lucky number 9 shirt in the bag. It is his favourite number as all the best strikers he has watched at the club have worn the number 9 shirt.

Katlego puts his number 4 shirt in the bag and TJ notices a tattoo on his ribs. It reads *'Nkosinathi RIP my brother'* and TJ smiles as a lonely tear forms in his eye.

"When did you get the tattoo, KT? It looks good!"

"About five days ago. I miss that man, TJ! He fought hard for his life and if we don't remember him then who will?"

"I miss him too and you're right. It is a really great tribute and I'm sure he appreciates it."

"You really think he sees us?"

"I have no idea, but I'd like to think he does. I'm sure he's proud that we are still wearing the Rustenburg Rovers badge on our chests."

Katlego smiles with solemn in his eyes. TJ begins remembering the wonderful times he had with Nkosi.

Nkosinathi died a year ago, contracting HIV/AIDS from his girlfriend. It was a sad time for TJ and Katlego who'd lost a best friend and a team mate. There isn't a day that passes by when TJ does not think of his lost friend with whom he shared so many great childhood memories.

The team pack their kits into the large yellow bag and begin emptying the dressing room. Some players live at the academy but most of them need to take a bus or taxi to their respective homes or townships.

Walking to the taxis outside the training complex, they notice their coach speeding off in his brand new silver Mercedes. He runs his own business of some sort in Hartbeespoort, driving an hour every day to coach the team as a hobby. He apparently played professional football in Europe many years ago. He often tells the players he is only hard on them to ensure they are ready for the harshness of reserve team soccer next season. Cut off time for the under-eighteen team is soon and most of the players will be told their dream of becoming a professional is officially over. Their options would then be to either leave Rustenburg to try finding a new club in Gauteng or to try finding another form of income in their home town.

"Will you be joining us this time, TJ?" asks Francis, climbing into a taxi. "It might be good for you to have a drink and forget about your shocking penalty miss."

"No thanks, my boy, need to be getting to work now. I'm already late," he replies.

"Eish, you so boring, bra! But fine, whatever, go to your job. Good luck making memories at work," says Francis as he gets into the taxi with the rest of the team.

"See you on Monday, TJ!" shouts Zavi, already in the taxi.

"You sure you don't want to come? It might be good for you to enjoy yourself once in a while?" asks Katlego.

"I'm good, thanks brother. You know I don't drink but enjoy it and I'll see you at training on Monday."

"Alright. Well, have an awesome weekend then, my boy," he replies embracing TJ with a handshake and joining the team on their mission to the local Shebeen.

The team go to the local Shebeen every weekend to drink alcohol together. They do this whether they win, draw or lose the game. TJ has found some of his team mates to be very arrogant people but they know how to enjoy themselves. A few players smoke – not just cigarettes – and many of them have more than one girlfriend at a time. He feels that maybe their arrogance and belief in themselves is why they have reached their current levels on the soccer field.

TJ gets into a separate taxi with the team's timid goalkeeper and travels to his part time job. He never joins the rest of the team on these outings, vowing never to drink alcohol because of what he saw growing up with his father. He'd tried smoking once but didn't like it. He has also never been a person who understands girls and he never takes the time to pursue them either. He has spent time with them before, but he feels that playing and understanding soccer is far less complex than understanding a girl. As long as he plays soccer every day, he does not crave or need anything else in his life. He is not scared of the judgment and influences of those around him. He is an authentic teenager who follows his own heart's desires.

He arrives at work lacking energy and focus, feeling mixed emotions. He is disappointed with his penalty miss but delighted that he'd scored another goal, taking his tally to thirteen goals for the season.

His part time job is at a petrol station. It is roughly seventeen kilometres away from his house. He spends many of his days working at the station.

He works with an elderly boss who spends most of his days fixing cars brought to him for repairs. It is just the two of them that work at the station. His boss does not say much, but when he does speak it is in short sentences and straight to the point. There is an air of mystery about the grey-haired man.

TJ puts his bag down in the small shop he takes care of four days a week and then greets his boss who is working on a car in a fairly large tin garage.

"How was your game today, son?" he asks TJ in a firm tone of voice.

"Went well, thank you sir. I scored a decent header today but the team drew, unfortunately."

"But you scored another goal? That's great! Just promise to get me tickets to the games when you are playing for the first team."

TJ laughs. "I will, boss, but only if you promise to give me a raise these next few months. Tickets aren't cheap," he responds cheekily.

His boss smiles cheerfully. "You can get a raise when you learn how to stop spilling petrol on the floor."

"It was one time! And you saw how beautiful that lady was. I'm surprised I only spilled such a small amount of petrol on the floor!"

They both laugh. "Fine, but you still need to earn that raise. Take good care of the customers today and I will see you at the end of your shift," says his boss, who continues working on his latest car arrival.

"No problem, boss, see you later."

TJ seldom speaks to his boss, but he feels very comfortable talking and being in the old man's company. He has always called him 'boss' or 'sir', terms of respect his mother, Lerato, has forced him to use. He has been drummed into being a well-mannered person all his life.

He has been working at the petrol station for just over two years. The job allows him to pay for his own food on weekends and it gave him the money he needed to buy the brand new boots he currently wears to training and matches. He is also saving money in case he does not get the professional contract he desires.

Throughout the day, TJ wipes windscreens, pumps petrol into cars and serves customers who would like to buy something to drink or eat. After seven hours, he ends his shift, bids farewell to his boss and takes another taxi home to the same semi-bricked house with a grey tin roof that he has lived in since he was born.

It is just him and his mother who share the house, with the occasional visit from her drug-dealing, alcoholic boyfriend. His mother desperately wants to leave the house but she has not found anywhere suitable yet. Her boyfriend comes to the house every night during the week but on weekends it is usually just her and TJ in the house. TJ tries to stay away from him because of his abusive tendencies when he drinks.

He arrives home and puts his kit bag down in his room. He takes a quick shower and then sits down at the small wooden dining room table to eat dinner with his mother. She is delighted to see him.

They immediately begin trading stories about the strenuous week they both had to endure, using their wonderful ability to talk incessantly.

"I trained really well this week, Mama. I think the coach is happy with how hard I'm working and I even scored another goal for the team today!"

"Ah, TJ, well done, my darling! I'm so happy! How many goals is that now? I've lost count."

"It's thirteen goals and I'm now officially the top goal scorer of the team!"

"I'm so proud of you, my boy. I know how things were with your father, but just know that he is very proud of you too. When does the season end? I want to come watch the last game."

"Thanks, Mama; and last game of the season is this weekend. Kick off at normal time. How were things at the hospital this week?"

"Not good. We are still too full and we can't give the patients the care they deserve. The quantity of patients doesn't allow for quality care, but the good news is they want to give me a promotion."

"Ah, that is awesome, Mama! More money then?"

"Eish, TJ, you and money. Yes, more money but hopefully I can also change a few things. They want me to be the head of the nursing sector I work in because they say I am very clean and that I have a very demanding personality, perfect for the job."

"Doesn't sound like you," replies TJ, smiling sarcastically.

His mother recently quit her job as a domestic worker and works her dream job as a nurse at the local government hospital they used to walk past every day on their way to school. She has always felt helping others is what she is meant to be doing.

TJ is her sixth child and she has always been proud of her youngest son's achievements in the game. She was ecstatic when he was accepted into the Rustenburg Rovers academy team at thirteen years old and she continued to support his rise through the ranks at the club. Whenever she has free time she goes to watch him play. They have a close bond that has not wavered throughout the years.

TJ has grown immensely from the young boy she used to walk to school every day. He does not spend much time with her anymore because of his commitments to soccer and his part time job. He has inherited her friendly smile, bright clear skin and his eyes are an earthy dark brown colour, just like hers. He has just recently shaved all the hair off his head as he sweats profusely when he trains. He is six feet tall with a thin frame; a body his father blessed him with. He is exceptionally fit, but not exceptionally fast or strong. His technical skills are good, but he is not the best player in the team. His mother always assures him that, as long as he is working hard, he will get what he deserves. She always supports him and makes herself available whenever he needs to talk.

After dinner, they say good night to one another and head to their respective bedrooms. Lerato does not have far to walk as her bedroom is in the kitchen. TJ's bed is surrounded by his older sibling's beds; they do not live at home anymore.

He puts the money he earned today into a silver tin underneath his bed. He then lies in his single bed, but after a long while he finds he is struggling to sleep yet again. It is a quiet evening in the township but there are loud noises in his head. His thoughts slowly begin to consume him as they do every night, streaming through his mind at a rapid pace:

I played well today, I scored a goal and that's all that matters. Who really cares about the penalty miss? I did everything else okay. I am the team's top goal scorer. Surely that means they have to give me a contract at the end of the season? But what if they don't think I'm good enough? I have sacrificed everything to get to this point in my life. I should be rewarded for all my hard work and perseverance. But what will everyone say if I don't make it? What will I do if I don't make it? Soccer is all I have in this world. I want to make myself, my family and the people in my life proud, but what if I fail? What if I get injured? I have never been naturally talented but I've worked hard to prove myself. I deserve this. My family deserves this for all the suffering we have gone through. I have given everything, surely I will be rewarded?

His mind continues for hours, creating a circular pattern of thoughts that do not stop. Most nights when he closes his eyes he struggles to cross over into a peaceful sleep, often having nightmares and waking up in a cold sweat worrying about his future or reliving his tragic past. On the nights he struggles, he puts his tracksuit on and jogs around the township in an attempt to take his mind off his endless thoughts.

He has countless conversations in his head, with rhetorical ques-tions that are never answered. The only time his mind is quiet is when he is on a soccer field. A soccer field is where he feels most alive.

He is trying to learn how to live with the noise machine in his head but, no matter how hard he tries, he cannot seem to rid himself of the edgy and nervous mood he is in as the season draws to a close. He is deeply worried he will not receive a professional contract. The time is coming for him to find a full time job so he can move out of the house and start providing for himself. There is only one game left in the season for him to prove to the academy that he deserves a chance to play in the reserve team.

Still tossing and turning in his bed he decides to pray to ask for help and answers from God. He does this every night in the hope that he will receive some form of guidance, but he never does.

He closes his eyes, clutches his hands together and asks, "Why didn't You just make me talented? Why do so many other people have all these wonderful natural skills but You have made me work so hard to improve? All these people have such nice things in their lives but You have given me nothing. You have given me nothing but pain and suffering. Why have You made it so difficult for me? I am trying so hard to make You and my family proud; I am giving everything I can. Please help me, please; I am in desperate need of Your help."

TJ opens his eyes and looks up at the tin roof.

There is complete silence; still no answer from God. He shakes his head disappointedly and begins to stress as he needs to wake up early for his job in the morning.

He needs to prepare for another week of training ahead. The team needs to prepare for their next game. He needs to be ready for any remaining challenges he may face if he is going to prove he deserves to be selected in the reserve team.

"I hope I can do this," he says, lying alone in his room staring at the tin ceiling.

TJ works hard throughout the day on Sunday, despite feeling ex-hausted from his sleepless night. He then travels to the academy, has dinner with a few of his team mates and gets into bed early. He listens to the local radio station in his single bedroom, trying his best to fall sleep.

Monday, he wakes up at 09:00, has breakfast with his team mates and then jogs out onto the field at 10:00. The frost has melted off the grass on the field and the players jog around the pitch to warm up. Mr Stevens arrives and begins the training session. He has the team working on defensive structure throughout the session. The defenders are taught to mark the attackers tightly, the midfielders are taught to mark the correct zones and the attackers are taught to close the angles for the opposition defenders to pass. The session lasts just under two hours; each player being reprimanded and pushed by Mr Stevens. TJ trains hard and spends the rest of the day listening to music, also spending time with team mates.

Tuesday, the team goes through the exact same training routine, the players being taught the importance of resilient defending. A few members of the team go to gym and TJ joins them, hoping to add more muscle to his lean body.

Wednesday, the team do fitness and passing drills, the players being pushed to their physical limits and learning to keep the ball under pressure. TJ impresses in the fitness exercises and manages in the passing drills.

Thursday is another day of fitness and passing drills as the players are put through the same regime as the previous day. Mr Stevens encourages the players to play long ball, hoping to play soccer in the oppositions half for as long as possible. It is another two-hour session and a few players go to the gym with TJ joining them again. He has worked hard and trained well throughout the week, hopefully cementing his place in the starting eleven for the penultimate game of the season.

On Friday, the team do a crossing and shooting drill for half an hour and then spend an hour playing a practice match, practising staying in shape, communicating effectively and executing the game plan for the match tomorrow. After the match, Mr Stevens calls all the players in.

"Your attitudes need to be spot on for tomorrow! With the right attitude we can achieve anything. The most talented players I have coached have never gone on to play professionally because they never had to fight a day in their lives! Life has always been too easy for them. The fighters, the great attitudes, the hungry players are the ones who go on to play professionally! So that is what I want tomorrow, lads! Hungry players, fighters, and players giving everything they have to win the game!"

The players nod their heads and agree frantically, feeling inspired by their coach's words.

Mr Stevens then spends another ten minutes talking about the opposition, preparing the players for their biggest game of the season. A first place finish in a very competitive academy league will look good on his CV as well as each player's CV moving forward.

The players spend the remainder of the day resting; keeping their bodies and minds fresh for the game. TJ spends the day with his team mates, talking excitedly about what they will do on the field tomorrow. TJ is desperate to add another goal to his collection. The team talk right into the early hours of the evening; talking openly with one another, feeling confident they will finish first in the league. There is real belief amongst the players.

On Saturday, the entire team arrives in the dressing room, putting on shin pads and socks in preparation for the vital encounter.

"We can do this, boys! The first Rustenburg Rovers academy team to win the league in five years," Katlego shouts passionately to TJ and Zavi.

"Yes, we can. Let's give it everything we have today, gents. One more big push and the league title is ours," says Zavi.

TJ smiles, feeling nerves and excitement all at once. He is tapping his leg up and down, agitated and raring to get onto the field, like a wild animal desperately waiting to be released into its natural habitat.

Mr Stevens enters the dressing room seeming confident. He looks around at the young talent in front of him.

"You need to play without fear today, lads! Be confident in yourselves. We finish first with a win today! Keep your shape and win your individual battles on the field, be comfortable on the ball and, most importantly, give it your best! That's all I can ever ask of any of you."

The players gear themselves up as Mr Stevens adds, "Don't forget to tuck in your shirts; you must look professional out there!"

"Come on, boys!" Katlego shouts to the team as they run onto the field ready to entertain the crowd and be remembered as one of the best academy teams the club has had.

TJ waves to his mother in the stands, the team has one final pep talk and TJ then runs to take kick off, ready to give everything he has for the team. He passes to Zavi and the game is underway as Rustenburg Rovers adopt the strategy of playing long balls immediately.

Ten minutes into the game, TJ receives the ball on the halfway line. He wants to play short but changes his mind and attempts a long pass to the left winger. It is intercepted.

"What's the plan there, TJ? That was telegraphed; he read you like a book!" shouts Mr Stevens as TJ then hunts the ball down, trying to win it back for his team – and he does. He passes it to a team mate but not long after that the opposition have the ball again. The opponents are dominating possession.

When they are attacking, TJ is trying to be an option for his team mates as often as he can, but the opposition centre back is marking him tightly, not giving him any free space. It is a while before he receives the ball but he eventually gets passed the ball on the edge of the opposition box. He thinks what to do on the ball for a short moment, looks around for his team mates and then decides to turn. He attempts to dribble the opponent but he is tackled with ease; a poorly-timed skill.

The opposition clear the ball, but it is picked up by Zavi who instinctively plays a through ball for TJ. He sprints into the space and he just manages to get to the ball as the opposition defender catches up to him. He runs with the ball, slightly unconfidently, not knowing what he wants to do with it as he struggles to hold off the opponent. He loses his balance slightly and the ball is kicked out of play for a throw in. He shouts loudly, upset with himself.

The opposition continue to dominate possession but Katelgo and his troops are defending with incredible aggression, not allowing the opposition near the goals. They have been defiant at the back.

Just before the first half ends, TJ receives the ball on the edge of the box again. This time he turns quickly onto his left foot. He has a gap to shoot but turns back onto his stronger right and manages to get a shot away, but it is soft and straight at the goalkeeper. He did well to create the space for himself but his shot was harmless.

The first half ends 0-0, with tough defending from Katlego and the rest of the defenders at the back. The opposition have been dominating the play, creating more chances than Rustenburg Rovers.

The players still feel fresh, their fitness levels not waning on them. The game is on a knife's edge.

"Brilliant defensive work, gentlemen! But we need to relax on the ball a bit more. Let's simplify our game and, another thing: what kind of chances are we creating? We need to know what we want to do in attack. Cross, one-twos, through balls? We need to decide! We were just playing and hoping for the best, hoping to create chances!" Mr Stevens shouts fanatically in the dressing room.

The whole team focuses their entire attention on their passionate coach.

"All this game needs is a hero. It is crying out for somebody to take it by the scruff of the neck! Who wants to be the hero today?" TJ feels inspired, wanting to be the player who wins this important game for his team.

The second half begins brightly for Rustenburg Rovers as they manage to retain the ball better, creating clearer-cut opportunities for themselves. They have asserted their dominance and the game has swung in their favour. TJ is playing well, doing as much as he can up front for the team.

Twenty-five minutes remain as the ball gets passed across the edge of the box by the left winger on the left hand side of the field. TJ runs towards the ball; he hears a loud shout from Zavi and he dummies the ball on the edge of the eighteen-yard box.

Zavi takes a great first touch away from the defender; he sets his sights and shoots immediately. The ball curves, the opposition goalkeeper dives desperately to his left as the ball curls into the bottom, right hand corner of the goals.

Rustenburg Rovers take the lead!

Their jubilant players sprint after Zavi to congratulate their goal scorer. TJ runs after his best friend who has run to the corner flag to celebrate. The team do a dance routine, smiling and enjoying the incredible moment shared together. TJ and Zavi hug each other passionately, smiling widely.

"Great dummy there, brother!" shouts Zavi, rubbing the top of TJ's head.

Mr Stevens applauds both of them as they make their way back to the half way line.

The game continues with the players doing everything in their power to protect their one goal cushion. The opposition are struggling to break them down as TJ continues to do everything he can up front for his team. He misplaces a pass with his left foot and shortly after that he is substituted with ten minutes of the game to go. He applauds the few supporters at the ground and taps the hand of the striker replacing him.

Sibongile, a player sitting on the bench, hands TJ a bib and looks at him.

"Yoh! You sweating badly, TJ bra, you look like a river. How hard were you working out there?"

"I gave everything but I hate it when I don't score," replies TJ still panting heavily.

"Chill brother, you did well. When it's not your day, it's not your day."

TJ nods his head, feeling it was an average performance according to his own standards.

There are a few more chances created by the team, and a few scary moments where they almost concede an equalizer, but the game finishes 1-0 to Rustenburg Rovers; a game of two halves with Rustenburg Rovers dominating the second half's proceedings. The players are ecstatic, extremely proud of their efforts throughout the thirty-game season.

The victory ensures the team finish top of the league. TJ ends the game without a goal but he ends as the top goal-scorer of the team with thirteen goals. He feels content, feeling he has done enough to prove to Mr Stevens that he is worthy of a place in the reserve team and a professional contract. Sitting on the bench in the dressing room after the game, talking excitedly about the future, his best friends feel the same way.

"We've done it, gents! I can't believe it! League champions! The team couldn't have done it without us," says Katlego, proud of captaining the team.

"Yes, we did, boys! Just imagine what we will be doing to teams next year. We're going to be the kings of the reserve team. Girls are going to want us, we going to be earning good money; it's the start of everything we have been dreaming of since we joined the academy together. They have to keep all three of us. They can't change a winning formula," says Zavi, with a huge excited smile on his face.

"It's going to be incredible! I'm going to double my goal tally next year with you boys behind me again!" shouts TJ in a confident tone.

"The Poacher!" shouts Zavi, laughing.

"The Great Wall, Slow Poison and The Poacher: the deadly trio," says Katlego with a wide smile.

TJ grins, trying to hide the whirlwind of emotions flowing through his entire body. He is confident of keeping his dream alive by moving up the ranks at the club, but is still feeling slightly anxious about not making it. Before he can say anything in reply to his friends, Mr Stevens walks into the dressing room, in a far more cheerful mood than usual. He smiles excitedly at the players.

"Congratulations on your first placed finish, lads. It's a wonderful achievement for this team and the club! We finished above some very reputable teams, which is a great advertisement for all of us. You made yourselves proud and you made me proud. Many of you have staked your claim to be involved in the reserve team next year."

A few of the players begin smiling proudly as Mr Stevens continues, "There is a meeting next week Saturday, in this dressing room, where all twenty-three of you will learn your fate for next season. The players chosen will report back here in five weeks' time to begin pre-season with the reserves. I have a fairly good idea who has what it takes to play at that level, but the coaching staff and I are going to take the week to discuss everything to make sure we make the best possible decision for the club. So, have a great week with your families and be back here next week Saturday. A big thank you to all of you for your wonderful efforts throughout the season, every single one of you mattered."

Mr Stevens shakes each player's hand as they leave the dressing room to thank them for their hard work throughout the year.

"Well done, TJ, a very good season," he says shaking his hand firmly.

"Thanks coach, I just hope I've done enough, I love this club with all my heart."

"You will have to wait and see, but you did yourself proud this year none the less."

TJ nods his head and then says goodbye to his best friends and team mates. He will not be joining them at the local shebeen for the end of year celebrations.

In one week's time, TJ's fate and the fate of all his team mates will be decided by the club. All he needs to do in this week is remain calm and hope for the best, although he is certain there are a few sleepless nights ahead.

· 2 ·

D-Day
....

The Rustenburg Rovers players are sitting huddled tightly around one another in the dressing room.

The tension can be felt in the air.

There is the sound of a few murmurs floating around the plain white room, but none of the players is speaking too loudly. Some players are sitting arrogantly, unconcerned about their role in the future plans of the club. Others sit nervously rubbing their hands together or blowing hot air into them. The cold, dry wind blowing outside the dressing room has left their hands ice cold. The grass on the field, which was green for most of the season, is now entirely yellow. The lifeless winter sun shines dimly through the one dressing room window, with each player silently waiting for Mr Stevens to enter.

TJ is sitting next to Zavi and Katlego, nervously bouncing his right leg up and down. He is proudly wearing his white Rustenburg Rovers training kit given to him to keep for life. He also has a bag with his boots in them, as the whole team is going to have one more match together before they leave for their post-season break. They know they might never see one another again.

There is a ball of nerves sitting in the pit of TJ's stomach and he knows it will only disappear when he receives the answer to whether he has made the reserve team or not.

"I have to make it, I have to. There is nothing more I could have done this year," he whispers to himself.

After what feels like an eternity, Mr Stevens eventually enters the edgy dressing room, looking far less angry and uptight than the players are used to seeing him.

He looks around at his team and slowly removes his Rustenburg Rovers cap so that his thin, messy hair is revealed. There is pure emotion showing on his face and there are heavy dark blue rings underneath his eyes.

"This for me is the worst day of the year, lads," he begins saying to the players. He clears his throat, rubs his hand vigorously through his hair and continues, "I do not want to end any of your football careers today but the sad fact of the matter is that I will be doing so. Most of the players sitting here will most probably not have a chance of becoming professional footballers anymore. It isn't enjoyable but sometimes in life we have to do the wrong things for the right reasons."

TJ gulps and looks towards the floor, not wanting to make eye contact with Mr Stevens in case his eyes give away the answer of where his future lies.

"Calm down and think positively," he whispers again.

Mr Stevens continues. "Just remember, it doesn't matter what happens to you in life, it matters what you do about it. It's not the size of the dog in the fight but the size of the fight in the dog. Every single day is an opportunity for you to improve so this does not have to be the end of the road for any of you. There are other pathways for you to take on your football journeys. Those new journeys can be discussed with me at any time if you are not offered a contract with us."

He pauses for a brief moment to sense the mood in the room and then continues. "I have the duty of doing what is best for this football club, not you boys, and although I am grateful for the effort and hard work each of you has put in for me and your team mates throughout the year, the football club comes first. To the players who have been chosen, I am very enthusiastic about your futures at the club. Each of you is a wonderful talent and your place in the team next year is justly deserved. Now, remember your attitude will determine your altitude; with a great attitude you can achieve anything you want in life. You will always get what you deserve with a great attitude."

Mr Stevens continues to ramble on, praising the players who have been chosen as well as trying to justify his choices; trying to explain the tough decisions he has had to make in this past week.

He eventually pulls out a piece of paper from his pocket and says, "Congratulations to those who have been selected. These players must please report to pre-season training in four weeks time."

He begins reading out the names of the players on the piece of paper: one name, another name and another. He continues as TJ waits patiently in anticipation of the news. He then abruptly finishes reading after the tenth name on the list is called out.

TJ looks up from his feet at his two best friend's delighted faces and suddenly realizes his name was not called out by Mr Stevens.

"TJ bra, I'm so sorry," says Katlego immediately trying to counsel him for not being chosen.

His heart sinks.

The world has just become a cruel and dark place with no hope, no joy and no way out of his nightmare existence. The total despair he is feeling is suddenly replaced by a burning and uncontrollable rage.

"Why?" he screeches, without realizing what he is doing. He stands up, takes his brand new boots out of his bag and throws them brutally against the dressing room wall, with no intention of picking them up.

"Relax brother," says Zavi trying to calm him down.

Mr Stevens looks at him, showing an understanding of the pain he must be feeling.

"I'm sorry, TJ. You don't handle pressure well and you are too slow. I know you were our top goal scorer, but the club already has four strikers in the reserve team, all better than you are. I think you are a wonderful boy, everybody loves you, you work incredibly hard, but you are not good enough to play further at this club."

TJ walks towards his coach, looks him in the eyes, a sign of disrespect in his culture and says, "You have just ruined my entire life". He picks up his bag and sprints out of the dressing room as fast as he can.

"TJ! Come back!" screams Katlego, but he ignores his best friend.

He leaves his boots behind and turns his back on his now former team mates with no intention of ever going back, beginning a difficult and lengthy run home.

"I will never kick another soccer ball in my life ever again," he vows as he runs, ignoring the pain in his legs and heart.

He arrives home and slams open the front door of the house. He drops his bag by the front door and lies on his bed, feeling utterly empty. He swears and screams into his pillow, hitting and punching it as if it were the cause of all his pain and misery.

His rage is gradually replaced by gentle tears. He has not cried since he was a young boy. Everything he has lived for his entire life has just come to an end and it feels as though he has wasted his entire life chasing a fantasy. He puts his face into his pillow as the tears slowly fall onto the soft blue cushion fabric.

"Why me, God? Why are You doing this to me? Why was I even born? Please help me. I need You! I can't take this pain anymore, please take it away! Please! I can't handle anymore suffering in my life!"

There is silence.

The intense depression he is feeling is replaced by anger once more as he throws his pillow onto the floor.

He stands up and aggressively kicks the bricks his bed is resting on, blasting them with a ferocious temper. He kicks his siblings' former beds and then moves into the bricked part of the house, breaking the rest of the furniture. He throws food from the shelves onto the floor and onto the walls, destructively breaking parts of the entire room.

He throws a tea cup against the wall and another and another. He throws a fourth cup and suddenly realizes what he is doing and looks around at the chaos he has caused. He calms down, feeling disgusted with himself as he looks around at the damage around him. There is glass, food and broken wood everywhere.

He returns to his bedroom, desperately wanting to just end his nightmare. He lies on his pillow on the floor, his rage cools and he falls asleep feeling emotionally drained.

Lerato arrives home late in the evening to find her entire house looking as if a herd of angry elephants has just stampeded through it. She sees her son sleeping on the floor of his bedroom. In complete shock, she stands in the doorway with no idea what to say or do. She assumes TJ is the culprit as she knows they were announcing the reserve team squad and bad news would have upset her son deeply.

He has broken the table, damaged the front door, thrown food all over the floor and broken the beds.

She begins trying to fix everything as fast as she can, in case her boyfriend comes home. She knows how angry and violent he can get, especially if he has been out drinking. If he sees the place in this state there is no doubt he will take it out on her or her son. He has lost his temper before for far less serious reasons.

She does her utmost to fix TJ's mess but all her efforts are in vain as her boyfriend walks through the front door to find her on her hands and knees picking up food off the floor.

"Who did this, Lerato?" he shouts aggressively, slurring those four simple words.

"I don't know. I came home and someone must of..."

He ignores her and marches straight towards TJ's bedroom. He pulls the sleeping teenager off the floor.

"Who did this, boy?"

TJ remains silent, looking through his still teary and gloomy eyes at the violent man clutching his arm tightly; unmoved by his terrifying aggression

"I'm going to ask you one more time! Who did this?"

"What do you care? This is not even your house?"

The drunk man snarls at TJ and without hesitation he slaps him across the face; the teenager hits the floor.

"No! Stop!" screams Lerato in desperation.

TJ gets onto his hands and knees, wobbles his head and slowly stands up.

He then looks at the vicious man in front of him and, for the first time in his life, he feels no fear. He feels he has nothing else to live for. All he has to look forward to is a life of trying to survive in a township that does not care whether he exists or not.

"Never disrespect me again, do you understand me, boy?"

"I don't have to do anything. I'm tired of this! If you want to hit me, hit me! I don't care! I'm not scared of you!" he shouts back at the violent man.

The man grinds his teeth and looks at TJ with a burning fire in his eyes. He lifts his hand and hits the teenager with far more force than before.

"Please, no more!" shouts Lerato bursting into tears as she begins pulling back on the giant man's shoulders. "Please stop!" she screams again; begging him to end the cruelty.

He swings his arm around sharply and hits her to the ground.

TJ jumps up off the floor immediately, trying his best to land a punch on this monster of a man. He swings and misses. He swings another and another and on the fourth punch he misses again as the man pushes him forcefully to the floor. TJ goes down for a third time.

The man rushes and stumbles his way towards a drawer next to the bed in the corner of the room. He reaches into the drawer and pulls out a gun. He turns around sharply and points it directly at TJ, who is standing up again.

TJ is in complete shock; frozen in the doorway.

"I could kill you right now and the world would never know or care! You are nothing, boy!"

TJ is speechless, staring at the end of the black gun barrel pointing directly at him.

His mother is sobbing on the floor, pleading. "Please don't shoot, I'm begging you, please don't."

TJ stands, unable to move a muscle, waiting to hear the sound of a gunshot, waiting to die, and all he can wonder is how painful it is going to be.

He suddenly remembers the night his older brother was shot saving his life and realizes he is about to experience the same fate.

I'm not ready to die yet, is the crystal clear thought that moves through his mind.

The fierce man holds the gun pointed firmly at TJ. "Get out!" he shouts.

TJ takes a few steps backwards.

"Get out of this house and never come back!"

TJ lifts his bag up off the floor at the door.

"If you ever come back into this house again I will shoot you and your mother."

TJ takes one final look at his crying mother on the floor. There is total despair in her eyes. He turns around and for the second time in a day he runs as fast as he can. He sprints, trying to escape a reality that no longer wants or needs him. He does not look back as he runs aimlessly into the space ahead of him.

There is nowhere to run to and nowhere to run back to. He runs, leaving everything he owns behind. He leaves his money, his clothes, his ball and his favourite possession of them all: the shirt given to him by Pitso Ngwenya, his childhood idol, when he was ten years old.

He cannot go left or right. He has no choice but to run forward into what lies ahead of him.

He runs directly into the empty darkness of the night.

· 3 ·

A Young Boy in the Township

Seven Years Ago

TJ is panting loudly, sprinting vigorously up a steep hill, pushing his small legs and urging them not to stop. He is breathing heavily, his legs are aching, but he needs to keep going. He is running to his grandmother's house, timing himself with his brother's old stopwatch. He needs to beat his previous best time, set just over three weeks ago.

It is 5:30am. The bars on wheelbarrow handles carrying a heavy load of bricks and wood are beginning to cause a searing pain in his hands. The brisk morning summer air is filling his lungs and causing him to drip with sweat. He keeps sprinting. His chest is burning, his body struggling, but he keeps going.

He stops suddenly at the top of the steep hill and immediately releases his grip on the wheelbarrow, letting it run out of his control. He clicks a button on the stopwatch.

"Yes! Yes! Yes!" he shouts with a beaming smile on his face, fist pumping the air.

He has just beaten his previous best time. He stands outside the house with a proud smile on his face, taking a few deep breaths to recover.

He then knocks on his grandmother's tattered wooden door.

She answers in her usual sour mood of this time of the morning. TJ shows her the wheelbarrow carrying the wood she needs for her cooking and the brick's she needs for the new wall TJ is building around her property.

She thanks him and puts a five Rand coin in his hand as payment for the three-kilometre run he just needed to do up the steep sand road from his own house in the township.

He picks up fallen bark from old trees, collects bricks from damaged and abandoned houses and then wheelbarrows them up this steep hill every morning before he goes to school in order to earn the desirable five Rand coin.

He is keeping himself fit and strong for the afternoon soccer games he plays with his friends each day; he plays every day of his life. He will be putting the five Rand coin he has just earned into a small tin container underneath his bed when he gets home. He is trying to save enough money to buy himself his very own pair of soccer boots; only a few of his friends own their own pair. He is forced to play soccer with bare feet every afternoon because the only shoes he owns are his school shoes.

TJ begins a fast jog back to his house. He needs to be ready before his mother leaves for work. They usually walk to school together but, if he is not ready in time, he will need to walk the two kilometres on his own.

He jogs down the steep hill and eventually arrives at a red, semi-bricked house with a grey tin roof. There is barbed wire fencing put on the decrepit wall around the house. One half of the house is built with bricks and the other half of the house is put together with tin. Mr Sibeko built the tin attachment to the bricked house after the third child in the family was born. The red paint of the house is peeling off the wall, a sight seen on many houses in the township. Walls and roofs, creatively made up of different kinds of materials, are not uncommon in the area either. A few of the houses are even completely abandoned.

The Sibeko household still has four children living at home. The children sleep in the tin attachment to the house, sleeping inches away from one another. The entire house is not bigger than the size of an eighteen yard box of a soccer pitch.

He greets his mother as he arrives home. She is already dressed for work and she aggressively taps on her watch.

"Get changed quickly. You know how angry Mrs Scott gets when I'm late," she says urgently.

TJ puts his five Rand coin in the tin located under his bed that rests on a few bricks barely rising above the floor. He puts his school clothes on in a hurry, grabs an apple and a piece of bread and picks up his school bag, untouched from the night before. They lock the door and begin walking.

His mother begins to settle down, knowing they have left on time. Her boss hates it if she is late for work.

They begin talking in a relaxed mood, as they do every morning together. His mother loves to talk and, when she starts talking, she does not stop. TJ loves this side of her personality and has adopted the same personality trait. Whenever he is with her or in class with his friends, his mouth never stops either. Lerato is slightly overweight but she is full of life and she has a bright, contagious smile that brings momentary happiness to any person she comes into contact with. TJ feels close to her and they spend many days talking to one another about their own lives. He often talks about soccer to her and, although she does not understand much about the game, she enjoys hearing her son talk about something he loves so dearly. She provides constant support and guidance in ways she feels is best for him.

They walk past a local hospital, which signals they are only a few minutes away from school.

"I don't think I have told you this before, my boy, but since I was a young girl, probably around your age, I have always wanted to become a nurse. I would love to be helping people every day of my life," she says, pointing at the hospital.

TJ looks up at the run-down building. It looks old and in desperate need of refurbishment.

"I don't know, I don't think nurses get paid enough, Mama. I would love to help those people too. A few of my friends go there for their medicine, but why would I do a job that is so sad and doesn't even pay me nice money?"

Lerato stops walking and looks into her young son's eyes. "You should always be willing to help others, my boy. Give love unconditionally to others. Just like the sun gives us warmth and asks for nothing in return, you should give to those less fortunate than you and ask for nothing in return."

His mother always encourages him to help those who are suffering, but he feels it isn't fair to help people without being rewarded. Her family lives a difficult life but she still feels they are blessed in many ways. She has a very optimistic outlook on life.

TJ doesn't quite know how to respond as they arrive at his school. His mother gives him a kiss goodbye and walks to a nearby taxi rank to get transport to Hartbeespoort, where her job is located. Her rich bosses pay her a monthly salary as a domestic worker. The job is an hour away and she does not enjoy the treacherous journey the fast-paced and uncaring taxi drivers take her on every day. They are aggressive on the roads and do not show any care for the human lives they are transporting, but Lerato has no other choice. She has to do the job as her family needs the money. It has always been a hand to mouth existence for them.

TJ sits in the front row of his class, away from his friends due to his incessant talking. He suffers throughout the day of school; staring blankly at the wall, talking, getting told to stop talking and just counting down the seconds on the clock in the classroom to when his friends and he can leave to play soccer together on the muddy pitch in the township. TJ is a clever boy but he only does just enough to pass each of his subjects, feeling soccer is more important than school. Like most of the students who attend, he does not take much interest in school. There are only a few children in his class who excel. Those who succeed in this particular primary school are the children who spend their entire lives studying on their own and reading books.

The schooling in the area is exceptionally cheap due to the quality of education the children receive. Classes are too full and the desks and textbooks used are in terrible condition. The education is at a low standard and most children aspire only to work in the labour industry or as domestic workers and subsistence farmers. Realiztically, the ambition of most of the people and children in the township is to survive each day and make the most of their circumstances.

The majority of people in the area speak Setswana but TJ's family speak Zulu. His father and mother are both Zulu but they always speak English to him, encouraging him to use the chosen language of the world as his first language.

The grey clock on the yellow wall ticks away and the school bell rings at 13:15. The teacher gives her permission for the children to leave class.

TJ and his soccer-loving friends hurry out of the classroom, running away from the small school as fast as they possibly can. Katlego and Nkosinathi, his two best friends, run next to him. They want to spend as much time as possible on the soccer pitch the children constructed for themselves a few years ago. It is a flat piece of mud and sand on the outskirts of the township. The pitch has two wooden poles on either side of it, serving as the goals. It is often muddy, either from the leaking drain pipe that runs next to the soccer pitch or the frequent thunderstorms in the area.

The only thing that truly matters to these children is soccer. A round ball provides them with escape from their reality and problems. They play soccer every day, regardless of any terrible weather conditions or the amount of studying and homework that needs to be done. They play every afternoon during the week, all day on weekends and all day during the school holidays. Soccer is all they live for each day.

The young boys arrive at their favourite place on the planet as two thirteen-year-old captains are being chosen to pick the teams.

The first captain scans his eyes across the children of all ages in front of him and his first pick is TJ.

"Ah, come on, why TJ?" exclaims Sihle, considered the best player in the group.

The thirteen-year-old captain turns towards the talented Sihle and smiles warm-heartedly.

"He never gives up and how do you beat someone that does not give up?" he says with conviction.

TJ smiles, joining the team he has been chosen for. They finish picking the teams and the children kick off immediately, running in all different directions, angles and areas, simply chasing and following the old white ball's every move. It is difficult in the mud, but it does not stop them from slide tackling, trying their array of entertaining skills and passing the ball as quickly as they can to their team mates in relatively open space.

TJ runs in every direction the ball is moving, trying his best to get on it as often as possible. He does not spend much time dribbling or passing the ball; all he wants to do is shoot. He just wants to score goals. He continuously hunts the ball down, even kicking his friends Katlego and Nkosinathi, willing to do anything to win the game for his team. He kicks other players, he gets kicked, but nobody sheds any tears or pulls out of any challenges. Each player quickly becomes tired and bruised, but they never stop running.

The ball gets played to TJ. Katlego slides in hard at his best friend's legs. TJ's determination gets him in front of Katlego who is trying his utmost to stop him. TJ shoots…

And scores. 1-0. There is no time to celebrate as the opposition restart immediately and the children begin running wildly again, TJ doing everything he can to help his temporary team win the game for the day. He scores another goal and another, continuing to provide goals for his team.

TJ is not the best player amongst his peers. He is not a very fast runner. He does not win many sprint races and he is not fast with the ball at his feet either. He is capable with the ball, but he is not naturally gifted with it like some of his friends are. Despite his lack of speed and technical prowess, in their afternoon games he is usually chosen first by the captains of the teams for his sheer determination, athleticism and love of scoring goals. He works harder than anybody else and he is extremely fit. He never stops running and he hates losing with all his heart.

After over five hours of nonstop, full throttle soccer in the simmering summer's heat, TJ's team are the eventual 19-16 winners courtesy of eight goals from the ten-year-old boy himself.

"Thank you, TJ!" shouts one of the older players in the team, who loves winning just as much as TJ does. The captain, three years older than his younger compatriot, gives him a massive, brotherly hug.

TJ is well liked and respected amongst his group of friends. He is a very talkative but very humble and down-to-earth young boy, who never looks to harm or bother anybody else. There is an innocence about him that makes him different from the rest of the children. He lives according to his own heart and mind's desires.

Katlego and Nkosinathi congratulate him on his great performance and begin talking about the match: the mistakes, the great moments, the goals. On the pitch they will do anything to win, nobody is friends, but off the pitch they are the best of friends.

"Great goals there, TJ" says Katlego, impressed with the way his best friend played.

"Thanks, KT. You guys both played well today as well."

"Yeah, good stuff, TJ, but you both know I was the best player on the pitch today," says Nkosinathi with a playful smile.

TJ smiles, "Yeah, right Nkosi! Are you forgetting the shibobo I put through your legs?"

They all laugh.

"So we will meet at your house before the game tomorrow morning, hey TJ?" asks Katlego.

"No problem, KT. We will have to leave my house at about two to make sure we get there on time."

"I can't wait, guys! The team needs a win tomorrow!" says Nkosinathi enthusiastically.

"It will be a great game, both teams fighting to stay in the premier league," adds Katlego.

"I can't wait either! See you guys tomorrow!" says TJ excitedly and they all begin their late-evening run home.

They will be going to watch Rustenburg Rovers first team play in the PSL tomorrow. They are the biggest club in Rustenburg.

TJ, Katlego and Nksoinathi all dream of wearing the club's badge one day as professional footballers. They often go to the Royal Bafokeng Stadium in Phokeng to watch the first team play. They will hopefully be going to the stadium on a more regular basis with the FIFA world cup coming to the shores of South Africa in a few months' time.

TJ arrives home and immediately gets into the shower, washing the dry mud off his entire body and face. The cold water burns the bruises and cuts on his shins and legs. He often has 'battle wounds', as his mother calls them. It does not bother him too much though, as he is not afraid of getting hurt.

Arriving late in the evenings after his soccer endeavours, he is usually forced to take a cold shower as most of the hot water is used by the other family members. The cold shower is great in the summer but he freezes and shivers in the winter.

He gets dressed and goes to the dining room/kitchen, hoping there is still dinner left over for him. He joins his two sisters, Bontle and Dineo, his one older brother, Phenyo, and his parents at the small tin dining room table. He sits in his usual wooden chair, which will almost certainly leave him with splinters.

TJ has two older brothers and three older sisters. He is four years younger than the fifth-born child in the family. Three of his siblings still live at home but none of them spend any time with him because of the large age gap. His eldest sister, Ayanda, is studying to become a teacher, but Bontle and Dineo are still in high school, living at home with TJ. His eldest brother, Siyabonga, works at a furniture store in Hartbeespoort and Phenyo works as a bartender at one of the local shebeens. The family barely has enough money to survive each day and if food is on the table each morning and night it is considered a victory. Being the youngest in his family, TJ is not able to do anything in terms of financial support for them.

TJ looks at the centre of the dinner table and sees there is no dinner left for him. His father is chewing a roll loudly. "If you don't eat dinner with the family then you don't eat at all. There isn't enough food for all of us," he says, unconcerned by the anguished look on TJ's face. It is a rare Friday night that his father has not gone out drinking. All the mining fathers of the township spend the remainder of their hard-earned weekly wage on alcohol at the local shebeen. They do this from Friday evening through to Sunday evening in an attempt to escape the harsh reality they are facing.

TJ swallows his spit, looks at his father, and wonders how he is going to feel without food again tonight. His stomach grumbles loudly; the last thing he ate was a piece of bread in the morning when he left for school. His mother discretely slips a piece of her mielie pap onto his lap, underneath the table.

"So, how was school, everybody?" asks Mr Sibeko, as he scoffs his baked beans.

Bontle replies, "It was good. I got over eighty percent for the two tests I wrote last week."

"Mine was okay. Nothing special happened," adds Dineo.

"The shebeen was busy. All the guys were asking where you are today, Baba," says Phenyo.

"I'm not drinking alcohol anymore. I've given up," says Mr Sibeko assertively. Nobody replies as it is not the first time he has told the family he is giving up drinking alcohol.

"What about you, TJ? I hope those marks are improving," he then says sternly.

"Not really, but I scored eight goals in the match after school today! Everyone was hugging me and congratulating me. It was awesome, Baba, you should have seen me," replies TJ excitedly, reliving his exploits on the muddy pitch.

His father lets out a deep sigh, shaking his head.

"What have I told you before, Thulani? Enough with this childish soccer dream of yours. School comes first. How many times do I need to tell you that you are never going to become a soccer player? There are far more important things for you to worry about. You are such a smart boy and still only ten years old so you can get ahead of many children your age. Study hard now; you don't want to end up as a miner like me."

He pauses briefly and then says, "I can't keep having this same conversation with you. I'm going to have to ban you from those afternoon soccer matches if this continues!"

TJ sits silently in his seat, not wanting to disrespect his father, and simply nods his head, hoping that will be the end of the conversation.

Mr Sibeko is always warning TJ about the hardships he will have to face in this life. He works on platinum mines in Rustenburg but he is not suited to the life of a miner as his body is very thin and not strong enough to deal with the harsh mining conditions. He struggles daily with the heavy work load and the dust, but he does the work reluctantly as it is the only way he is able to provide for his family.

Mining is not what he wanted to do with his life; he'd wanted to become a lawyer. However, mining was his foretold destiny as many generations of his family were all mining men. TJ's grandfather was a miner and so was his great-grandfather. Mr Sibeko believes it is a fate that will be bestowed upon his youngest son in the future too if he does not work hard at school.

TJ takes each family member's plate to the sink and washes the dishes; a ritual he performs every night. It is a tradition for the youngest person in the family to wash the dishes.

After packing the thin yellow plates with green patterns on them away, he fetches his dirty clothes from his room and begins hand washing them under the tap outside the house. He does this each day when he returns from his soccer endeavours. His school clothes consist of just one plain, white collared T-shirt with grey shorts and socks. His only other outfit, worn everyday, is black shorts with a bright red soccer shirt, given to him by Mrs Scott, his mother's employer. He has no idea what team it is, but he simply loves the fact it is a soccer shirt he can wear every single day when playing in the mud with his friends. He also spends some afternoons playing soccer with Mrs Scott's children.

Lerato walks outside to check on her washing hanging on the line as TJ asks her, "Why do I have to do this every day, Mama? I am so tired; I just want to go to bed."

She adjusts the clothing on the line and replies, "I wash dishes and do laundry for other people's children every day. I have earned the right to relax in my own home."

He pulls a face, knowing he was trying his luck to get his mother to wash the clothes for him. Often, if the dishes or clothes are not done properly, then she ends up doing them anyway, unable to control her obsessive need to keep things clean and in order. Under her watchful eye, the house remains immaculately clean with everything kept in its correct place. Outside of the house, however, is dust and dirt. The streets in the township are littered with beer bottles and waste.

Phenyo walks outside, rubs TJ's head and says, "Enjoy your night, superstar. Don't stress too much about Dad. He's just worried and saying what he thinks is best for you. Play soccer, but focus on your school work as well. Sound good?"

"That sounds good, Phenyo. Thanks bhuti," TJ replies with a grateful smile, pleased his brother is offering him support.

Phenyo smiles and begins walking towards the back gate, to exit the property.

"And where do you think you are going, my boy?" Lerato asks, poking her head around the washing on the line.

"Just going to chill at a friend's house. You mustn't worry all the time, Mama, everything is fine," he says, walking to his mother and giving her a loving kiss on the cheek.

Phenyo leaves, much to the concern of Lerato. She is worried he is involved with the wrong crowd of people.

The family say goodnight to one another as TJ climbs into his small single bed, thinking about the wonderful goals he scored earlier in the day. He smiles, reliving the great moments in the match but his wide smile is suddenly replaced by anxiety as he thinks about what his father said at the dinner table.

He thinks maybe he should be more focused at school and not spend so much of his time kicking a ball. After many hours of contemplation, he eventually decides he is going to ignore his father's comments.

He closes his eyes dreaming of becoming the best soccer player the world has ever seen.

"Don't forget to say please and thank you, TJ. Treat your elders with respect!" shouts Lerato as TJ, Katlego and Nkosinathi hop into a taxi at 14:15.

They travel to the Royal Bafokeng for the 17:00 kick off of Rustenburg Rovers VS Cosmos City. Nkosinathi's mother is a receptionist at the club. She organizes the boy's free tickets to the games and often gives them any available merchandise from the club. TJ is wearing a Rustenburg Rovers cap, Katlego a shirt and Nkosinathi is holding a flag. They talk excitedly as they make their way to the stadium.

Today is a special day as Nkosinathi's mother has organized for the boys to go into the Rustenburg Rovers' dressing room and meet the players after the match.

They arrive at the game, the earliest people to arrive although there isn't a large crowd expected for the grudge match between two teams in the relegation zone. They wait for the gates to open and they take their seats behind the goals in the recently renovated and expanded stadium. They are given a free lunch by the club. TJ eats his food like a starving lion.

He is incredibly excited to see his heroes play in the flesh. He dreams of wearing the club's badge one day as a player. He also feels slightly nervous, hoping his team can snatch a victory to send them further up the league table.

A quarter of the seats are filled in the 44 000 capacity stadium as the teams kick off. There is singing and dancing in the stands as the teams grit it out on the freshly cut green grass. There is an intense mood on the field, with both teams desperate for the victory. Neither team allows each other any time on the ball, as the game moves at a frantic speed, without any major chances being created by the teams. TJ feels as though the minutes are passing by in seconds.

Forty-four minutes gone and Rustenburg Rovers finally score the opening goal. The crowd celebrates and blows their vuvzela's loudly. TJ and his friends jump up and hug each other with pure ecstasy in their hearts, smiling wildly and chanting the goal scorer's name.

"Ngwenya! Ngwenya! Ngwenya!" is the chant from the ecstatic crowd; a vital goal scored just before half time.

The second half continues in the same manner. It is a tightly contested match with each moment vital to the league standings. It is a nervy game, both teams missing clear cut chances with each pass and chance mattering more on this day than it would on other days.

With one minute remaining in the game, Joseph Mbengwa scores a goal from outside the box for Rustenburg Rovers and that goal should put the game beyond doubt. An eruption of noise bellows out from the crowd once more.

A final chance for Cosmos City goes wide and the game finishes 2-0 to Rustenburg Rovers, earning a vital three points for the team.

TJ and his friends are over the moon about a well deserved victory for their team in an important fixture. As soon as the final whistle blows, they make their way to the dressing room in a hurry, excited to congratulate and meet their victorious heroes.

TJ enters the dressing room to the laughter and loud shouting of the players towering above him. He is star struck and in awe of getting to see his idols up close and in the flesh. He smiles with his mouth wide open as he looks at Pitso Ngwenya, the striker who scored the opening goal. He is TJ's favourite player and the clubs all-time leading goal scorer.

Mr Ngwenya notices TJ out the corner of his eye and calls the young boy over to him.

TJ walks hesitantly towards him, in disbelief that he is about to meet is favourite player.

"So, tell me, do you like Rustenburg Rovers?"

"Yes, Mr Ngwenya sir, I do! It's the best club in the world!"

Overhearing the young boy, the team members laugh, and Mr Ngwenya chuckles and smiles at TJ.

"Well, would you like a shirt from the striker of the best team in the world?" he asks TJ.

TJ cannot believe what he has just heard. "Yes, sir! I would! More than anything!" he replies without hesitation.

Mr Ngwenya hands him the shirt he'd played in.

TJ's eyes fill with tears of joy. "Thank you, Mr Ngwenya, thank you so much!" he shouts, hugging the topless striker. Pitso Ngwenya returns the passionate hug and the boys are asked to leave the dressing room as the manager enters to give his post match team talk.

The boys walk past the manager, holding shirts given to them by the players. They are ecstatic and, as soon as they exit the dressing room, they immediately begin jumping up and down uncontrollably, comparing stories. Katlego received a shirt from Joseph Mbengwa, the goal-scoring midfielder, and Nkosinathi received a shirt from Norikazu Mazibuko, a hard-working winger.

They thank Nkosinathi's mother repeatedly and they head home in the taxi, feeling the happiest they have ever felt in their young lives, knowing this is a day they will never forget. They arrive back at the Sibeko household late in the evening and say goodbye to one another.

TJ relives the match over and over in his head, replaying the great and nerve wracking moments. He hangs his brand-new shirt above his bed, never wanting to forget the wonderful moment he experienced meeting his hero. He gets into bed and goes to sleep feeling like the luckiest child on the planet.

TJ is woken up by his mother shouting loudly. She is in a jovial mood. He puts his pillow over his head. Lerato is always energetic on Sunday mornings as it is the day for church. She wants to sing, dance and praise the Lord.

TJ reluctantly gets up, not wanting to disappoint his mother by telling her he does not want to go. He joins the rest of the family on their walk to the local church around the corner from their home. Lerato wants them all to pray for better lives. She loves church, but Mr Sibeko is not a very spiritual person. He does not understand why God allows his people to suffer as they do. Lerato forces the family to attend church in the fear they will be punished if they do not go. TJ believes in God, praying every night to ask God to help him become the best soccer player in the world, but he does not understand why God never talks back to him.

The family fulfil their duty, listening and doing what they are told in the passionate service, along with the rest of the church-lovers in the township. Once the service is complete, the family begin walking home.

Mr Sibeko is hung-over and Lerato is jumping with jubilation as she does every Sunday after church. TJ is curious and feels this is the perfect time to talk to his parents about something that has been on his mind recently.

"I pray every night to God and I ask Him to make me the best soccer player in the world. I know He can't do anything right now because I am still small, but why does He never talk to me? He never says anything. Doesn't He like me?" he asks curiously.

"God loves all of His children, my boy, but the problem is the prayer you are saying. It's nice that you love soccer so much, but there are more important problems in the world to pray about," is his mother's reply.

His father, in his hung-over state, then says, "Again with the soccer. Rather ask for food in your mouth instead."

TJ listens to his parents but chooses to believe that God will talk to him some day; it is what his own heart is telling him.

Unlike Mr Sibeko, Lerato is happy he plays so much soccer. She feels the sport keeps him focused and out of all the trouble on offer in the township. As he grows older, he may possibly get involved in things like taking drugs, drinking alcohol, having premature intercourse, stealing or even joining a gang.

The township is a dangerous place, with HIV and AIDS very prominent in the area too. Many children and adults battle against the virus on a daily basis, often losing the fight. These people do not have the money for quality medical care and the government hospital in the area is too full and understaffed, without enough resources to provide the right quality of care to the patients. Many children in the area are orphaned because of the virus. There is drug abuse, alcohol abuse and gangs that operate and run their separate areas within the township at night. There are major gang wars over drugs and illegal weapons. Many young adults are trapped in the lifestyle due to a lack of finances or having no family to support them.

The reality many children TJ's age are facing in the township restricts each of their options for what they want to do in this life. It is not something TJ thinks about, as all he cares about, more than anything in the world, is a round ball. Despite the possible problems and restrictions on his life, he refuses to give up hope of achieving his only dream. He does not feel condemned to a life of mining platinum or trying to get great school marks he doesn't feel he is capable of.

He has a bigger dream.

He dreams of playing soccer in front of millions of people. Scoring the winning goal for his country and becoming a hero who is worshipped by his fellow man. This is the dream his closest friends have too. There are no soccer teams and no soccer coaches at his school, nor any soccer clubs in the township. All he has is a burning desire to play soccer and a group of friends who love the game just as much as he does. He lives and breathes soccer and it is the only thing he ever speaks about.

They arrive home and TJ's father immediately leaves the house to begin another day of drinking alcohol. His mother begins cleaning an already clean house and his brothers and sisters make their way to their respective girlfriends or friends' houses. A few of TJ's friends are going to the muddy pitch, but he cannot join them as he will be going to his grandmother's house to help build her wall. It is to earn a bright green ten Rand note from her. He is upset he won't be joining his friends, but he will be earning valuable money in his quest to afford his very own pair of boots.

He spends the entire morning and the early hours of the afternoon putting cement on bricks and seeing the slight formation of a wall beginning to form.

"Maybe you could build houses instead of kicking a ball all day, young man," says his grandmother, impressed with TJ's building skills.

"Thanks, Gogo, but I'm afraid the pay isn't really good. I only earn ten Rand from my boss," he says with a cheeky smile.

She laughs and smiles cheerfully at her youngest grandson.

He finishes working for the day, gets a kiss on the head from his grandmother, and then receives the much needed ten Rand note. He runs home, delighted with the sacrifice he has made, and upon arriving home he immediately puts the precious green note into his money tin under his bed. He then stretches further underneath his bed to grab a small white ball; another gift given to him by Mrs Scott. He takes the ball and goes outside to practise on the patch of sand his family calls their garden.

He juggles the ball; he passes and shoots it against the wall, much to the annoyance of his mother. He attempts different skills and tricks with it throughout the afternoon, having incredible fun with his favourite object in the world. He pretends to be the heroes he sees playing for Rustenburg Rovers every weekend at the stadium. In his own world, he passes to his heroes, scores amazing goals and wins important games for the club. He spends the entire afternoon living in this imaginary world with the ball; escaping from reality.

When the evening arrives and most of his family members return home from their day's activities, TJ barely acknowledges any of them walking past him in the sandy garden. He never ventures too far away from his house when he practises because "there are dangerous men in the township at night all running their own illegal businesses", as his mother puts it.

He continues juggling the ball calmly. The stars and moon in the late evening sky shine brightly above him as he counts how many times he can keep the ball up off the floor. He continuously kicks the ball up in the air until suddenly he hears a loud gunshot in the near distance. A few birds scatter from the trees as the sound sends shivers down his spine. He immediately picks up his small white ball, stops training and sprints inside to the comfort of his own bed.

He feels safe, having become accustomed to the noise a gunshot makes, however he does not allow the sound to cut his training short. He begins imagining himself as the best soccer player this planet has ever seen, picturing himself scoring amazing goals and doing all kinds of tricks and skills. Soccer is an escape for him; it is his only escape and the only thing he believes has the ability to take him out of a life he feels condemned to live.

He is training as hard as possible every day in the hope that Rustenburg Rovers will want him in their academy team when he turns thirteen. There is nothing he wants more. Only a few boys from the township in the past have made it into the academy and he wants to be one of them.

"Please help me become the best soccer player ever, God," he begins saying, clutching his hands together. "I promise I will do anything to be the best and I promise I will make You proud. Please help my dad get more money and help my mom become a nurse. Help my friends be happy and please help Rustenburg Rovers to stay in the league. I hope one day You will talk to me and tell me I made You happy."

He opens his eyes, satisfied with his request and ready to make God proud of him.

Five days later

TJ takes two bites of his brown bread as the front door of the house swings wide open.

Mr Sibeko walks through the creaking wooden door, stumbling into the old brick walls and haggard furniture of the house. He slurs a few words and eventually manages to fall into a seat at the table with the rest of the family.

His eyes are bloodshot and glassy as he slouches heavily in the chair. TJ can smell the alcohol's odour seeping off of him.

Mr Sibeko stares blankly at his family; nobody utters a word. He then lets out a deep sigh. "This world is not fair!" he bellows, looking around the table.

Everyone stops eating immediately to look at the grey-haired man in his dirty orange work overalls.

"Nobody cares about the human being next to them. You are just put on this earth to suffer for as long as possible and then you die! It's torture! And there is never enough money for us! I am doing everything I can! Everything! I just don't know what more I can do for you people!"

The family can barely hear him as the drunk man slurs each word he says.

TJ keeps his head down, trying to avoid making eye contact with his resentful father. He picks off a small piece of brown bread with his hands, hoping to flee from the uncomfortable conversation and experience.

"Lift your head and look at me, boy," says Mr Sibeko assertively, sensing his son's timid reaction.

He lifts his head and looks at his father.

"You need to do things differently to what your brothers and I have done. Study hard at school so you don't ever have a hard life like us, struggling to survive every day. You must never have to worry about your survival."

TJ sits in silence, not wanting to say what is truly on his mind in case he upsets his intoxicated father. This is a conversation they have had on more than one occasion.

"Do you understand me?" his father asks more sternly.

TJ feels anger rising in the pit of his stomach and decides he is not going to just sit and listen tonight.

"You never care about my soccer or ask me how I'm doing! You don't believe I can be a professional player one day! It's always about school and just doing anything not to become a miner like you. There has to be more to life than just surviving!" he shouts, losing control of his emotions.

His father and mother are both shocked by his random outburst of emotion.

"Listen to me, boy!" his father shouts in a more aggressive tone, "You will never become a soccer player. Nobody from this township has ever become a professional soccer player and nobody ever will. The faster you forget about this unrealiztic dream of yours, the better it will be for your life!"

"You're wrong! And I will be the first professional from this township!"

"No you won't!"

"Yes I will! I don't care what you say!"

"That's it. You are banned from playing soccer ever again. If you play soccer again, you can go live on the street!"

"How could you do that to me?"

"I am trying to help you! Remember my words: you will never be a soccer player. I am not telling you this to hurt you. I am telling you this to protect you. People like us are in this world to work and survive. Forget about soccer, start focusing on school and thinking about getting a real job one day. My father never gave me this advice. He told me I had to become a miner to survive. I am teaching you to stay far away from this life."

TJ feels a tear escaping his eye as his anger turns to sadness. "Why don't you believe in me?" he asks in a soft sensitive tone. He looks at his mother and two sisters for support as each of them sit in silence, in fear of angering the man even more.

TJ stands up suddenly from the dinner table, his small meal barely touched. He runs towards the front door, tears falling from his eyes. His mother tries to stop him from leaving, but he escapes her desperate grasp and runs out of sight.

He sprints far away from the house, eventually stopping at an old, abandoned house a couple of streets down. He sits at the foot of the front door of this empty, dilapidated house, crying uncontrollably. He does not want to believe what his father has just told him. He fights the voices in his head, the voices telling him he should just forget about becoming a soccer player.

Over an hour passes by as the tears continue streaming down his face. He sniffs loudly, staring at the sand on the empty, silent street. The silence is faintly broken as he begins hearing loud voices coming from further up the street. The voices are getting closer to where he is sitting. He stops crying immediately and quickly runs inside the abandoned house, hiding away from any possible danger.

He finds a spot in the corner of the house furthest away from the dusty street. He gets on his knees, puts his hands on a window sill and looks out of a broken window as he sees a young man running away from what looks like a large gang of other young men. The moon light is the only light dimly illuminating the street.

This young man stops running directly in front of the abandoned house. He looks at the front door briefly and runs into the house in an attempt to escape this gang that is chasing him. He enters the house, panting heavily and trembling with fear. He looks up and suddenly sees TJ in the dark corner; he immediately takes a knife out of his pocket in an attempt to defend himself.

TJ recognizes him instantly.

"Phenyo? What are you doing here?" he asks completely stunned.

"TJ? What am I doing here? What the hell are you doing here! You need to leave! Get away from here as fast as you can! There are dangerous people out there!"

TJ is frozen with fear as the voices of the gang chasing his brother are now directly outside the abandoned house. One member of the gang points towards the front door of the house, leaving TJ and Phenyo with no chance of escaping the situation.

Phenyo looks at his innocent younger brother, realizing these dangerous people are about to see the both of them.

"Stay here and be quiet. Don't move a muscle," Phenyo whispers.

"Phenyo, no! Don't go! Those men will kill you!" says TJ, whispering loudly in a panic.

"Don't worry, superstar. Your older brother can talk his way out of any trouble," he says softly and gives TJ a warm hug. TJ grips his brother tightly.

Phenyo looks up, smiles at him and then pushes his younger brother into a dark corner as his warm smile disappears into a look of pure trepidation. He jumps out of the abandoned house to stop them from finding TJ.

He walks out of sight as TJ sits dead still, completely frozen and incapable of processing what is happening. He pokes his eyes out the broken window again and he sees Phenyo walking towards this gang with his hands above his head. His older brother slowly takes something out of his pocket to give to one of the gang members. It must be the leader. It seems as if Phenyo has stolen something from the gang. The leader looks him in the eye, shaking his head as he grabs the item from him.

"So, you've got what you wanted and, if you do anything to me, my boss will kill every single one of you," TJ hears his brother saying.

The leader laughs and the rest of the gang follow suit. The leader then reaches into his pocket, pulls out a gun and points it at Phenyo. There is pure shock on TJ's face.

"No! Please don't!" Phenyo shouts but, without any hesitation, the leader shoots him twice, directly in the middle of his chest. The gun shots make a deafening noise that echoes along the hollow dusty street.

Phenyo falls to the floor, clutching his chest and screaming in agony. The gang members flee the scene as quickly as they possibly can.

TJ screams. He cannot believe his eyes; he has a look of pure disbelief on his face.

The gang members disappear into the dark night air as he sprints to help his older brother. He sees Phenyo shivering uncontrollably, his eyes filled with pure fear. TJ kneels by his side, not knowing what else to do. Phenyo stares blankly at him, moving his mouth, trying to talk, but there are no sounds coming from his vocal chords.

"What is it Phenyo? Tell me what I must do! What do you need?" he shouts in desperation.

The moon's light shines across his brother's face as TJ simply stares helplessly back at him, not knowing what to do, not knowing who to call. The light from Phenyo's eyes slowly disappears and his breathing suddenly stops.

"No! No! No! No! No! Phenyo!" he shouts, bursting into tears, lifting his brother up and rocking his body. "Please! Somebody! Somebody help us! Please!" he shouts crying loudly.

The street is completely silent, with no police sirens or ambulances on the way and no one around to tell him what to do.

He sits crying, swaying up and down, hoping somebody will hear his call.

A light suddenly comes on at a nearby house as an elderly man rushes to the scene. He sees TJ holding his brother and immediately takes out his phone to contact the emergency services. The elderly man then lifts him from his brother's limp body as TJ clutches on, not wanting to let go. The elderly man pulls him off, TJ squealing and kicking wildly. The man grips him and hugs him tightly.

"It's okay, boy. It's okay, just breathe," says the elderly man in a comforting tone of voice.

He puts TJ down and immediately begins performing CPR.

It takes the emergency services over twenty minutes to arrive at the scene. They do some tests and then put Phenyo's body in the vehicle. As soon as they speed off, TJ is walked back to his house by the elderly man.

Eventually arriving at the house, the elderly man knocks firmly on the old wooden door. It is answered by a dazed Lerato who immediately sees her youngest son's clothes covered in blood.

"TJ? What happened?" she asks flabbergasted.

The elderly man explains the passage of events and Lerato bursts into tears while he talks.

"No, it can't be true," she says, crying loudly, putting her face in her hands.

The rest of the family join Lerato and TJ as they all mourn the loss of a member, holding one another and shedding many painful tears. Other family members are called as an evening of grief takes place deep into the early hours of the morning at the Sibeko residence. Tears are shed, stories are told, gifts and flowers are given to TJ's mother and father.

Once the last family member has paid their tribute, and after a night he will never forget, TJ climbs into bed in the early hours of the morning. He is in complete shock as he tries to calm down and make sense out of what he has just witnessed.

"Breathe TJ, breathe," he says softly to himself.

After a long while of panting and nerves moving through his young body, he slowly begins to relax, thinking more clearly. He thinks deeply about the events that have just occurred. It feels like a dream. He suddenly realizes that what his father had told him earlier in the evening was not as detrimental as he had thought. Phenyo saved his life and his untimely death has helped him realize that life is precious and it can be taken from him at any time.

He is now completely calm as he comes to an important decision. He decides that he might as well spend his life going after his dream rather than living a life he does not truly want to live. He feels his father is wrong and he will do everything in his power to prove it is possible for him to achieve his dream.

He stares at the tin ceiling above him, clutches his hands together and then closes his eyes.

"God, please take care of Phenyo up there. He should be joining You soon. I don't know if he is. Please forgive him for anything he did wrong. He saved my life and I will do anything to make You and him proud. I promise I will do anything to become a soccer player. I will never give up, no matter what, and I will do whatever You need me to do. Please God, help me become the best soccer player ever. I want it more than anything in the world," he says emotionally in prayer.

He breathes out heavily and begins shutting his eyes as he silently hopes God is listening and willing to help Phenyo.

He drifts off into sleep, feeling peaceful and protected.

· 4 ·

The Mechanic
....

TJ opens his eyes gradually as the rising suns light slowly creeps through a small window above his head.

"Where am I?" he says looking around at the beige painted walls.

He blinks a few times, widens his eyes fully and jumps out of bed, completely startled. He looks around and finds himself in a strange room he does not recognize.

He then begins hearing a few familiar noises and recognizes a few of the smells around him. He suddenly remembers he is in his boss's house at the petrol station.

The last thing he recalls is lying on the side of the road outside the petrol station, using a cardboard box as a blanket to protect his body from the freezing cold winter night. He'd knocked on the door but his boss didn't answer.

The petrol station is the only place TJ could think of to come to. His boss had found him when leaving for an early morning walk. His boss is known in the town, as well as in nearby towns and townships, as 'The Mechanic' because any car or machinery that has an issue will be brought to him for repairs. Most people bring cars; some people bring old tractors; other people bring farm machinery and even household appliances to be fixed by him. The mechanic is very popular in the Rustenburg area because he provides quality service and charges reasonable fees to the local people who cannot afford expensive car repairs.

TJ opens the white door of the bedroom, immediately entering into the dining room and kitchen. He puts his bag down on the black tiles of the kitchen and, still in his clothes from the previous day, he searches for the mechanic. He walks towards a tin garage, where he sees two cars parked. This is the place the mechanic spends the majority of his days at the petrol station.

Looking from the street, the house, which includes the room TJ slept in, cannot be seen.

The petrol station is not an exceptionally large piece of land. It has just one petrol pump underneath a thin roof and a separate, small, freshly painted white shop that sells items like rice, eggs, milk, tea, bread and water, the essential foods and drinks a person needs for their day to day survival. It is different to other petrol stations in that it does not sell any junk food to eat or cigarettes and cigars to smoke.

There is a separate tin garage that parks two cars at a time for the mechanic to work on. The station is situated in a small town on the outskirts of the township that TJ has grown up in. Houses and properties are widely spaced and there are a few farms not too far away. There is a large amount of dust in the town and the surrounding area, especially now in winter, from the open and dry terrain.

TJ looks around the tin garage and finds the mechanic underneath one of the cars, doing what he does every single day of his life without question. He is hesitant to disturb his boss, but he plucks up the courage and bumps the end of the mechanics black and dusty shoe with his own white shoe.

The mechanic slides from underneath the car with grease on the side of his face and a spanner in his right hand. He looks directly at the teenager with a strong gaze.

TJ becomes uneasy as the mechanic's deep stare makes him feel as if he is searching into the depths of his soul.

The mechanic is a fairly old man, probably in his late sixties. He has short, grey hair but he looks very fit for a man his age; he seems younger than he probably is. His body is lean, strong and healthy and his skin does not show any form of wrinkles or old age. When he speaks, he speaks with a deep and calm tone, never rushing whatever he wants to say. The clothes he wears are worn and their colours have faded. He wears similar clothing and the same black boots every single day. He has a wide smile, always seen whenever he greets a customer or person who enters the station. He is very approachable and most customers tell TJ how easy it is to talk to the old man, but TJ has never really had anything of real importance to talk to the mechanic about. They share the odd joke and chat about soccer, but it has never gone further than that.

There is a long pause as they both look at one another.

The mechanic eventually smiles cheerfully and says, "It was a long way to sleep walk last night, champ."

TJ does not laugh. He looks to the floor and the mechanic immediately senses something is wrong.

"I have food, but I suggest you go home first to get some breakfast before you come to work today, TJ."

TJ continues looking down. A single tear slowly escapes the courage he is trying to show as he stutters, "I don't... I don't have a home, boss".

The mechanic looks at him with concern. Then he puts his spanner on the floor next to him and, as he begins to stand up, TJ begins speaking hurriedly.

"I can't go back home or I lose my life and my mother loses hers. I don't know what to do. My whole world is falling apart and I feel like..."

"Go to the kitchen. Grab four eggs from the fridge and four pieces of bread out the bread bin," says the mechanic, interrupting his emotional outburst.

TJ swallows the words on the tip of his tongue, nods his head and wipes the lonely tear off his cheek.

He then walks inside the house to do as he has been told. The mechanic wipes the grease and sweat off his face with a white handkerchief from his pocket, stands up and begins walking to the kitchen.

TJ grabs the eggs, takes the bread out and puts the ingredients on a small, rectangular dining room table in the middle of the room. The mechanic puts a green kettle on the stove. Four eggs boil next to the green kettle and he then puts the bread in the toaster. The old man silently prepares breakfast and a warm cup of rooibos tea each for them.

TJ is sitting calmly at the dining room table in the mechanic's quaint and pleasant home as he waits for breakfast. It is not a very large house, but he feels surprisingly calm and comfortable sitting in it. He feels protected from the harshness and misery of the outside world.

The mechanic finishes cooking, puts their food down on the table and takes a seat opposite the teenager at the brown antique dining room table.

TJ thanks him and begins eating.

After only five minutes he finishes his food and takes the last sip of his tea. He then looks up at the mechanic. In the time he took to finish his food, the mechanic has only just begun.

TJ watches him eat for a short while and it seems as though he is savouring every bite and every sip, like he is trying to get full value from the food and drink.

The mechanic looks up, notices TJ's empty plate and says, "did you not eat this week, champ? If you slowed down, you might have found out what the food actually tasted like."

TJ smiles, but the longer the mechanic takes to finish, the more agitated he begins to feel. He begins bouncing his leg up and down, waiting for the old man to finish eating and say something to him. He has not said anything in regards to the troubles of his life and he has not shown any pity or offered any comfort.

There is a long silence as the mechanic eats. TJ continues bouncing his leg, waiting for the old man to speak. There are many thoughts moving rapidly through his mind.

"Well, aren't you going to say anything about what I told you?" asks TJ impatiently, breaking the silence.

Before the mechanic can answer, he continues to speak. "That actually doesn't matter. I really need a place to stay, boss. I can even start working here full time. I will pay rent and help you around the petrol station the entire day. I promise I will pay my way. I am a fast learner, I can learn how to fix cars and I will help customers the entire day, every day and not just on weekends like now. I will do anything, sir. I am in desperate need of a home and a job, so is there any chance I can stay here and work full time with you?"

The mechanic listens, takes a sip of tea, slowly puts his blue mug back on the table and then looks into TJ's eyes. "What about your dream of becoming a professional footballer?" he asks in his usual firm tone of voice.

TJ leans back slightly in his chair, not expecting the question. He then lets out a deep sigh.

"I was cut from the academy team, sir. It sucks, but I'm not good enough, so my dream is officially over," he tells the mechanic, feeling ashamed.

There is a short silence before he adds, "And it's soccer player, not footballer".

The mechanic smiles and replies, "No champ. It's football, not soccer."

The teenager rolls his eyes. "Fine, football, whatever. I was the top scorer of the team and I always gave my best. I have sacrificed so much throughout my life and given my whole life to the sport. I did not give up when things got hard in my life or when I was struggling on the field. I have given my entire life to football but it has just filled me with hopes and dreams, used me and pushed me aside without any rewards.

"Instead of working to support my family, being home with my mother, going out to do fun things with friends and trying my luck with girls, I was on a football field or with a ball by my feet. And for what? So I can end up homeless, leave my mother with a drug-dealing maniac and have no football. All that time wasted! It could have been spent doing something far more meaningful."

The mechanic sits in complete silence, just listening without offering any response.

TJ becomes frustrated. He is pouring his heart and soul out, but it feels as though he is pleading for help from a complete stranger.

"Why are you ignoring me? If you're not going to help and give me a job, then just tell me and I will leave."

Still, the mechanic sits in silence.

"Fine then. Thank you for helping me last night but I need to find something else to do with my life and I need to do it now."

TJ stands up hurriedly, the chair screeching as it scrapes against the tiles. He picks up his bag and begins marching out the front door.

The mechanic looks disappointedly at TJ; his back is turned towards the old man. The teenager is about to disappear as the mechanic says, "Suffering is our greatest teacher, TJ."

The boy ignores the mechanic.

"If you do not learn to handle your emotions, you will continue to suffer and struggle your way through life."

TJ halts his dramatic exit as the mechanic continues, "You talk too much and when you talk you are only repeating what you already know, but if you listened you may find you will learn something new."

He turns around to face the mechanic and the old man stares sternly at him. "I believe you said something about not giving up on your dream when things got hard. So tell me, why are you giving up now?"

"Because I have no other choice!" the teenager says defensively. "I can't take the hurt anymore. It's time for me to grow up and become a man. I need to stop living in this fantasy world of becoming a footballer. Everyone has always told me since I was a child that I was wasting my time and they were right. No one from my township of one muddy football pitch and no coaches could ever become a professional footballer."

"You can find a million reasons why you should do something and a million reasons why you shouldn't do it, for the man who says he can and the man who says he can't are both right."

TJ remains silent, not knowing what to say in reply.

The mechanic takes a deep breath and then asks, "Are you badly injured?"

"No, sir," he replies, surprised by the question.

"Do you have a life-threatening illness that stops you from running or kicking a ball?"

"No, sir."

"Do you have air in your lungs right now to breathe and live?"

TJ, shocked by the question, replies, "Yes, sir."

"Then you do not give up on your dream. As long as you have air in your lungs and a heart that is beating, you give everything you have to achieving your dream and you never, ever give up!" The mechanic speaks passionately, looking deeply into the teenager's eyes.

TJ cannot maintain eye contact as he looks to the floor and replies softly, "But I have nowhere to go, nowhere to train and nobody to train me. I have always been too slow and I have never been naturally talented. I've had to work hard to get to where I have got to. I've done all I can and now I have no money to support myself to go on trial in Gauteng. I have hit a dead end in my journey, with no other choice to make."

"You always have a choice to make!" the mechanic says enthusiastically. "No excuses or looking for someone to blame. 'I'm too slow, I have no money, there were no coaches where I grew up or I am not naturally talented.' These are all excuses! Stop making them. You have the power to change your current circumstances, regardless of what they are."

"I do?" asks TJ hesitantly.

"Yes, you do. There is no one to blame. Take responsibility for your own life, champ. Take responsibility for your own actions and choices, no excuses or blaming."

"But sometimes bad things happen and there is nothing I can do about it. I'm not making excuses; I am just saying that I can't take responsibility for everything that happens to me."

"No, you don't need to take responsibility for everything that happens, just take responsibility for your own choices and actions."

"Okay, but you say I can't blame anyone. I can blame someone, like my coach for cutting me from the team. He had his favourites. He is the one to blame for my football career ending."

"If you were already a great player, you would not have been cut from the team. If a team really needs you, they will do everything in their power to keep you. A coach needs to be able to trust you. The moment you lose the trust of the coach you are done for."

TJ is hurt by the comment and replies, "But I have no control over his decision."

"You're right. You don't have control over it, so accept it. If you cannot change the situation, then you have no other choice but to accept it. Am I right?"

"Yeah, I guess so."

"So right now you can choose to accept Rustenburg Rovers and being a footballer was not meant for you or you have the power to change your current circumstances. It's your choice, but don't make any excuses."

TJ is looking down at the floor. The mechanic stands up out of his chair and walks towards him. He lifts the teenager's head with two of his fingers and says, "Always look into a person's eyes, champ. Eyes are the doorway to another human being's soul. You will find all the answers you need to know about another person by looking into their eyes. You can see how fearful or hungry a person is. Whether it is me, a team mate or even an opponent, look into a person's eyes."

He pauses briefly, looks at TJ with his usual strong gaze and says, "I see pure fear in your eyes, son".

TJ stares back at the mechanic, noticing the strength and conviction in the old man's eyes. He maintains eye contact with the mechanic and says, "I agree with everything you said. No blaming or excuses, but I have to give up on my dream, boss. I just don't know what else to do."

"Let's take a seat and talk, or are you still adamant about leaving?"

"No sir, I'm happy to talk."

They calmly take a seat and sit comfortably.

"So you say you want to give up, but do you believe you are meant to be a footballer or not?"

TJ does not respond.

"Just be honest with yourself, my boy. It's okay if it is not what you truly want to do. You are allowed to make whatever choice you want to make in this life."

TJ sighs and replies, "I don't know. I mean, I think I am meant to play football. It's all I've ever wanted to do and there must be a reason for why I have always had this urge to become a footballer. I think that's a good enough reason."

"Don't think, feel. Have the courage to listen to your own heart and follow your own heart's desires. Trust yourself. When you want meaningful answers from within, always listen to your heart and intuition. They already know what you are meant to become."

"My heart already knows what I am meant to become?"

"Yes, you are already everything you want to become in this life, TJ," says the mechanic firmly. "Life has all the answers you need. All you need to do is start asking the right questions."

"What are the right questions to be asking?"

"Well, in this moment, simply ask yourself: do I want to be a footballer?"

"I do! But I have no team and nowhere to train!"

"You are searching for excuses again. Being cut from the team is your new training. Life is all about choices. You are making choices constantly, moment by moment. And can I tell you the most important choice you will ever have to make?"

The teenager shrugs his shoulders and the mechanic, answering his own question, says, "The next one. The very next choice you make in your life is always the most important one. Life is only ever one choice at a time."

"What do you mean?"

"Now, that's a better question. Understand this: the only thing that truly exists is right now, this moment in time. The present moment is all that ever exists and it is fleeting. It passes by in the blink of an eye. Try enjoying every single moment to its fullest as you never, ever get the moment you are currently living over again in your life; so give it your full attention and focus."

"Huh? I don't understand. What about the past and the future? They exist."

"They only exist in your head, in your thoughts. Every moment in this life is brand new. When you think about the future, you are thinking about it in the present moment. When you think about the past, you still only think about it in the present moment. The future and the past only exist in your mind."

"That doesn't make any sense."

The mechanic chuckles and says, "It won't. What I am talking about requires discipline and dedication, but truly living in the present moment at all times will transform your life in ways you can't even imagine. When you are fully focused on what you need to do in the present moment, you will be amazed at what you can do and how well you can do it."

"How do I do it then? How do I become fully devoted to the present moment?" asks the teenager, somewhat curious.

"Well, what other moment are you going to live in, champ? It's not like you can just live in the future, now is it?" asks the mechanic with a cheerful smile.

"No, it's not sir."

"Correct. So simply calm your mind, look around you and remind yourself that you are here and not in the thousands of thoughts in your head. It's the thoughts in your head that are confusing you right now, not the circumstances."

"So I need to stop thinking?"

"Not necessarily. It's a wonderful ability. We are the only species on the planet that can see past and future events in any moment we choose. It is spectacular, but you should be able to choose when you want to think and when you don't want to think. Like a light switch, your thoughts are there for your convenience and when you want to you can switch them on."

"I'm beginning to understand."

"Good. Just be fully focused and devoted to whatever you are required to do right now in your life or on the football field. Focus on whatever you need to do in this moment; that is all you can ever do."

"Well, that's cool to know, but I have no idea what to do in this next moment! What do you think I should do, boss?"

The mechanic grins and answers, "Again, that is a much better question to ask, but words are limited. Ten thousand words are not as great as one single action. It is like saying that you want to be a footballer but you are not giving your best in training to become a better footballer. It requires action from you to improve yourself and move forward, not words. So decide and then do."

"But I have been giving my best my entire life and I've used action to improve myself and not words! I have worked so hard and given my absolute best every time I stepped onto a football field!"

"You need to be honest with yourself, TJ. You can lie to everyone else but the one person you cannot lie to in this life is yourself. Deep within, you always know the truth. Honesty is vital if you are going to grow as a footballer and a person."

"I am being honest! I have given my best and there are no more improvements for me to make! I have reached my full potential."

"Who told you that? I can promise and guarantee you have not reached your full potential. A person can always learn and grow. Every single footballer on this planet, even the best, can still learn and improve every day of their lives. So let me ask you this, are you the best footballer in the world right now?"

"No, I'm not."

"The correct answer would have been 'not yet', as you can always improve and become the best, but you definitely aren't the best in the world in this moment. As I said earlier, if you were already a great player, there is no chance you would have been cut from the team."

TJ is hurt again by the comment. "I am good enough. Football just never wanted me, and it never needed me," he says, defending himself.

"Ten minutes ago you weren't good enough, now you are good enough. Which one is it?"

TJ remains silent.

"Tell me: why did you start playing football in the first place?"

TJ thinks about it for a short moment and answers, "Because I love it. It is the only thing in the world I am certain that I love. It's fun and it makes me happy. A football field is the one place I can truly be who I am and express myself."

The mechanic smiles, having anticipated hearing the answer TJ has just given him. The old man then says, "If you ask any child in the world why he or she plays football, every single one of them will tell you 'because it is fun'. Somewhere along your football journey you forgot this and it became a job, a duty, or even a pressure for you to play football, like your life depended on it. Instead of playing for the happiness it brings you, you played it because you felt you needed it more than anything. Life is not so serious. Yes, be dedicated, work hard but enjoy it; understand that your life can be taken away at any time."

TJ nods his head, already knowing how thin the line is between being alive and not being alive.

"So, whatever your dream is in this world, you have to enjoy it, it has to be your passion and you have to love it. That is exactly why you want it more than anything else in the world. It makes you feel alive and worthwhile, like you were meant to be alive at this time. Football is played from your heart, TJ. It's an emotional game. You need to begin understanding what your heart is telling you and what it is driving you to do."

TJ feels inspired as he remembers why he began playing football as a child. He begins to feel guilty for putting so much pressure on himself to succeed, instead of just enjoying being on the field with his team mates.

He has been entranced by the conversation with the mechanic and now he suddenly wonders where the mechanic's understanding and knowledge has all come from.

"How do you even know all of this stuff? Who are you, boss?"

The mechanic takes a deep breath and then walks towards his own bedroom, down a small passage way from the dining room and kitchen. TJ waits patiently as he hears the mechanic opening and closing cupboards and drawers.

The old man eventually returns, holding a photograph in his hands. He puts it on the table in front of TJ. The teenager looks at the black and white photograph for a short while and suddenly notices a younger-looking version of the mechanic standing alongside his team mates in a team jersey.

"You were a professional footballer!" screams the ecstatic teenager.

The mechanic nods his head.

TJ continues excitedly "When? How did you do it? What is your name? You have to teach me everything you know, sir!"

The mechanic sits down and calmly replies, "It was a long time ago and there is no value in talking about it now."

TJ looks disappointed.

The mechanic continues, "However, I am willing to teach you everything I know. I do not believe it is a co-incidence that we are in each other's lives."

"You would do that for me? Teach me everything you know?"

"Yes. All I need to know from you, TJ, is how much you are willing to give to achieve your dream? If you tell me that being a footballer is what you want more than anything in the world, and you are willing to push yourself and your body harder than you have ever pushed them before, then I will train you to be the best footballer and person you can be."

"I will give everything I have! I promise sir!" shouts TJ without any hesitation, still shocked and excited by the fact that his boss has played for one of the biggest teams in South Africa.

The mechanic nods his head and lifts his blue mug to take a sip of his now colder tea. "When the student is ready, the teacher appears," the old man says, putting his mug back on the table. "I want you to know that you do not have to agree with everything I say to you. Some things I teach you might make sense, other things might not. Some things I teach you might help you improve, other things might not. As long as you are willing to learn and ask questions, then I am here to help. Just like you can learn from me, I can learn things from you. We do not know it all. There is always something new to learn each day."

"I understand, sir."

"Good. To be a footballer will require hard work and dedication, but never forget that football is meant to be enjoyed. You need to love the game and love what you are doing, but it still requires sheer determination from you. I want your absolute best! You are going to need courage as the things I am going to show and teach you might not be easy, but anything worth doing will require some level of difficulty."

TJ nods his head, stands up and holds out his hand to shake the mechanic's hand as a promise to always give his best. "So, does that mean I can have the full time job at the petrol station too?" he asks nervously, as they shake hands.

The mechanic smiles and replies, "Yes, your job starts today, but as of five o'clock tomorrow morning you will be begin your training as a footballer."

The mechanic lets go of TJ's hand, puts their dirty dishes in the sink and walks outside the kitchen door to continue working on the car he had been working on earlier.

TJ smiles blissfully and follows the mechanic out the door as he goes to the cash register in the shop to start his first day as a full time employee. He cannot believe how excited he feels. Moments ago he'd felt he had nothing left in this world, no family or friends, no home, no dream. He was without any hope of a bright future, but now it is suddenly possible for him to keep his football dream alive, being trained by a former professional South African footballer.

Life is very strange, he thinks as he opens the cash register.

· 5 ·

A Large Grey Rock

"It's time to wake up, champ! It's a beautiful day and time waits for no man!" shouts the mechanic, knocking on the door loudly.

"Huh?" is the reply from TJ, who is feeling slightly disoriented. The light of the moon is still shining through his small bedroom window.

"You will never get another day like this again in your life. So let's give it the full attention and enthusiasm it deserves," says the old man, unfazed by the unenthusiastic response.

TJ wipes his eyes in an attempt to gain some focus.

The mechanic's voice begins to fade as he walks away from the bedroom saying, "There is no value in starting your day off on the back foot, son!"

TJ suddenly realizes it is the first day of training and he jumps excitedly out of bed, despite the green digits on the clock in his bedroom showing 5:04am. Usually he would attempt running the clock down to the final few seconds before getting out of bed. However, this morning, his eyes have widened quickly and he is ready for the day.

He puts on the full white Rustenburg Rovers training kit he ran away in, and walks through to the kitchen, fully dressed.

"Morning, boss!" he shouts, greeting the mechanic with a more lively tone of voice.

"Morning, champ," he replies, busy preparing breakfast.

"So what are we doing today, sir? Are you going to make me run until I vomit?"

TJ chuckles and before the mechanic can answer he continues, "I think I need to do a lot more work on my ball skills. I'm a good athlete, I could be faster, but I need to improve my skills and ball control. I think that's why I didn't make it at Rustenburg Rovers."

The mechanic hands him a glass of water and a bowl of freshly cut fruit with various kinds of nuts and seeds in it, and then puts a separate plate with two boiled eggs on the table.

"The first thing you need to know is that your diet will be changing. You will be eating more fruit and vegetables with no junk food, sweets or chocolate to be eaten at any time. Sound good?" the mechanic asks sharply.

"No problem at all, sir. Whatever you need me to do."

"The next thing you need to understand and accept is that you are not a professional footballer. So, you are going to need to trust me and accept that you can still improve and learn. Even if you were a professional, you would still need to accept that you can always improve. Like I asked you yesterday: are you the best footballer in the world?"

"Uh, no, um, I mean not yet, sir."

"Good. Now put a tracksuit top and pants on. It's cold outside and the wind is blowing today so you are going to need to keep warm out there."

"I don't have a tracksuit. All I have is my football kit and the old running shoes I ran away with."

"No problem. Go to my cupboard and borrow mine. You already slept in my spare clothes last night so you may as well use the rest of my outfits too," says the mechanic jokingly.

TJ is pleasantly surprised by the warm-hearted kindness the mechanic has shown towards him.

He walks to the mechanic's bedroom and puts on a black tracksuit with white stripes. He then begins eating the most nutritious breakfast he has ever had and, as soon as he finishes eating his last mouthful, the mechanic asks him to stand up.

"Do you see that massive grey rock outside there, down the small hill and in between the two rows of tall trees?" asks the mechanic, pointing outside a large window facing towards the back garden behind the petrol station.

"Yes, sir."

"I need you to go outside and sit on it."

"That's it?" asks TJ, disappointedly.

"That's it. You do not leave that rock until I tell you to. Don't worry about work today or coming back in when you get hungry, I've got you covered."

TJ lets out a massive sigh and the mechanic taps him softly on the top of his head. "Hey! Focus!" he says. "When you are on the rock, focus on your breathing. Breathe in deeply through your nose and out firmly with your mouth. Stay conscious of your breathing."

The mechanic imitates the breathing technique and TJ nods his head.

"Always listen very carefully to any instructions I give you. It is the small details that are the most important in life."

The teenager reluctantly agrees to the mechanic's instructions and walks outside the back door of the kitchen and dining room towards the large, grey rock. His shoulders are slouched and there is dissatisfaction showing all over his face. He'd thought that he was going to be learning about football and not sitting on some ice cold rock in the freezing cold winter air.

The grey rock is situated behind the petrol station. It is surrounded by leafless trees, yellow grass, with a long sand patch below it and flowers that are not currently blooming. It is the mechanic's very own back garden that overlooks a large part of the Rustenburg terrain. There is green fencing surrounding the property, with a black gate at the bottom of the garden.

TJ climbs on top of the dark grey rock that is big enough for two people, crosses his legs, sits uncomfortably and then looks out into the distant fields. He sits for a while as the minutes that pass by feel like hours. He attempts the breathing technique, but he becomes bored and agitated. His mind immediately begins to drift as he begins thinking about his entire life.

He thinks about the joy he had playing football as a child on the muddy pitch with his friends; the place he learned all the basics of football; the place where his love for the game was moulded and formed. They were the happiest times of his young life. His thoughts begin to drift as he begins thinking about the tragedies that have happened to his family throughout the years he was growing up and how much the events have completely changed his life. He thinks about his mother, her terrible boyfriend and the unfortunate life she has been given.

"I actually miss my father," he mutters out loud. They are painful thoughts, so he begins thinking about the day he made it into the Rustenburg Rovers academy as a thirteen-year-old boy and the happiness he felt that day. He relives the wonderful memories he has made over these past few years with his team mates since that proud day, and all he has learned from the great coaches at the club. These thoughts suddenly cause him to worry about what is going to happen with his football in the future. He tries to accept that the chances of him going on to become a professional footballer are minimal. He grows anxious. He has absolutely no idea what is going to happen to him in the future.

"Think positively, man TJ! Come on! No more negative thoughts!" he shouts aggressively at himself.

His mind begins to drift again as he begins questioning what life is actually all about.

These thought patterns continue for hours, as hundreds of thoughts stream through his mind, some great ones, some not so great ones. He is uncomfortable and after eight long hours he has had enough spending time on his own.

The sun is shining in the middle of the blue sky as the mechanic walks down the small hill to get to the grey rock; it is situated slightly below the house. He hands TJ a healthy meal for lunch: a tuna salad and water.

"When can I come inside? I don't know if you are trying to punish me or what you are trying to do but this is wasting my time. I would rather be working in the shop than sitting doing absolutely nothing. I need to be doing real training boss!" whines the teenager.

"This is your training. If you cannot even spend time with yourself, then who else is going to want to spend time with you?"

TJ frowns and does not reply.

The mechanic continues, "Keep your focus. I will be back to get you after sunset. Do not leave this rock."

"But I'm so bored!" he complains.

"Good, boredom breeds creativity," replies the mechanic.

"I'm serious, sir, this is terrible," says TJ as he puts his food down and climbs off the rock.

The mechanic edges closely towards him and looks into TJ's fearful eyes. He then takes a deep breath. TJ stares back feeling uneasy.

"Learn to use this," says the mechanic, as he pokes at TJ's forehead.

"Learn to use this," he says, tapping TJ's chest. "And then I will teach you how to use those," he says, pointing towards TJ's feet.

He looks at the mechanic with understanding, nodding his head, accepting his fate.

"Fine, I will get back up on the stupid, dumb rock and just sit on it," he says reluctantly.

"Good. I will see you later," replies the mechanic, and he turns and walks back up the small hill towards the house, whistling a cheerful tune.

TJ mumbles angrily to himself, eats his lunch and, as soon as he finishes, he immediately begins thinking again.

He spends another hour living in his thoughts.

"I can't do this nonsense anymore!" he shouts, letting out a loud, frustrated groan.

He refuses to spend any more time thinking. He lies down on the uncomfortable rock and looks up at the pure blue sky. He feels his eyes slowly beginning to close as he drifts off and falls asleep.

TJ feels the sudden splash of ice cold water over his face as he wakes up in a complete panic.

"Come inside, it's getting cold," says the mechanic.

"Why would you do that!"TJ shouts. The old man ignores him and walks back towards the house.

TJ sees the stars in the night sky that have replaced the pure blue sky from earlier in the day and he begins to shiver. He walks inside to find the mechanic sitting in the dining room, reading a newspaper and rocking his chair. A fire is burning brightly in the corner of the dining room, warming and shielding the house from the cold weather outside. Opposite the mechanic is a cup of tea and dinner for him to eat. He does not say anything to the mechanic and simply sits in the red cushioned chair sulking, upset with the day he's had.

He begins eating his dinner, which has more vegetables than he has ever eaten in his life. The food is slightly cold as it has probably been waiting a while for him to come inside. The old man and teenager sit in silence throughout the dinner, as the mechanic reads his newspaper.

TJ finishes eating, puts his plate in the sink and then goes back to his cushioned seat. There is pure frustration flowing through him. The mechanic, sensing TJ's anger, folds up his newspaper, puts it on the table and enquires, "So, what did you learn today?"

"I learned nothing!" the boy shouts, banging his hands on the table. "I learned how to waste my time and freeze to death. If you are trying to make me stronger I get it, but can I please start with the real training tomorrow morning. Every day that passes by is one less day for me to improve. This is not the training I expected."

"I see. So what did you expect from the training today, then?" replies the mechanic calmly.

"I don't know. Maybe to actually work on my football ability and not waste my time."

"Expectations… You should never expect anything, champ. You expected a certain training today but it brought disappointment. Never have expectations."

"Why?"

"Because, if you get what you expected then you don't feel any happiness because you expected it. If you don't get what you expected, then you feel massively disappointed."

"I still don't understand."

"How do I put this then... Well, it is like a football team who is expected to win every game. It is not possible and it will always bring disappointment. Even if they do win every game as is expected, the satisfaction isn't as great, because they were expected to do that. I'm not saying don't set goals for yourself or try to achieve certain things, but don't expect anything from life. Life owes you nothing."

"So, no expectations at all then?"

"No, expect nothing, appreciate everything."

"Okay, I agree that maybe I shouldn't have expected anything, but I still don't feel sitting on some rock is going to help me improve as a footballer or as a person. I am just sitting there, doing nothing, just thinking the entire time and it sucks. I need to improve and I need to improve quickly if I am going to achieve what I want."

"What is the hurry? Where exactly are you rushing to?"

"I don't know. The future, I guess. That doesn't matter. All I know is that I need to work as hard as I can now and get there as soon as possible. There is no time to waste."

"So you sacrifice being happy now to rather be happy in the future?"

"I don't know. I think the best thing..."

"Stop there. You are like so many people I have met, rushing to get to some wonderful destination while all the while missing out on everything that is happening right in front of their eyes. But where are you actually rushing to?"

TJ does not know how to answer the question, never having thought about what the mechanic is saying.

The mechanic looks the teenager in the eyes again and continues, "Listen carefully, TJ. I admire your eagerness and your will to improve, but if you are going to do this, you are going to have to trust me. You promised me you will give your best. I warned you this journey you are about to go on will not be as easy as you would like it to be. It takes a courageous soul to pursue his or her dreams or to push past his or her limits. If football is not what you truly desire, then you do not need to keep going, there are other paths for you to choose. Life is all about your momentary choices."

"But, like I told you yesterday, I don't know what choices to make! Sitting on some dumb rock is not going to help me make those choices. I just sat there all day with terrible thoughts that would not leave my mind."

The mechanic clicks his fingers loudly. "You need to focus," he says assertively. "The rock is teaching you how to focus and to not get distracted by insignificant issues inside you or insignificant issues from the world around you. Focus. Don't be distracted by any thoughts."

"That's impossible."

"It's not. Focus on the specific job you need to do right now, not what those around you are doing or what others think you should be doing. Focus and concentrate on whatever you need to do in this moment and, another thing: you are not your thoughts. It is essential you empty your mind and keep it clear in order to get full value from the present moment. Being a footballer requires you to rely on natural instinct, not your thoughts."

"What do you mean, I am not my thoughts? They are who I am. You sound crazy!"

"You are not your thoughts. Your mind produces thousands of random thoughts a day and most of these thoughts are the same ones you had yesterday. None of these thoughts are who you are. They are beliefs, ideas, opinions, concepts, perceptions. Most of them aren't even what you have chosen to believe."

"You've lost me."

"Your life is currently being run by the thousands of thoughts in your mind. Your mind does not control you, you control your mind."

"What do you mean?"

"Well, when you are on the football field one on one with the goalkeeper and your mind says, 'you are going to miss this chance', did you choose that thought?"

"No," replies TJ.

"Of course not. Why would you choose a thought that you did not want. It's the same as thinking, 'I am a terrible person'. How does that make you feel?"

"Not so good."

"Now think, 'I am the best footballer in the world' and how does that feel?"

"Much better."

"Of course it does. Now those are chosen thoughts. Most thoughts are not actually chosen by you. You are simply listening to them and reacting to them, but you have the power to choose your own thoughts. Choosing thoughts will help you attract whatever you want from life."

"Whatever I want?"

"Yes, whatever you want. If you say to yourself, 'I'm going to hit the crossbar or misplace this pass,' what do you think is going to happen?"

"I am going to misplace the pass or hit the crossbar."

"If you say, 'I'm going to score this chance'?"

"I will most probably score the chance."

"Exactly. You attract what you think about or tell yourself and others. It is not just on a football field but in your entire life that you need to learn how to master your mind. You have the power to turn what is in your mind into reality. You should choose your thoughts and what you want to focus on. Don't let the mind choose for you. Why would you purposely choose thoughts that make you suffer? And yet human beings purposely choose to suffer by believing everything the mind says. The mind only knows how to live in the past or future. Teach it how to live in the present moment. This moment is the only moment that truly exists."

With a confused look on his face, TJ asks, "What about using my mind to learn from the past? Or using my imagination to help me picture myself becoming better? I need to use what I have learned and I need to imagine the future to get a better understanding of what I am currently doing."

The mechanic can sense the teenager's eagerness to learn and replies, "Those are wonderful questions. You are very insightful for your age, but listen: your mind only knows how to live in the past or future. It struggles to live in this moment. The past is gone and you cannot change it. Accept it and learn from it. Forgive yourself and others for any harm caused, as the past cannot be changed. Don't worry about the future either, like worrying when something terrible is going to happen to you. Understand that the future does not exist yet, only in your imagination.

"Your mind and thoughts will tell you that when you get to a certain goal or achieve certain things then you can finally be happy, but the only place to find true happiness is in the present moment, right here and now. Focus on the present moment to create a better future for yourself. If you need to, use the regrets of your past to teach you and use the worries of the future to inspire you, but do not live with them constantly, moment by moment and throughout your days on earth. *That* is the definition of wasting time."

"Okay, so I understand that the past and the future only live in my mind as thoughts and they don't really exist at this moment, but what about education? You need your mind to educate yourself and become smarter. You need knowledge to survive in this world," he replies, slowly beginning to grasp what the mechanic is saying.

The mechanic is impressed by TJ's understanding and curiosity. The old man happily replies, "Your thoughts and your knowledge are two very separate entities. Your brain is an incredible tool that should be used to gain knowledge and learn new things. Your brain is capable of learning and remembering anything you want to put into it; it is an incredible piece of creation."

"No, its not. I can't remember anything I learned in Maths last year, not a single thing!"

"Yes, but that is because we all learn in different ways and when we care about something, we will remember everything and know everything about it. For example, you can probably tell me what your friend said or taught you about football when you were very young but you won't remember what Maths assignment you had to do just over a year ago."

"You're actually right," says the teenager, admitting defeat.

"Learning and adding new knowledge to your mind is very important for your growth as an individual but reacting to your thoughts is not."

"But then that means I do need my mind and I must not get rid of the thoughts in my head! They are helping me."

"Let me try this from another angle. There is so much power in education and knowledge, but your thoughts are separate from what you have learned. A thought is thinking about a past memory and reliving it in your mind, where as your knowledge will be using that memory and learning from it to help you in the present moment. Another example of thinking is worrying if you will become a footballer in the future, where as knowledge is learning how to become a footballer."

"So, learn and gain knowledge, but try thinking as little as possible in my day to day life?"

"Yes, don't think, do. Actions speak louder than words. Learn not to become your thoughts; they make life seem far more serious than it actually is. Your brain stores knowledge that you need to pass school, make money and do whatever is needed for you to do. Your thoughts distract you. Am I making sense?"

"You are making sense, sir. I should always be learning but I should not always be thinking."

"Yes, but be more concerned with your character than your knowledge."

"What is my character?"

"It is who you are as a human being. Your true character is what you show in times of adversity and struggle. It's not what you know that is important. It is who you are as a human being that truly matters; your strength and conviction. Your character is everything."

"That's cool to know, but back to my thoughts. What about positive and negative thoughts? Surely I need positive thoughts. They are very useful and they make me feel good."

"Yes, there are very nice positive thoughts and very revealing negative thoughts that do help you, but do not ever let your thoughts distract you in this moment. Saying, 'I am going to score a goal today,' is very positive and healthy, but telling yourself you are going to have a terrible game or being fearful that you will get injured is unhealthy. Just remember, you can tell yourself and think anything you want to, even a lie."

"I can?" asks TJ inquisitively.

"Yes. You can tell yourself you are the greatest footballer in the world and it makes you feel great, but does it make it true?"

"No, it doesn't."

"It's the same way you can tell yourself you are a terrible footballer; it still does not make it true. Your eyes see what they want to see, not what is really happening in front of you. Choose what you think, but it is best to always clear your mind. Clearing your mind will help you see every situation for what it actually is, not what you think the situation should be like."

"Will learning how to clear my mind help me on the football field?"

"Yes. You do not have time to think on a football field. You need to rely on your natural instinct in football and the emptier your mind is, the better decisions you will make on the pitch. Play with a clear mind and a heart full of passion."

"That's cool sir. A clear mind and a heart full of passion. I really like that."

"I'm glad you do. I used that saying as a reminder throughout my football career."

"How do I clear my mind? How do I empty my mind and stop my thoughts from distracting me. There are so many problems in the world and so many problems in my life; I need to be thinking to fix them."

The mechanic replies, "Look around you and tell me what actual problem you have right now in your life?"

The teenager looks around the room, pauses briefly to think about it and answers, "There are a lot of problems in my life. I don't have enough money, I'm not a professional footballer, I have no home of my own, I can't get into university, I have no close friends or a girlfriend who loves me. Oh, and the only family I truly have left in this world might die if I go and see her. Did I leave anything out?"

The mechanic smiles at the teenager's ignorance and replies, "No, TJ. Look around you right now, in this room, and tell me what problem you have. Right now in this room, what is the problem?"

TJ looks around the room and it is as if he sees the room for the first time.

His eyes widen and his breathing begins to slow. He feels calm. He notices the red hot burning coals and wood in the fire place, he hears the fire crackle. He notices the light yellow paint on the walls. He feels the comfortable, cushioned seat he is on as he sinks deeper into it. He rubs the smooth wood on the brown dining room table slowly. His heart beat slows. He looks at the mechanic, realizing what a wonderful conversation he is having with the old man. He feels a subtle peace within.

The moment lasts a mere few seconds as he reacts to his mind again and says, "There is no problem in this room, but there are many problems in my life."

The mechanic chuckles and replies, "Those are all mind problems. They are not real. Do you really want to live your life in your head, thinking about the millions of wonderful or terrible things that have happened in the past and things that might happen in the future? And then miss out on everything that is actually happening right in front of your eyes? Life is extraordinary! Honestly, what real problem are you actually facing right now, sitting in that chair? Is there anything in front of your eyes right now to be truly upset about? You have a roof over your head, you have just eaten, you are sitting by a warm fire out of the cold winter air and you are speaking to a very pleasant old man."

The teenager laughs and says, "I guess so, but there are problems in some moments in life, like when my mother's boyfriend pointed a gun at me. I know it is in the past, but how can I feel happy and not worry in that moment."

"Is that happening to you right now?"

"No, but…"

"There are many wonderful moments and there are many moments when you will struggle or suffer," says the mechanic, interrupting him.

"There will be pain and misery in this life; there is no doubt about that. Life is a constant test, so accept that there will be times when you will struggle. I am simply saying there are enough things in the world that bring pain, so try not to create your own pain. The mind finds thousands of problems to solve every day, week and month. As soon as it solves one problem, it wants to solve the next one. It is an endless cycle of talking within you, never silent. I am simply saying, quieten your thoughts, understand that all there is in this life is this present moment and, when you become overwhelmed by your thoughts and emotions, just look around you and ask yourself, 'what problem am I actually facing in this moment?' You will find life is not that serious."

"But what do I do if I am facing a major problem in this moment?"

The mechanic pauses. He scans around the room, gets out of his seat and then walks towards the fire place. He picks up some tongs and takes a hot coal out of the fire with them. He walks towards TJ with this hot burning coal and the teenager immediately jumps out of his seat.

"What are you doing?" TJ shouts. His eyes widen and he becomes entirely focused on getting away from this hot coal.

The mechanic chases him around the room, the entire room, and eventually bursts into laughter when he looks at TJ's petrified face.

"I don't think I've ever seen someone with such a scared but focused look on their face," says the mechanic, laughing loudly.

"What is the matter with you? Why would you even do that?" says TJ, panting and trying to recover from his minor adrenalin rush. "You're not well, sir!"

The mechanic puts the tongs back by the fire place, looks at the defenceless teenager and says, "Now tell me, TJ, what were you thinking about while I was chasing you?"

"I don't know!"

"Were you thinking about football?"

"No!"

"Were you thinking about your life?"

"No! I wasn't thinking about anything. I just needed to get away from you!"

"You had your full attention on the present moment, no regrets from the past or worries about the future. Not complaining about what has happened or anxious about what is going to happen. You were completely focused on what you needed to do."

TJ listens intently.

"This is how your entire life needs to be. Quieten your mind and give your full attention to whatever you are currently doing. When an actual problem arises, you will then know how to deal with it because you will be fully focused on the present moment. Whilst you are still learning this and learning to be the master of your own destiny, just let life show you the way."

TJ is calmer as they take their seats again, recovering from the chaos that just occurred.

They sit in silence as TJ begins choosing certain thoughts in his mind while the mechanic sits in his seat, staring at the fire. TJ watches his mind, chooses his thoughts and then suddenly laughs out loud as he sees and hears how silly, defensive and repetitive his mind can be. The mechanic notices the teenager laughing and smiles as they both stare at the fire.

A question comes to the forefront of TJ's mind. "Sir, I've realized that you always say 'life' like it exists. It's not like life actually knows or cares about who I am."

The mechanic smiles and replies, "Of course it does. You are not alone, son. You will begin to understand this if you complete your training. Life is constantly leading and guiding you towards where you want to go. Everything is connected. Listen to life and do not fight the signs. The more you resist something, the more it will continue; so just let go. If you embrace and listen to what life is telling you, you will be a far happier person."

"Okay, boss, I trust you."

"That's great, but it is more important that you trust the universe."

"I will."

"Good. Just try your best with whatever situation you are given or challenge you are facing. Give your best to what you need to do, or don't do it at all. What is the point of doing things at half your ability?"

"So one hundred percent effort or don't do it at all?"

"Yes, half an effort is wasting time. So, when you are on the rock choose your thoughts wisely and be aware of everything around you. Give your best to what you are doing. Like right now, you are giving your best and paying full attention to what you are learning."

"What kind of thoughts should I be choosing on the rock?"

"Just be completely honest with yourself and ask yourself the right questions. Questions like, 'can I still improve? What can I still improve? Do I feel I am giving my absolute best to whatever I am currently doing? Who am I? What does life really need from me?' Pay attention to the answers and pay attention to what is happening around you at the time. Be aware of what is around you at all times. Don't react, be aware."

TJ understands and he develops a weird feeling in the pit of his stomach as he notices he has been listening to his mind his entire life, believing every thought that has entered into his mind.

He yawns loudly and looks up at the clock in the kitchen; it shows 00:06.

"I can see you're tired, champ, and you need to get some rest for tomorrow's training but, before you go to bed, the last thing I want to say is this: understand that your life will have a few key moments. Pay close attention to those moments, TJ. The success of an individual is determined by the smallest of margins. Enjoy this life as much as you can and give everything you can to each moment that passes by, as it will be over sooner than you think. You never get the current moment you are living ever again, so pay close attention to it. Just let go of everything you are holding onto, enjoy life, take the pressure off. If you are meant to become the best footballer in the world, you will be."

TJ nods his head. "I am very tired, but thank you for everything you have taught me tonight, boss. I will never forget and I will try applying everything I have learned. I do want to become the best footballer in the world and I promise I will try my best tomorrow."

"Sounds good. Sleep well, champ."

"Thank you, sir. You too and see you in the morning," TJ replies as he gets out of his chair and walks towards his new bedroom. Shortly after he leaves, the mechanic pours water over the fire and switches off all the lights in the house.

TJ climbs into bed and vows to give his best throughout the training. He tells himself that it has only been one day and that the mechanic has played at the highest level in the country and must know what he is talking about. He promises himself that he will try to focus and be more aware of things around him tomorrow. He does not pray tonight, never wanting to speak to God again.

TJ is tossing and turning uncontrollably in bed. He is breathing heavily and sweating profusely. His eyes are closed; he has not realized he is sleeping.

He hears gun shots, he hears people screaming and shouting. He sees his father on the floor.

"Get up, Dad! Get up!" he shouts, but his father does not move. There are bullets flying in all directions, people in a panic, men lying face down on the rocky sand.

He is crying, shaking his father's body. "Please get up! We need you!" he shouts and he then wakes up suddenly, sitting up sharply and panting heavily in his bed. He sees the quiet and calm bedroom around him. The green digital numbers on his clock show 03:19 and he slowly begins to relax.

"It was just a dream," he says as he lies down, trying his best to fall asleep again.

A few hours pass and TJ is sleeping deeply. The sound of loud music suddenly comes bellowing through his bedroom door. He wakes up, startled.

The mechanic follows the sound of the music, dancing awkwardly to the vibrant instruments coming from the radio. The teenager pulls his white pillow over his head and lets out a loud groan.

"Come on, TJ, there's life to live today, son! You will never get this day in your life, ever again. Let's enjoy it!" says the old man, smiling and still dancing gracelessly to the beat. The teenager takes the pillow off his face and sees the mechanic bopping and smiling above him.

"I'm not in the mood today, boss."

"So, you are not in the mood to live? Come on, champ, wake up! Let's not waste a single day we get given. We need to make each day count!"

The mechanic pulls the blanket off the teenager's body and leaves the room, singing to the vibrant African tune.

TJ wipes his eyes and yawns loudly. He is exhausted and not in the mood for the mechanic's lessons this morning. His early morning dream has left him tired and he has woken up without the same excitement he had the previous morning, knowing he needs to do training he does not really want to do. He does not truly believe it will improve him as a footballer. He enjoyed the lessons he learned last night, but he is not excited about sitting on the rock again today. He slowly steps out of bed, gets ready and goes to the kitchen.

As he eats his breakfast, the mechanic puts a list down on the dining room table in front of him.

It is a list of chores he needs to do around the petrol station. TJ reads the list and sees he is required to do chores like washing the floors, cleaning the toilets, dusting the shelves, as well as washing and cleaning the inside and the outside of the cars.

He pulls a disappointed face at the list, as it is not ideal training, but he feels it is at least better than sitting on some big rock.

I guess I shouldn't have had any expectations about training today, he thinks.

Although it is terrible labour and not what he really wants to be doing, he is willing to do it in the hope that it will somehow help him become a footballer. He is going to blindly follow his instincts and trust that the mechanic's training methods are going to help him.

"Focus on your breathing today. Every task you do, you need to inhale slowly and deeply through your nose and exhale firmly out with your mouth. It is vitally important you do this, so focus on it," says the mechanic as he walks passed the dining room table fully dressed and ready for work.

TJ says nothing in reply. He finishes his breakfast and goes to the shop. He grabs a mop out of a cupboard behind the shop counter and begins mopping the floors. He breathes in slowly through his nose and out firmly with his mouth focusing all his energy on mopping the floor, trying his best to focus on the present moment. He watches his thoughts and tries keeping his mind clear.

After mopping the floors, his next task is to scrub the floors of the toilet in the customer's bathroom.

He scrubs the urine and faeces around the toilet as he starts to gag, trying his best not to vomit. It is terrible. He scrubs and scrubs the horrifically dirty toilet and he suddenly vomits uncontrollably. He pants heavily and realizes he is going to have to clean up his own mess now too. He looks around at the hideous scene and then picks up the soapy cloth in the bucket next to him and throws it into the water with pure rage. He begins swearing incessantly, complaining about this torture he is being put through. He then punches the wall of the bathroom as hard as he can.

He wants to confront the mechanic, but chooses instead to ignore the frustration he feels and the harsh words he wants to say to the old man. He needs to focus and give his best, no matter what.

He finishes cleaning the small bathroom, washes the cars and dusts the shelves. He tries his best not to react to his thoughts, to live in the present moment and focus all his attention on his breathing whilst doing each of the non-football related tasks.

The only support he receives throughout the day is the occasional, "Breathe in, breathe out," from the mechanic.

Once the day of hard, demeaning labour has ended, TJ gets into bed after a quiet dinner and feels as though the day took a lifetime to finish.

He lies in bed, still breathing in through his nose and out through his mouth as he rubs his bruised knuckles. He begins reflecting on everything he had to do throughout the day. He wonders if he had actually learned anything.

Alone in bed, the house is quiet. He chooses his thoughts and thinks: *I did actually notice how calm I was when I was fully focusing on my breathing during the chores today. I noticed how child-like my mind can be. Some things I think about, if I said some of them out loud I would be sent to a mental hospital. I felt relaxed and at ease sometimes but most of the time it was frustrating. It was difficult trying to focus on the pointless tasks I was doing.*

It must be because I didn't want to do all the stupid chores I had to do. I suppose living in the present moment is harder than I thought it would be. I mean, I did try to give my best to whatever I needed to do but, to be honest, I struggled. I just really hope all these things I'm being forced to do will actually make sense sooner or later. It had better help me with my life and help me become a professional footballer because I don't think I will handle doing all this stuff for nothing. I suppose I must just trust the mechanic. I must push myself through whatever mind-numbing task he has in store for me tomorrow and see how it goes. I just hope it all works out okay.

· 6 ·

One touch, One pass,
One Moment at a Time

TJ is staring out into the distant fields. The early-morning sun is weak and an icy breeze blows onto the skin of his face. He is struggling to keep his focus.

Just over twenty strenuous days have passed by. He has had to do his job as a petrol attendant and shop caretaker every day, and he has spent most of the days doing the gruelling labour around the petrol station as well as sitting on the grey rock. There were occasions when he felt relaxed and focused. He felt as though he was learning something, but on the whole he has felt agitated and unnerved. He has had to constantly remind himself that the mechanic is trying to help him become a footballer and that by doing his job at the petrol station he has food in his mouth as well as a place to live.

TJ lets out a deep sigh as he feels anger pulsating rapidly through his veins. "I can't take this anymore!" he shouts, slamming his hand against the rock's hard surface.

He jumps off and marches towards the tin garage to confront the mechanic. He finds the old man working on some red car's engine.

"I've had enough, boss! I can't do this anymore! I am done with these stupid tasks and worthless exercises that are not getting me any further with my football or training me to be any better at some other profession. All these tasks are teaching me is that I can go on to become the first rock model or the greatest domestic worker this country has ever had!"

The mechanic pauses to look at the rage-filled teenager as TJ continues to shout. "You gave me hope of being a footballer again! I was happy to give it all up! The world was telling me that I was not meant to become a footballer and you have done nothing but waste my time and fill me with some philosophical mumbo jumbo. I don't even know who you are. For all I know, you only ever played one game for your team because there were no other players available. So, thank you for taking care of me, feeding me and giving me a home, sir, but I need to go find something of true value and start building an actual life for myself."

The mechanic puts his screwdriver down on a small brown table next to him and wipes the sweat off his forehead with a white cloth. He then looks at TJ and asks, "What colour is the floor in the shop bathroom?"

"You see what I mean? Why would you even ask me that? No more pointless questions, boss. I think it's definitely time for me to move on!"

The mechanic repeats, "What colour is the floor in the shop bathroom?"

"I don't know, white or brown, I don't actually care."

"No, the tiles are blue."

The teenager frowns as curiosity gets the better of him. He goes to find out if the mechanic is telling the truth.

The tiles are blue.

He returns to the tin garage and confirms, "The tiles are blue, but what does that even matter?"

"And tell me TJ, did you see any birds in the trees whilst you were sitting on the rock?"

"I don't know."

"From where you were sitting, did you notice where the sun rises and sets?"

"No."

"Or even how many houses there are in the distance. Did you see the wonderful farms growing large crops as well as the farms with livestock on them?"

"I didn't, but..."

"What sounds did you hear? Were there sounds coming from the town or were there any noises coming from the insects and birds?"

"No, I don't think so."

"How hard was the wind blowing?"

"I don't know, I can't remember!"

"Describe what the rock felt like as you were sitting on it, all its details?"

"It was like hard and cold. It doesn't matter!"

"Did you notice the fruit trees next to you?"

"No."

"Was the mop you used to wash the floors made out of wood or plastic?"

"I think wood, I'm not sure."

"And in the..."

"Enough!" shouts TJ. "Why are you asking me all these ridiculous questions?"

The mechanic remains silent. TJ cannot provide any adequate answers to his simple questions. He begins to feel a huge wave of anxiety in his stomach. The old man looks into his eyes yet again, not showing any signs of anger or animosity.

"I didn't focus on the moment, did I, sir?" he asks the mechanic with caution.

"No, you didn't, son. You lost control of your emotions again too. Come with me. We're going to take a walk."

"What about the station?"

"It will just have to remain closed for the rest of the morning."

The mechanic locks the tin garage, the shop and the house and they begin walking along the only straight dusty road that runs through the entire small town that the petrol station is situated in.

The sky is blue. There are birds chirping in the many leafless trees and there is a cold winter breeze blowing against their bodies as they walk. The town is made up mostly of houses and a few small shops. There are a few houses in poor condition made out of tin or old red brick, but most of the houses are in better condition and are predominantly painted white. The town is surrounded by a large amount of open terrain, farm land and mines, with the majority of the inhabitants working outside of the town's boundaries. There are miners, farm workers and other labour men who stay in the town with their families. It is pleasant and not dangerous like the township TJ grew up in.

A few people are walking in the street as the mechanic greets a random gentleman who passes by. They walk at a steady pace, hearing each crunching step they take on the dusty and stone-laden road. Their surroundings are quiet and calm.

"As I have told you before, TJ," the mechanic begins saying, "when you do anything in your life, you need to pay full attention to what you are currently doing in this moment. What are you doing in this moment?"

"Walking on a sand road, in a small town and having a conversation with you."

"Yes. Notice and be aware of all the details the present moment is currently offering you. Nothing else truly exists but this moment in time. I need you to truly understand this."

The mechanic is talking slowly and methodically as he continues, "Life is always only one moment at a time. Football is no different. You need to be able to focus and be aware of what is around you at all times. You need to be constantly analysing and scanning what is happening on the field. Focusing on this moment will allow you to make fast, intelligent decisions on and off the field."

"Surely this isn't the most important thing to teach me about football, boss? What you are saying is completely true, but does it really matter that much?"

"Nothing matters more than right now. It is the only thing that is real and true. I am trying to prepare you mentally to become a footballer. What most footballers do is they focus on their technical and physical skills before they master the mental side of the game and life. There is nothing wrong with doing this. However, to receive full value from your training, matches and your life, you need to pay attention to the mental side of the game and your life."

"What do you mean by the mental side of the game?"

"The mental side of the game are things like: Are you calm in pressure situations? Are you making intelligent decisions? Are you confident in your own abilities? Do you work harder than anybody else? Do you lead and encourage those around you? Are you determined, brave, driven and always giving your best in training and in matches? How focused are you throughout training and matches? Football is played from your heart and mind before it is played with your legs and feet."

"I see. So, by simply focusing on the present moment I will be able to do all of that?"

"Yes. Breathing in deeply through your nose and out firmly with your mouth will help you too. It will help you stay calm, focused and keep your emotions in check. It will also help immensely during physical and technical training. Try to focus and be aware of every detail around you. The smallest details are the most important in life."

"I understand. But how was noticing things while sitting on a rock or doing house work helping me with my awareness on a football pitch?"

"Good question. Noticing the colour of the bathroom floor, on the football pitch for example could be noticing a tiny detail like where your opponent's weak foot is.

"The houses in the distance that you did not notice on the rock, on the football pitch could be noticing where the opposition goalkeeper or defence is positioned and how you can take advantage of their positioning.

"Noticing the small details of rock you were sitting on, on the football pitch could be noticing where the defender is in the moment. Is he on your right or left and how far away is he from you? Will you be able to turn him if he is tight to you or do you just need to hold up the ball and wait for your team mate to come and support.

"The sounds of the birds, on a football pitch could be noticing what your team mates or coach are communicating with you: what are they saying? Communication is vital on and off the field and it doesn't have to always be with your mouth. You can use your hands, body movement, eyes and telepathy to communicate with your team mates.

"How hard the wind was blowing on the rock, on a football pitch could be noticing what the weather conditions or pitch conditions are like. If the field is wet and slippery you should make softer passes. Do you have to play short or long passes because of the wind? The wind is one of the biggest enemies in football, by the way.

"These are all things that you need to be processing whilst you are playing the beautiful game. Am I making sense?"

TJ listens in astonishment and replies, "I was learning all of that just by sitting on a rock and cleaning floors?"

He puts his head in his hands, lets out a disappointed sigh and then says, "I do feel really embarrassed about not trying harder, sir, but still everything you just said needs me to be focusing on so many things at once. How will I possibly be able to concentrate on doing all those things at the same time?"

"When you are giving your best and you are fully devoted to each moment, everything I have just mentioned will happen naturally. Of course, it will take time and practice, but focus on the small details that you can do right now in this moment. Achieve small momentary victories. Don't focus on the big goal. There will be daily tests and battles in your life and in football. All you can do is try to win these small daily battles. Small daily victories lead to the large victories in life. It is like trying to win your fifty-fifty tackles or taking the clear cut chances that are presented in a match. You need to win the small battles on the pitch to win the overall match."

"That's it? Just focus on whatever small details I have to take care of right now?"

"That's it. Simple isn't it? You also need to understand that you are capable of far more than you realize son. You are an unbelievable creation. The incredible things your body is currently doing moment by moment without you even realizing it will astonish you."

"What could my body possibly be doing right now that is so amazing?"

"Well, at this very moment your heart is pumping and returning blood throughout your entire body every single second and it does this one hundred thousand times a day without you even realizing it. You never have to tell your heart to beat, it just does. At the same time, there are twenty-five million new cells being created and destroyed in your body every second that passes by. Twenty-five million!

"Then, at the same time you are consistently breathing in and out without your ever having to ask your body to do it; it just does. You have cellular, nervous, digestive, immune, muscular and skeletal systems all working in perfect harmony with one another, right now in your body.

"This all happens, even while you are running as fast as you can on the pitch and kicking a ball at the same time. Without you ever needing to tell your body to do these things, it just does them. This is all happening in a few split seconds. It is a miracle: you are a walking miracle.

"There is intelligence inside your body that your mind will never begin to understand. You are capable of far more than you realize and the only way to awaken this vast intelligence inside of you is to focus on whatever you are doing right now. I am not asking you to 'think' about improving your awareness on the pitch. I am not asking you to 'think' about improving your composure and calmness in pressure situations all at one time, as it is impossible, just like telling your body to pump your heart and destroy cells right now. I am asking you to devote yourself to whatever task you are currently doing, internally and externally. Trust that your body will do it. Trust yourself.

"If the situation requires you to pass, then focus only on that pass and make it a pass of the highest quality, even if it is only a two-metre pass. If you need to shoot, then shoot and devote all your power and attention to shooting. If the coach needs you to run twenty kilometres for training, that is what you focus on. You need to be comfortable dealing with any situation you are faced with."

TJ feels inspired, realizing what his body is capable of doing and the enormous potential he has at his disposal. His feelings of amazement and wonder are suddenly replaced by a terrible feeling of guilt; for not trying his hardest to focus on the rock and constantly complaining each day he was doing the chores around the petrol station. He takes a deep breath as he walks along the dusty road and tells himself silently: *it's in the past. You cannot change it, so just enjoy the walk.*

"So, it is all about making the correct decisions in each passing moment?" he then asks the mechanic.

"Yes! That's it! That's all it is", replies the old man. "The difference between the best footballers of this world and the average footballers is a few split seconds in making a decision on the pitch. Most players at the top level have similar technical and physical attributes, but the difference is that the best players make a decision a few split seconds quicker than the average player. You should already know what you want to do with the ball before it gets to you. Don't receive the ball and then think about what you should do with it; you should already know. So make a decision as quickly as you can and never change your mind or make no decision at all."

"Why do you say that?"

"Because, if you make the right decision, you will learn. If you make the wrong decision, you will still learn. If you make no decision or change your mind, you learn nothing and you let your team mates down. Never hesitate. If you do not have the ability to make a fast decision on the football pitch then you are a menace to your team mates. Your team mates need to be able to trust you. Always make a decision and do it as fast as you can. Never change your mind as there isn't enough time on the field to do so."

"How do I learn to make a quick decision?"

"Again, if you're focusing entirely on the present moment this will come naturally to you, but it is about learning how to read the situation and not reacting to it. Reading a situation means anticipating the outcome. You need to have awareness. There is nothing wrong with reacting to a situation because if, let's say, your team mate misplaces a pass, you will need to react quickly and get into your appropriate defensive position. Things don't always go to plan on a football pitch, so you will need to react to certain situations and improvise; however it is far more powerful to read the game.

"Begin to read the game in a way that, if the ball goes left for example, you know where to be and you can estimate where you think the ball will be going next. It is the same in life. Read the situation and don't react to it. You need to be able to anticipate the outcome. This comes with making mistakes and gaining experience."

"Okay, so I must try to read the situation and not react to it. I must only react and improvise if something happens that is out of the ordinary. So, I understand my mind and eyes will always be looking around to analyse and be aware of what's around me, but what spaces should I be looking at exactly? What should I be analysing on the field to help me read the situation?" asks TJ, now thoroughly enjoying the lessons he is learning.

"Good question. Always look to move into an area that will create the most time and space for you, or create space for your team mates to move or run into. One simple equation you will always need to remember on the football field is space equals time. The more space you create for yourself will equal more time for you to make the right decision. The less space you have, the less time you have on the ball. In football, a few extra seconds on the ball can be the difference between a misplaced pass or an accurate pass and even scoring a goal or not scoring a goal."

"That makes sense. It's probably the only maths equation I've ever understood in my life! But what spaces should I specifically be looking to move into on the field?"

"In order to understand space, you need to understand what channels there are on the field. There are three vertical channels and they are the right side channel, the left side channel and the central channel. Then there are four horizontal channels and they are the goalkeeper channel, the defensive channel, the midfield channel and the striker channel. You need to position yourself in the best channels to have the best chance of receiving the ball. You will learn more about the tactical side of the game later in the training; if you complete the training."

"I feel anxious again, sir. How do I even remember everything you have just told me? I can barely remember anything you have said and now I need to do it in an intense football match!"

"It may feel like I am giving you an impossible amount of information to process, but when you are feeling stressed and overwhelmed on the pitch all you need to remember are these nine words: one touch, one pass, one moment at a time. Take a deep breath in through your nose and just focus on the next job you need to do. No matter how badly you are playing or how unfocused you have been, you are one moment away from doing something magical and creating wonderful memories for all those around you."

"One touch, one pass and one moment at a time?"

"Yes, TJ. Just take a deep breath and say those words to yourself. When you remember these words, all the things I have told you will happen naturally without you needing to think about doing them, as you will focus on the next job you need to do, whatever job it may be."

TJ nods his head and walks in silence, with his hands behind his back and his eyes gazing firmly at his feet walking on the sand road. He is processing and thinking deeply about everything the mechanic is teaching him.

He then asks, "I know I am not my thoughts, but I'm still confused about the past and future. What about everything I've already learned on the football pitch that is part of the past that I need to use on the pitch. And what about imagining the future. They say your imagination can take you anywhere you want to go."

The mechanic is pleased with the question and responds, "Of course you need the past and the future for certain moments in your life. For instance, in the past you might have tried to dribble a player and got tackled instead of passing to a team mate in open space and now, when that situation arises again, you know what to do. Or, in the future you could imagine yourself scoring a goal in front of thousands of people and it makes you feel good. Your imagination has the power to create a moment that could possibly come true in the future. It's an incredible ability. That is when the past and future are very useful.

"It is only when you are constantly living in your mind, thinking about the past or future. Regretting past decisions you have made or worrying about making a mistake or failing in the future. Then the past or the future will affect you negatively and will take your focus away from the task in front of you. Do not look to the past to figure out who you are and do not use the future for your salvation. You are who you are in this moment. That can't change, so embrace who you are."

"It's truly special, sir."

"What is?" asks the mechanic.

"The incredible power of being aware of everything that is happening around me. If I am aware of everything around me, on and off the pitch, life and football actually becomes way easier to do. I just need to focus on the present moment."

"That's right, champ. Focus on this moment. It is not just being focused on what's around you, but focusing on what's happening inside of you too. Also, don't forget your breathing as it will help with your emotions."

"I actually struggle with handling my emotions. They tend to take hold of me and then I can't control myself. I do things I wouldn't normally do. I also feel pressure when I'm playing. I don't know how to handle pressure situations."

"That is where the breathing part of your training comes in."

"How will breathing help me with handling my emotions and pressure?"

"It will. Simply notice your breathing when you become anxious or angry on and off the pitch, breathe deeply and relax. Football is an incredibly emotional game and you need to be able to handle your emotions as you will make decisions that you don't truly want to make if you are too emotional. When playing, passion and courage are healthy emotions; anxiety or fears are not."

"I can't choose my emotions, can I?"

"Emotions are natural, and they arise in any moment or situation in life. Do not hide away from them. Feel your emotions fully, but do not let them control your behaviour. You should be able to choose how you want to react. If you want to be angry or defensive, then do that if you feel it is best. I find it's best to remain level headed and balanced at all times. There is enough negative emotion in the world; I don't need to add to it."

"I understand, but what if an opponent upsets me?"

"If an opponent upsets you, you can still feel the anger, but channel that emotion and use it to serve you. The moment you lose control of your emotions, you are out of the game. You do things you regret and you say things you can't take back. Use positive emotions to make you better and do your best to turn negative emotions into positive ones. Turn anger into passion, jealousy into acceptance, resentment into forgiveness, nerves into excitement and hatred into compassion. It is not easy, but it is necessary."

"So, when I get frustrated I just need to breathe and understand that it is natural. I have the choice not to react to the emotion I'm feeling?"

"Yes, that is the choice you have. Next time you feel angry, try your best to notice the anger, take a deep breath and notice if you still feel angry. It is not easy to do, but when you calm down you will be amazed at how much this technique will help you in life."

"Okay, cool. I will try my best to monitor and handle my emotions just as I will try to monitor and handle my thoughts. But what about handling and dealing with pressure situations?"

"Pressure is self-created and, when you feel it, smile and understand that the pressure does not even exist. You have created it for yourself with your thoughts. Take a deep breath and understand the situation isn't as serious as you have made it for yourself. Your emotions constantly respond to everything that is happening around you and within you. It is completely healthy and natural to feel your emotions as it shows you care about what you are doing. Emotions are a necessity in the game; football without emotion would not be as entertaining and what is football without entertainment?"

"You're right, boss. Emotions make the game interesting but, as you say, it's about using the emotions I feel to benefit me and my team mates, not make things worse. When I feel pressure, I must smile and understand that it isn't real. I now understand what you told me the other night. You said I need to play with a calm mind and a heart full of passion, and that is exactly what I will try to do."

"Good. You are beginning to listen more than you talk, TJ. It is a valuable life skill. Most people listen to respond, they do not listen to learn. Another thing: always be aware of distractions."

"What kind of distractions?"

"On the field there are supporters, opponents, personal problems and even your coach and team mates, all distracting you. You need to be able to keep your focus. Our society has many distractions that take you away from the present moment, which is why I do not have a cell phone or television. This world is full of distractions and you need to be focused on what you need to do."

"I understand, but I'm a bit scared by what you've just said. I'm starting to realize that people will judge me if I start living my life in the way you are teaching me to. Nobody lives their lives like this and if I tell anybody what you have been telling me they will think I'm weird. I'm not really scared of judgment, I generally follow my own heart. I'm just saying that this is extremely different to how most people I know think or behave."

"Never judge yourself and never fear the judgment of others. It does not matter what your parents think of you, what your coach thinks of you, what your team mates think of you or what I think of you. Let people think what they want to think about you, you can't change it. As long as you are not harming others and you know in your own heart what you are doing and what you want to achieve, that's all that matters."

"But other people's opinions are important to me. I don't want to be lonely. I enjoy being with people. Yes, I don't always agree with them and many people have always told me what to do, but I don't want to be lonely."

"That's good, TJ, but understand that people don't want you to use your own answers. They want you to use theirs. It is wonderful that you want to be with people, but I am talking about the judgment of other people. Many people would rather prove that they are right than actually search for the truth. Instead of discussing, people argue, to prove that their point of view is right. But do not fear judgment, TJ. Embrace who you are as a person. Some days you are a great son to your parents, other days you are not. Some days you are a great footballer in people's eyes and then you miss an easy opportunity in front of goal and you are the worst player in the world. You pull off a great move, then you are a hero. You mess it up, then you are a clown. Do not concern yourself with the thoughts or opinions of others; do what you feel is right in your own heart."

"I completely agree with that, sir, and if you ask my mother she will tell you I have always followed my own heart, but what about the great advice I have received from other people? I needed them at certain times and they helped me."

"You do need other people and there is a lot of great advice other people will give you, but always decide for yourself what you want to do. If you want to take people's advice, take it, but before you start believing everyone else's answers, find your own, ask your own questions and run your own race. You cannot control what other people think. In fact, there isn't much you have control over in this life, not much at all. You control a few body movements, your attitude and that's about it, so surrender control. When you think you are in control of everything in your life, change comes. Change is constant, so you need to understand that anything can happen at any time, nothing ever stays the same. Be grateful for what you have right now in your life because it may be taken away from you at any moment."

"I'm learning a lot, thank you sir, and I understand everything you are saying. Before I listen to others I need to listen to my own heart. There are many things that have happened in my life that have been out of my control and there was nothing I could do to stop them. I have no control over what happens to me but I can control my attitude. I understand all of that, but I don't understand the last thing you said. How can I still be grateful for things when I am not happy about them?"

"Gratitude is the key to abundance in life, TJ. If you learn to love what you already have, more will come to you."

"But there are bad things that happen. How can I be grateful for the bad things?"

"Remember, when you suffer, you learn and you can be grateful for the lessons you learn from the supposed bad things that happen."

"What about people who treat me badly? Do I still need to be grateful and treat them with respect?"

"Yes, always treat people, especially your parents, with respect, but you must be who you are and not who your family or friends want you to be. If someone hurts or disrespects you, don't associate with them anymore, simple. If someone fights you, stand your ground but forgive them, forgive yourself and move on. This life is about being who you are and making the choices you truly want to make. When you do what is best for you, then you will be at your best for those around you."

"But people won't accept me if I don't listen to them or don't do what they tell me to do, boss."

"Do you accept yourself as a person?"

"I think I do."

The mechanic smiles and stops walking; which causes TJ to stop too.

The mechanic puts his hand on TJ's shoulder and says, "You cannot change your true nature, champ, so you might as well embrace yourself for who you are. Trust in your own capabilities. You feel truly happy when you are being who you are. You have probably felt this happiness on the football field, where you can express yourself and be yourself, which is why you love the game so much."

The mechanic pulls his hand off as TJ replies, "But, like you said, boss, change is constant. People change all the time. I've changed a lot, so how can I accept some of the terrible things I do and say. I'm not perfect, so how can I truly accept myself?"

"Your thoughts, your words and your actions change constantly, but who you truly are never changes. You can change your thoughts and actions, but who you are, your true nature never changes. Embrace who you are. There are not two of you, there is only you. Your thoughts, emotions and actions are not who you are. There is only one you and the real you is limitless."

TJ pauses for a moment and then has a sudden realization as he thinks: *so the only person who needs to accept me, is me. I need to accept myself as a person first, for all my great qualities and not so great qualities.* His silence tells the mechanic he has understood everything that was just said to him. It is the middle of the afternoon and the sun is shining brightly. They have walked a fair distance away from the petrol station, out of the town and along a road with farm land on either side of it.

"I think we should start heading back. We have walked for a while and I still have a lot of work to do back at the garage," says the mechanic as he turns to face the teenager.

TJ agrees as they turn around and begin walking back home. They walk in silence as TJ processes everything he has learned about football and life. They do not say anything to one another throughout the entire walk home.

Arriving home, the sun is beginning to set along the Rustenburg horizon. Walking towards the front door of the house, the mechanic breaks the silence and says, "We have spoken a lot today, champ, but there is one more thing that I need you to ask yourself."

"Okay, boss."

"What is most important to you in your life?"

"I don't know, sir."

"I don't want you to answer it now. I want you to ask the question in your own time and be patient to receive the answer. If being a footballer is the most important thing to you, then you need to ask yourself the next questions. Why do you want to become a footballer? Why do you love the game so much? What is it that is driving and motivating you? The answers you receive to those questions will keep you going whenever you feel like giving up or want to stop playing the game when it becomes gruelling and tough. You need to start asking the right questions to receive the right answers you are looking for. Life has all the answers you need but understand that life will only give them to you when you are ready to receive them. When you are not ready, you will not hear or understand the answers you receive."

TJ then begins to wonder why he fell in love with football in the first place. They stop at the front door of the house. The mechanic looks at TJ and puts his hand on his shoulder again.

"I do not believe in coincidences, my boy. You are meant to be here with me and I am meant to be here with you. There is a bigger plan for both of us here; a plan we do not understand. There is a reason for us being in each other's lives and that reason might or might not be revealed in the future. Everything has its reason and its purpose."

He takes his hand off TJ's shoulder and unlocks the door. The old man pauses and then says, "One more thing."

TJ smiles. "Yes, sir?"

"Anybody from anywhere in the world can go on to be a wonderful footballer but why do you think it is that people who grow up in tough and harsh environments or circumstances are the people that generally go on to become great footballers?"

The teenager shrugs his shoulders, having never really thought about it before.

The mechanic answers. "It is because they have an unrelenting fire in their belly to succeed. It is because that without football they feel they cannot live or breathe. Football fuels the passion in their veins and drives them further than anybody else to escape a life of pain or poverty. Everybody has this desire within them and it is up to you to ignite the fire in your belly every single morning when the sun comes up. Every morning I wake up, I am grateful just to be breathing. Thousands upon thousands of people on the planet will not be breathing tomorrow morning, so be happy to be alive.

"It is up to you to be excited and enthusiastic about the challenges and growth you can experience each day. There will be tests, there will be tough times and you will toil, but it is how we grow as individuals. There will be great times and bad times. You will fall and you will rise, but do not let that fire within you disappear. That fire in your belly is the passion you need to drive you and if you have scored a winning goal for your team or saved a ball off the line before then you know what burning feeling I am talking about."

"I do know what feeing you are talking about, boss. I had it on the first day you told me you were going to train me but it disappeared the next day when I didn't want to do the training you wanted me to do."

"That's it! Now you need to spark that fire in your belly every single day, with however you know how to. You will be amazed at how far enthusiasm can take you and the things it will encourage you to do!"

"I know what I need to do," says TJ as he walks past the mechanic, into the house and out the back door into the garden. The mechanic nods his head, puts his keys down on the dining room table and then walks in the opposite direction to continue working on the red car he was fixing earlier in the day.

TJ plants himself on the grey rock. He sits comfortably and stares out at the horizon. He breathes in deeply through his nose and he feels the fresh air slowly filling his lungs. He breathes out slowly through his mouth. Although he has spent over twenty days in this position, he looks around and it is as if he sees his surroundings for the first time. He notices the dark orange and red skyline being created by the setting sun in the west. He sees mountains, farms and houses in the distance. He hears the different sounds the different birds are making in the trees and flying high in the sky. He feels the rock's surface as he rubs its hard texture with his hands. He notices a few brown leaves slowly falling, one by one from the lifeless trees. He feels the warmth from the sun slowly disappearing as it sets in front of him.

He closes his eyes and for the first time he sees himself from within. He feels pure joy and peace. He feels boundless and whole; the world is in perfect balance. There are pure and calm emotions flowing gently though his body. Happy pictures move in the forefront of his mind as a subtle smile forms on his face. No emotions, no thinking, just a clear mind and a happy heart living in the moment. It is as if he knows who he truly is for the first time in his life.

"So this is what the old man was talking about," he says softly, his eyes remaining closed.

It is late in the evening and the mechanic has not seen TJ for quite some time now. The old man decides to walk through the house, trying to find the teenager and, as he looks out of the kitchen window, he sees TJ sitting on the grey rock staring out in to the distance. The mechanic grabs a faded brown leather jacket hanging in his cupboard and walks outside to check on TJ. The winter air bites at the old man's face as he steps outside. He walks down the small hill towards the grey rock. He settles next to TJ, who acknowledges him, and they both look out into the distance together. There is nothing but the bright stars and full moon lighting up the earth's dark surface.

"So, what are you doing?" the mechanic asks after a few minutes of silence.

TJ sits extremely still and answers, "Just sitting on a rock... Have you seen how awesome the stars are tonight? It's breath taking and the sounds are amazing. I had no idea nature made so much noise in winter. Only difficult thing at the moment is this rock is stinging my hands. It's freezing but I do feel incredible."

"It's rather pleasant living in the present moment, isn't it champ?"

"It is, boss. I can feel it! I feel calm and happy at the same time. It's awesome!"

The mechanic smiles, nods his head and looks up at the stars together with TJ.

"So I received the answer to why I love football so much sir."

"That's great. And why is that?"

"It was never actually about being the best in the world or earning money from it. It has always been about the memories it creates. The power football has to bring people together. It allows people to share stories of great moments and feelings they have experienced together. It has always been about bringing happiness to those around me. My team mates, my coach, the supporters that watched and my family. The same way I felt growing up when my hero scored a goal or when my team won, that is the feeling I want to give to other people. I want to help create those stories, memories and joy for people and help them forget all the worries and troubles that they are facing in the real world, even if it is just for a few moments. The way I want to do it is by becoming the best player this world has ever seen. I know if I am meant to be the best, I will be."

There isn't a flicker of emotion in TJ's voice or doubt in his mind as he speaks. It is as if the answer has come from somewhere deep within him. The mechanic feels every word and responds, "Some players just want to have some fun and be with their team mates. Why are you so serious?"

They both laugh.

"Get your football kit on when you wake up tomorrow morning. You are finally ready to begin the next part of your training. Brace yourself, TJ. The hard work begins as soon as your eyes open tomorrow."

The old man pats the teenager on the back and begins walking back into the house as TJ says, "Before you go inside, boss… I have one more question for you."

The mechanic turns around and he asks, "Why did you really make me do all those terrible cleaning jobs? I could have learned the power of focus, breathing properly and awareness by just sitting on this rock."

The mechanic smiles and replies. "Well, the entire station was in desperate need of some quality cleaning!"

TJ pulls a face and shakes his head.

"No, I needed to see how far you were willing to go to become a footballer. Any teenager willing to devote himself to scrubbing floors, cleaning toilets or washing cars with no extra pay and no clue why he is doing it must really want to become a footballer. It also taught you to give your best to whatever job you are doing. You might not like to defend on the football pitch but you have to do it and you have to give your best when doing it. It taught you the value of working hard. When I was your age, a few of us often had to scrub the floors, clean the toilets and paint the walls of the training ground and stadium for the club we were playing at. It was initiation for being the youngest guys in the first team. I hated it, but I always made sure that the part of the job I was doing was better than the guy's next to me. Focus on the job you need to do, your team mates needs to focus on theirs. We need to do the small jobs to the best of our ability, on and off the pitch. As I have said before: the smallest jobs and details are the most important."

TJ looks at the old man with amazement in his eyes suddenly realizing he is being taught by a very special human being.

"Well, I think that is enough talk for one day. Rest well tonight and I will see you in the morning," says the mechanic as he continues his walk back towards the house.

TJ smiles, jumps off the cold rock and heads to bed, feeling as though he can overcome any challenge he may face tomorrow.

· 7 ·

Do Ten More

....

It is 5:00am and TJ is already out of bed, fully dressed in his white Rustenburg Rovers training kit. He is preparing a cup of tea, hydrating himself for whatever the mechanic has in store for him today.

The old man returns from his morning walk as the green kettle finishes boiling and he looks at TJ with a startled smile on his face as he opens the front door.

"TJ! Good morning, champ! I was just about to wake you," he says in his usual energetic tone of voice.

"Morning, sir! Well, I wanted to be sure I was up before you could come give me some profound lecture to start my day again," chirps TJ.

The mechanic chuckles and replies, "Well, if you could see how depressed your face looks in the morning you would lecture yourself too."

TJ smiles. "So how was the walk?" he asks.

"It was great. Beautiful and fresh weather out there today. Winter is slowly starting to lose its battle to spring. Earlier sunrises and warmer air will be here soon. I think today is a perfect day for a run."

TJ has anticipated he would be running this morning so he is not surprised by the old man's comment.

The mechanic continues, "But before you go on your run I want you to do fifty push ups without stopping."

"Seriously? I haven't done push ups in ages."

"I can see that, champ," says the mechanic, smiling.

"Very funny, sir. Why do I need to do them?"

"You need to do them because your body looks like a treeless leaf at the moment."

"A treeless leaf?"

"Yes. If the wind blows too hard you will blow away with it. You are terribly thin for an athlete, son."

"I don't need to have massive muscles to play football!" says TJ, defending himself.

"You're right, but you don't need to be a twig either."

"Fine!" says TJ in a dejected tone, "I will do the push ups then. Fifty doesn't sound too difficult. Must I do them right here?"

"Yes."

The teenager gets down on his hands and begins doing the push ups intensely. He starts off well but as he goes past fifteen his arms begin to burn, each push up becoming increasingly difficult to do.

He reaches thirty push ups, panting and in agony. He bends down, his arms burn and he shouts, "I can't do anymore, boss!"

"If you fall down, you start all over again, so push yourself! It's a mental test not a physical one. Be strong mentally!"

TJ keeps going, bending his arms slowly and pushing up in agony, each push up taking him longer and longer to do, his arms shaking and his muscles burning.

"Forty eight... Forty nine... Fifty!" and he collapses.

"See, that wasn't so hard, was it?" chirps the mechanic.

TJ bites his tongue to stop himself from swearing in reply as he lies with his chest flat on the floor, panting heavily, purposefully ignoring the old man's comment. He then slowly sits up and rubs his arms.

"Now I need you to do ten more," says the mechanic.

"Are you joking? I can't sir! I can't! I wouldn't even be able to do one more! I've reached my limit!"

"No you haven't! He who says he can and he who says he can't are both right. You need to develop a strong, resilient mind. Anything you set your mind to you can achieve. Don't listen to it when it's telling you to give up. When you feel pain, there is growth."

TJ sighs, clears his throat and then reluctantly gets into a push up position once again, not wanting to argue with the old man. His arms are weak but he readies himself for ten more.

"One... Two... Three... Four... Five... I can't!"

"Come on, TJ! You can do it! Be strong!"

"Six... Seven... Eight..."

TJ takes a deep breath and tells himself, "Come on, you can do it. Only two left!"

"Nine... Ten," and his arms collapse onto the floor once more.

"I thought you said you couldn't do anymore," says the mechanic jokingly.

"You're just lucky I can't move my arms to throw a punch at you," replies TJ, panting.

"Now do you see what a wonderful creation your body is, champ? The things it is capable of? You thought you were completely finished, not able to even do one more push up, but you managed to do ten. Your body can do spectacular things and your mind is extremely powerful."

"Yeah, I honestly never thought I even had a chance of doing ten more, not a chance with the way I felt after doing fifty. Usually, I would have been telling myself that it is okay to give up."

"Exactly. Push past any fears or limits you have within you. Use your mind to achieve what you want in life. Whatever it is that you want, develop a resilient mind and it will help you achieve what you want to achieve. You need to be strong. When you grow, there will most likely be pain involved; as you have just seen with these push ups."

"I understand, boss. I will never forget this lesson and I don't think my arms will let me forget it either... I'm just saying. If I don't have some form of a bicep tomorrow morning then I'm going to be very upset."

The mechanic laughs and takes a piece of paper out from his pocket. He hands it to TJ, who is still sitting on the floor and breathing heavily.

"You need to do what's on that paper now" says the mechanic.

TJ opens it up and it reads:

Daily gym routine:

3 sets of: 150 push-ups, 150 sit-ups, 100 pull-ups on the bar on your door, 100 triceps dips on the edge of your bed, 100 lunges, 100 jump squats, 100 calf raises and a 7 minute plank.

TJ looks at the paper with pure fear on his face as he thinks about the strain he will be putting on his body. The mechanic looks at the teenager's fearful face and says, "Just give it your best. The stronger your muscles are the easier training will be for you. You need to condition your body. A footballer does not need to be big and strong, but he needs to be mobile. He needs to have a firm, lean body and he needs to be light on his feet."

"I'm not looking forward to it at all but I will give it my best, sir, to get into the best shape possible for the training."

"Good, and just remember to always stretch your body first. Stretch your ankles, calves, groin, hamstrings, gluts, quads, hips, arms, neck, everything. Stretching is vitally important. If you are flexible, you lower the risk of getting an injury, so don't treat stretching lightly. I will prepare breakfast; just let me know when you are done."

TJ goes to his room, stretches each of his muscles and attempts each exercise until they become unbearable.

He gives his best, his muscles burn and after one set of the gym routine he only manages to do twenty more push ups, forty sit-ups, twenty pull-ups, fifty dips, fifty lunges, fifty jump squats, sixty ankle raises and a one minute plank. His body is in pain and he is not even going to attempt another set.

He walks to the kitchen and the mechanic, who has only just begun preparing breakfast chirps, "That was quick!"

"I can't push my body anymore, sir. I didn't even come close to the targets and I could only do one set."

The mechanic smiles. "It's understandable, champ. Your body is not accustomed to the intense work and you don't want to overdo it today, but that will be your gym routine. Three mornings in a row you will do the routine and then you will take one morning to recover. Then you will do it again. If there are days you cannot push yourself, then listen to your body and rest. The recovery you take is just as important as the load you put on yourself, but you are going to need to push yourself when you feel pain. Pain equals growth when it comes to physical activity, unfortunately, and if getting stronger was easy then everybody would do it."

"I promise I will push myself, boss. You know I will, but is it healthy to do my entire body in one gym session?"

"No, you need to balance it. One morning, focus on your upper body. Developing strong shoulders and arms is vital when needing to protect the ball or win the ball from an opponent. The next morning you will focus on your legs and core. If your legs are strong, you will be faster and staying on your feet will be easier. Having a strong core, your stomach muscles, will improve your balance and movement. Stretch as soon as you wake up and stretch as soon as you are finished the workout, every day. Flexibility is vital to your physical training. If your body and muscles are tight, it will prevent you from performing at your best. You are going to need to be strong and flexible."

"I understand, and will my diet be staying the same?"

"Yes, still vegetables, fruit, carbohydrates and protein. The only thing you will add to your diet is a health protein shake that I order from a shop in Hartbeespoort. You need to drink it every morning after you do the work out."

"Sounds good, sir. Thank you."

"Have this bowl of fruit now, drink some water and when you feel ready I want you to go outside and stretch again. I will show you the route you will be running."

"I still need to run? No ways, boss, that's way too hectic! You will break my body."

"Are you the best footballer in the world?"

TJ lets out a huge sigh. "Not yet, sir," he replies reluctantly.

He eats his bowl of fruit, has his protein shake and makes sure he is mentally prepared for the run. He walks into the garden, towards the long flat patch of sand below the large grey rock and does a few stretches to prepare for his run. After a short while of stretching, the mechanic joins him, holding a stop watch in his hand.

He looks at TJ and immediately asks, "What are you doing?"

"I'm stretching," the teenager replies innocently.

"That is static stretching and it is not the kind of stretching you need to be doing. Before you do any extreme football activity you should do dynamic stretching."

"What's that?"

"It is stretching, but you are jogging at the same time. So you do the specific stretches with a bit of movement. You stretch all the major muscles I mentioned earlier with dynamic stretching."

"When will I do static stretching then?"

"For your arms and neck you can do static stretching. You also do static stretching when you have finished your physical activity. Static stretching will prevent your muscles from tightening and stop you from feeling stiff the next day. It is to prevent lactic acid from building up in your muscles. Lactic acid builds up and stops you from training at a high intensity or on a regular basis; it will harm your recovery too. Football is a very explosive sport, using all of your muscles, so, as I've said, stretching is vital."

"I understand, but why do you place such importance on the recovery after exercise, sir?"

"The way you recover from extreme physical activity is just as important as the effort you put into it. If your body is extremely tired and exhausted, listen to it and rest. If you train too hard you could become sick or injure yourself. Same thing will happen if you don't train hard enough. Push your body as hard as you can, but rest if you are taking strain. Does that make sense?"

"It does. I must push myself as hard as I can but I should recover when I feel I can't give my best."

"That's right. Now this is how you do dynamic stretching."

The old man begins demonstrating and TJ copies him, move for move. It is a unique sight to the petrol station as they run up and down the sand patch, doing dynamic stretches.

"Your task now is to run three kilometres in twelve minutes," says the mechanic as soon as the stretching is complete. "Why such a short distance? We would run fifteen kilometres in pre-season training at Rustenburg Rovers."

"There will be long distance runs ahead for you, but not too many. We need to build up your fitness levels first. Most professional footballers will run between nine to twelve kilometres during a match over ninety minutes, but in those nine to twelve kilometres are many short sprints, jumping and lateral movements. You do not need to train like a long distance runner to be a footballer. You will never have to run more than a hundred metres at one time on the field. It is all short distance, high intensity sprinting; so three kilometres is a great distance to build your endurance with."

"I understand."

"Good. These three kilometres will build up your stamina and doing it in twelve minutes will ensure you can run long distances in a short space of time. Being fit is so important because, if you are not fit, you can't play this game. You need to be able to give your best throughout the ninety minutes of a match. If you can only give your absolute best for twenty minutes of a game you are letting your team down and if I was coaching you I would make you warm the bench."

"So I need to be able to focus for an entire ninety minutes without getting tired? That's impossible."

"It's not impossible. It is vital for you to be able to give your best throughout the entire game without losing your focus or your legs and lungs stopping you from pushing as hard as you can. When eighty minutes of the game has passed and everyone around you is fading away, you will be able to keep going. The greatest teams and players come alive in the final ten minutes of a game; they push beyond their limits right until that final whistle blows."

The mechanic notices TJ listening intently to everything he is telling him. He then begins pointing his finger, showing the route he needs to run in order to complete the three kilometres.

He will need to exit the gate at the bottom of the mechanic's self-made garden and run along a sand road that leads out of the small town and past the array of farms he has been staring at from the grey rock.

TJ nods his head and the mechanic says, "One more thing… Concentrate on your breathing, deep breaths in through your nose and firm breaths out your mouth; take it one step at a time. Keep your mind empty, focus on one moment at a time and, if you are in pain, remember what an incredible creation your body is. It is capable of doing things you never thought were possible."

"Okay, boss. I will push, no matter what, no excuses."

"Alright, you're all set then. Good luck, son."

TJ prepares his mind, takes a few deep breaths and then takes the first step and another and another as he begins jogging out the black gate and onto the sand road the mechanic had pointed to. His legs are moving slowly but as he continues his pace increases.

"I won't give up," he promises himself as he runs past a small forest of trees beginning to grow their leaves back. He tries to stay conscious of his breathing and attempts noticing everything around him. The wind is blowing gently against his face as he enters a different part of the small town he has not seen before. He sees children playing games in the street, avoiding school, birds in the trees, people talking to each other at different shops and, as he exits the town, he sees men working hard on the farms. His chest suddenly begins to burn and it becomes increasingly difficult for him to focus on what is going on around him as his mind says, *Slow down.*

His feet are thumping hard against the sand road as he tries pushing his legs, constantly urging them not to walk or slow down. He hears his every step landing firmly against the ground. After eight minutes of running it feels as though he has been running for a life time. He turns around where he was told to and makes his way back to the petrol station. His legs are in agony, his heart is pounding and his lungs and throat are burning. He is in immense pain. Everything inside of him is telling him to stop and walk.

It's okay to just relax, his mind tells him

TJ fights as he runs back past the farms, the town and small forest. He is coming to the end of the run. He focuses on taking it one step and one breath at a time. The mechanic's back garden is approaching as he sees the old man in the near distance, standing on the flat piece of sand, waiting for him to arrive. He is utterly exhausted, but he feels a burst of energy from within and he starts sprinting to finish as quickly as he can, pushing his legs and lungs right to the end. He reaches the mechanic and stops. The old man clicks the stop watch and shouts, "fifteen minutes and four seconds! Not bad!"

"I can taste blood! I'm dying!" shouts TJ, as he heaves in the air, trying to catch his breath. He puts his hands on his knees, breathing heavily, trying to gasp in as much air as possible to recover.

"I could have run that distance in half the amount of time and I am more than triple your age," says the mechanic, handing him a much needed bottle of water.

"You're lucky... I can't... talk back..." says TJ, still trying to catch his breath as he stands up straight, gulping the water given to him.

"Stretch properly. Drink plenty of water and eat well throughout the day. Pasta, you need to eat lots of pasta to recharge your energy levels," says the mechanic assertively.

TJ is panting intensely. He gives the empty bottle of water to the mechanic and puts both his hands on his head as the mechanic tells him, "That is all you will be doing today."

"Oh, is that all? Only three kilometres and all the gym work I had to do," says the teenager sarcastically.

"Get used to it. Over the next few months we will be working on the physical side of your game. The highest recorded amount of time spent on the ball in world football during ninety minutes is four minutes and twelve seconds."

"Only four minutes?" asks a surprised TJ.

"Yes, so what do you think you are doing the other eighty six minutes?"

TJ is still out of breath but replies, "Running".

"That's right. You can be the most skilful player in the world, but if you are not an athlete or do not have the required physical attributes to play football you will struggle to play the game professionally. What is the point of having all these wonderful skills if you don't have the ability to move into the correct space and protect the ball when you get it? If you don't know how to get the ball, it doesn't matter how good you are with it."

"That makes sense."

"Good. I want you to be able to keep running no matter what. We need you to form the essential habit of moving constantly on the pitch in training and in games. Don't get into the bad habit of needing to walk or standing still on a football pitch. There is always something to do. Sometimes you need to walk to recover, but remember there is always something happening. So, stay on your toes and always be aware of what is happening around you. Keep on your toes. There is nothing worse than a flat footed footballer. So, work hard when you train. The more you sweat in training, the less you will sweat in a match."

"The more I sweat in training, the less I will sweat in a match, I like that. It makes me feel like if I train hard then it will be worth it in the games when it matters most."

"I like the saying too. I used to train harder than anybody else and because of that the games were easy. Everybody has the ability to improve their physical attributes. Some need to work harder than others, but everyone has the ability to improve their strength, speed, acceleration, fitness or whatever. Whenever your mind says stop pushing yourself or begs you to give up, don't listen. Give your best, or don't do it at all."

TJ is recovering gradually from the run. There is no wind, but the air is fresh and the sounds of nature can be heard as they talk to one another. The old man continues, "You will never ever be at one hundred percent for an entire ninety minutes. You can be the fittest man in the world, and it helps, but as soon as that whistle blows to kick off the game, your energy levels begin to decrease. You need to get fitter and learn how to keep your focus even when you are exhausted."

"So you are saying I can be as fit as I want to be, but I will still get tired in the games?"

"Yes. Being fit is essential; the more you train, the longer you can run for and the more comfortable you become with being tired. It is about being comfortable and focused, even though you are feeling tired."

"What about injuries? Won't I get exhausted if I work too hard and, when I get exhausted, doesn't it make it easier for my body to get injured?"

"Injuries will occur if you over work yourself. They will also occur if you don't work hard enough. When you need a rest, take it. If you are stiff and tired, then stretch, eat recovery foods or even get a massage, but don't come to me for one. The stronger your body is and the fitter you are, the less prone you will be to injuries."

"How will I know when I need to recover?"

"Just listen to your body. It will give you all the signals, but you are going to feel pain and you are going to need to work hard. You get the body you earn, not the body you want."

"So I will only get the body I deserve and work for. Sounds fair enough."

"Yes. The most intelligent footballers in the world never feel extremely tired for two reasons. One reason is that they are incredibly fit and the other reason is that they know where to move on the pitch; they don't do any aimless or pointless running. You need to work exceptionally hard, but work intelligently. Sometimes not moving is the right movement to make. This comes with experience."

"Let's hope I can learn to do that, but right now I am so tired, boss, and in need of a rest. Can we continue this conversation another time?"

The mechanic smiles and says, "Yes, we can but you still need to do your job today, TJ. You don't get days off from work at the station because of training."

"That's chilled. I just need a bit of time to rest before I start working."

"No problem. One thing is for sure, you are going to sleep very deeply tonight. It will be needed for the week of training you are about to go through."

"Sounds like fun, sir."

The mechanic laughs and begins walking back to the tin garage to work on the latest machinery that has arrived for repairs. TJ, feeling exhausted, goes to his room, takes off his football kit, puts on his new white and black working clothes given to him by the mechanic and then opens up the shop. It is 9:00 and TJ already feels as though he has lived through an entire day. He goes to the petrol pump to serve a customer and he greets the middle aged woman in a friendly manner.

He keeps himself busy throughout the day, not complaining he is tired or worrying about the week ahead of him. He serves customers who purchase items at the shop and pumps petrol into cars that pass by. He drinks water throughout the day and eats healthily too, over-loading on pasta as he was told to do. Before 20:00 arrives, he goes to his room and collapses into bed. His eyes glue shut and he does not move a muscle until the morning.

TJ wakes up to the sound of a small bird outside, tapping its beak against a tiny window above his bed. The sun has already risen and the mechanic must have allowed him to sleep in later because of the hard physical work he'd done yesterday. He gets up and, still in his pyjamas, he attempts the upper body gym routine that he has been instructed to do.

He completes three sets of the routine, with great difficulty, and it is taking longer than he had hoped it would. However, he feels proud of completing it.

He showers and washes the sweat off his body. Feeling fresh and ready for the day, he puts on his football kit and then walks through to the kitchen. He makes himself a protein shake and sits down at the dining room table. Looking at the table he notices a note resting on pieces of paper. He begins reading the note:

Out of town for the week. I need to be in Gauteng. I have locked the tin garage. No repairs to be done until I return. I need you to please run the petrol station and take care of the house while I am gone. I have written all the exercises you will need to do this week. Read the instructions carefully and give it your best. Don't forget to do your gym routine each morning too. Thank you very much and see you soon.

TJ takes the note off the three pieces of paper it is resting on and on these pieces of paper are all the physical exercises he will need to do throughout the week. He begins reading:

Day one: Agility, movement exercises and skipping

This will teach you how to become lighter on your feet and it will also improve your balance. Footballers who are too heavy on their feet will struggle in the professional environment. It will teach you how to glide with or without a ball on the field. Which is what you see when some of the best players are running with the ball and they look as though they are just effortlessly floating whilst they are running. Mobility is vital.

Put at least 10 rocks down on the ground. Those rocks will be your cones. You will run in between the rocks with quick feet for 15 minutes. Then put the rocks wider apart and sprint and touch each rock with one hand for 10 minutes. You need to complete as many agility sprints as possible in those 25 minutes.

After doing the agility work, you will need to start skipping. The skipping rope is in the cupboard of your bedroom. Skip for 10 minutes. It will help you improve your balance as well as help you become lighter on your feet.

Day two: Three 100-metre, Three 200-metre, Three 500-metre sprints and jumping

Measure the distance of the sprints yourself by taking big steps, each step is a metre. Use any flat surface that will allow you to sprint without any turns. There are no targets for the sprints just run them at the quickest speed you can. Time yourself and try to beat your time every single sprint you do. Speed is king in modern day football and the faster you are, the more valuable you are to your team. The more you work on your speed, the faster you will become.

You will also need to do 5 sets of jumping. One set is jumping 15 times onto the rock.

A footballer will usually jump between 10 and 15 times during a game. So you need to improve your leap off the ground and jump higher than anybody else on the field. Being able to jump and hang in the air will help you win headers to score more goals. It will also help you win valuable defensive or offensive headers for your team.

Day three: Recovery day

Use this time to sit on the rock and practise living in the present moment. Think about what parts of your physical game you can still improve. Stretch often, take a walk through nature and visualize and imagine yourself doing wonderful and spectacular things on a football pitch in the future. Your imagination has no boundaries, so use it. Remember to stay focused on whatever job you are doing.

Day Four: 10-metre sprints and balancing

You need to measure 10 metres with your steps and do 30 sprints. Try doing the 10 metre sprints in 1.7 seconds. Use my stopwatch and time yourself. 10 metre sprints will improve your acceleration. In football, you only need to be extremely fast over a short distance to get past your opponent or to get into the appropriate space. Your burst of speed is vitally important.

You will then need to stand on the edge of the rock, balancing on one leg. Lunge with one leg at a time, doing it with your eyes closed. Keep your balance on the rock without falling off. Lunge for 5 minutes on each leg. Your legs will burn, you will wobble but you need to attempt to stay on the rock for 5 minutes. Look at the stop watch when you think 5 minutes is over. This will improve your balance. Balance helps you stay on your feet easier and move with ease when you are running with or without the ball. Focus on your breathing and keep your mind clear while doing it.

Day five: Hill runs

When you exit the station, turn left on the main road. You will need to walk just over a kilometre and you will be faced with a steep hill that is 200 metres long. You need to do 12 sprints up this hill. Once you have sprinted up the hill as quickly as you can, you will walk back down to recover. You need to attempt to do it in 24 minutes. These sprints will improve your speed and fitness levels and also improve your leg strength and power.

Day six: Cycling

You need to cycle 20 kilometres in 22 minutes with my old bicycle in the garage. Turn right, leaving the station. Stay on the same road the entire ride and cycle until you get to a small chicken farm on your right hand side. There will be a few uphills and downhills. Pedal as fast as you can on the uphills and rest on the downhills. Cycling will improve your leg strength and fitness levels.

Day seven: Recovery day or the 3 kilometre run in 12 minutes

TJ reads through everything again, making sure he understands exactly what he needs to do throughout the week. Every exercise has its own instructions, what physical part of his game it will be improving and the goal that he needs to reach. Reading the information, he realizes the power he has to improve his physical attributes.

All my life I've just accepted that I'm not as strong or as fast as my team mates and friends, but I actually had the chance to improve everything, he thinks.

He then notices the benefits of setting targets and goals. Setting goals like this actually makes a lot of sense, he thinks. How can I shoot at the goals if I don't know where the goals are? I need a target to aim for, otherwise it's pointless. Also, how will I know if I've improved or not? I think I should start setting small goals first, before I go after the ultimate goals.

He uses the pen on the table and begins writing the small goals he wants to achieve. The first one he sets for himself is to try running the three kilometres in fourteen minutes. When he achieves that target, he will try to do it in thirteen minutes and thirty seconds before attempting the ultimate goal of twelve minutes. He continues writing every small goal he wants to achieve in each exercise.

He finishes, puts the pen down and then puts his goals in a wooden drawer next to his bed.

He makes a healthy breakfast to fuel himself for the agility exercises. As he sits down to start eating, he hears a loud knock on the wooden front door. He opens the door and greets a customer who has been waiting for someone to serve him at the petrol pump. It is 8:30am and the petrol station is usually open at this time. TJ apologizes to the middle aged man and walks outside to unlock the pump. He puts petrol into the man's car and realizes that during this week he is going to need to serve customers throughout the day before doing his physical exercises in the evenings.

He bids farewell to the customer and then opens the shop. He changes into his work uniform and begins his day as temporary petrol station manager.

He treats the petrol station as he would treat his own business, greeting each customer with a smile and serving each of their needs without any complaints. He serves people the entire day, but is forced to tell unhappy customers who need car repairs that it will have to be done next week. They tell TJ they will wait until next week, all having heard of the mechanic's expertise. When there are no customers at the petrol station, TJ cleans the shop and house.

At 17:00, he finishes serving an elderly woman in the shop and then locks everything. It has been a fairly busy day and he feels tired but excited because it is time for him to complete his football exercises for the day.

He puts on his football kit again, takes the skipping rope out of the white cupboard in his bedroom and walks towards the patch of sand below the grey rock in the back garden. He finds a few rocks in the sand beds the plants and fruit trees are growing in. He puts the rocks on the long patch of empty sand and then begins pushing himself, doing as many quick feet and agility exercises as he can. He immediately realizes how heavily he lands on his feet as he tries to do as many agility exercises in the twenty five minutes he's been told to do it in. It is exhausting, but he needs to improve his balance and become lighter on his feet.

After completing the agility exercises, he picks up the skipping rope in the sand and reluctantly begins skipping, feeling exhausted. After only a minute he is forced to stop as he can barely breathe. He skips for one minute at a time. His chest burns, his legs ache, but he slowly makes his way towards the ten minute target.

In the final minute he collapses in the patch of sand, holding the skipping rope in his hand and panting heavily.

"That was insanely difficult. I thought today would be easy," he says as he sits up panting in the sand. He looks around at the trees and birds; the sun setting on a small hill in the distance.

"Another beautiful day in Africa," he says as he stretches his body. The night sky slowly replaces the light and he jogs inside as soon as he finishes stretching. He cooks his own dinner, feeling it is slightly strange being alone in the house, but he is being kept busy with everything he has to do throughout the day.

Let's hope I can find the motivation to push myself without the boss here to teach or inspire me, he thinks as he takes the boiling vegetables off the stove.

Day two on his own, TJ does his leg gym routine in the morning and then completes his work at the petrol station. Once he has locked everything up, he walks through town and finds a flat sand road. He measures out one hundred metres, two hundred metres and five hundred metres. He sprints each distance three times and by the end of all the sprints, he is utterly exhausted. His times were not as great as he'd hoped in the first two runs of each distance and by the third run, they were shocking. He walks back to the petrol station and then practises leaping off the ground onto the grey rock. The rock is about a metre above the ground and, after jumping fifteen times, his legs are burning. He does five sets, bit by bit, and by the time he is finished, he can barely walk up the small hill to get to the house; his legs wobble and shake with each step he takes, the muscles feeling extremely fragile. He goes to bed utterly exhausted again.

Day three, he does his morning upper body gym routine and operates everything at the petrol station. After finishing work, he sits watching the sun set, visualizing scoring amazing goals for the best teams in the country whilst listening and watching everything that is happening around him. He breathes deeply, quietens his mind and simply lives in the present moment, staying focused and thinking about the improvements he could still make physically by doing what he has been told to do. He feels inspired to keep working as hard as he can. His under fifteen Rustenburg Rovers coach always told him that hard work will beat natural talent every time. He believes that, in time, with constant dedication and commitment, he will reach the goals that have been set for him by the mechanic. He just needs to keep pushing. He is not going to give up.

Day four, he does not do the gym routine. It is his recovery day and he runs the petrol station again without any problems before locking up and going to the long sand patch. He measures out ten metres; he holds the stop watch in his hand and he sprints the short distance in two seconds and thirty split seconds is his first time. He needs to reach one second and seventy split seconds. He attempts another twenty-nine short sprints and, just like every other day so far, he is completely worn out when he finishes, his best time at two seconds and fifteen split seconds. He needs to improve his burst of speed. He then walks up to the grey rock, gets on it, closes his eyes, stands on one leg and lunges, trying to balance on the end of it for five minutes. He keeps lunging and then suddenly falls off, having lost his balance.

He looks at his watch. Forty-five seconds was all he'd managed. He tries again. He attempts to do it on both legs, but the longest he manages to stay on the rock is just over one minute. He collapses into bed after dinner.

Day five, he does his morning leg gym routine, serves customers and at 17:00 he locks the petrol station. He turns left at the main road and walks to find the steep hill the mechanic had told him to find. After walking over a kilometre he sees the steep hill. It looks far steeper than he thought it would be. He starts the stop watch, sprints up as fast as he can and then walks down quickly, trying to recover. He needs to complete twelve of these hill runs in twenty-four minutes.

He ends up completing them in thirty five minutes. Every muscle in his legs is in agony as he makes his way back to the petrol station, walking gingerly. His legs feel extremely heavy and he is breathing uncomfortably. He arrives back and has no energy to even cook dinner, and he falls into bed without eating.

Day six, he does his morning upper body gym routine, pumps petrol, serves customers and locks up the shop, house and petrol pump. He opens the tin garage and finds the mechanic's light grey and black bicycle hanging on the wall. He takes it down, locks the tinned garage and begins pedalling. He turns right at the main road and cycles a long distance until he sees the small chicken farm on his right hand side. He turns around and starts pedalling back. There are many uphills and downhills, and his thighs burn on the uphills and he recovers on the downhills. He arrives back at the petrol station feeling exhausted yet again. He manages to cook dinner and he gets into bed.

I'm taking a recovery day tomorrow, he thinks. *My legs and body are in so much pain. I won't be able to move in the morning. I can now see why the boss told me recovery time is just as important as the load; I'm finished.* He falls into a deep sleep.

It is the seventh day since the mechanic left for Gauteng. TJ has eaten dinner, done his football exercises and he is putting petrol into a customer's car late in the evening. The customer was in desperate need of petrol and asked TJ to help him; the teenager duly obliged.

As he pulls the pump out of the car, he notices the mechanic walking along the flat sand road approaching the petrol station without his normal work attire on. He must have been dropped off by a taxi higher up the road, and TJ wonders about what the old man needed to do in Gauteng.

The mechanic mumbles a greeting as he walks past the teenager, barely acknowledging him. TJ notices an extremely tired look on his face. He does not seem to be his normal friendly and energetic self. He finishes serving the customer and immediately walks towards the shop to find out if his boss is feeling okay. He walks into the shop and sees the mechanic checking the cash register.

"Thank you for taking care of the petrol station and the house while I was gone, champ. I really appreciate it," he says more assertively than his earlier greeting. He then closes the cash register and shakes TJ's hand. He smiles uncomfortably, pats him on the shoulder and walks directly into the house without uttering another word.

TJ feels offended that he hadn't even asked if he had completed all the training he was meant to throughout the week. He suddenly feels anger pulsating through his body. He takes a few deep breaths trying to calm down and on the third breath in he says, "No. I'm not going to control my emotions now. He should have asked how everything went with my training this week!"

He follows the mechanic into the house to confront him. He walks down the passage and sees the mechanic sitting on the edge of his double bed.

"I worked as hard as I could to do all those exercises the entire week and you don't even care if I did them or not! You don't care how well I did them either! What kind of coach doesn't care about his own player's progress?" shouts TJ.

The mechanic, who seems extremely fatigued, is taking off his shoes on the edge of his bed. He doesn't look up at TJ, which is strange for the old man as he always looks into the teenager's eyes when being spoken to. He looks at his right shoe, unties the laces and replies, "Do you become a better footballer if you don't do the exercises?"

TJ suddenly realizes he has just lost control of his emotions, reacting unfairly.

He takes a deep breath and replies, "No, I don't, sir."

The mechanic kicks off both his shoes and then looks up at him. "Motivation is always more powerful when you are self motivated," he says. "You should not need anybody else to motivate and push you. If you want something, you are the only one who is going to be able get it. You know in your heart if you have pushed yourself past your limits or if you have done everything correctly this week. I don't need to check up on you; the results will show if you are doing the right things."

TJ knows there is truth to what the mechanic is saying. He suddenly feels a great sense of pride at having done all the exercises correctly. He did them on his own to the best of his ability, without needing anybody to motivate him.

"Your true character is what you are doing when nobody else is watching you, TJ. Be more concerned with your character than your reputation."

"What's the difference?"

"Your character is who you are and your reputation is what others think of you. Who you are matters more than what other people say about you. Do not limit yourself or allow those around you to place limitations on you."

"But we all have limitations, boss. We can't just do anything we simply want to do. Sometimes we must understand there are things we are not good at."

"Why should we accept that? Yes, some things are done more naturally by some people than by others, but we can all do anything we want to do in this life. The only limits are the limits that you place upon yourself. They are created by your mind to protect you from failing or not succeeding. They do not exist."

"So you are saying I can do anything I want to do?"

"Of course you can. Yes, some things that you do your natural talent will make easier for you. Other things you will have to work hard at to improve. I am not saying you can be the best at everything. I am simply saying, don't limit yourself. Allow all possibilities to come to you, whatever they may be."

"I understand, sir."

The old man lies down on his bed, begins closing his eyes and says, "I'm very tired, champ. We will talk more in the morning. Go and get some rest."

TJ realizes that something is definitely wrong with his boss. "Are you okay, sir?" he asks, feeling concerned.

The mechanic lies still for a while, looking as though he is contemplating whether to answer TJ or not.

He eventually opens his eyes again and sits up on the edge of bed. He takes a deep breath and then says, "I received a phone call last week telling me that my brother died in a car accident. He hit a tree late in the evening as he veered off the road at a high speed. The police said he was drunk and driving." The mechanic does not show any emotion and sits extremely still as he makes eye contact with the teenager.

"I am so sorry to hear that, boss. Were you close to him?" TJ responds empathetically.

"We were very close. We could speak about anything and we spoke every week on the telephone. He was my older brother. He helped and guided me when I was growing up. When I was a child and a teenager he took me to my football games and never missed a single one of them. He always gave me advice and was hard on me when I had strayed off the path, like drinking or spending too much time partying with friends and girls instead of focusing on my football. He used to protect me when I got myself into unnecessary trouble. He was like the father I never had."

"Sounds like a great relationship. How do you not even get upset when you talk about him, though? Whenever I speak about the tragedies of my family, I can never hold my emotions together."

"Death isn't sad, TJ. The sad thing is that most people don't truly live."

"That's deep, sir."

"It's true. You should never fear death. It is necessary and it will happen to you inevitably. You come into this world to live as best you can, learn your lessons and then you leave. We all have our own choices to make in this life but, as much as we have our own choices, we are also all fated and destined to do certain things. My brother made the choice to drive drunk, right or wrong, and he is not here anymore. I do not question the universe. If my brother's time is over on this planet, then his time is over. I am not saying I will not miss his presence or our conversations, but holding onto him would be living in the past. I do feel the terrible and painful emotions, but I understand that these emotions are natural."

"I honestly don't know how you handle your emotions so well, boss."

"Some emotions feel great, some emotions feel terrible, and you need to truly feel all of them when they come, but do not lose yourself in them. It is the same on a football pitch. When you're angry, or fearful emotions take hold of you. Take a deep breath and relax because as soon as you get angry, the opposition has succeeded in distracting you and taking your focus away from the job you need to do."

"It's okay to leave the football lessons out of the conversation tonight, sir."

The mechanic smiles and replies, "There is a lot football can teach you about life."

"So I've learned, but whether it was fate or not fate that your brother died, I am still very sorry for your loss."

"Thanks, champ. I have shed many tears these past few days, but it does not change the situation. You have to accept what has happened and what is currently happening. You cannot change it, so why punish yourself with something you cannot change. It's a lot easier said than done, but always remind yourself that there is actually nothing terrible happening in this current moment in time. There are painful emotions, and I will miss him terribly, but nothing horrible is actually currently happening to me right now in this moment, only in my heart and mind."

"Change and loss is hard to deal with though, sir."

"It is, TJ, but always know that nothing will ever stay the same in your life. Change is constant. Learn to deal with change. As I have told you before, there are no co-incidences; things have their reasons and purpose. My brother's death does not stop me from living my life in this moment. Life goes on."

"I suppose you're right."

"It's good that you can understand what I'm saying, my boy. Always remember that the best way to honour the dead is to live our lives fully in this moment."

"I understand what you are saying, sir, but when I lost my father and two older brothers, I really struggled."

"I am so sorry to hear that, son. Do you want to talk about it?"

"Not really. I just want to ask if you think we will ever see the dead again? Do you believe there is life after death?"

"Okay, champ. Well, whenever you need to talk, I am here and, to answer your question, yes, you will see them again. There is life after death; they are not truly lost. But this is a conversation for another time. Your focus now is to get a good night's rest and prepare for your training tomorrow morning."

"Okay, boss, I hope you sleep well," TJ replies disappointedly. He turns off the lights in the bedroom and in the rest of the house, locks the front door and then gets into his own bed.

Lying in bed with his eyes wide open, he begins wondering about death and where we all go once our time has ended.

He thinks of his own family.

I wonder if I will ever see my own ancestors and family members ever again. I hope they are okay; I'd like to think that they are guiding me right now...

Eight weeks later

TJ finishes his dynamic stretching and sets off on a three-kilometre run, focusing on one breath at a time. It is Saturday morning in week nine of the physical training programme. These three kilometres are the final piece of the puzzle in reaching all the targets of the programme. He has not come back in twelve minutes yet.

The fresh spring air blows onto his face and flows through his entire body. He strides, feeling his chest burning and his legs aching, but his mind is not telling him to give up. He feels the same pain he felt when he did the run for the first time, but his mind has become accustomed to dealing with the hurting. His heart and lungs have also become accustomed to the intense physical activity he has been doing.

He pushes his body intensely, breathing in deeply and blowing air out, trying his best to achieve the target. He runs past the forest, through the town, past the farm land, turns around and maintains his speed on the way back.

He approaches the back garden. His legs speed up as he sprints the final three hundred metres and returns to the petrol station, running the three kilometres in what he feels is his record time. He looks at his new watch and it shows eleven minutes, forty three seconds.

"Yes! Yes! Yes!" he shouts with enthusiasm as he smiles widely. He is fist pumping the air, filled with pride and passion. He immediately jets into the house, still panting from the intense run but unbelievably excited, to tell the mechanic the wonderful news.

Eight gruelling weeks of working and training have passed by. TJ has continued to do the physical training programme, focusing on one moment at a time. He does his gym routine every morning, he works at the petrol station and he does his physical training to the best of his abilities each day. He even went to one of the local shops in the town and bought himself a cheap watch so he could record all of his training times. He has pushed himself every day and on some days his times for the exercises improved and on other days they did not.

The spring months have officially arrived and his training arena has now become far more attractive to look at and train in. It is warmer and the fresh spring air feels lighter and purer to breathe in. Flowers are beginning to blossom, fruit is beginning to grow on the fruit trees, the bees and birds are out of hiding, doing their daily duties, and the air feels more pleasant than the cold, dry winter air. TJ's formerly thin and skinny frame has been greatly enhanced. His body is firm and he is looking lean, fit and strong, with a six pack showing on his stomach. His stronger core muscles have naturally improved his balance. His arms are firmer, his lungs and legs stronger. His stronger arms will hopefully aid him when protecting the ball and his stronger legs have helped improve his speed and balance.

The mechanic has kept a watchful eye on the teenager's progress throughout the weeks he has been training. The old man has begun to notice the changes in TJ's body and the improvements he is making in his times for the exercises. It is over two months since he started the physical programme and there has been a radical transformation in the way he lives his life and the way he trains. He is growing and improving as a human being, just as much as he is growing and improving as a footballer.

TJ walks hurriedly into the shop and shouts, "I did it, boss! I just ran the three kilometres in less than twelve minutes!"

The old man looks up from beneath the counter and grins.

"Well done, champ!" shouts the old man, gripping the teenager and patting him enthusiastically on the back with pure pride.

TJ smiles warmly.

Throughout week nine, he reaches every target he needed to reach. He is completing all of his push-ups, pull ups, dips, sit ups, lunges and jump squats, and he is doing a plank for seven minutes. He is doing the hill runs in less than twenty-four minutes and he can balance on the rock with one leg and his eyes closed for ten minutes. He is completing the agility exercises in the twenty-five minutes with ease and it is noticeable he is becoming lighter on his feet. It seems as though he is floating when he runs, running with such ease and grace. He can do the ten-metre sprints in just under one point seven seconds, which means he now has a very impressive burst of speed.

The mechanic continues, "It has been a long and hard nine weeks for you but you can be proud of yourself for how hard you have pushed your body, my boy. Your body is looking strong, maybe even stronger than mine now!" he says jokingly. "You are definitely fitter and faster and there is no doubt in my mind that you have improved. You are light on your feet now as well, not running like an elephant anymore. There actually isn't much more you can do to improve yourself physically."

"Thanks, boss, but I thought you said we can always improve as footballers?"

"Yes, of course you can always improve every day, but you have reached a level where your growth will not be as rapid and substantial. What that really means is I think you are finally ready to begin training with a ball at your feet."

"No ways! Are you being serious?" shouts TJ ecstatically.

"Yes, I'm being serious! If it weren't for your massive physical problems and restraints, you probably would have been using a ball sooner," jokes the mechanic.

"Not funny, boss."

"Honestly though, champ, I have noticed a massive improvement in your agility, burst of speed and the strength of your body. You can be very happy with yourself as it is you and only you who has achieved this wonderful progress. I have only given you the programme. You are the one who has taken the words on a piece of paper and used them for positive action. It was not always easy, but I'm sure you will say it has been worth it."

"It has been worth it, sir. I feel awesome. Even my diet has improved my energy levels and I have never felt this good in my life. The training is still difficult, but when I look in the mirror and love how I look, I feel good. I feel fit and I am so happy to hear that I can finally start using a ball. I've missed it so much."

"I would hope you have missed it. You will continue to sit on your best friend the rock, and you will continue to do your physical training, but a less intense physical programme. You need to maintain the progress and improvements you have made. It is a tough journey to get to the top, but it is even harder staying there. So you still need to push your body. However, you are finally ready to begin your technical training. Tomorrow you will begin working with a ball."

TJ, feeling slightly tired after the run, is happy that he can finally start playing with a ball again. It has been a long time and he has missed it immensely. They walk to the kitchen together. TJ pours himself a glass of water as the mechanic opens the fridge, pulling out a white cubed cardboard box. TJ takes a seat in his usual red chair, drinking the glass of ice cold water. He knows he still needs to stretch before he can shower and start his work at the petrol station for the day.

The mechanic puts the white cardboard box on the table in front of him and says, "Come with me, I want to show you something."

TJ stands up and follows the mechanic to a cupboard in the old man's bedroom. The mechanic pulls out a brown box from the top of the cupboard; it looks like a box of shoes. The old man puts the box into his hands.

"These boots are for you, TJ. I got them on my trip to Gauteng all those weeks ago. You have earned them with all your hard work and dedication. I also know it's your birthday next week, so consider it an eighteenth birthday present as well. It is perfect timing."

"You got me boots! Why? You really didn't have to do that, boss. And how did you even know it is my birthday next week?" he asks, slightly bemused.

"It's not important, but if you remember you signed an employment contract and you wrote your birth date on it."

"You don't miss a thing," says TJ with amazement in his eyes. He opens the brown box and sees his brand new boots lying next to one another. The boots are black and white and, as he rubs them with his fingers, he feels the strong material that they are made of. *Copa Mundial* is written in gold on the side of the magnificent boots.

TJ is stunned and cannot contain his happiness. "I don't know what to say other than thank you, boss! Thank you so much. These are the first boots that have ever been given to me. I promise I will treasure them and treat them with nothing but total respect."

He gives the mechanic a massive hug, squeezing the old man tightly as the mechanic smiles and returns the love shown. TJ runs off, feeling like a young child on Christmas morning; he wants to try them on immediately. He stops running suddenly when he notices the white cardboard box on the kitchen table. He curiously opens the lid and inside is a brown chocolate cake with the number 18 on it.

"I thought you said no junk food, sir?" he shouts.

The mechanic smiles. "Who said it was for you?" he shouts back from the bedroom. TJ laughs and immediately goes to his bedroom and begins trying on his brand new boots.

The mechanic walks to the kitchen and cuts a slice of cake each. "We will have a piece of cake today. I don't want you eating this nonsense while doing your technical training!"

TJ ignores the mechanic, "The boots fit perfectly!" he shouts back, feeling thrilled.

"Well, put them on again when you wake up tomorrow morning. Then meet me on the flat piece of sand below the rock; where you have been doing your stretching and different physical exercises! I will be waiting there for you!"

"Okay sir!"

TJ smiles as he looks down at his feet, admiring his new boots. He can't wait to feel a ball on his feet again. He has completely forgotten what it feels like.

· 8 ·

A Ball in the Mud

TJ is walking down the hill towards the long flat piece of sand, wearing his new black and white boots with his old plain white Silver Star's training kit. He sees the mechanic standing on the flat piece of sand with his usual work overalls and black boots on; his right foot planted firmly on top of an old white ball.

As TJ approaches he sees the mechanic has created a miniature football pitch. There are two sets of goals opposite one another over a twenty-metre distance. The goals are made with large sticks planted firmly in the ground, roughly two metres apart with no crossbars on either goal. The pitch the old man is standing on is entirely muddy. The mud is not thick, but it reminds TJ of his childhood, when he used to play football every day with his friends on the one muddy pitch in the township. This pitch is smaller, but he smiles as the happy memories of playing in the township begin moving through his mind. He completes a short walk down the hill and steps onto the muddy pitch with the mechanic.

"It's great to be alive, isn't it son! All you need is a ball and a flat surface," says the old man, greeting him with his usual enthusiastic grin and tone of voice. TJ smiles and looks around at the green trees, flowers and birds. He scans the miniature football pitch.

"Not bad," he says softly.

"It's amazing, TJ. You can put two terrible pieces of wood in the ground opposite one another and it is still the same beautiful game. The same game played in Africa, Europe, South America and all over the world. We are all the same, sharing the same love for the beautiful game."

TJ can feel the mechanic's enthusiasm for the game emanating from his voice and he recognizes that this is a man who truly loves football.

"I'm excited, sir, but why did you wet the sand? I'm not complaining, I'm just curious. The last time I played on a muddy pitch was when I was still a young boy in the township."

"Well, you are going to have to get used to it again. Mud is tougher and heavier to run on; difficult conditions to control or use the ball the way you want to use it. If you can play on mud, grass is going to feel a whole lot easier for you."

"Yeah, it's chilled. I spent my whole childhood playing in the mud. I'm probably more comfortable on it than grass," jokes the teenager.

"This pitch should suit you perfectly then. Now, I want you to remember that as a footballer you need to be training a minimum of ten hours a week by yourself or with your team mates. Unfortunately, you have not being doing this due to the amount of mental training you needed to do as well as the major physical issues you had."

TJ pulls a face at the mechanic, as the old man smirks and continues, "You will still be working on the mental and physical aspects of your game, as you need to maintain the progress you have made, but you will now be working primarily with a ball."

"I honestly can't wait, sir!"

"Good. Now I want you to be focusing on improving every single day you spend with the ball. If you simply improve your football ability by just 0.1% every day, it is more than enough. If you are improving by 0.1% every day for the next few years, just imagine how great you will eventually be."

"That's a cool way to look at it and improving by just 0.1% every day doesn't sound too hectic to do at all."

"It's not. Another thing you need to know is that your technical training is all about creating great habits with the ball so that when you are on the pitch you do not have to think, you just do it naturally."

"So I need to create great habits; like the habit of constantly moving on the pitch?"

"Yes, you will just do things without thinking about them and using your natural instinct instead of your mind. Even when you do need to think in certain situations, you will still be able to make a quick decision. One habit you need to learn quickly is keeping your head up at all times. You cannot see what's going on around you if your eyes are looking at the ball or your feet. So you need to do your best to feel the ball, feel the ball with your feet and not drop your head! Do you understand?"

"I understand, sir."

"Great. Now I need you to answer a vital question before we start," the mechanic says sternly.

"Okay."

"What is the most important thing in football?"

TJ takes his time to think about the answer.

"Having fun, focusing on the moment, bringing joy to others, scoring, shooting, passing, my first touch, teamwork, supporters, defending," he says, giving a series of quick fire answers.

The mechanic responds "no" to each of them.

"I don't know, boss, maybe, um…"

"The ball," the mechanic interrupts him. "The most important thing in football is the ball."

"The ball?" asks TJ, slightly baffled.

"Yes, the ball is the most important thing in football. If you do not have a ball, you cannot have fun, you cannot shoot or take a first touch and you cannot bring joy to others. Or any other wonderful suggestions you gave. Without a ball, there is no football. So treat it with the respect it deserves."

"I can't believe I never thought of that before, but you're right. The game does not exist without it, so I guess it's fairly obvious it is the most important thing."

"The ball is the most important object on the football pitch, so when you have it, you do everything in your power to protect it and use it wisely! When you don't have it, you do everything you can to get it back!"

TJ smiles at the simplicity of the lesson. "That's pretty cool," he says. "Well, then I promise to treat the ball like a man would treat water when lost in the desert."

"I like that," replies the mechanic, grabbing the ball off the ground. "A great player once said that he learned everything he needed to know about life with a ball at his feet. This magnificent round thing can teach a person so much about himself and life. So the first thing you are going to be doing is improving your relationship with the ball, and the only way to do that is to spend plenty of time with it. Truly feel the ball on your feet. Learn the way it moves and reacts to certain touches."

"I can do that, sir."

The mechanic lobs the ball at the teenager's chest. "Now show me how you juggle the ball," he says as TJ catches the ball.

TJ looks at the ball with fear, remembering he has not juggled a ball since he was a child.

"Why? Juggling is a waste of time," he says, in an attempt to avoid any embarrassment.

"You need to juggle because I'm asking you to."

"But sir, I…"

"Are you the best footballer in the world?" interrupts the mechanic.

"Um, no, I mean not yet," replies TJ.

"Yes. So I am simply asking you to juggle to help you improve."

"Fine! I'll juggle the ball!"

He sighs, takes a deep breath and then drops the ball onto his right foot.

"One, two, three," he counts and after three nervous juggles, the ball lands firmly in the mud. He feels embarrassed, but he picks the ball up immediately and attempts to juggle it again, trying his best to keep it up off the ground. It hits the floor again after four terrible touches.

He tries again and again, constantly kicking the ball away, only using his right foot and not being able to keep the ball up for longer than ten seconds. It is uncomfortable for him and he just wants to go inside and hide. The mechanic is silently watching his futile attempts.

"Never be afraid of making mistakes, TJ. It is the only way you learn. Have the courage to make mistakes and do not be afraid of what I think or other people think. How do you grow if you are not making mistakes?"

"I know I need to make mistakes to improve, that's why I'm not giving up, but it still feels terrible. I haven't juggled in such a long time. Just give me some more time and I'm sure I'll get it right soon."

"Great attitude, champ! It's also great that you're willing to make mistakes because you're going to spend the entire day juggling."

"Awesome," replies TJ sarcastically.

"You are going to juggle using both your feet and always alternating between your right foot and left foot. You must use the laces of your boot, the insides of your boot, the outsides of your boot, your thighs and your head. Try different combinations, whatever works best; be creative."

"All parts of my leg and foot? I've never juggled like that before!"

"Well, you are going to start today. You need to do one thousand juggles in a row without the ball hitting the floor before you can sleep tonight."

"One thousand juggles!" exclaims TJ.

"Just start with the next touch. Try keeping your mind clear and don't have any expectations. Just juggle and enjoy. Have fun with that ball! Express yourself!"

"It's so frustrating when the ball drops, though, sir."

"It can be frustrating, but stay calm, stay patient and remember that each time you drop the ball it is not a mistake but a lesson. The mistake belongs to the past and any worries you feel belong to the future, so just focus on every touch you take, one touch at a time."

"Okay, boss, one touch and one moment at a time."

"That's right, son, one moment at a time. Celebrate the small victories and improvements in life."

The mechanic gives TJ an encouraging smile and then begins walking away, leaving the teenager alone with the ball. The calm spring sun shines on the miniature football pitch as TJ begins juggling without any pressure or expectations, feeling relaxed and focusing on taking it one touch at a time.

"It is just you and the ball, TJ! Nothing else matters! Don't allow anything to distract you!" Shouts the mechanic as he opens the back door of the house at the top of the hill.

"It's just you and the ball. It's just you and the ball," TJ whispers to himself as he juggles the ball with both feet.

He continues to juggle the ball for the next few hours without breaking his concentration or worrying about the target. Right foot, left foot, right foot; he can barely do ten juggles.

Hours pass by of constantly picking the ball up and dropping it, picking the ball up and dropping it again. His frustration begins to show as half a day disappears and he has only managed to do twenty juggles. He refuses to be hard on himself and, each time he drops the ball, he tries to understand why he dropped it and he does his best not to make the same mistake again.

A few more hours of mistakes and constantly picking up the ball pass by and he eventually begins to do thirty juggles. Then he begins to do fifty as the more he gets the feel of it, the easier it is becoming. Soon after reaching fifty juggles, he reaches one hundred. He is exhausted and, even though the sun is not excessively hot, he is still sweating profusely.

By the early hours of the evening he has managed to reach just over three hundred juggles, using all the parts of his foot and body: using his laces, his insides, his outsides, his thighs and his head. Everything the mechanic told him to do. He has not taken a break to eat. He has only had a few quick glasses of water.

He continues tapping the ball with both his feet and thighs without breaking his focus. Right foot lace, left foot lace, right thigh, outside right foot, left thigh and on and on he continues for the next six hours. Lifting the ball and eventually dropping it again without reaching one thousand juggles.

He is still continuing to juggle. He is exhausted, tired and his body is weak from a day of pure frustration and unwavering effort. He refuses to give up and vows he will not sleep until he reaches the desired target of one thousand juggles. His clothes, his body and his face are covered in mud. His plain white Rustenburg Rovers kit is now entirely brown; the exhaustion and frustration is showing in his body language and facial expressions. His clothes are drenched in sweat; his energy levels are almost depleted. The cheap watch on his arm shows 1:42 in the morning and he still continues to juggle. He is relentless.

He continues tapping – right foot inside, left foot lace, right foot lace – and his left foot then misses the ball and it falls in the mud. After dropping it yet again on nine hundred and six, he collapses to the ground, desperately needing to rest as the sweat rapidly drips off the edge of his nose. He lifts his arms and smacks the ground with the palms of his hands before letting out a loud scream. While the rest of the country is sleeping, he is working on his dream and refusing to give up on what he needs to do.

"Come on TJ! Come on!" he says as he stands up and picks up the ball again. Right foot lace, left foot lace, right foot lace, left thigh, inside left foot, outside right foot as he slowly makes his way to the magical number he craves.

After a further fifteen minutes of juggling the voice in his head eventually begins saying "998,999,1000!"

He cannot believe it as he drops the ball purposely and he falls to the floor with a huge, exhausted smile on his face. He lies in the mud, flat on his back. After many hours of toiling away, just him and the old white ball, he has reached the goal.

He stands up suddenly, feeling an unexpected burst of energy. He sprints up the hill and through the house. The watch on his arm beeps to say it is 2:00 but he does not care.

"I did it, boss! I did it! I cannot believe I did it!" he screams with excitement and pride.

The mechanic wakes up, startled by the lively TJ. The old man opens his eyes slowly and looks at the ecstatic teenager standing in the doorway.

"Well done. You learned the art of juggling in less than twenty-four hours. I am impressed, but what would be more impressive is if you allow an old man to get some much needed rest and sleep," he says in a husky voice.

TJ laughs. "Sorry, sir," he replies insincerely as he runs off to the shower to wash all the mud and sweat off his clothes and body.

He gets into bed feeling extremely happy and proud but completely and utterly exhausted. It was not easy, but after over twenty hours of one on one time with the ball, TJ feels their relationship has definitely improved.

It's awesome that I kept my focus and patience for that many juggles; don't know how I did it, he thinks, feeling proud of his achievement. *It was like I was in my own world with nothing but me and the ball, no distractions or thinking. What a cool feeling.*

He digs his head into the pillow, hoping that with all the hard work he has done throughout the day, he will have earned himself the opportunity to sleep well past 5:00 tomorrow morning.

Sleeping deeply, and not knowing he is dreaming, TJ finds himself at the foot of a large mountain. He looks up, but he cannot see further than a few centimetres above his head as there are thick grey clouds just above him, surrounding the entire rocky mountain. He feels anxious. He does not want to climb in fear that he falls; also in fear of not knowing what he will find if he starts climbing.

He takes a deep breath and puts his hand on the rock, trusting his inner strength; going against his natural instincts.

He climbs gradually as the cloud begins to block his vision of the ground below him. He looks down and realizes there is no going back now. He climbs one hand at a time. The mountain's rocky surface is cold on the palms of his hands and he cannot see anything above him. He climbs, and climbs and climbs, just trusting he will reach what he desires. He begins to see a bright yellow light piercing through the dark clouds and feels a wave of peace wrap around him. He hesitates.

"You are almost there, TJ, keep going," says a melodic voice in the distance, as he nears the top of the mountain. He is about to see what is on top. He steps up and...

"Meet me at the football pitch after work today. We will have to do a late afternoon session," says the mechanic waking TJ up from his deep sleep.

TJ looks around the room, slowly realizing he was dreaming as he looks at the clock next to his bed. It is 11:00. He has been allowed to sleep well into the morning.

"That was a weird dream," he says as he puts on his work clothes and immediately goes to the shop to begin working. He nibbles on fruit the entire day for energy and, after a day of hard work, he and the mechanic make their way down to the muddy pitch. The mechanic is wearing football boots that look as old he is. TJ once again notices the flowers beginning to bloom and the trees beginning to grow their green leaves and fruit after a bitterly cold winter.

"I planted these flowers and trees about five years ago. They are beautiful aren't they?" says the mechanic admiring the vegetation.

"They are, sir. I probably wouldn't have noticed them if I hadn't spent most of my life on the famous grey rock."

"You're probably right, but I'm glad you did notice them. There is much you can learn from nature."

TJ breathes in deeply through his nose as if to breathe in all the beauty around him. The sun is setting as the horizon's usual pure blue is replaced by a bright gold and fluorescent orange. They arrive at the muddy training arena surrounded by the luscious trees, colourful flowers, tweeting birds, the breath taking sun set and busy farms in the distance, a perfect setting to be playing football.

"Today we'll be working on the most fundamental elements of the game; your first touch and passing."

"Awesome!" replies TJ, feeling excited.

"Your passing needs to be firm and accurate; I want to hear the sound of the ball when you pass it; also keep your first touch tight!"

"Who or what will I be passing to, boss?"

"Me," replies the mechanic firmly.

TJ looks up and down at the old man.

"Are you sure, sir? I don't want you to pull a muscle or something."
"I'll be fine. Just make sure you keep up with me. I've seen how slowly you run."

"Please man, sir, I'm a beast now!" replies TJ with a playful smile.

The mechanic grins, shakes his head and then says, "Listen carefully. I want you to record everything you learn about your technical training in a diary. I have a small book you can use. I want you to write down everything you learn after every training session you complete. Write down any lessons you learn over the course of the entire technical program. Write down what parts of your game need improvement and what parts of your game you think are your strengths. It is your personal diary, so record the lessons that you feel are most important to you. So listen carefully during the sessions."

"It will be quite cool to have my own personal football book. I never wrote in a book while I was at school, so this will be a new experience for me, but I guess I will be more willing to write in a book about football than parabolas."

The mechanic drops the old white ball he is holding onto the ground. He plants his left foot on top of the ball, takes a deep breath and smiles as he looks around at the surroundings. TJ smiles at the old man.

"I can't wait to show you what I've got, sir. Since the day you started training me I've wanted to show you how I play so you can see for yourself. I've wanted to show you what you would be working with," he says eagerly.

"It has never bothered me. Whether you were a horrific footballer or the best in the world, I was willing to train you just because of your love for the game. The love you have for the game is more important than your talent."

"Okay, but still I can't wait to show you what I can do."

"That's great. I always want you to show me what you can do, never tell me. Words are easy to say but actions speak louder than words. Don't forget to breathe in deeply through your nose and out through your mouth throughout the training."

"Okay, sir."

"Now, enough talk. Let's get to work!"

The mechanic passes the ball firmly towards TJ's feet and they begin a passing and first touch session together. They begin doing things TJ has never done on a football pitch before. He is doing high intensity drills that are getting him to open his body as well as pass firmly. He is constantly moving into the open space around him, focusing on keeping his first touch close to him. He is not allowed to stand still after making a pass and every time his first touch is poor the mechanic instructs him to do ten short sprints up and down the pitch or twenty push ups. It is first touch, pass, move, repeat.

TJ is using all parts of his foot to take a first touch as well as using all parts of his foot to make a pass. His passing needs to be firm and accurate, and he needs to time the pass correctly. He is making constant short passes and trying to manipulate his first touch to where he wants the ball. The mechanic is calm throughout the training session as he continually urges the teenager to work harder.

The training is not interrupted until TJ holds onto the ball for too long in the drill they are doing. He should have passed the ball sooner but he panics, takes an extra touch, rushes the pass and he passes it five metres wide of the old man.

"Why are you taking the extra touch?" yells the mechanic. "I have told you that you need to make quick decisions. Even if you make the wrong decision, make a quick decision. Think quickly, do things quickly, but do not ever rush as that will lead to panic and mistakes. Never panic! Never ever panic on a football pitch!" shouts the mechanic passionately as he breathes heavily.

"I don't understand. I need to be quick, but I mustn't rush?" enquires TJ, also panting slightly.

"That's it! Be quick, but don't rush. You should know what you want to do with the ball before it gets to you. Don't delay the pass. Take as few touches as possible on the ball. Only take the extra touch if you have time and space. Never hesitate and play quickly! Your first choice when you receive the ball should always be to pass to a team mate."

"Why?"

"Because the ball moves faster than any man can run. If you want to race this ball now I can prove it to you."

"I can run faster than the ball!" argues TJ.

The mechanic jogs to the ball and tells the teenager to come to stand by him.

"Okay. As soon as I pass this ball, try beating it to the other side of the pitch," says the mechanic.

TJ sets himself and the mechanic passes the ball firmly. TJ sprints as fast as he can but he is beaten comfortably by the ball. The ashamed teenager fetches the ball that has run off the pitch into the bushes and brings it back to the mechanic.

"So, do you still feel you are faster than the ball?" asks the old man rhetorically. TJ shakes his head knowing it wasn't his best idea to argue with him.

They continue training with intensity, the mechanic constantly shouting, "Quick feet! Quick movement! Quick decision making!"

The play is suddenly stopped once again when TJ tries to be too fancy on the ball and then holds onto it for too long.

"Don't think! Play! Play the situation how you see it, TJ. Stop thinking and stop dancing with the ball! Just play the way you face. Keep it simple!"

"Sorry, sir," replies TJ, out of breath.

"Don't be sorry, be better. Listen, champ. Football is not an easy sport to play but it is a simple sport to understand. All you really need to do is pass to an open team mate with the same colour shirt as yours and then move into the correct space. That is how simple it is. The simplest option is generally the most effective option."

"But won't I be a hero if I can make a long pass that opens up the opposition defence?"

"It is not about making a short pass or a long pass. It is about making the correct pass."

"That's a cool saying. I won't forget that, but it's hard to know what the correct pass is all the time. I'm sure with more experience I will start learning and understanding what the right pass is in each moment."

"Yes, you will, but football is like life in the way that it is about risk and reward. In life, if you take a high risk, then make sure there is a high reward for what you are doing. It is the same as passing and decisions on the pitch. If a pass is high risk and has a low reward, do not pass the ball. Ultimately you want a situation with no risk and full rewards, but when you find rewards that didn't require any risks then wake yourself up because you're dreaming," says the mechanic with his hands on his hips, still panting from the earlier running on the pitch.

"Well, what is a risk? And what is a reward on the football pitch?" asks the teenager.

"A risk is if you try passing the ball and there is a chance that an opponent can intercept the pass and score a goal. A reward is, if you attempt passing a through ball, will the through ball give your team the reward of creating an opportunity to score a goal?"

"I understand."

"Good. The goalkeeper and defence are always judged on the number of mistakes they make because there are a lot more risks for them to take closer to their own goals. They need to keep their game simple. The fewer mistakes they make, the better they are as a goalkeeper or defender. The midfielders and strikers are allowed to make more mistakes and take more risks as they are further up the pitch with less risk of conceding a goal, and they have more chance of getting rewards for the team than the defence or goalkeeper does."

"I see. So, as an attacker I need to be taking risks and looking for rewards. When defending, then I should take fewer risks and minimize my mistakes, but when exactly should I be taking risks as an attacking player?"

"My advice is to take risks close to the opposition's box. The opposition's box is all about your decision making. Keep things simple and do everything you can to just keep possession in your own half, but take risks in the opposition half or box. I encourage you to take as many risks as possible. Be creative, for fortune favours the brave."

"Won't my coach be upset with me if I take a risk and make a mistake?"

"He shouldn't be. Mistakes are proof that you are trying, so personally I don't care if you make mistakes when you are giving your best. I will only have a problem if you are not giving your best. When you finish training you should be able to say, 'I couldn't give anymore'. You know how I feel. You either give your best or nothing at all. Practising wrongly is more harmful than not practising at all."

"It is a lot to process, sir."

"Remember, it is just one touch, one pass and one moment at a time. Focus on the very next thing you need to do and everything will fall into place naturally. It will take time, but remember a great moment or a bad moment immediately belongs to the past, so focus on whatever is in front of you. Do what you can to the best of your ability and I promise you will get what is meant for you."

"Give my best and I will get what I deserve?"

"That's right, TJ. Life is fair even though it might not always seem that way."

The mechanic wipes the sweat off his forehead with the bottom of his brown shirt and then picks the ball up out of the mud. "I think that's enough training for today. Go get your diary and write what you have learned. After that we will have some dinner."

It is completely dark as they walk off the pitch. They take their boots off on the grass at the top of the hill and smack one boot against the other to get the mud out from in between the studs. TJ walks inside the house bare foot and picks up a white diary on the dining room table. He picks up the pen next to it and goes to his bedroom to write about the training session. He reflects on each passing and first touch drill he was required to do and each lesson the mechanic taught him throughout the session.

He opens up the small white book and begins writing on the first page:

Training day one: First touch and passing
My first touch and my passing both need to improve.
I need to know what I want to do with the ball before I receive it. I can use the sole of my boot when taking a first touch.

If my first touch is poor, I will most probably not be taking a second touch.

I need to take a positive first touch, cushioning the ball. I should be able to manipulate the ball and put it into the space I want to put it in.

My first touch needs to be into an area that creates the most time and space for me. I must also have the ability to stop the ball with either foot and also be comfortable using all parts of my foot to trap the ball.

I need to always OPEN MY BODY when I receive the ball because opening my body gives me a full view of the pitch. If I close my body, I am narrowing my view and limiting my options. I need to always be aware of where my opponents and team mates are. Sometimes a great first touch can take my opponent right out of the game when he's near me and have him chasing my shadow.

Passing is incredibly important. If I cannot pass, I cannot play this game. There are only 3 rules with passing: make sure the pass is the correct speed, make sure the pass is accurate and make sure I have timed the pass correctly. I need to be comfortable passing with all parts of my foot, using both feet, as well as have the ability to make short or long passes using those 3 rules. Never pass the ball with my toes, ever. I can shoot with my toes if needs be.

Remember, the ball is quicker than I am. Passing to a team mate is all about making the situation easy for my team mate to receive the ball. Always pass in front of my team mate because if I pass behind him it slows down my team's momentum. I must also always pass to a team mate who is in a better position than me, the team mate who has the most space. If there is no one open, then I can run with the ball but

I just need to do what the situation requires from me, don't think too much. I can reflect after the match or training.

Receive the ball correctly, look up and then pass. Never just kick without looking first. It is vitally important to keep my head up! It will help me analyse where the opponents and my team mates are. I also need to know how to keep the ball and pass the ball in tight spaces.

Play one-twos with my team mates if I can, as they are simple but extremely effective. Don't admire my pass or get upset when I make a mistake. Just keep going. Often the simplest option is the greatest option of them all. Football is not an easy game, but it is a simple one. Just pass to a player with the same colour shirt as me and then move into space.

A great moment or a bad moment immediately belongs to the past. Move on to what is required next from me.

TJ reads over his notes again to make sure he has written down everything he wanted to. He then closes his new training diary, feeling he has learned a great deal today. He stretches, gets into the shower and then joins the mechanic for dinner. They sit at the table, discussing football as they do at every meal they share together.

Their plates are nearly empty as TJ says, "I noticed you made me do a lot of passing and first touch work with my weaker foot today, boss. Why's that? Surely I must focus on making my right foot stronger before worrying about my left foot's ability. I hardly use my left foot."

"I could see that. Your left foot is broken and in desperate need of repairs. It doesn't work at all, but you need to know that there is no such thing as a weaker foot. You just don't want to use the weaker foot. That's the problem."

"What do you mean?"

"You were told as a young child that your left foot is your weaker foot and you believed it, or you just enjoyed using your right foot more. But what happens when you practice with your weaker foot?"

"It gets better."

"Yes, it gets better. So every drill you do will require you to do it with both feet. It is the same as people who say all footballers have to be naturally talented. Yes, some things do come more naturally to some people than others, but what tends to happen when you work hard and practice every day?"

"I get better."

"That's it! Hard work and talent need to work together. That applies to any job and it applies to football. You need to have the passion, patience and perseverance to achieve what you want out of life. The three Ps as I call them."

"I think I have the three Ps."

"I'm sure you do. They come naturally when you are living in the moment," says the mechanic as he slowly stands up, taking the empty plates to the sink and beginning to wash them.

TJ is sitting in his usual chair in the kitchen, tapping his finger against the wooden table as a thought enters his mind.

"What is the biggest difference between average footballers and the best footballers? What would make me the best?"

"Consistency," answers the mechanic without hesitation as he dries one of the dishes with his back turned to the teenager.

"What is consistency?"

"Consistency is how frequently you do something. The best players do great things more frequently than other players do," says the mechanic as he turns off the tap and faces TJ.

"I still don't understand, boss."

"Well, have you scored a wonderful goal before?"

"Yes."

"Have you dribbled a player or completed a pass before?"

"Obviously."

"Well, the best players do it more often than you do," says the mechanic, leaning on the kitchen sink. "They make better decisions more often than you do. They dribble players on a regular basis and they complete more passes than you do. Everyone has the ability to dribble an opponent, complete a pass and score wonderful goals, but the best players do it more consistently. What they consistently do in a match, they will be doing in training too. Any person who is considered the best in their field has used the power of consistency to do it. They have woken up daily and been consistent with how they work and how they go about doing things. Even the best teams in the world are the most consistent teams. It is about achieving small victories and making small improvements every single day. That is all you need to do if you want to be the best."

TJ listens intently as the mechanic takes a seat in his usual, comfortable, cushioned rocking chair.

"Not to live too far in the future, boss, but what will I be doing this week? I want to prepare myself mentally. I still need to be improving my focus and awareness as well as my physical attributes, so I need to plan how I am going to also incorporate the technical side into my weekly training."

"There is absolutely nothing wrong with planning your week before you start it because, the moment the week starts, time begins to move quickly and you need to have a plan of action. Living in the moment does not mean you don't plan for the future. But, to help you plan this week I recommend you sit for four hours per week on the grey rock and do four hours physical training per week. You can decide what physical training you want to be doing each day; it does not have to be intense. The technical sessions will be two hours every day, but your normal hours of work will take place as well."

"Sounds like a lot I need to be doing each day."

"Do you want to become a better footballer or not?"

"I do, sir."

"Then doing what I'm telling you to do will help. You will need to juggle before you start every technical session, to get you focusing and comfortable with the ball before you start training, and if there are days you cannot give your best then rather rest. You will know in the juggling if you are in the mood or not. As I have told you before, your recovery is just as important as your work load."

"No stress, boss. I will balance my load and recovery. I learned how to do it in the physical training, but how is the technical training going to work? Like what will we be doing each week?"

"Well, we will be doing passing and first touch on the first day of each training week. Day two will be basic moves, as I call them. Day three is running with the ball, day four is a recovery day where we will discuss the tactical side of the game, day five is skills and turns, day six is shooting and crossing and day seven is a match where you will play against me."

TJ laughs.

"What's so funny?" asks the mechanic.

"You are going to hurt yourself coming up against me, sir! Those old brittle bones are going to struggle."

"We will see about that," says the mechanic with a light-hearted smile. "Just be prepared this week. The first week I will be doing more talking during the sessions, but as the weeks go on you will begin training at a higher intensity, with no distractions."

"Sounds like a plan. I'm pumped up and ready, sir!"

"Good man."

"Well, I'm off to bed now. Thank you for today, boss. Let's hope tomorrow is another day I improve."

"Let's hope so. Sleep well, TJ."

One month later

TJ launches his body and blocks a firm shot from the mechanic. He gets up and they both run to compete for the loose ball on the small muddy pitch. It is partly cloudy. The wind is blowing wildly as TJ shields the ball from the mechanic. The old man is kicking at the teenager's legs, desperately trying to get the ball off of him.

He manages to snatch the ball away from TJ. The old man turns gradually and runs with the ball at his mediocre full pace. TJ puts in a half-hearted tackle and the mechanic goes past him with relative ease, running towards TJ's goals.

The mechanic puts the ball in between the two wooden sticks in the mud, turns around and yells, "What did I tell you the most important thing in football was?"

"The ball," replies TJ without hesitation.

"Then why do you treat it as something that requires a half hearted effort! When you have the ball, you treat it like gold and when you lose it you have to hunt it down like you need it just as much as you need air to breathe. You have to want that ball more than anything! You need to be aggressive when you defend, be brave and get stuck in. If you are scared when you tackle, you are the one who is going to get hurt, not the opponent. Be strong on the ball and protect it, TJ! Shield the ball with aggression. I won that ball far too easily off of you. Don't feel sorry for me. You need to be strong and hard. This is a physical sport."

"I understand, sir."

"I can't keep telling you what to do the entire time, champ. A player needs to express himself and learn on his own. If I have to keep telling you what to do, you will never learn. And another thing, please use your left foot! You are half the footballer you can be if you can only use one foot!'

"I will. I'm trying my best to get into the habit of using it more often sir, I promise."

"Good! Try things! Learn! When you leave this pitch today, is it about the ten goals you scored or about what you learned?"

"It's about what I learned."

"Yes. We won't remember the score two years from now but you will definitely remember the lessons you learned."

"I understand."

"Good. You are creating habits with every touch you take, so make sure that they are good ones. Get the small details right and don't lose the courage to make mistakes. Now focus and give your best!"

They continue to play the game in an intense manner; competing for each ball, showing off their skills and wanting to win as if it were a world cup final. Their clothes are completely muddy and their faces and bodies are sweating as they both give their utmost to end as the victor. The first player to score ten goals is the winner.

Over an hour of competitive football is played as TJ tackles the mechanic and accelerates through the mud. The mechanic tries to pull his shirt to stop him but TJ finishes the ball wonderfully to make the score 10-9 to him.

The mechanic, who is heaving in air, walks slowly to shake TJ's hand to congratulate him. It is the first time he has lost to the teenager after four games.

"It was like you were trying to wear my shirt, you were pulling it so hard!" says TJ, laughing.

"I'm not a big fan of losing, son. If I wasn't so exhausted I would force us to keep playing until I'm in the lead," replies the mechanic, still breathing heavily.

"Unlucky, sir, but if you are second, you are first loser," he says with a light-hearted smile. The mechanic laughs and gives him a friendly punch on his arm.

The old man then gingerly walks up the small hill in search of some much needed water. TJ sits in the mud, smiling widely, feeling confident in his abilities after one month of gruelling, one on one technical training with the mechanic. He breathes in deeply, acknowledging another training week that has just passed by in a flash.

The next day arrives. It's a Monday and it is a passing and first touch session. The mechanic joins the teenager after working in the tin garage throughout the day.

TJ juggles while the mechanic stretches. Before they begin the mechanic says, "I want you to focus on your movement today. When wanting the ball passed to you, you need to ask yourself: How do I get the ball in this situation? You either need to support your team mate or open the space for him. Play one touch under pressure, two touch if you are in space and never turn your back on the ball, ever! Always know where the ball is on the pitch. Communicate with me as well. If you don't talk, if you don't move, you don't get the ball, simple."

TJ nods his head and they begin the session, passing and moving, keeping his first touch close, passing it firmly and keeping it simple. Half an hour passes by as the mechanic shouts, "You are going to sink in that mud you are standing so still! Come on, TJ, keep moving. You never stop moving on a football pitch."

They keep passing and moving as another half an hour passes by. TJ then unnecessarily passes the ball in the air to the mechanic. The old man stops the session and says, "Don't argue with gravity, son. Try keeping the ball on the ground as often as possible."

"Yeah, but I was bored, sir. When am I going to learn how to spin or curve my passes?"

"When you learn how to keep your game simple! Every touch matters! Basics! Basics! Basics! The simple things are the most important!"

"Yeah, but I need to learn cool things to impress the coaches when I go on trial in a few months."

"Stay in this moment, son! Where you are right now! Don't worry about a few months' time. Right now you need to be passing and moving, not going on trial."

"You're right, sir."

"Another thing. You are still passing too softly. Don't be afraid to hit the pass! I want to hear that ball when you pass it. Wah! I want to hear it!"

TJ smiles and they continue training for another hour. They complete the training session and then they stretch. TJ writes everything he learned in his diary, then eats dinner and goes to bed.

Tuesday, TJ does a morning leg routine, skips for twenty minutes, practises jumping and balancing on the grey rock and then eats a healthy breakfast. He finishes working at the petrol station, puts his boots on and walks to the training arena on his own. The mechanic wets the pitch while he waters the bushes, flowers and fruit trees with a hose, as he does every day.

TJ juggles and then begins a basic moves session on his own. The mechanic watches him over his shoulder as TJ does each move at a high intensity. These basic movement drills have him moving the ball in different combinations with both his feet. The moves are static; he stands in one spot doing them. They are tiring, tough, and he needs to reach certain targets in a certain amount of time. He is required to manipulate the ball in certain directions, open his body, use all parts of his foot and do them quickly, getting as many touches on the ball as possible whilst keeping his head up. The mechanic turns around to continue watering the plants and when he turns to face TJ again, he notices a drop in his intensity levels.

The mechanic drops the hose and shouts, "Do you want to be the best footballer in the world or not?"

TJ is startled and instinctively replies, "I do, sir."

"Well then, why, when I turn my back do you stop working hard? You need to be self motivated!"

"I am, sir. I'm just really tired."

"I need a better excuse than that, TJ. Listen to me carefully. The players who become great footballers aren't always the most talented, they are the players who do more than they are asked to do because they are hungry to be the best. If I say, 'Do fifty juggles,' you should do one hundred. If I say, 'Do ten sprints,' you should do twenty. You need to be self motivated and hungry to be the best in the world! Do you understand what I am trying to say?"

"I do, sir."

"Good. Now keep pushing past your limits." The mechanic switches off the tap for the hose and sits on the grey rock watching him train. The old man offers him a few words of encouragement and advice as he continues to do the training on his own.

TJ completes the training session; stretches and then writes in his diary:

> Ball manipulation is vital to improving the speed of my feet and how quickly I can do things with a ball. My foot speed needs to improve. These basic static exercises with the ball also help improve my balance, my ball control and my leg strength.

It is important that I have strong ankles and these moves help my ankles become more flexible and sturdy. If my ankles are flexible, I am naturally more skilful and if they are strong and sturdy I will manage to keep my balance easier, as well as prevent unnecessary injuries.

Be self motivated, do more than what is required.

Wednesday, the session is running with the ball.

TJ juggles then walks to the nearby bushes and collects eighteen fairly large rocks and places them all in the mud. He takes the white ball and begins running through the rocks using the inside and outside of his right foot. He then uses his left foot. The mechanic has taught him that he needs to run through the rocks at speed, shifting his body with his head up. He needs to constantly change his speed when running through the rocks, slowing down and accelerating. When using his burst of speed he needs to keep the ball close to his feet.

The mechanic stands, arms folded, keeping a watchful eye on TJ who is trying to improve his ball control and ball manipulation. He gives TJ a few pointers and after one hour of shifting his body, changing his speed and trying different running combinations with the ball he then does agility exercises before stretching and going inside. He showers and reads through what he has already written about running with the ball in his diary:

Learning how to drive with the ball is a vital skill for me to have on the pitch when I find myself with space in front of me. I always need to keep the ball in front of me.

If there is an opponent next to me, I need to keep my body between the ball and my opponent. I need to use my body to protect the ball. It is called keeping it on the safe side. When I run with the ball using the insides and outsides of my boot, it will give me more control and also put the defender off balance.

I need to keep the ball close to my feet at all times and try to keep my head up as often as possible when I am running with the ball. I need to notice and be aware of what is happening around me. I need to shift my body as much as possible with the ball too. This will give me the ability to put opposition defenders off balance, as well as deceive them.

TJ then takes a black pen and adds what the mechanic has taught him during the session today:

When I run with the ball, I need to imagine I have the strongest super glue in the world put on my boots and that is how close the ball must stick to my boots when I run with it. I need to be able to keep the ball tight at all times.

Thursday, TJ wakes up knowing that on these days he does not need to do any training. It is a tactical day where he will do some physical training and focusing on the grey rock. He opens his diary to read what he has written about the tactical side of the game so far:

I use these days to reflect on my progress and to figure out what areas of my game need improvement. I need to think about and understand what my strengths and weaknesses are on the pitch.

I have learned that there are 3 moments in football and they are attack, defence and transition. Attack is when my team has the ball and has to open the space to try and score. Defence is when the opposition has the ball and we have to close the space to prevent the opposition from scoring. Transition is the moment that my team regains possession or loses it; the mechanic says it is the most important moment in the game.

TJ then closes his diary, stretches, does an upper body gym routine and walks through for breakfast.

"Morning, boss! How's it going today?"

"I'm feeling great thanks, champ! I made some poached eggs this morning. Haven't done it in a while so hopefully you keep them down."

"Let's hope so."

They begin eating and TJ finds himself enjoying every bite of the well prepared meal.

"I was wondering, sir, why did you say transition is the most important moment in the game?" he asks after the last bite of his breakfast.

"Great question to start the day," says the mechanic, finishing his mouthful of food. "Because your opponents are always at their weakest when they are attacking. As soon as a team wins the ball, they need to be quick on the counter attack to try and get a goal as soon as possible while the opposition are all committed to their attack. It is the same in defending. The team needs to learn how to either press or organize themselves quickly in transition. Great transition is all about speed."

"Where did you learn about this?" asks TJ inquisitively.

"From the head coach of the national team. His rule in the small five-a-side games that we played was that, when the attacking team gets the ball they have ten seconds to get to the other side of the pitch to try and score. When the attacking team loses the ball, they have ten seconds to try to win the ball back. My coach believed in pressing as soon as the ball is lost and countering as soon as it is won. If we weren't able to win the ball back immediately, then we would sit deep, tighten the space and wait for the opposition to make a mistake. He encouraged our team to play football in the opposition's half and get to the opponent's box as quickly as possible. There is more risk in our own half and more rewards in the oppositions half. My coach was an angry man who was always aggressive during training sessions but calm during a match. I learned from him that a coach needs to do his coaching during the week, not on match days."

"Sounds cool, sir. I will definitely remember that. So he loved to play attacking football, then?"

"Yes, he did. He believed the best form of defence is attack. Which is fine, but if a team is too focused on attack then they are unbalanced. If they are too focused on defence they are still unbalanced. Focus on both equally. A team needs balance. Just like your life. If you are too positive, you hallucinate. If you are too negative, you become depressed. You need balance."

"Okay, so teams need to balance their focus on attacking and defending?"

"Yes, but let me ask you this: what exactly is attacking in football?"

"It is when my team has the ball."

"Yes, but what do you want to do with the ball?"

"Score goals," TJ answers immediately.

"Yes! Attacking is all about putting the ball into the back of the net! Not passing, skills, turns. Those are all part of the attack, but ultimately you want to get to the opposition goals and score a goal."

"I understand, sir, and defending is all about stopping goals."

"Yes, stopping goals in whatever way possible: tackling, marking, pressing, being aggressive. There are many ways, but ultimately you just want to stop the ball from hitting the back of your team's net."

"Makes sense, boss. I won't forget that."

"Good," replies the mechanic as he takes the dishes to the sink before taking a seat again.

He then says, "I actually want to talk about your position on the field today. Are you happy with that?"

"I'd like that, sir."

"Great. Well, the first thing you should know when choosing a position is that it should suit your personality. If you love stopping attacks and you are an aggressive person, then you need to go into defence. If you love passing the ball and creating chances for others, then you should play in midfield. If you love scoring goals, then you should play in attack. A position should suit your personality and your physical and technical attributes. Just always remember that a footballer needs to defend just as well as he or she attacks, because you will need to do both on the field."

"I love playing striker, sir. I love scoring goals and it is the only position I want to play."

"I assumed you were a striker when you told me you were top goal scorer of the Rustenburg Rovers team. I was a striker too, also fascinated with scoring goals and winning games for my team. It's great that it is the only position you want to play because, if you want to be the best in the world, you need to perfect your position. Just don't forget that it is also valuable to be a versatile player, who can play in the variety of positions for the team. A versatile player is a team player and the great thing about him is that he is always willing to sacrifice himself for the team. He is always willing to put the team's needs ahead of his own and that is a wonderful quality to have in life and in football. You should be able to play in a variety of positions, but you need to make one position your own."

"I will be happy and willing to play anywhere the coach needs me, sir, but I do want to become the best striker the world has ever seen."

"I agree. Why aim for the sky when you can aim for the moon? Just remember that, if you are meant to be the best striker in the world, you will be."

"Well, let's hope I am meant to be, then. Do you have any tips for me, boss? What do I need to be working on as a striker?"

"First thing you need to know is that a striker's prime purpose is to put the ball into the back of the net. That is what the greatest strikers in history have all done consistently. Also remember that your movement is your greatest weapon and it needs to be intelligent. You need to be constantly moving to create space for yourself and your team mates, but make sure that you are timing your runs correctly. There is no such thing as a wasted run. If you run into a certain space, you will drag an opponent with you, opening up more space for a team mate to run into. You need to always make runs as a striker, no matter what and, like I said, the timing of the run is the most important thing when running into a channel."

"I won't forget that, boss! So, putting the ball into the back of the net and my movement are both vital. I got it."

"Yes, you need to be an outlet for your team at all times. They need an outlet when they are building up their attack or need to clear the ball. You need to give your team different options. Like being able to come short and offer an option, or being able to take the ball out of the air and hold up the ball when it is played long, as well as have the ability to run in behind the opposition defence. You need to be a complete striker."

"I will learn to be a complete striker, then," says TJ with a glow in his eyes, fascinated with what he is learning.

"Good. There is one more thing you need to know. Anticipation is imperative as a striker. Always anticipate receiving the ball. Anticipate you will receive the ball, whether it is from a through ball, a cross, a pass and even anticipate rebounds whenever a team mate shoots. You need to know what you want to do with the ball before you receive it. You must be aware and know where the defender's weak foot is, target it. Is the defender slow or fast? Can you beat him for pace? Where will you finish the ball if you are one on one with the goalkeeper? You need to anticipate what you want to do: not think, anticipate."

"I will! You're making me feel excited, sir. Opposition defenders will be fearful whenever I get the ball. I will put them on the back foot whenever they see me running at them."

"I like the confidence, son! Just remember that the most important job as a striker is to put that ball into the back of the net."

"I will. I can't wait for our shooting practice this week."

"I'm glad," replies the mechanic, sipping his fruit juice. There is then a loud knock on the front door; a customer wanting repairs.

"Sorry, champ. It looks like we are going to have to cut this conversation short."

"No problem, sir. I will wash the dishes now and then open up the shop."

"Great. Enjoy your day and see you later."

TJ writes in his diary and then works at the petrol station throughout the day and, as the sun sets, he does a three-kilometre run in under twelve minutes again. He is feeling better than he has ever felt in his life. He stretches and then sits on the grey rock, noticing and becoming aware of all the small details around him and within him.

On Friday, TJ juggles and then puts a fairly large rock in the middle of the muddy pitch; it is skills and turning today. It has been an exceptionally hot day and heavy rain clouds settle above the town and the petrol station. He had cycled early in the morning and returned to sit on the grey rock before breakfast.

The rain begins falling as TJ runs at this large rock in the middle of the pitch, performing a series of skills and turns with both feet, imagining the rock is a defender. He has been taught over thirty different skills and turns by the mechanic, only a few of which he has seen before. He has been taught that he needs to just create one metre of space for himself when he is under pressure from an opponent. The timing when doing a skill is vitally important. He needs to do the skill just before the rock or opponent as, without the perfect timing, the skill will be worthless. He needs to then perform a burst of speed after the skill to make sure he gets away from the defender.

The mechanic is watching TJ from the kitchen window as the teenager does the different skills and turns. The mechanic puts on a rain jacket and walks towards the pitch as the rain begins to fall harder. He stops TJ, throws the large rock off the pitch and stands in its place.

"I'm going to be your opponent now, to make it more difficult for you. You need to look at what my feet are doing when you run at me. If I lean too far left, you need to go right. You need to unbalance and deceive me. Confidence is key when performing a skill!" shouts the mechanic, trying to yell louder than falling rain. The rain is creating puddles of water on the already muddy pitch.

TJ begins running at the old man, trying to unbalance him and accelerate past him. He uses an array of different skills. Some of the skills work well and some don't work at all.

After a short while, the mechanic stops him and says, "There are hundreds of different skills and turns in the world. You need to just pick two skills and one turn that you really love and feel you are really good at. When you perfect the specific skills and the specific turn, then you can move on to adding more skills to your artillery. The best players in the world only have a few moves they rely on and that they have perfected. It is all about which skills best suit your style of play. The simplest skills are the most effective skills."

"I understand, sir. Well, I love step overs and the chop. I want to try those two."

"Two world class skills. Let's work on those then!"

TJ opens up some space for himself and then runs at the mechanic as the rain darts into his face. He attempts the two skills for the next ten minutes and then suddenly becomes bored and he tries another skill: the skill called the elastico. The mechanic stops him.

"So, you think you've perfected those two skills after a few minutes then?"

"Well, I got them right at the end there, sir. I felt I was ready to try something else."

"Don't practise until you get it right. Practise until you can't get it wrong, TJ. I repeat: don't practise until you get it right. Practise until you can't get it right. That goes for everything you do in training. You need to create great habits for yourself. When you have great football habits, you can do things on the pitch without needing to think about doing them. It will just be natural instinct. Don't get bored; keep working on them until you can't get them wrong."

"I won't forget, that," says TJ, feeling slightly disappointed with what he'd done.

"Smile, champ. There's no point in playing football if you're not even enjoying yourself."

TJ smiles widely as he feels the pressure he has been putting on himself disappear.

"Let's work on turning now," says the mechanic, looking at TJ's grin.

He continues, "You will only ever use a turn when you run out of space or if you do not like what you see in front of you. If you have your back facing towards me, then you should try and turn me. Playing the way you face is great advice, but if a defender is tight behind you when you receive the ball, why not turn him as soon as you receive it to get in behind him. If possible, try and move towards the opposition goals as quickly as you can."

"Okay, sir."

TJ begins attempting to turn the mechanic. It is difficult. "You are turning like a truck! It's too slow. You need to be sharper!" shouts the old man after only a few minutes.

They continue for another half an hour. The rain is beginning to fall softly, bringing an end to the lightning and thunder in the African sky. TJ is feeling exhausted and the mechanic feels it is time to conclude the training session. They stretch together and then go inside, drenched from the rain. TJ writes every lesson he learned in his diary and at the bottom of the page he writes in capital letters:

DON'T PRACTISE UNTIL I GET IT RIGHT. PRACTISE UNTIL I CAN'T GET IT WRONG

On Saturday, TJ stretches, does an upper body and leg gym routine and sits on the grey rock before starting his day. He decides to read his diary on the rock. He reads last Saturday's notes:

We did crossing and heading together. We alternate between who crosses the ball and who headers the ball. The crossing requires me to cross with both feet, to aim for the near post or far post and to decide whether to hit the cross low or hit it high. I need to cross in front of my team mate, so he can attack the ball. I must never cross behind my team mate.

When I am heading the ball I need to anticipate the cross and attack the ball. I need to jump as high as I can, attack the ball fiercely and head the ball into the ground first, as this makes it more difficult for the keeper to save it. When the cross is too low for a header or too high for a shot, I need to control the ball on my thigh or chest, and then volley the ball, cushion the ball when I take it out of the air. If I want to, I can volley the ball first time and keep my volley controlled.

When volleying, I need to keep my eyes completely focused and fixed on the ball and also turn and twist my hips to generate more power. I need to anticipate any kind of cross and to do what makes it easiest for me to score.

TJ closes the diary and then showers before opening the shop and petrol pump.

In the late afternoon, he walks to the muddy pitch with the mechanic. They did crossing last week, so it will be shooting this week. The mechanic stands between the two pieces of wood in the mud as goalkeeper; he will be intent on keeping TJ's shots out of the goals.

"Who do you think are the most expensive players in the world?" asks the mechanic, readying himself in the goals.

Before TJ can answer he says, "They are the players who regularly put the ball into the back of the net. It is an art and an incredibly difficult thing to do. If it were easy, every player would be able to do it. So I want you to be ruthless with your finishing, son."

TJ nods his head and then immediately begins shooting, eager to learn and improve.

They train for hours. TJ takes close distance shots, long distance shots, and learns to dribble the goalkeeper 1v1 as well as learning to chip the goalkeeper. He needs to use both feet in each situation. There are many different opportunities and he needs to stay calm in each pressure situation. He loves shooting; he smiles and laughs throughout the session.

After many hours of constant shooting and with the mechanic trying to save as many shots as he possibly could, the old man eventually calls an end to training.

"Ah, why boss?" asks TJ, not wanting the session to end.

"Because my hands are about to fall off! That's why!" he shouts, rubbing his aching fingers and stinging palms.

They take off their boots off the muddy pitch and begin stretching together.

"The art of finishing is all in the mind son," the mechanic begins saying. "You need to have the ability to pick your spot in the goal before you shoot. Picking where you want to shoot is the most important part of finishing. Try shooting across the keeper as it is where there is the most space in the goal but, as always, just play the situation how you see it. If you see the smallest of margins to shoot, you shoot! Don't hesitate."

"I won't."

"I want you to be creative with your finishing. You should be able to chip the keeper, beat the keeper with skills and be able to finish in any possible circumstance that arises. It comes down to the two Ps: power and placement. Put plenty of power on the ball and the keeper will struggle, so hit the ball with venom! Put the ball in the right place of the net and the keeper will struggle too. So, whenever you are faced with a shooting opportunity: whether it is a long shot, a one versus one situation, it doesn't matter. Look up, pick your spot and shoot as hard as you can. You can even just pass the ball into the back of the net if need be, but it is about whatever shooting style works best for you and also whatever the situation requires from you."

"When can I learn to curve or spin the ball?" TJ asks, hoping the mechanic will teach him now.

"When you are good enough at finishing simply. Then you will be able to learn how to curve the ball, spin the ball or make it dip. All I really want to emphasize to you today is that you need to take your chances as a striker, just like you need to take the chances you receive in life. There are many chances presented by life and on a football field. If you take them, you will be successful. The most successful teams take their chances."

TJ nods his head. They finish stretching and then walk inside. It is the end of another training week. TJ is continuing to grow and improve each day that passes by. He showers and writes in his diary before going to bed. He needs to be ready to beat the mechanic in their weekly 1v1 match tomorrow.

He settles into bed and begins thinking.

What a cool week. I'm going to have the quickest feet, sharpest mind and strongest body in the world if I keep going like this. I wonder how Mama is doing, she would be so proud of me he thinks, staring at the white bedroom ceiling.

Three months later

It is a hot summer's afternoon. TJ is doing a basic moves, training on his own in the sweltering African heat. He is pushing himself even though he is feeling extremely frustrated.

He completes the training, sweat dripping off of his face, mud all over his pants and in between his boot studs yet again. He walks off the muddy pitch, feeling agitated and restricted. He has been feeling this way for the last few days and these sour feelings do not want to disappear. He feels his growth is not as rapid and any improvements he is currently making are now far smaller than they were in the first two months of the technical training. The training has become tedious and he feels he is stagnating.

It is a hot afternoon. The temperature is well above thirty degrees Celsius as he gets into the shower to cool down and freshen up. He puts on casual clothes he bought for himself at one of the local shops and lies down on the freshly cleaned white blanket of his bed.

The mechanic believes in repetition and he always tells him that the more he does something, the more natural he will become at it. He won't need to think on the pitch anymore; he will just do it. However, he is beginning to feel the drills are becoming monotonous.

He leans over, opens the top compartment of the old light brown drawer next to him and takes out his training diary. He gazes at the front cover which simply reads:

Thulani J Sibeko
Give your best or do nothing at all

He has not written in his diary for over a week. He is hoping that reading his diary will help him relax and ease his frustration. Reflecting on everything he has learned in the past twelve weeks, and seeing what he could still possibly improve on, might take away his restricted feeling.

He opens onto page one: the passing and first touch page. He reads through his notes and realizes he did not write what he learned yesterday in the training session, so he takes a black pen and writes:

It is vital I communicate on and off the pitch. Football has a universal language, but if I want the ball, I must talk. If I have a problem with the coach or a team mate I must say how I feel. People cannot guess what I am thinking or feeling. I must tell my team mate exactly where I want him to pass me the ball, either to my feet or into the space. Shout "man on" if my team mate is under pressure. I need to earn the trust and respect of my team mates and I need to trust my team mates.

There are four forms of communication on the pitch and they are with my voice, with my eyes, with my hands and telepathy. I can use my mouth to talk, I can use my eyes to show where I want the ball and I can point with my hands to show where I want the ball. Telepathy is being on the same wavelength as my team mates and knowing what they want to do with ball when they get it without having to waste time communicating.

He turns the page to begin reading the next page, the basics move page. He reads through all of his notes and then writes:

I have reached all goals with my basic moves. I know I can always improve, but I feel the training is becoming slightly repetitive and my improvements are not as rapid.

He turns the page over and he begins reading his notes on running with the ball. After reading through it he writes:

I feel I have improved a lot when I am running with the ball, it is one of my strengths and it is not a weakness anymore. I could still work on protecting the ball better with my body. I feel capable of keeping the ball close, shifting my body, getting my head up and adding a burst of speed.

I feel so comfortable with the ball at my feet now; I wish I'd learned all of this when I was younger, he thinks as he turns the page to read his day four notes.

He has written many things about the tactical side of the game. He and the mechanic have spent many days talking about football and he continuously wrote down everything he learned. However, he had not written down last week's lesson, so he takes the pen once more and writes:

I need to be able to operate in any formation the coach chooses and any style of play the coach adopts. I should never limit myself and say that I can only play in certain formation or say I can only play in a team or against opposition that plays in a certain way. I need to be flexible and capable of playing with any instructions given to me or against any opposition I come up against, no excuses.

I've learned so many things from this great man, he thinks as he finishes writing the latest lesson in the diary. He reads his latest entry in training day five of his diary:

Skills and turning with the ball

Only use my skills on the pitch when I do not have an option to pass or if I see there is space behind my opponent in a 1v1 situation. The ball moves faster than me, so I must always look for a team mate who is open first.

I love doing step overs and the mechanic has taught me the 360 degree skill done by many players around the world. He calls it the Maradona. I love the 'Cryff' turn as the mechanic calls it. I feel I am very comfortable with doing these skills and turns now. I will not hesitate to use them in a pressure situation.

Remember that supporters pay money to be entertained. They pay money to see exciting, skilful players, so I need to be able to entertain the people who watch the game.

He turns the page over, reading through all of his crossing and shooting notes. He then picks up the pen and writes:

I feel confident with my heading, crossing and shooting and they have all improved massively. I love scoring goals more than anything else in the world.

TJ reads his latest entry about taking penalties and it says:

I always struggle dealing with the pressure when I have to take a penalty. I need to remember that pressure is a mind-made thing. It is not real and I have created it for myself.

When taking a penalty I need to remind myself of the 3 Cs 😁 confidence, composure and corner 😁 and I will never miss a penalty.

Be confident in my ability, believe in myself and relinquish any doubts that creep into my mind. Remain calm and composed as it is the exact same sized goal I shoot at in training with a keeper that wants to stop the ball just as much. Then I need to pick a corner I feel most comfortable with. Take a deep breath, deceive the goalkeeper with my eyes or body and hit it into that corner with power. A player without confidence or composure in his finishing will never score a goal.

It's a good thing I wrote that lesson down, I might need it, he thinks as he reads the final pages of his diary: the 1v1 matches he and the mechanic played against each other at the end of every technical training week. He reads:

The rule of the 1v1 matches is the first player to reach 10 goals wins. Another rule we have is the 'shibobo rule'. When one of us gets the ball put through our legs, then that player that gets the 'shibobo' and has to do 10 push-ups. A player has to do 20 push-ups if an easy chance is missed; I am being forced to take my chances.

The 1v1 games allow me to work on my defending as well as all the skills I have been learning throughout the week.

I need to be an aggressive defender. I must not deliberately hurt the opponent, but I need to be aggressive and keep my eyes on the ball and not the attacker's feet.

I have been working on my tackling, learning how to put an opponent under pressure and also forcing an opponent onto their weak foot. I have learned how to mark the man by staying goal-side of the attacker. I need to tackle but tackle while staying on my feet. If I cannot win the ball immediately then I need to jockey the opponent. Jockeying is when I allow the opponent to run with the ball and I simply need to jog backwards, not allowing the opponent to get past me.

I need to stay on my feet as long as possible and try not going to ground. I am no use to my team when I am on the ground and there is valuable time wasted when I have to get back up.

The games also give me the opportunity to work hard on my skills and turns in a pressure situation. There is always a way out of a situation. No matter how hard it seems, I have learned how to get out of tight situations using my turns and skills, and by understanding which space to accelerate into.

TJ looks up from the diary, thinking about the 1v1 games played every Sunday.

They played each game in a child-like manner, with pure enjoyment and smiles on their faces, both giving their utmost to win each match they played. They would walk off of the muddy pitch looking like two tired boxers after twelve rounds of endless punching and moving, full of mud and utterly exhausted, both of them giving everything they had to win every game. Some games lasted over two hours with neither of them wanting to lose. The mechanic had won the first few games. He is not as fit and agile as the teenager, but he played the games more intelligently. The more games they played, the more frequently the mechanic lost.

TJ still practises focusing on the moment, visualising the future and clearing his mind on a daily basis. He sits on the grey rock as often as he can, looking out into the distance, trying to be aware and to notice the surroundings as well as the thoughts and feelings within him. He is still pushing himself physically too, working on trying to improve his times and making himself even fitter, stronger and quicker, whilst doing the technical programme seven days a week.

He has been training in all kinds of weather conditions throughout the technical programme. There were windy days, extremely hot days and some cold days, but there was nothing he loved more than training in the rain.

His technical skills have improved more than he could ever have imagined. He is able to do things with a ball that he was never able to do before. He is juggling with ease and it has become more of a relaxation exercise than a training exercise. His first touch is more polished and his passing has become firmer and more accurate. He rarely makes a mistake when doing his step overs or Cryff turn, and he can do them under intense pressure. He has never before been fast with the ball at his feet, but he feels he is now. His weaker left foot is not his weaker foot anymore and he is now using it without hesitation. He is also shooting the ball with more power and better placement.

TJ did not notice his progress on a daily basis. He needed to stay positive, patient and persistent throughout the programme and constantly remind himself that if he improved by just 0.1% every day, it would be enough. He understands he can still improve and learn every day. People at his old club had always told him that once he reached a certain age he would stop growing and improving, which he now knows is not true. He understands why the mechanic had not allowed him to just give up on his dream all those months ago.

TJ closes his training diary and puts it back inside the wooden drawer. He goes in search of the mechanic to ask him the question that has been on his mind throughout the day.

He finds the old man working on a rusty blue car, concentrating hard with his head hidden behind the car's bonnet. The teenager stands next to the car for a short while, not knowing how to ask the question. The mechanic senses something is on his mind.

"Is there anything I can help you with, TJ?" he asks, twisting and prodding the broken car's engine.

TJ takes a deep breath. "Do you think I'm ready to go and trial at a club?" he asks hesitantly.

The mechanic grins. "Maybe," he replies, not lifting his head.

TJ is saddened by the answer, feeling that the old man does not truly believe in him. The mechanic looks up and notices TJ's distressed facial expression.

"There is no certainty in this life, only opportunity," he says, putting his tools down and leaving the unrepaired engine as it is.

"What do you mean, sir?"

"It is like a chance you get given during a match. You will be presented with many chances to score and you are going to have to take them if you want to be successful. It is the same with life. You will be given many opportunities in your lifetime and it is up to you to seize them. There is no certainty you will seize them, only opportunity, and only you know when you are ready. No one else needs to tell you or convince you. When you know the truth, you do not need to be convinced or persuaded."

TJ shakes his head. "Do you ever just give a simple yes or no answer, boss?"

The mechanic grins, showing his usual contagious smile. He picks up his tools and starts working on the old blue car's engine again.

He then replies, "Don't do any training tomorrow morning. I feel you are ready for the final part of your training. We will be leaving early to go on a short journey. There is a place I need to show you."

"Really? That's awesome! No offence, boss, but I'm excited that we're going to do something different and learn something new. I was wondering what more I could do to improve. I have loved the training, don't get me wrong, and I am so grateful for everything you have taught me, but I was beginning to feel frustrated."

"No offence taken. I have been waiting for you to get to this point as there is only so much individual training a player can do before he wants to show and test what he is really capable of. It's like a stallion that trains extremely hard every day but never gets to go to the big race day to test how good he is against other horses."

"You have some weird analogies, boss, but thank you, I'm looking forward to tomorrow!"

"No problem, champ. Just make sure you are up early and ready to go."

"I will, sir."

TJ has grown from the fearful and timid boy who'd woken up in the old man's spare room all those months ago. The mechanic can hear the confidence in his voice when he speaks. He can feel the enthusiasm radiating from the teenager's body. He can see the hunger and desire in his eyes.

He is ready for the final part of his training.

· 9 ·

A Dark Blue Metal Bench

It is early as the sun begins to shine through TJ's bedroom window. He wakes up with enthusiasm. He gets changed and then eats a large breakfast with the mechanic. They pack lunches with bottles of water into a small blue cooler box with a white lid and they walk to the nearest taxi rank to start the short journey to wherever the mechanic is taking them.

TJ is very eager to see what the mechanic is going to show him today. He could barely sleep last night, excited to know what the final part of his training entails.

They hop into a taxi and begin the journey. TJ notices the bright green grass and trees as they drive away from the small town and the surrounding farm lands. As he stares out the window at the back of the taxi, he feels every bump on the road pocked with potholes. He smiles thinking it must be some place special if the mechanic has waited for him to finish his training before taking him to see it.

They travel in the old, worn taxi for just over half an hour before the mechanic taps the driver on his shoulder, says something to the man and the taxi turns off onto the side of the road. The mechanic tells TJ to get out as they step onto the road to find themselves standing in the middle of vast grassland with a few trees and nothing of any importance to be seen around them.

TJ is slightly disheartened.

"So this is what you finally wanted to show me boss? You wanted to show me an empty piece of land with some green grass and trees."

"We had better get going. We have a few kilometres to walk today," replies the old man as he energetically paces off the paved road.

"But I don't even know where we're going."

The mechanic turns around and says, "Well, where else are you going to go? It's not like you can just run home from here. Trust me and try enjoying the journey. Sometimes things are more than they appear to be."

"How long is it going to take to get there?"

"Where are you rushing to, TJ? I've told you before: don't be like so many people, rushing to get to certain destinations without even enjoying the journey of getting to their rewards. The journey is far more rewarding and exciting than the destination will ever be. So come, let's get going."

TJ opens his mouth, thinking about replying, but decides against it as he swallows his words and walks off the paved road, joining the mechanic on the grass. They begin striding along.

He walks slightly behind the mechanic, holding the small blue cooler box's handle in his hand. Shortly after stepping onto the grass, they begin walking along a sand path on which it seems other people's footsteps have been too. These footsteps have created a clear path for them to walk along. TJ assumes this path is leading to the destination.

They walk along this path for a few hours, sometimes trading football stories, memories and ideas, but for the most part they walk in silence, simply admiring the untamed African bush that surrounds them. The mechanic begins veering off the trodden path as they walk through a few bushes and trees. They walk purposefully through the thick bush until they reach the bottom of a small mountain.

TJ is reminded of the dream he had four months ago. He looks up at this small mountain, realizing that the mechanic wants to climb it, and slowly they begin ascending it together. It is not too steep, but they use their hands and feet, clenching and climbing slowly up the rocks.

They eventually reach the summit and, as they take their final few steps, they reach a small, flat piece of ground on the top with green grass and sand. Opposite the edge they have ascended, there is a dark blue, metal bench made for two that overlooks the vast African plain, showing off its summer beauty. They walk towards this bench and TJ feels in awe of the view he sees circling below the top of this mountain. He feels a deep, peaceful feeling at the root of his belly as he looks across the magnificence that surrounds them. There are many unique trees, fauna and bushes to be seen below them and many small mountains similar to the mountain they have just ascended. They can see the main road and sand path they walked from and a few towns and houses in the distance. It is still and silent, but for the occasional noises from birds that pass by in the sapphire sky.

They sit down on the bench and spend a few minutes admiring the spectacular view. It is the middle of the morning, but the unwavering summer's heat has already started to heat the Earth's surface as they wipe the sweat off their foreheads and gulp a few sips of their water.

"Isn't it great to be alive, TJ? Breathe in deeply and feel it! Feel the breeze, feel your heart beating. There is life flowing through you and all around you," says the mechanic as he breaks the peaceful silence with his enthusiasm.

"It's breath taking, sir. Thank you for bringing me here."

"It's great to hear you say thank you. Gratitude is so important. And I'm happy to be here with you. This place always reminds me what an unbelievable creation this world is and how fortunate we are to be a part of this miracle we call life. We are all unbelievable creations, filled with unbelievable potential, TJ. It would be such a waste to live life without joy and enthusiasm!"

TJ smiles, having grown used to the mechanic's random outbursts of passion.

"I was nervous when we moved off of the road to find this place. I didn't know what part of the forest you were taking me to, but I'm glad we left the road. It is an amazing view and worth the long journey, boss."

"That is the same as life, champ. You need to follow other people's footsteps as success always leaves clues but, if you want to get what you really want out of life, sometimes you have to walk off the well worn path and go your own way. Do what your heart truly desires."

"How long were you waiting to use that analogy, sir?" asks TJ playfully.

"The entire walk here!" replies the mechanic, laughing loudly.

They sit in silence for a while, admiring the scenery, feeling the serenity of living completely in the stillness of the present moment.

It is quiet and calm.

"I played professional football for fifteen years. I would have most probably played internationally too had it not been for what was going on in our country at the time," the mechanic begins saying.

TJ pricks his ears, ready to listen.

"After I retired from football I began coaching young players at the academy of a big club in the country, but after ten years of coaching at the club I grew frustrated. I loved coaching and the greatest lesson I learned on the side lines is that a good coach can improve a team but a great coach can improve a life. The chances were that maybe three players from my team each year would go on to play professional football in the future, if they were lucky, so for me it was more about helping each child or teenager to get through life, teaching them valuable life lessons through football rather than just simply coaching him or her football.

"Great football skills and ability were secondary to me. I grew increasingly frustrated the longer I coached because things were not done in the correct way, in my view, and there was nothing I could do to change it. Parents and opposition coaches celebrated winning matches like they were playing in the biggest games of the century. It was all about who the best team was and who could win the most matches. My bosses wanted results instead of producing quality footballers.

"I've never seen an under fifteen team win the world cup final, but still the focus was on results and not development. Of course, the team should work hard, but youth football is supposed to be about having fun, children and teenagers enjoying and learning the game of football. These were not my only issues but, anyway, I made the difficult decision to stop coaching and end my involvement in football.

"Every now and again I will watch a local game, but I don't get involved anymore. I will always love the beautiful game as, once a football person, always a football person but I had to move on.

"After I gave up coaching I then moved from Gauteng to the North West Province to open up the petrol station. I used all the money I had earned playing professional football. My grandfather was a mechanic and I learned how to fix cars and machines from him as a child. I always knew it is what I wanted to do if I ever left football. I found this spot on the mountain not too long after I moved to the province. A gentleman whose car I fixed told me how to find this place. I would often come to this mountain spot when I had spare time and wanted to contemplate all of life's greatest questions. It gave me time and space to really understand everything that was happening around me but, more importantly, also to understand who I am."

He pauses briefly and then says, "Life has all the answers you need, champ. You just have to ask the right questions. And when you are ready, you will receive the answers. So that is what we are going to do today. Ask all the questions you have ever wanted to ask about life or football and hopefully we can find the answers together."

TJ has always been a curious person, as a young boy and even now as a teenager. He has finally found an opportunity and someone who can delve into life's deepest questions with him.

"Thank you for sharing that with me, sir. It's quite a cool journey you've had in football. I've always wondered why you opened the petrol station and why you're not coaching a team at the moment. I feel I understand more about you now and I'm very keen to talk today. There are so many questions I've wanted to ask you ever since you began training and teaching me. I didn't know if we would ever get an opportunity to talk like this so I'm glad we get to talk now."

"Good. I will help and answer as far as I can, son. Feel free to ask anything and talk about anything your heart desires today."

"Thanks, boss. I suppose I will start with the one question I have desperately wanted to ask you but never really had the right moment to ask it."

"Go for it."

"Well, as I told you before, my father and two older brothers died when I was younger. Their deaths have always made me wonder if I will ever see them again."

The mechanic looks saddened as TJ continues, "I know you have told me I will see them again but how do you really know? How can you be so sure that there is life after death? I always tried to speak to God and ask Him but I have not found God either. I think it's because there are more important people for God to worry about than me."

"I will answer your question in a moment, champ, but I just want to say again that I am deeply sorry about your father and brothers. It is never easy losing a parent or siblings, especially at a young age. I don't like to dwell on the past, as you know, but something tells me you have never had the opportunity to talk about their deaths. So, if you want to, you can tell me what happened."

"I haven't ever spoken to anybody about it. My family's only words were that it is a natural part of life and I just need to accept it. So maybe it will be good for me to talk about it," he replies emotionally.

"Maybe it will, maybe it won't. You must do what you feel is best, my boy."

TJ takes a deep breath.

"Well, my father was shot by a policeman and died in the Marikana Massacre, as it was known," he says remembering the events as if it were yesterday.

He continues, "I remember being dragged out of school by my mother to watch my father fight for his life in hospital. He had an emergency operation and the doctors did all they could as he lay in a coma after the surgery. We tried to tell him how much we love him and pleaded with him to keep fighting."

TJ takes another deep breath. "There were many tears shed and after three long days of talking to my unresponsive father, he died in the hospital and his legacy was that he died striking for higher wages. My father was never around much for me or us and I never really got to know him. He once tried banning me from football to get me to work harder at school, but it didn't work. He never really understood my fascination with the sport, but I guess he didn't have to. He did his job by always providing food and putting a roof over my head.

"We were always a poor family so I guess I understand why he went to strike that day, but it was extremely tough for the family when he died. My mother only recently received remuneration from the government; it took five years for us to receive the money. At the time of the shooting, we did not have enough money to support our family of seven, so each of us had to find work to survive. I sold newspapers every morning for three years until I came to you at the petrol station. My one older brother was already involved in drug dealing to earn money before my father died and was shot by another gang when he apparently stole their merchandise. I saw him get shot. It was hard. It changed me a lot."

There is a distressed look on the mechanic's face.

"My eldest brother died of AIDS; he contracted the virus from his girlfriend. He didn't have enough money for medication and the quality of care he received was not of a high standard, as the demand in the hospital was high. He was not the only one. A few of my friends also died after contracting the virus. I never really knew my brothers as they were much older than me, but the loss hurt my family deeply.

"My one older sister is a domestic worker now. The other is a nurse, like my mother, and my eldest sister is a teacher. They have all moved out the house and have started their own lives and families. I am the youngest in my family by a long way. Some people said I was a mistake and my parents didn't actually want to have me, which is why I always thought the world didn't really need me. It is also why I thought life has made it so difficult for me to become a footballer. It was an excuse I liked to use."

A single tear escapes TJ's eye as he relives his painful past. The mechanic simply pats the teenager's leg briefly to comfort him, understanding that sometimes the best thing to say is saying nothing at all.

"Do you believe there is a God, boss? Why are we all here? What loving God lets his people suffer as they do?" asks TJ emotionally.

The mechanic sits comfortably on the dark blue metal bench overlooking the wide open fields. He breathes deeply as if to summon an answer from within himself.

"The death of a family member is one of the most difficult things a person will ever have to face. It grounds a person and helps them realize that all the unnecessary things they worry or stress about on a daily basis are of not much importance at all. I'm sorry for your losses, my boy... you know how I feel about death and you know the lessons I taught you when my own brother died."

"I do remember that conversation, sir. I learned a lot that night, but when I asked you about life after death you told me we will talk about it another time."

"Yes, I did, but before we talk about that you need to know that you are not a mistake. If the world does not want or need you here, then you would not be here. So you can stop living with that misperception of yourself. Understand?"

"Yes, sir."

"Good. Now you asked me if I believe there is a God or if there is life after death. These are two very powerful questions. The questions I used to ask when I was a younger man were, 'Who am I? And what does life want with me?' These questions gave me the answers I was searching for. Ultimately, a person needs to find their own answers to these questions. There are thousands of beliefs and opinions in the world and then there is the truth. The truth cannot be argued or disagreed with because it is real. You cannot argue with the truth and you need to find the truth for yourself."

"I promise I will do that, boss, but what is the truth you have found?"

"Like I say, I would prefer you find the answers on your own, but maybe what I have found will help you along your journey. But, before I talk, if you are going to understand me you are going to need to change the perception of God in your mind as being someone or something. You are going to need to let go of everything you have learned and be ready to open your mind to receive the truth."

"I can do that, sir."

"Alright, it may be confusing at first, but the truth I have found is that God is every living thing on this planet and beyond. God is every living thing you see, touch, taste, smell and hear. God is everything around you and everything within you. God is pure love and creation. God is every tiny rain drop and the entire ocean; every rock on the earth and every breath of wind in the sky; every flame of a fire and every fibre of your body. Every living thing! The universe is made up of space and matter, both of which is God. Nature – your best friend and your worst enemy – and you are intrinsically linked. Everything is connected and has a designed purpose, whatever the purpose may be."

"That was a lot to process, sir. So you believe everyone comes from the same God then?"

"Everyone and every living thing, TJ. The person who sweeps the streets in the city and the person who runs and operates a billion dollar business in the city are both essentially the same. Both with a purpose on this planet and both required to do their jobs to the best of their abilities. The groundsman of a football club and the owner of the club are both equal men in service of the same football club.

"There is a plan and we all need to live it, whatever the plan may be. We live the plan by simply being who we are as individuals, but the thing is most people don't actually know who they are and they have never taken the time to find out. It is a mad world we live in. Everyone in opposition to one another, taking from others to satisfy our own needs and not realizing that what we do to others, we actually do to ourselves, as we all share the same creator. We need to be helping one another."

"But we all look so different and believe such different things. How can we all come from the same God?"

"As I said earlier, there are beliefs and then there is the truth. You need to find the truth, not new beliefs. The truth comes to you when you give up believing you know it all. Yes, we all look different on the outside and we all have different talents or attributes. We are outwardly different but essentially the same. We are all one, expressed in different forms."

"We are all one? Nobody is one. We are all separate and you can see that by the way we treat each other. So what happens if someone treats me badly? Do I have to put up with him because we come from the same god?"

"If someone treats you badly or you don't like how someone behaves, you can choose to not associate or be with those people. You cannot change or control someone else's behaviour. There are many people who will hurt you, the same way you might hurt others. Do not take it personally, as you or they have forgotten your true natures and that we are all here to help one another. If a person murders, punish them. If they steal, punish them, simple.

"If someone wants to cause you pain, then there is pain inside of them. People to whom you struggle to show kindness towards are the people who need it the most. You have the ability to sense when another human being is not well, the same way they can sense if you are not well."

"Like I sensed when you were not well after your trip to Gauteng?"

"Yes. We all have that innate ability. We just need to care about one another more. Compassion needs to be shown. We need compassion. The universe needs us and we need the universe. It is the balance required."

TJ is struggling to grasp what the mechanic is saying.

"The universe? Is that your term for God?"

"Not really."

"Okay, well, I just want to know why God would not have said anything to me this entire time. Why does He allow me and others to suffer?" TJ asks in desperation.

"I do not question the intentions of the creator and I do not want to lecture you or change your beliefs. There is so much for you to learn still. It is difficult to talk about God because ultimately God is not someone or something that can be spoken about or truly understood on the surface level of existence. God cannot be understood in words. God needs to be understood within your own spirit.

"I have found my answers and this is what I have found to be true. Most people just enter the planet, exist and then they die. Have the courage to find the truth and it will come to you. All I can tell you is that there is a higher purpose to why we are all here that we do not understand. You need to accept that. The higher purpose might be no purpose at all. So live a little more, relax a bit and simply enjoy being alive. Use your time given here to learn and grow. The way to bring God into this world is to do whatever makes you feel most alive, whatever drives you and pulls you towards it. Do what you love and be with whom you love and you will find God in that love too."

"But why does He never talk to us?"

The mechanic closes his eyes. "Listen to the silence, TJ," he says. "God, as you currently know 'Him', speaks in the silence. If you are too busy talking, you cannot receive an answer. You will always receive an answer and the answer isn't always in words or directly spoken to you. The answers come in many forms and ways, when you least expect them."

The mechanic opens his eyes to notice the teenager's confused look on his face, but TJ is still listening to everything being said.

"Just live in the present moment. When you live in the present moment you will feel God. Be still, keep silent and feel your connection to all living phenomena. Look deep into nature. Along your journey you will ultimately discover that service to others is the greatest gift we can offer to the world. Give to others and it shall be given back to you. Everything I have said might make sense to you and it might not but as I said before, a person needs to find their own answers. Most people would rather prove that they are right than actually find the truth."

"It's really hard to understand everything you're saying, sir. All I can promise is that I will try and find my own answers and hopefully everything you are saying will make more sense in the future."

"I'm happy to hear that, TJ. You are already one step ahead. Having the courage to find the truth is the first step. To answer your other question about where we all go when we die is that you are not ready for the answers yet. However, I will tell you that you will see your loved ones again, so don't have sleepless nights about that. Just always keep in mind that death is necessary. Don't argue with the natural process of death as the old needs to be replaced by the new to maintain growth."

"You've lost me."

The mechanic smiles. "There is still much for you to learn so if I say any more I will just confuse you. All I will promise you now is that you will continue to exist, even when your body dies. You will continue to exist, so do not fear dying."

TJ struggles to believe or understand what the mechanic is saying. He feels confused, but he promises himself that he will go in search of his own answers.

"I will contemplate everything you have said, sir. There is a lot to process but I will spend time finding my own answers."

"Good. Just use the time you are given on this planet to do the best you can with the circumstances you are given."

"Okay, boss."

"Great. Let's move on, champ. I'm sure there are quite a few things you want to talk about today."

"Yes, there are, sir. I wanted to ask: what is your opinion on drugs, smoking, sleeping with girls, gambling and alcohol? All those sorts of things we are encouraged not to do. Most of my team mates were involved with these kinds of things and I've never known what the right thing to do is."

"Good question. A person needs to do what is best for them. I had team mates who would get very drunk the night before a game and the next day they played their best game of the year. Others would get drunk the night before and the next day would be completely lost on the football pitch. Some players enjoyed being with girls the night before and played a great game, some players would not. Some players loved to gamble and it brought them happiness and a thrill, others would not.

"It comes down to whatever works best for you. Do I believe you should drink, smoke, sleep with random girls, watch lots of television and take drugs? No, I do not. I believe all those things lead to an unhealthier body and unclear mind. If you have a healthy body, there will be less chance of injury. If you have a clear mind, you will make more intelligent decisions on and off the pitch. You need to be conscious about your choices and actions and be responsible for the consequences that come from them."

"I understand, sir. And what about tattoos?" TJ replies.

"Some are beautifully artistic, some are not, some are meaningful and some are not. There is nothing wrong or right with them. It's a personal preference. Just be who you truly are and decisions and choices such as these will come easily to you."

"Well, that doesn't really answer my question at all."

The mechanic smiles. "Life is all about balance, champ, Anything in moderation is fine. It is addiction and habit that lead to pain and stress. Addiction always leads to unbalance, which will inevitably lead to pain and suffering. There is nothing wrong with suffering because, when a person suffers, he or she changes their previous actions and that is a sign of growth. So ultimately there is nothing wrong with suffering, it is the greatest teacher. If you do have an addiction or a compulsive desire, try to remain calm when it arises and do not judge yourself."

"That makes more sense now. I have never really been addicted to anything other than football, so I guess I'm lucky, but what I will work on is not judging others who do enjoy these thrills in life. I agree everyone must do what is best for them, but personally I will try doing what you said boss: keep my body healthy and my mind clear."

"That's good, TJ."

"Another thing that scares me is getting injured, sir. I have never been injured before but if I were to get injured then what is the best way to cope with an injury? It must be the toughest thing to go through as a footballer. Have you ever been through it?"

"I have. It's difficult. However, it is not how we fall down but how we stand up that truly matters. Injuries are just another challenge for you to face in football. Sometimes an injury occurs to slow you down if you have been training too hard or it occurs to wake you up to tell you that you have not been training hard enough and your body needs more work. Injuries also occur frequently in a negative state of mind.

"Some player's bodies struggle more than others, but if you are eating the right things, training hard and doing your recovery exercises, you lower the risk of injury. Football is a contact sport, though, and if you expect not to get hurt or bruised on the pitch then you need to find another sport.

"You are going to get kicked, you are going to fall down but do not seek revenge as that will only end badly for you. You need to be strong, you need to be tough and, when the opponent kicks you, you need to have the courage to look at your opponent in the eye and ask 'is that all you've got?'

"Try to stay on your feet and never let the opposition know that they have gotten the better of you. There will probably be injuries in your life, but do the recovery to the best of your ability and don't become a victim. It is just a challenge given to you for you to learn and grow as a footballer and as a person."

As the sun approaches the centre of the pure blue sky, TJ nods his head, satisfied with the answer. It is hot as TJ takes a big sip of his water, hoping it will help cool him down. He puts it back in the blue cooler box and then takes their home made lunches out. He hands the mechanic his sandwich before taking a small bite of his own sandwich.

Busy chewing, TJ says, "Many people in my team were arrogant. Even some of the coaches I met were arrogant people. A lot of the players believed they were the greatest people on the planet and that they knew it all. Is arrogance what you need to be the best?"

The mechanic begins eating his sandwich too, finishes chewing and replies, "Confidence is far more powerful than arrogance. There is a difference between being confident in your abilities and arrogant about your abilities. Being confident means you know how good you are and you don't need to tell anybody else or need recognition from anybody else. You already know in yourself how capable and great you are.

"Arrogance shows weakness and insecurity, as when people have an ego they are trying to protect a weakness they feel they have. Do not seek validation from others if you want to do or become something. Have the confidence and faith in your own abilities. Think about it: why would a player feel the need to tell people they are the best player in the team if they know they are?

"Actions always speak louder than words do. If you know you are great, why do you need to tell people you are? If you are confident, then you will not need any recognition from others as you already have enough belief in yourself to achieve the things you want to achieve. The moment you feel the need to brag or gloat about anything it is your ego talking. As long as you are happy with your own achievements, then that is all that truly matters. You don't need the approval of anyone else to do something in this life. In fact, most people I have come across do not actually care what you achieve either. Most people generally want to talk about themselves and only want to know about you if it's negative, as it makes them feel better and more superior.

"So don't do things to impress others. I've found most people want you to fail as it means they are now succeeding and you are not, which is sad really because we need to be helping one another. It's a part of the human condition that needs to be mended. The football world is filled with egos, many people who all have the best answers and keys to success, never understanding that we are all in service of the same game. We all have a duty to improve the game together."

"So confidence, not arrogance. That actually does sound right, but what do you mean we all have a duty to improve the game together? There are opponents and other teams that you need to beat in order to be the best. How can we all be working together? We need to work against one another to be the best."

"There are different teams and different opposition with different styles of play, but no one is right or wrong. There are so many different types of players and managers who have all played or managed a team in their own unique ways and they have been successful using different methods. We are all students of the game. Some people have been more successful than others and even then you do not have a right to be arrogant. We all need to help one another on our journeys through football.

"Your opponents are footballers, just like you, with fans just like yours. When one team wins, one set of players and supporters go home with the best feeling in the world whilst the other set of players and supporters go home totally distraught and depressed. It is why we love the beautiful game. It is to experience those highs and lows with those around you. To feel and experience the intense emotion. To belong to a community of people who all want the same thing every weekend."

"So, what you are actually saying is that winning is not important? As long as we all helping the game of football improve."

"No, I'm not saying that at all. I don't agree with the attitude that winning does not matter. Of course it does. That is why you are playing, to beat an opposition that wants to beat you. I am simply saying that we need to remember that it is only football and that everybody who is employed because of the game needs to do what is best for football. But, by all means, give your absolute best to win every single game you play in; try to be the best player or team in the world of football. Just remember that you won't always win. Sometimes, you have to learn how to lose before you learn how to win. The victory is always sweeter when you have tasted the bitterness of defeat. If you are beaten, accept it and shake your opponents' hands after the game with respect. If your team is victorious, win humbly and do not ever ridicule an opponent. Let your football ability and the score do the talking for you."

"I understand. So, do everything I can to win, but I must always remember that all football people need to help one another and support one another."

The mechanic nods his head in agreement. "Yes, we need to support one another. The greatest obstacle with arrogant people and people with egos is they do not believe they have anything more to learn. They believe they know it all already, and how do you teach a person who does not believe he has anything to learn? How does someone improve if they do not believe they need to improve? None of us are perfect. It is essential to wake up every day knowing we can improve on the previous day and it is possible to learn and grow more."

"What about competition? Isn't competition between players and teams healthy?"

"Competition is extremely healthy within a team because it pushes a player to improve and be better than the player who is trying to take his place or to take the place of someone who is ahead of him in the team. Competition is healthy in any organization and you need to want to be the best at what you are doing. You need to be hungry to be the best! Competition also pushes coaches and managers to be more creative and innovative with their training and tactics. It motivates teams to always strive to improve and finish as the best team at the end of the year.

"Remember, football is a team sport and you cannot win a game on your own, just like you cannot lose the game on your own. We all need one another as there is no success unless the entire team or club is successful. Football is constantly growing and evolving and teams need to keep up with the evolution of the game."

"I suppose you're right, sir. We do all need one another in football."

"Yes, we do. The greatest football people of our time all have one thing in common and that is that they love the game with all their hearts. They know that we are all in service of the same beautiful game."

"Thanks, boss. I understand everything you are saying. I've never been an arrogant person, which is why I always felt that maybe I needed to be more outspoken and arrogant to get what I want. Now I see that I just need to be confident in my own abilities and understand that, as much as we compete with opponents and our own team mates, we are all students of football and we need to help one another. I need to let go of needing to be right all the time. If I am meant to be the greatest footballer in the world, I will be and I will not need to prove anything to anybody."

"That's right, champ."

"Another question that has been on my mind is what is your opinion on school? Why do we need it? Most of us at my school didn't even need all the stuff we learned and, to be honest, school was so boring for me. I studied just enough to pass because if I didn't my father wouldn't allow me to play soccer. Why must we suffer and go somewhere we don't really want to go?"

The mechanic smiles as he remembers dreading going to school as a child too.

"I didn't enjoy school either, TJ. It was so bad that when I played football as a child I used to pretend my teacher's face was on the ball whenever I used to shoot it. It helped me shoot the ball with more power!"

TJ laughs as the old man continues, "But as a child you have no choice but to go to school, so you might as well enjoy it and give it your best. I do believe the school system is outdated, but school is vitally important – not essential but vitally important – in the development of your brain. However, it is my opinion that the school system only serves certain children who study in a certain way.

"If every bird is judged on its ability to swim in the ocean, many would fail. Just like many students in school get tested in a way they are not comfortable with. Each of us learns differently and we will learn the things we care about and are passionate about far more easily without ever being forced to learn them.

"We all have our own unique interests and passions that need to be practised. You need school to add knowledge and give you options when picking a career but, just because you are successful at school, that doesn't mean you will be successful in life. Just like if you are successful in school, you have every opportunity to be successful in life too.

"The human being you become in school is far more important than loving or hating school. It is about the person you are and the character you show. If your best is fifty percent for all subjects, then so be it. There are other paths for you to choose in life and make money from. If your best is not fifty percent and you have the potential to be an eighty percent student, then you are selling yourself short and letting yourself down if you only get fifty percent, which will lead to regrets later in life. Regrets that will have you telling yourself that if you had just studied harder, life would be okay now.

"University is the same. Just give your best to whatever is in front of you or do nothing at all. If you do nothing, accept the consequences that come because you made the choice but, like I say, you have no other choice but to go to school so you might as well try enjoying it and making the most of the experience and knowledge learned."

TJ begins remembering all the times he messed around in class, not paying attention and not giving his best. He knows he underachieved at school but he has come to terms with the fact that his mind and personality did not enjoy school and that is okay.

There are many people who love school and have been successful because of it, so good luck to them, he thinks.

They finish their lunch. The sun is slowly lowering in the sky and the heat is lessening. The day is nearing an end and TJ wants to make sure he asks every question he wants to ask. He begins thinking about money.

"What about the crazy amount of money spent and earned in football? I was watching TV at one of my friend's houses before and I saw a news report that showed the amount of money players are bought for and the amount of money they earn. It motivated me even more to become a footballer. Do you believe footballers are worth this money? What are your beliefs about money, sir?"

"Money is just an object," replies the mechanic instantaneously. "It is given to you by the universe for the services you render. If you are good at something, you will get paid for it. Ultimately, you want to be earning money every day from a job you love doing and hopefully the job gives you enough money to live the lifestyle you want to be living. Money is a wonderful tool, but try not to let it be the only motivating factor for doing something.

"Give your best in any job or position you occupy and the money will come. Footballers who get to the very top of the game have earned their money as they are competing with millions of other footballers on the planet to get to the highest level. The footballers on television also entertain millions of people around the world. I do not watch television, so I do not know the prices of players and money earned, but I do know that there are more important things in the world than football that need financial help and aid. There are starving and sick people on this planet and that should take preference over excessive amounts of money spent on a human being to play football. The planet and its occupants are more important than profits."

"That is very true. I agree with you, boss, but I grew up very poor and have never had much money and neither did my family, so I am motivated by the fact that I can make a lot of money in football. It was very difficult growing up without money and I've seen how it can change a person's life when that person has it. I understand what you are saying, that it is just an object and it mustn't be my main motivator, but I feel that it's okay to be motivated by earning money. I will always try doing something I love in order to make money for myself, though."

"That's good, TJ. There is absolutely nothing wrong with that attitude."

"What is your opinion on diving and cheating to gain an advantage? We were never encouraged to cheat at Rustenburg Rovers but other teams would do it."

"There was once a great football man who said that he would break his wife's legs if he played against her but he would never cheat. This is extreme, but basically what he was saying was that you do everything you can to win the game, but never cheat. I don't want you to ever break someone's legs on a football pitch on purpose and I don't want you to ever cheat. What you give out, you receive back. The wheel always turns and if you harm someone else, that harm will return to you. That is why you never need to seek revenge, because the universe keeps a scorecard for you. This I promise.

"If you cheat to win a penalty and your team scores it to win the game, in an important game your team will concede an illegal penalty to cost you the game. Or if you deliberately get someone else sent off, someone will get you sent off or something else along those lines. It is the universal law called karma. It is how the world works. Play the game in the right way and if everybody does this it will end a lot of controversy."

"What about referees? What's your opinion on them and the treatment they receive?"

"Referees are human beings with one of the toughest jobs in the world. One half of the supporters and players think the referee is the greatest person ever when he awards a decision in their favour, while the other half think he or she is the biggest idiot to walk the face of the earth. There is not enough money in the world to pay me to become a referee, but you have to accept that they are in charge.

"The problem I had with some referees as a player and a coach was that they understood the rules but they did not understand the game. However, this does not allow anyone to speak to a human being like people speak to referees. As upset as you are, even if the referee has made the wrong decision you have to accept it. It's not easy to do in a pressure situation and intense game, but I have rarely seen a referee make a decision and then change his mind in all my life in football. You can be angry and question him, but treat him with respect. All you can ask for is that the referee is objective and unbiased. They should judge the situation entirely on its merit."

The sun is beginning to set on top of a small mountain in the distance, creating a copper coloured sky along the horizon. They have been sitting on the dark blue metal bench for almost an entire day.

"We need to leave before it gets too dark," says the mechanic, but TJ isn't ready to go. He does not want this moment to end.

"Last question, please sir."

"Okay, last one, TJ. There aren't too many lights to guide us back to the road when it gets too dark."

"Thank you, last one, I promise."

"Okay, go for it."

"There are so many people who complain about the state of South African football and the truth is I feel we could be doing better. Why do you believe South African football is not at the highest standard in the world? What do you believe is the problem?"

"I have spent many days contemplating this question," says the mechanic, letting out a deep sigh. "I believe we have everything we need to be successful. South Africa has some of the best technical and physically gifted footballers in the world. There are players who are hungry to succeed and be the best. We have some of the best stadiums and training facilities at our disposal, but we need to face the fact that we are very far behind. We are not fulfilling the amazing potential we have.

"Remember what I said earlier, about arrogance and having an ego? In this country we have some of the most arrogant people in the highest positions of our football. We believe we have all the right answers and we do not need help from the person next to us or from the rest of the world, who have been far more successful than we have ever been. We need to stop making excuses and start working together to do what is best for our footballers, no matter what the colour of a person's skin is or what background they come from or who their grandfather was."

"Maybe we're not fulfilling our potential and we're not the best in the world, but I think we still have the best league in Africa, boss, with some awesome players and coaches."

"Yes, we do. I am not disputing that. We do have some wonderful teams, players and coaches and our league is somewhat entertaining. There are so many great people trying to improve the standard in the country, but we are not fulfilling our potential and there is nothing worse than when something or someone is not fulfilling their full potential.

"Let's look at the facts. Our national team do not play in major tournaments and we struggle tremendously to qualify for them. We have only produced a handful of players who have gone on to play at the highest levels of the game. We have not produced one coach or manager who has worked at the top levels of the game overseas. The youth coaches in the country are undertrained and do not work full time. They are paid terrible salaries and there are not many qualified, full time youth coaches as it is not a profession a person can survive on.

"Coaching our young children is exactly where the best coaches need to be coaching and our best coaches are managing in the professional league because that is where the money is. An under-eighteen academy team in Europe will have maybe seven or eight backroom staff members with the head coach. They will be doing sport science, scouting, coaching, video analysis and all sorts of advanced things, while most of our under-eighteen teams have just one or two coaches trying to produce footballers for the reserve teams."

"So the coaching system needs to be fixed?"

"Not just the coaching system. The systems we have in place in our football do not allow for young, talented players to be nurtured or identified. There is corruption. There is age cheating. Football played at school level is abysmal. No one in the country cares about school football and the focus in schools is predominantly cricket and rugby. The country has produced wonderful cricketers and rugby players who play around the world, but no footballers, and yet football is the most loved sport in our country.

"Young children do not spend enough hours on a football pitch. As I have told you before, a footballer needs to spend at least ten hours a week on a football pitch, but our children are too busy with other sports or doing other things. Young footballers in Europe commit themselves entirely to the sport and the entire country lives and breathes for football. We claim to live and breathe for football but our actions suggest otherwise."

The mechanic is becoming slightly emotional. "There is a worrying amount of match fixing and corruption in the lower leagues. Women's football in this country is also in desperate need of a better system and support structure. Then there are thousands of children in the townships who have unbelievable natural ability and spend all their lives with a ball at their feet, but they never receive the adequate coaching or have the right paths to follow to being identified by a professional academy or club.

"The more privileged children do not care about local football and are more interested in getting overseas and as far away from this country's football as possible. They know all the results from professional overseas teams but do not even know who is playing ten kilometres away from their own home. They would rather sit on the couch watching a game ten thousand kilometres away than go to a live game that is ten kilometres away, and I don't blame them either. Most weekends, our stadiums are empty. It breaks my heart, but people pay money to be entertained and watch quality football."

"What do you believe needs to change then, sir?"

"The country as a whole needs to recover, not just our football system. We are all very quiet and we do not want to talk about the truth or face reality. It is time to shed the shackles and the conditioning of the past that we are all chained to and being dragged down by. We need to start changing the present moment to generate a healthier and happier future. It does not start with the leaders or government; it starts with each individual in the country. It is time for people to stop being victims of the past or believing that they are superior to another race.

"It will take a long time for this country to recover from a racial point of view, but we all need to remember that every single one of us comes from the exact same creator. And whether you like it or not, we all belong to the same country; we need one another to grow and survive. We have everything we need in this country to succeed and it does not matter what the colour of your skin is. Who you are as a human being is what truly matters.

"We all share the same humanity and we need to start working together to achieve everything we are capable of. No more excuses or blaming others but joining together in a common fight in doing what is best for this beautiful country. Not just in football but in all aspects. Let us do what is best right now and do what is best for our youth and future generations of this country! Let us finally realize and fulfil our wonderful potential!"

TJ sits in silence, in admiration of what the mechanic has just said. The old man takes a deep breath, calming his enthusiasm.

"You've just inspired me, boss. I felt every word you said. You've made me want to make a difference to the football and people of this country now! If I become a professional footballer I will echo your same beliefs to the football community!"

The mechanic could see that TJ was speaking directly from his heart.

"I'm glad you feel that way, TJ. I could sit here all night talking with you, but we have to go now."

The sun is hidden behind the horizon. They stand up from the dark blue metal bench and leave. There is only a faint light left in the sky as they begin descending the mountain.

They reach the bottom and walk through the same thick bushes before, eventually finding the sand path. They begin jogging towards the tarred road. It is dark and they are struggling to see, but the moon's light and bright stars give them just enough light to work with.

They make it back to the tarred road and wait, waving their hands in the dark hoping a taxi will see them. Fortunately a taxi eventually arrives and they climb in, feeling relieved to have found transport back to the petrol station. They take the same route home, after many hours of sitting on top of the small mountain.

What a day, TJ thinks, sitting in the taxi travelling quickly on the dark road.

They arrive home safely, make dinner and sit at the dining room table eating together. TJ eats slowly and silently, reflecting on everything he has learned throughout the day. Every question the mechanic answered for him has given him more clarity and a better perspective about life. The answers he's received have improved his understanding of how the world and football operate.

"I think I am ready to go and trial at clubs in Gauteng, boss," he says, after taking the last bite of his dinner.

The mechanic looks up from his plate. "You think or you know?" he asks.

TJ smiles. "I am ready but I will continue the programme for more time if you feel I am not ready to go yet. I have learned so much and I am sure I can learn so much more while I am with you."

The mechanic wipes a piece of food off the side of his lip with a serviette. "You have learned all you can from me, TJ," he says. "I believe you are ready to go on trial at the big clubs in Gauteng. You have work experience to find a job if you need to and you know the programme and all you need for the programme is your mind, body and a ball."

TJ's spirits are uplifted, knowing that the mechanic feels he is ready for an academy team too.

"It's great that you also believe I have what it takes to make it. I can't wait to fulfil my purpose."

"Remember, son, your job is not your purpose. Your purpose could be anything on this planet. Just be who you truly are and your purpose will be revealed to you. And maybe you have what it takes, we don't know. There is no certainty in life, only opportunity. Just remember to take it one touch, one pass and one moment at a time."

"How could I possibly forget that?"

"I've said it once or twice, haven't I? But here's a new one for you: give your best and let the football gods take care of the rest."

"That's cool, sir."

The mechanic smiles as he takes the last bite of his food in front of him.

"Well, I will finish working at the petrol station this week, get an ID book for proof of my age and on Friday I will head to the bus station and take a bus to my cousin's house in Gauteng. I'm sure he has room for me to stay with him," says TJ assertively.

The mechanic nods his head. "Sounds like a plan."

The old man stands up, collecting the plates to take them to the sink.

"Don't worry about it, boss, I'll do them."

"You sure?"

"Yes, of course. It's the least I can do with everything you have taught me today and these past six months."

"You taught me just as much as I taught you, my boy, but thank you," says the mechanic with a smile. "I'm off to bed then. Good night, TJ. Sleep well and I will see you in the morning," he says shaking the teenager's hand.

"Night, sir," he replies, shaking the mechanic's hand and looking into his eyes with pure gratitude.

He washes the dishes until they are spotless and then goes to his room, lies in his bed and feels a wave of mixed emotions moving through his body.

He is extremely excited that he will be pursuing his dream, but he is also deeply saddened that he will be leaving the petrol station and the mechanic, a person he has grown so fond of. He has never left North West Province in all his life and he knows saying goodbye will not be easy, but it is something he needs to do. All that is left for him to do this week is to finish off his final days as a petrol attendant and shop caretaker before preparing to say a very hard goodbye.

Rain begins to trickle on the red tin roof above his bedroom. A white flash of lightning penetrates through TJ's small bedroom window in the blink of an eye. It is followed immediately by a loud crack of thunder.

Listening to the beauty of the late night thunder storm, TJ feels a radiant peace.

"Thank you for everything you have given me, God," he says, hearing the soft tranquil sound of the rain drops on the roof.

The silence in his room beams with a warmth and comfort he has never felt in all the years of his young life.

10

House Number 19

An early morning storm has made its way over Rustenburg as the rain plummets down from the dark grey clouds in the sky. It is the end of the week and it is time for TJ to begin his new journey.

He puts his clothes, ID, training diary and his boots into his black bag and then swings the bag onto his back. He picks up the old white ball he trained with each day and puts it underneath his arm. He begins walking around the house, saying his mental goodbyes to everything that mattered to him.

He says goodbye to his bedroom and the kitchen. He steps outside into the pouring rain and walks slowly towards the large grey rock, the mud on the ground dirtying his shoes.

He approaches the rock and rubs the wet surface of it with the palm of his hand as if it were a living creature that cared deeply for him. He spent so many hours on it, contemplating life and learning how to live in the present moment. He looks down the small hill at the rain falling down on the muddy training arena that taught him just as much as the grey rock had. As he looks around at the trees, flowers and plants, a slight smile appears on his face and he nods his head as if to show appreciation to his now former training arena.

TJ turns around and walks back towards the house. The rain is dripping off of his face as he wipes his muddy feet on the plain brown mat just in front of him. He walks through the back door of the house, his damp clothes dripping water onto the clean wooden floor. He is readying himself to say the hardest goodbye of them all. He knows he might never see the mechanic ever again. He is an old man and TJ does not know if or when he will ever return to Rustenburg in the future.

He steps outside, passes the shop on his right hand side and the petrol pump on his left as he walks towards the tin garage. Entering the tin garage, he sees a yellow tractor and finds the mechanic doing what he does best: fixing machinery in need of his expertise.

TJ stands next to the mechanic who is hunched over the yellow tractor, focused on repairing the vehicle. The rain is making a loud noise a it lands on the tinned garage roof.

"So I will be going now, sir. I don't know when or if I will ever see you again," he says, and his voice rattles with emotion. "When I arrived here, you were my boss. Leaving now, you have become my coach, the best coach I could have ever asked for."

The mechanic stops what he is doing and looks at TJ with his usual strong gaze as he notices the young man's teary eyes.

"Try your best not to become attached to anything in life, TJ," he says in firm tone of voice. He then puts his spanner down on the table next to him and looks into TJ's eyes once more.

"No attachments. You should be able to find happiness whether you have absolutely nothing but the clothes on your back with no-body who loves you, or if you have millions in your bank account and hundreds of people who love you. Let go of your attachments as nothing ever stays the same. Change is constant. Accept that we were meant to have the experience we had together, and now it is time to move on."

"I don't understand. Why can't I be attached to this place? I love it and I've loved learning from you. I'm allowed to be attached!"

"I know what you are trying to say, my boy, but can I tell you a little story about attachments?"

"Okay."

"The story is about the woman I love with all my heart, who left me for another man."

"Oh wow, I wasn't expecting that. What happened?"

"We were married for just over twenty-three years. She hated Rustenburg, met another man whose lifestyle appealed to her and, in the blink of an eye she was gone. She had a different path to travel and I was not seen as helping her on that path. I love her with all my heart and I always will. Maybe our paths will cross again in the future, but I do not question why she left me. She found a man who suited her needs better than I could.

"I could choose to be a victim and feel sorry for myself, or choose to accept it and move on. I accepted it and moved on, but it was easier for me because I was not attached to her. If I only lived for her, or thought I only knew who I was because I was with her, I would have had a major crisis.

"That is why it is important to be who you are, embrace who you are and be comfortable enough in your own skin to not need anybody else to make you happy. You need to be able to make yourself happy with whatever you currently have. Whatever else comes into your life is a bonus. The chances are you will meet a wonderful woman along your life journey and you are going to need to understand and accept yourself first before any woman will understand and accept who you are."

"How can you be so sure that I will find a girl out there for me?"

"Because a human being is created half complete. A man needs a woman just as much as a woman needs a man, and it is that balance that is required in this universe. Every positive has an equal negative. There is light and darkness, up and down, left and right. There are thousands of examples and one extreme is created because of the other. It is possible to love all things on this planet but a love between a man and a woman is a love felt right in the depths of your heart. When you feel it, you will not have the words to describe that feeling.

"In saying this, you need to be able to function on your own before things that you want come into your life. Understand who you are, understand that the universe supports you and you will never become attached to anything. You should be able to function and be yourself with or without me and this petrol station. The same way I can be myself and live a happy peaceful life without the woman I love. When something leaves your life, it is creating space for something else to arrive. Do you understand what I am trying to say?"

"I do, coach. You are saying I need to be comfortable with who I am and whatever situation I am in right now before I receive anything else in life. Even if I do receive awesome things in my life, then I still need to be able to live without them when they disappear. I must not get attached, but I do hope I can find a girl that I truly love with all my heart someday."

The mechanic smiles gently. "Don't worry, TJ, you will find each other," he says. "Your path has already been laid out for you; you just need to have the courage to follow it, even if it leads you off society's conventional path. Trust your gut and trust that the universe is looking out for you because it is. The universe wants you to be happy. Just remember that suffering and pain are wonderful teachers, because if life were too easy it would be boring. Life is constantly asking if you can still be kind to others and enthusiastic about your hopes and dreams, even when things are not going your way. So, be grateful for what you are because everything you already are is extraordinary."

TJ drops the old white ball underneath his arm and grabs the mechanic, hugging him uncontrollably. The mechanic is startled, but then calmly returns the hug, embracing the young man with affection.

"I will miss you and our conversations, coach. I will tell everybody about the amazing life lessons the Mechanic of Rustenburg has taught me. I have learned so much from you."

TJ lets go of his tight grip. The mechanic then picks up the ball and lobs it at the young man.

"I will miss you too, champ. I have truly enjoyed our conversations and times together. I have grown very fond of your company. The lessons and memories will be with us forever, but those memories and lessons now belong to the past and, who knows, our paths might cross again in the future too, but it is time for you to move on."

"Thank you for all you have done for me, coach. I don't have the words to tell you how grateful I am."

"In times like these, words are not needed, my boy."

The mechanic begins walking into the rain. "Wait here," he says, covering his head with his shirt.

TJ waits patiently and, shortly after leaving, the mechanic returns dripping from the rain. He hands TJ two folded pieces of paper.

"I almost forgot to give these to you," says the old man.

"What are they?"

"A short paragraph of why I love football and the other is a sonnet. Both pages are important. They will always remind you of what you have learned in case you forget along your journey."

"What's a sonnet?" TJ asks curiously.

"A fourteen line poem, ten syllables in each line and a rhyme scheme. I enjoy writing them."

"Thanks, coach," he replies, putting the two folded pieces of paper into the bag on his back.

"Before you go, TJ, you need to know that life will always test you to find out how much you truly want something, but understand that life will never give you something you cannot handle. Life is fair, even though it might not always seem that way at first. You will always be rewarded for the risks you take and the courage you show. If you risk and win, you will be happy. If you risk and lose, you will learn, but nothing is ever just given to you without you earning it first and proving you are ready to handle it. Obstacles are put in your way to see how badly you want something. When these obstacles arrive, just remember that you are already everything that you want to become in life. Everything will come when you are ready for it."

"You couldn't resist one last lesson, could you, coach? I don't know how I am going to cope without your constant support and advice."

"You'll be fine. In challenging times, just remember that you have two choices: accept the situation or change it. There is nothing else you can do."

"I will."

"Good. Now, get on that bus, give your best and let the football gods take care of the rest."

They shake hands firmly. "And don't forget what the good looking old man at the strange petrol station in Rustenburg has taught you," says the mechanic with a cheerful smile.

TJ laughs and begins walking into the pouring rain.

Walking towards the unknown.

Walking towards his lifelong dream of becoming the best player the planet has ever seen.

"Oh, and TJ! I have one more question for you!" shouts the mechanic.

"Oh yeah, and what's that?" TJ shouts back, standing in the rain.

"Are you the best footballer in the world?"

TJ smiles. "Not yet, coach! Not yet!"

They smile at one another. TJ waves goodbye and walks onto the main road leading out of the town towards the nearby bus station. The mechanic immediately begins working on the broken yellow tractor again, focusing on the job at hand.

TJ strides away from the petrol station with no intention of looking back. The petrol station belongs to his past, finding a new club belongs to his future, taking a bus to his cousin's house in Gauteng belongs to the present.

He arrives at the bus station. The rain is falling at a slower rate. He pays for a ticket on a blue and white bus that must seat just over forty people. It is in decent condition and, as TJ walks up the steps, he greets the bus driver and notices other passengers already seated. He finds a seat at the back of the bus and waits for the bus driver to begin the short trip to Gauteng. The bus fills up quickly and is almost completely full as a young woman steps onto the bus and walks towards the back, taking a seat next to TJ. He greets her politely. She greets him back and she takes a magazine out from her handbag. The bus driver then pulls off to begin their journey to Gauteng.

The blue and white bus travels along the tarred road, avoiding each dangerous pothole that approaches it. TJ looks out the window at everything he is leaving behind. He is calm, knowing that he is doing the right thing for himself. As the sun begins creeping through the grey storm clouds that are slowly disintegrating, he sees the beautiful North Western landscape passing by: the bright green trees, open land and full bushes.

He suddenly remembers the pieces of paper the mechanic has just given him. He reaches for the papers; they have slipped right to the bottom of his bag.

He unfolds them, eagerly anticipating what they say.

He reads the first page:

May I tell you my favourite moment?

Do you really want to know?

It is a moment of indescribable proportions.

It lasts a mere few seconds with no logical explanation for what occurs within it.

Time stands still, everybody holds their breath and, for the briefest moment, you can hear a deafening silence fall amongst thousands of people.

Friends and families then suddenly hold one another and show no care of who sees; they temporarily forget the hurts of their past and the worries of their future.

It is a moment that unites people.

The latest political or economic problem does not hold any importance over what is currently happening and the colour of your skin does not matter. People become unified and one.

Your blood pumps, you jump uncontrollably and you hug the person jumping next to you. A happy memory is created and spoken about for a lifetime.

It is a moment in time everybody has experienced in the beautiful game.

It is that moment a football flies into the back of the net.

TJ smiles delightedly as the passage reminds him of why he loves the beautiful game with all his heart.

He pictures the times he has given people wonderful memories by scoring important goals, as well as the great moments his own heroes have given him when he watched football as a young boy and teenager.

He feels a burning desire within him to continue giving people these incredible moments in the future.

He then looks at the sonnet and reads:

Football sonnet

This game is all about one thing, a ball
And that ball always moves faster than you
Never dive and try stand up when you fall
Always focus on what YOU need to do
It's not about the fame and the glory
Or about the team who scores less or more
It's about the game and each one's story
And the team who give their best to try score
Fun and enjoyment is what matters most
It is one touch and moment at a time
The same game in Spain or Ivory Coast
Potential for all to become sublime
All you can really do is give your best
Let the football gods take care of the rest

He reads the passage with joy, every line reminding him of the important lessons he has learned over these past six months.

Pretty cool, he thinks.

TJ then notices writing on the back of the sonnet and it says:

Trust the universe, trust your team mates and trust your own instincts on and off the field. Good luck on your journey, TJ.
014 318 1563 if you ever need anything

TJ smiles, refolds the pieces of paper and puts them into his wallet with the money he has been saving whilst working at the petrol station. He paid the mechanic rent each month and he'd bought himself new clothes and a pair of shoes, but he has still saved more than enough money to survive on his own for a while as he trials at different clubs in Gauteng. He puts his wallet into his bag and looks out of the bus window again, at everything he is leaving behind. He thinks of his mother.

After over two hours of travelling, the bus stops at a petrol station in Midrand, dropping off every Rustenburg passenger sitting on it.

"Sorry to disturb you, ma'am, but how do I get to Soweto from here?" TJ asks the young woman sitting next to him.

"You see those taxis over there at the corner of the street? They will get you there. You might have to take more than one," she answers politely.

"Thank you."

The young woman smiles, puts her magazine back in her handbag and they both climb off the bus. TJ walks towards the street corner where three taxi drivers stand talking to one another outside of their parked cars.

He approaches the taxi driver nearest him, who is chewing on the end of a toothpick.

"Excuse me, sir, how much to get to Soweto?" he asks.

"Thirty bucks," replies the man.

TJ hands him the money and climbs into the taxi with three other passengers silently waiting to depart. He is in no hurry, but he is excited to begin the journey to his cousin's house.

His cousin's name is Marley. However, TJ calls him Bob because he was named after the legendary singer Bob Marley. He is a few years younger than TJ, fairly short, and he wears thick glasses to improve his poor eyesight. He loves football just as much as TJ does, but he does not play the game. He is an only child and he lives in Soweto with his family who left Rustenburg over five years ago. They are not extremely wealthy, but they did help TJ's family financially in whatever way they could when Mr Sibeko passed away.

TJ remembers the name of their street; they'd told him and his mother over a year ago when they came to visit. He has saved enough money and he will offer Marley's parents money to pay rent or ask them if they know of a cheap, safe place for him stay.

The taxi pulls off and begins driving towards Johannesburg. They pull onto the highways and TJ is amazed by the number of cars on the road and the speed at which they drive. He notices the anger and frustration on the faces of many of the people who drive past them in the taxi.

These people need to relax, he thinks. *They can't change the fact that they are in a car.*

He gets into three separate taxis on the journey to Soweto, with each taxi driver just pointing him in the direction of the next taxi he needs to take. The third taxi drops him off in the middle of the street he needs to be in. TJ stands in the street, not knowing exactly where to go. He decides to knock on the door of each house and hope that his cousin answers one of them. He knocks on several doors with each person telling him to 'get lost!' in no uncertain terms, thinking he is either begging or wanting to sell them something.

He arrives at a house with the number 19 on the front door and he knocks firmly. The door opens and Marley is there, absolutely surprised and delighted to see his face.

"TJ!"

"It's me, Bob."

"Are you lost, cuzzy? What are you doing all the way in Soweto?" he asks with excitement.

"Thought you might be missing me," replies TJ with a smile.

Marley cannot control his happiness and he grips his older cousin, giving him a massive, brotherly hug.

"Come inside. Can I get you a Coke or something?" he asks, eventually letting go of TJ.

"Water will be good, thanks Bobby," he replies as they walk inside the house together and find a seat in the lounge.

They settle down and immediately begin talking about their lives, with Marley doing most of the talking. TJ laughs constantly at the few stories his playful younger cousin shares with him about his friends and funny moments at school.

"It's so great to see you, TJ! But seriously, why are you here?" he asks suddenly, after having spent the last fifteen minutes talking.

"It's good to see you too, Bobby. It's an odd story but basically I got cut from the Rustenburg Rovers academy, left home and started living with my boss, the mechanic at the petrol station I worked at. My boss then became my coach. He trained me. He showed me how to improve my life and become a better footballer, which leads me to now, where I am here to trial at clubs in Gauteng."

"That is so cool! I remember you telling me you were playing at Rustenburg Rovers but I didn't know you had a job. It's awesome that your boss coached you, but tell me, cuzzy: what could a man at a petrol station possibly have known about soccer? If he's a mechanic he must just fix things all day, he couldn't have known much about the game."

"He knew one or two things," says TJ with a gentle smile, "and it's football, not soccer, cuzzy."

"Alright, Mr Professional, football it is. What was your boss' name?"

"I never asked him. He was always just known as 'boss' to me and all those that greeted him knew him as 'The Mechanic', well known in Rustenburg for how well he repairs cars and machinery. I guess I never really wanted to know. He will always just be known as 'coach' for the rest of my life."

Marley listens while looking up and down at his cousin.

"I must admit, you do look and sound different, TJ. A good different, but I don't know what it is. Your body definitely looks stronger and... I don't know... like you are speaking with more confidence and stuff. You look happy."

"I don't know, Bob. Maybe I am different, but whatever you see now would not have been possible if it weren't for the mechanic."

"What kind of magic dust did he throw onto you?"

TJ laughs. "It's not magic dust. It is just clearing your mind and living in the present moment."

"Huh?"

TJ laughs again. "Don't worry, Bobby. I'll teach you in time because hopefully I will be in Gauteng for a long while. I just need to know if you have any idea how I get to the Impi Football Club's training ground."

Marley is shocked. "Are you mad, bra? You got cut from Rustenburg Rovers academy and now you want to go on trial at one of the biggest club's in the country, if not the biggest club in the country?"

"I think I can give it a try. What's the worst that could happen? They tell me I'm not good enough, and then I will try finding somewhere else. Why aim for the sky when you can aim for the moon, Bob? If the best club tells me 'no' then I just go somewhere else."

Marley shakes his head. "I just don't want you to get hurt if you don't make it. That's all."

"Don't worry about me. I'll be fine, my boy."

"By the way, where are you going to be staying while you're in Gauteng?"

"I actually wanted to ask if it's okay to stay here while I try finding a club. I have enough money to pay rent for the next three months."

"You want to stay here?" he asks excitedly.

TJ nods his head.

"That will be so cool! I will ask my parents right now! It should be fine!"

"Thanks, cuzzy."

"I'm so excited, TJ! I've never had a roommate before."

"Just check with your parents first. And you still haven't told me how I get to the Impi training ground?"

"Oh yeah, my bad. I will show you the route tomorrow morning. Come, let me show you my room. I think you will be staying here with me."

Marley shows his older cousin his bedroom and then immediately goes to phone his parents.

TJ puts his bag and his ball on the floor and then lies down on the comfortable double bed. He puts his hands behind his head, takes a deep breath and looks up at the ceiling, feeling extremely content with his current circumstances.

"My parents say it's fine if you stay, TJ!" Marley shouts ecstatically. TJ smiles. "Thanks, Bobby!" he shouts back.

Tomorrow is a day when the course of my entire life may change forever, he thinks, staring at the ceiling.

TJ shakes Marley awake at 7:00 to make sure that he gets to the Impi Football Club training ground before they finish training.

They'd slept in the same bed together during the night, but Marley had not heard him get up earlier to do his morning stretches and exercises. TJ is assuming the reserve team will be training in the morning and he knows he is going to have to convince the coach he is worth a place in the team. All he wants is just one training session to show them what he can do. That is all he feels he needs, to just show them exactly what he is capable of doing.

Marley wakes up extremely tired. It is school holidays and he has become accustomed to sleeping in late every morning.

He looks up with his eyes half open. "Go away, TJ, let me sleep," he says as he swats his hand in the air, trying to get his older cousin to leave him alone.

"I'll let you sleep now, Bob. Just tell me the directions to Impi Football Club," he whispers, not wanting to wake up anybody else in the household.

Marley groans. "Turn left when you walk out my house, walk to the end of our street. There is a taxi rank to your right and just ask one of the drivers to take you to the Impi Football Club training ground. It will cost you about twenty five Rand to get there," he says grumpily.

"Thanks, cuzzy!"

TJ puts his boots in his bag, has a quick breakfast, and runs out the house into the bright sunshine. He finds a taxi, tells the driver his destination and his next short journey begins.

"Are you an Impi player?" asks the taxi driver, curious to know about his only passenger.

"Not yet, sir, but I am hoping to become one."

"Well, I'm a Soweto Giants supporter, so if it doesn't work out at that small club you are going to today, then you should go to a real club afterwards."

TJ smiles, knowing the intense rivalry that Impi Football Club and Soweto Giants share. He continues having a conversation with the football-loving taxi driver and after twenty minutes of constant chatter they arrive at the Impi Football Club training complex. TJ gets out the taxi with a massive fire in his belly.

"Good luck, kid" says the taxi driver as TJ walks towards the training complex. He is mesmerized by the facilities he sees. There are two gateways to enter through and looking through the gates he can see the football fields are in immaculate condition. He chooses to go to the gateway nearest to him on his right hand side. There is a security guard sitting at the gate.

"Excuse me, sir, where do I go to speak to someone about having a trial here?" he asks the overweight security guard.

The security guard smiles in a friendly manner.

"The reserve team train in here but I am very sorry I cannot let you in. Players that come on trial have to be invited or recommended to the club," he answers assertively.

"I understand, but can you please just let me in for a few minutes. All I need is a few minutes just to speak to the reserve team coach. I've travelled all the way from Rustenburg."

"Sorry, but the rules are the rules. Now please leave the premises before I make you leave," says the security guard, adopting a more impatient tone.

TJ looks at him and then looks at the half open gate.

He sprints through the gap as the security guard lunges to try and grab him. He sneaks through and escapes the security guard's desperate grasp to get hold of him.

"Stop!"

"I just need a few minutes to talk to the coach!" replies TJ, escaping as fast as he can from the overweight security guard who jumps out of his chair to begin his pursuit.

TJ runs passed a few parked cars, turns around the corner of a large building and to his right he sees players training on the field he'd seen from outside the gate. He takes a chance and runs onto the field, hoping he is going to find the right person to speak to. He runs straight towards the coach, who is shouting out instructions to the group of players. The coach stops yelling when he notices TJ and the security guard approaching him at a rapid speed.

"What are you doing, boy?" asks the surprised coach with a smirk on his face, watching the comical events unfold in front of his eyes.

Before TJ can say anything, the security guard grabs his arm and says, "This boy has just run onto the property without my permission," and he explains the peculiar events.

"Please, sir. Just give me one training session to show you what I can do," pleads TJ as the surprisingly fast security guard drags him away. "I have travelled all the way from Rustenburg to have a trial here! I even played in the under-eighteen Rustenburg Rovers academy team last year. Please give me a chance, sir, just one chance to show you what I've got."

"Alright, Joseph, leave the young man alone. I will sort this out," says the coach with authority.

Joseph turns around, mumbles angrily to himself and then reluctantly lets go of TJ's arm, walking off the field upset after being told what to do.

The coach asks his assistant to handle the training session for the time being as TJ walks nervously towards him.

"What is your name, boy?" he asks in a firm tone.

"It's Thulani Sibeko, but you can call me TJ, sir."

"Alright, TJ. I don't know if you are aware but this is Impi Football Club's reserve team and we have already selected our team for the season. This is an elite team and we do not just choose any boy who comes off the street to join us. You have to be recommended or invited down. Our season ends in five months' time. Come down for a trial then and we will have a look at you."

"Respectfully, sir, I don't have five months to wait. I have left everything I know behind and I don't have a home of my own. I have risked everything to be here."

"I'm sorry about that," the coach sympathizes, "but there are hundreds of players a year coming off the street asking for a trial at the best club in the country. I gave none of them a chance and I will not be giving you a chance either."

"I am not like any of those players," says TJ, with pure confidence in his voice and hunger in his eyes.

The coach looks into his eyes and notices the intensity in them. He then looks up and down, as if to examine TJ's body.

"You look very fit. They must have excellent gym facilities at Rustenburg Rovers."

"I have not been training at Rustenburg Rovers for over six months sir. I've been doing my own training in that time. I want this more than anything in the world and I have wanted this more than anything in the world since I was a young boy. I need this!"

The coach seems intrigued.

"All I am asking for is one training session for you to have a look at me," TJ continues. "If you don't think I'm good enough, I trust your judgment and I will not be back to bother you again."

The coach stands in silence and simply stares at TJ as his assistant coach continues doing the training session he has been pulled away from.

It seems he is thinking about giving TJ a chance.

"I have had players come and ask for a trial before, but none of them have had the courage to outrun a security guard or the ability to persistently try and convince me of what they are capable of. I feel inclined to give you a chance, boy, but only one chance. I cannot have you disrupting my season midway through it if you are not good enough."

"One chance is all I need sir. Can I come tomorrow?"

"Yes, you can. Bring your boots with you in the morning and do not be here later than nine. I know the Rustenburg Rovers' coach well, so I will phone him after training today to see if he knows who you are. If he cannot confirm who you are then you must not expect to have a trial here tomorrow."

TJ cannot contain his smile.

"Now, get out of here. You have disturbed my session enough for one day!" shouts the coach, adopting an angrier tone.

TJ gets a fright and sprints off the field in a hurry.

He smiles arrogantly at the unimpressed Joseph as he jogs past him and tries to find another taxi that will take him back to his cousin's house. He does find a taxi around the corner and, as he climbs in, he struggles to contain his excitement.

This could really happen, I need to give it everything I have tomorrow, he thinks as he travels in the rusty white taxi.

TJ returns to his cousin's house and, as he opens the door, he sees Marley sitting in the kitchen staring at the front door almost like he's been waiting for him to arrive home.

"I spoke to my parents again this morning and they will allow you to stay in the house rent free for the next three months, but you will need to find somewhere else after they are over," Marley tells him.

TJ nods his head. "Thanks, Bob. I really appreciate it."

"How did the trial go, by the way?"

"I didn't train today but I will be training tomorrow morning. I'm sure you can come watch me train if you want to?"

"That's so cool, TJ!" shouts his younger cousin. "You're going to have a chance of becoming an Impi player! What time is training?"

"It starts at nine, but I want to leave an hour and a half earlier to make sure I'm not late."

"No problem. I'll definitely come with you. I promise I'll be in a better mood tomorrow morning. Today was too early for life."

"Sound's good, cuzzy. It's really great to have your support."

Marley smiles widely.

"Wow, my cousin wearing an Impi Football Club badge on his chest tomorrow. So cool! I'm going to tell all my friends when we get back to school."

TJ smiles and replies, "I hope you don't mind, but I am going to spend the rest of the day preparing myself for tomorrow, Bob."

"No problem, TJ. If you need anything, just let me know."

TJ pats Marley on the back, grabs an apple from the fruit bowl, and then spends the entire afternoon stretching his muscles, juggling the white ball and visualising what he will do on the field tomorrow. He begins feeling the fire in his belly that the mechanic told him he would feel if he is doing something he loves. He channels any nervous energy he feels and uses it to fire himself up even more. He keeps his mind clear of any negative thoughts, worries or expectations.

He juggles the ball on the small patch of grass in a small garden outside throughout the afternoon. As the sun begins to set, he drops the ball and takes a seat on the grass. He looks up at the sky and thinks about what he will do in training tomorrow.

I'm not expecting anything from tomorrow but to just take it one touch, one pass and one moment at a time, he thinks.

The darkness arrives. He eats dinner with the family and he gets into bed early, feeling ready to take on any challenges tomorrow may bring.

He sleeps deeply throughout the night, despite Marley's incessant snoring next to him, and he gets out of bed at 5:00 to clear his mind and stretch before eating a healthy breakfast. Waking up early has become a habit now.

After eating his breakfast, his watch showing 7:20, he shakes Marley to wake him up and tells his cousin that they will be leaving in fifteen minutes in case there is traffic.

Marley gets ready in a hurry. They close the front door of the house and, as they begin walking to the taxi rank together, it starts drizzling. TJ had seen the dark clouds in the morning, but no rain had fallen yet.

They start jogging and, as they approach the taxi rank, they do not see any taxis, much to their dismay. They look around the area, baffled.

"Excuse me, sir. Do you by any chance know where all the taxis are?" TJ asks an elderly man walking nearby.

"The taxis are striking today. There will be no taxi service the entire day," he answers politely.

"Thank you," replies TJ, not reacting to the bad news.

He then looks up at the sky, sighs loudly and then laughs shaking his head.

"He said life will test me to see how much I truly want something," he thinks out loud.

"What's so funny?" Marley asks. "You are going to miss the most important day of your life!"

"No, I'm not," replies an adamant TJ. "I paid attention to the route in the taxi yesterday and I know how to get to the training ground. It's a good thing I was focusing."

"Well, it's impressive that you know the route there, TJ, but you're forgetting one very important thing."

"What's that?"

"There are no taxis, you moron!"

"I'm going to run there, I don't know how fit you are, Bobby, but you can join me if you want to."

"You mad, bra. There's no ways I will make it! It must be over ten kilometres to get there! But good luck, cuzzy! Hopefully you get into the team so I can come watch you another day."

"I hope so too."

They give each other a firm farewell hug and then TJ starts running, the bag on his back carrying his boots weighing him down slightly as the rain begins falling harder.

The run must be just under eleven kilometres and it is not a run he wants to do, especially before a training session where he needs to prove himself. He did ten-kilometre runs at the petrol station during his training and he knows he will be able to get there in just under an hour. It is lucky that he'd left the house early, but now he will be burning off much-needed energy for the training session.

He runs as fast as he can, resting at certain points in an attempt to save energy and, when he does eventually arrive at the training complex, he is on time but he is one of the last players to arrive. The watch on his arm shows 8:50.

He sees the head coach talking to the assistant coach and another staff member of the team under the roof of a large building that overlooks the field.

TJ goes to greet them.

The head coach is tall and lean, and looks exceptionally fit. He is bald and, when TJ looks into his eyes, it as if there is a world of experience looking back at him. The assistant coach is short and slightly overweight. The other man they are talking to is tall and fairly well built with blonde hair.

The head coach greets TJ in return and then introduces him to the assistant coach and sports scientist of the team.

"I spoke to your old Rustenburg Rovers coach yesterday and after everything he said about you I am willing to let you train today," says the head coach, lobbing a training kit at TJ. He then continues his conversation with his coaching team.

I wonder what my old coach said about me, TJ thinks as he follows the signs to the dressing room. He puts his training gear and boots on as quickly as he can. He joins the rest of the team who are all talking to one another on the field. He introduces himself to a few of the players and those players introduce him to the rest of the team. He is pleasantly surprised at how respectful each player is towards him. Some players openly welcome him; others are wary of a new player trialling out, while others greet him as if they are not too concerned about the situation. Everybody he has met at the club has been exceptionally well-mannered and respectful towards him, apart from Joseph the security guard.

The rain has almost completely stopped as the coaches emerge from their shelter. TJ is still feeling jaded from the unexpected eleven-kilometre run.

The coaches greet the players and tell them they will be doing a full field practice match for training today, in preparation for their game against Tshwane Tigers this weekend. The coaching team say they want to analyse where the team's strengths and weaknesses are before the Tshwane Tigers game.

Two players arrive late while the head coach is giving his pre training talk. He glances at them once and simply says, "*Gijima!*"

"Ah, but coach, there are no taxis," replies one of the players.

"Did you not hear me? I said run! I don't care about your excuses. If you're late, you run. Simple."

The head coach then looks around at the rest of the team and notices a few players not wearing the correct training socks or pants and he tells those players to join the two players who were late.

"*Hamba!*" shouts the assistant coach.

The guilty players reluctantly begin running around the field at a fairly fast pace.

"Rustenburg boy," says the head coach looking at TJ, "you are going to do a beep test with the sports scientist. I need to know if you are fit enough to join us. If your beep test result is horrible, go home."

The rest of the team begin doing a warm up and passing drills together as TJ walks to the other end of the field with the sports scientist of the team to do the beep test. He feels nervous, wondering if the run he just had to do has ruined his chances of impressing the head coach.

"Okay. You are going to run from that cone to that cone every time you hear the loud beep from my cell phone. It is twenty metres. Don't stop running and do it as fast as you can. Every time you hear a beep, you run. If my phone beeps before you reach the other side then stop running. That will be your final score," says the sports scientist.

TJ nods his head, gets ready and, as soon as he hears the first beep, he sprints to the other cone, twenty metres away from him. He continues sprinting, trying to beat each beep. He breathes deeply through his nose, firmly out with his mouth and keeps his mind clear. It is exhausting, his energy levels are depleted, but he does not stop. The earlier run has made things difficult, but he takes it one breath at a time, staying strong mentally, pushing his body and not giving up. His confidence grows with each beep he beats. He feels his body is fit enough and strong enough to handle this difficult test.

"Everything I have worked for my entire life depends on this. Whatever you do, do not stop," he says softly to himself.

He continues sprinting and giving his absolute best for what feels like an eternity. He then sprints to one side, touches the line just in time and immediately sprints back, making it to the other side again. He turns and sprints once more but this time the cell phone beeps before he makes it to the other side.

His legs collapse and he sits on the ground, panting heavily. He looks up at the sports scientist, desperately hoping he has done enough to impress him. The sports scientist writes in some book without uttering a word to him.

"Well, how did I do, sir?" he asks, breathing heavily.

The sports scientist looks up from his book. "Excellently. Thirteen: ten is your score," he replies.

"What does that mean?"

"It means you are very fit."

The sports scientist then walks off to let the head coach know. TJ sits on the floor, recovering and waiting to hear the verdict as he sees the head coach nodding his head.

He then calls TJ and the young man jogs over to him.

"Are you still feeling okay? I don't allow players to train at fifty percent," asks the head coach as he approaches.

"Yes sir, I'm feeling good!" he replies enthusiastically, trying to hide the fact that he is completely and utterly exhausted.

"Okay then, you will play in the practice match. My reserve right winger isn't wearing his socks today, so he will be running the rest of training. So I'm going to put you on the wing. Show me what you've got."

"Okay, sir," replies TJ, not knowing whether to feel excited or nervous. He is extremely tired, but he still needs to do a training session to show what he's got. He feels he has no other choice but to simply give his best.

TJ's team put on purple bibs. He has a quick sip of water and then readies himself in the right wing position. He is going to find out if he is as versatile as the mechanic has taught him to be.

The assistant coach blows the whistle to kick off the game. TJ moves forward into the open space trying to find the best channel to settle into. His nerves settle and he begins focusing on each moment. He analyses the left back marking him, to see if the left back is marking him tightly or giving him space, he is assuming the left back's left foot is his strong foot, so when he receives the ball he will target his right foot. He looks to see if the striker he is playing with is short or tall.

The striker is tall, so he will put a high cross into the box if he gets the ball on the by-line.

Fifteen minutes pass by. TJ is moving intelligently into the spaces, calling for the ball, but none of his team mates are passing it to him. Every time he screams for the ball, his team mate chooses another option. They do not know his name and it seems as if they are not going to allow some player to come off the street and take one of their team mate's positions.

More time of moving and trying to get the ball passes by and the ball eventually lands at his feet by chance. The left back has not been marking him tightly so TJ immediately decides to turn with the ball and run directly at the full back. He wants to play a one-two with the central midfielder but decides he needs to show his team mates what he is capable of so they will pass him the ball.

He takes on the left back, inside of the boot, outside of the boot, shifting his body and putting the defender off balance. He then knocks the ball past him with ease, adding a burst of speed to get away from the man.

He glides with the ball.

The opposition central midfielder sprints to tackle him as TJ gets past him too with a superb double step over. The midfielder nudges him hard from behind, but he keeps his balance. He runs towards the by-line and crosses the ball, aiming towards the tall striker's head at the back post.

It curves in the air, the striker rushes into six yard box, jumps up high and he heads it wide.

The assistant coach screams with fury at the striker for missing the gilt-edged chance.

The game continues with the coaches giving out a few instructions, concerned with what decisions each team and each player is making.

TJ's team are beginning to pass the ball more regularly to him as he constantly stays on his toes, moves into the spaces and keeps things simple. He is doing the basic things extraordinarily well, just passing and moving into the correct space.

The score is 0-0, with neither team's strikers taking their chances. The defenders have been hard and disciplined but the attackers have been woeful.

The ball goes out for a corner to the purple bibs team. The ball is crossed into the box. TJ attacks the ball, leaps higher than all those around him. Hanging in the air, he makes firm contact with the ball, heading down into the ground with power, and it beams towards the corner of the goals.

The opposition goalkeeper flings himself towards the ball, stretches his arm out and saves the ball. Their defender then hoofs the ball clear and the game continues.

Nearly an hour has past by when the assistant coach shouts "ten minutes left! *Dlala* fast! I want that ball moving fast! I want a high intensity!"

TJ is utterly exhausted, but he is still pushing himself, not wanting to let this opportunity pass him by. He is taking it one touch at a time. He doesn't know if he has done enough as the ball goes out for a throw in on the left hand side of the field, near the opposition's corner flag. TJ has shifted inwards as his team's right back provides the width for the team. He settles just outside the eighteen yard box, creating an overload of purple attackers on the opposition's box.

The assistant coach shouts, "Down the line, always try throw down the line!"

The purple bibs teams left back throws the ball to the left winger, the left winger passes the ball to a central midfielder in the middle of the pitch. The central midfielder passes the ball directly to TJ's feet and usually in this situation he would pass it back to the central midfielder and move into the space.

He quickly decides: *Why play the way I face when I can turn the defender?* As the ball rolls towards him, he flicks it up and around the central defender, marking him tightly. He twists his body around the centre back as the ball bounces in front of him in the box. He is surrounded by opposition defenders, all sprinting to close down the ball. He picks his spot in the goals. He pulls his right foot back and a defender hurls his body towards the ball.

TJ volleys the ball with pure power.

It beats the defender's lunge and cannons into the bottom left hand corner of the goals, with the goalkeeper having nowhere near enough time to dive for it.

"Yes!" he shouts softly to himself, passionately fist pumping the air to celebrate. A few of his team mates tap him on the back and rub his head to congratulate him as the team jog back to the halfway line. TJ struck the volley with real venom making it 1-0 to the purple bibs.

The opposition kicks off and push hard for an equalizing goal, but it is to no avail as TJ's team wins the practice match. There aren't too many celebrations as a few players shake hands and chat to one another. They cool down and stretch, TJ feeling more tired than he has felt in his entire life.

They gather and listen to the coaching staff's post match team talk. The head coach and assistant coach tell each player directly what they need to improve and what they did well. They were happy with the defending and the way each team kept possession, but they were disappointed with the finishing in each team.

They have firm and lively African accents, speaking English most of the time but also using many Zulu and Xhosa sayings as they speak.

"Rustenburg boy," says the head coach, trying to spot TJ in the group, "I liked your decision making. It's quick and intelligent. It was a great goal too. You have earned yourself a two week trial here. Two weeks to show us if it is worth registering you at the club," he says and, just like that, TJ has earned himself a trial at Impi Football Club.

He is elated but utterly exhausted after everything he has been put through. Eleven kilometres, a beep test and then a high intensity, hour-long match against players who did not make it easy for him. The team shake each coach's hand to thank them for training.

TJ shakes the head coach's hand firmly. "Good luck," the coach says, looking him in the eye.

TJ looks back. "Thank you for the opportunity, sir," he replies confidently.

He then walks off the field, feeling the happiest he has ever felt in his life. He takes a shower and begins a long walk back to Marley's house feeling excited to tell his cousin the great news.

After two hours of walking, he arrives at house number 19.

"I've gotten myself a two week trial, Bobby!" he tells Marley as soon as he opens the front door.

"What? That is insane, TJ! I am so proud of you, bra!" he shouts, immediately jumping up off the couch and hugging his older cousin.

"Thanks, my boy. I want to savour this moment with you, but the truth is the hard work has only just begun. There is still a two-week challenge that lies ahead of me."

"Yeah but it's already such an awesome achievement, cuzzy! I can't believe you did it! I'm so happy for you!"

"Thanks, Bob, but I'm not getting too carried away. There are still more hurdles I need to jump over if I want to put the Impi badge on my heart permanently. But yeah, I've jumped over the first hurdle and I am definitely ready for the next one."

11

Derby Day

....

"Today is a gift. You never get another day like today so give your best and enjoy it," says TJ softly, sitting in the back of a taxi travelling to Impi Football Club's training complex.

The taxi pulls off the highway and he arrives at the grounds for the first day of his two-week trial with an enormous smile on his face and enthusiasm rushing through his veins.

It is early Wednesday morning and the summer's heat has already begun its flaming assault on the training grounds. TJ eats breakfast with the team, puts on the training gear with pride and reminds himself to focus on taking it one touch, one pass and one moment at a time. He has received the best individual training he could ever have asked for from the mechanic, but now it is time to prove he is ready for team training and competitive action.

"Remember, the more I sweat in training, the less I will sweat in a match," he says to himself as he runs out onto the training field.

The players laugh and joke amongst each other. TJ keeps his distance, knowing he still has a lot to do before he is considered a member of this team. The reserve team head coach arrives on the scene and welcomes the players to the training session.

The players warm up with light jogging, stretching and then do some agility exercises with explosive sprinting. The sports scientist oversees the warm up. They then begin playing separate rondos, where one player marks and the rest pass the ball as quickly as they can around him.

TJ does well until one of his passes gets intercepted and he is told to go in the middle and mark.

"Make him dizzy, gents!" shouts one of the players and he chases the ball that is being moved around at an intense speed.

"It's two touch, boys! Not seven touch! Create angles for each other. You can't play football in straight lines! You need to make it easy for your team mate to receive the ball!" shouts the determined sports scientist.

TJ eventually intercepts the ball and joins the rest of the team again in manipulating the players forced into the middle of the rondo.

After the warm up, the head coach calls the team in. He is holding a large book in his hand that reads 'Training Notes' on the front cover.

"We will be testing and pushing all of you to the maximum of your capabilities," he says to the players. "We are going to squeeze every bit of potential out of each one of you. There will be a lot of possession-based drills today; learning how to keep the ball, moving into the correct spaces on the field and practising building our attacks from the back. The best way to learn is to be on the ball as often as possible." He pauses briefly. "Now listen to me carefully. The game this weekend starts today in training! The game starts today. Whatever you do in training is what you will be doing this weekend, so make sure you are focused and pushing yourself! Do the right things!" shouts the head coach as the players ready themselves for the session.

The team then begins with high intensity individual training that has them doing passing, heading, first touch and all sorts of things that improve them as individuals. They move onto a low intensity, long and short passing drill, which has the players passing in pairs and working on their passing technique. After that, there is a group passing drill, working on different combinations and patterns of play without any opposition. After the combination play, they move onto

5v5 possession games against one another, with the focus on keeping the ball. If the ball goes out of play, it is a goal to the other team.

TJ is training well and does not look out of place during the drills; he is getting the basics correct. The coaching staff are constantly emphasizing the importance of always passing and moving. There is no time for him or anybody to just be standing around: each player is always involved in the session. The only time the assistant coach stops the session is when the players are doing something wrong or if he needs to motivate and inspire the players to push even harder than they are pushing. The head coach simply watches the session, simply analysing everything that is happening in the training.

During the 5v5 possession drill, one player passes the ball behind his team mate and, for the first time during the entire session, the head coach loses his temper.

"*Wena wenzani?* What are you doing?" he shouts. "You have slowed down the entire drill! Always pass in front of your team mate! If you pass behind him, you slow down our attack and you allow the opposition more time to get back! So always pass in front of your team mate and keep our momentum moving forward. If you are under pressure, play one touch to an open team mate. If you are not under pressure, you can take an extra touch and choose the best option."

The guilty player nods his head and they continue with the possession drill. The drills are testing the players physically, technically and mentally. There is no time for thinking or rest and the player's are forced to just keep passing and keep moving: forced to play high-intensity football.

The assistant coach calls an end to the possession games and tells them they will be playing a game. He speaks in Zulu and the instructions are to open the space as much as possible when attacking and tighten up and close the spaces when they are defending. They want to focus on building the attacks from the back.

TJ starts upfront for the team that seems to have the weaker players in it. It is an 11v11, full field game and, having watched the possession drills, he assumes he is in the weaker team.

They begin the game and, as it goes on, the coaches constantly yell out instructions but they do not stop the play. They are letting the game flow.

Ten minutes in, TJ receives the ball, turns easily and starts running at the opposition defender. He dribbles him and the head coach stops the game for the first time.

"Never let an attacker turn!" he shouts at the first choice centre back. "The moment he starts running at you it is difficult to defend him. So, get tight and don't allow him to turn with that ball. You have to want that ball more than he does! And if you are the attacker, never wait for the ball. You need to go to it! All of you need to want to be on the ball more than your opponent does. Want the ball more than he does! The opponent must never, ever want the ball more than you do! That goes for fifty-fifties, headers, second balls, anything!"

The game continues with each team working on keeping possession, building from the back and opening the space in their attack. In attack, the wide players need to create width for the team and the central players need to create depth. The head coach explains that the width stretches the opposition and the depth allows for penetration. The defending team works on closing the spaces when they don't have the ball, and keeping their shape rigid, making sure there is less space for the attackers to play in. The attackers need to press when they are defending.

After thirty minutes of game play, the head coach calls an end to training and the players all cool down and stretch. TJ did not feel out of place on the field, coping admirably with each situation he faced.

The coaches review the session with the team, talk to individual players who need to work on certain aspects of their game and also use the time to ask players what they have all learned.

The assistant coach then looks at TJ. "So, Rustenburg boy, what did you learn today?"

"Keep passing, keep moving and pass in front of your team mate, coach," he answers instantly.

The assistant coach nods his head, "Good and good session today, gentlemen. Tomorrow we will be working on transition. Have some lunch together now and, if your bodies are feeling okay, then do a gym session. The focus is on building your leg muscles today. We need to fix some of the pigeon-legged players running around on this field."

The players laugh.

"I would like all of you to spend as much time together as possible off the field," says the head coach. "You might not like one another but you need one another, so get to know each team member as if he were your brother."

TJ attends lunch with his new team mates, but enters the canteen quietly on his own. He does not want to get too close to anybody as he might be told to leave in two weeks time. He feels it is best if he just focuses on what he needs to do, keeping his distance from the team and not disturbing the team chemistry.

The chef puts a large amount of food on his plate, which will help load his energy levels before doing a gym session. He takes a seat by himself and has a small bite of his roast potato, reflecting on the training session. He realizes each drill followed a sequence from individual work to paired work to combination play to possession play and then game play.

Taking another bite of his potato, a player from the team sits down next to him.

"*Ngubani igama lakho?*" he asks.

"It's TJ, and yours?"

"I'm Bongani. How did you find your first real training session today, TJ?"

"It was good, thanks. I definitely learned a lot."

"Well, you might have learned a lot today but the drills we do are similar most of the time, doing the same things over and over again."

"So lots of repetition then?"

"*Yebo*, lots of repetition. Just make sure you are never late, always be correctly dressed and always be aware of what's around you on the field. The coach hates it if you don't know what's going on around you, so keep your head moving and scanning around the field, always looking both sides."

"Thanks for the advice, Bongani."

"No stress. I just really wanted to tell you that you shocked a lot of us in the team yesterday during the practice match. Your volley was awesome. Everybody is talking and asking who this new guy is that's arrived."

"I guess it was just one of those days, hey. Everything seemed to work for me, but thank you for telling me that."

"No problem. Have you signed a contract already?"

"No. It's a two-week trial."

"A trial? That's pressure!"

TJ smiles. "We'll see. Are you coming to the gym session?"

"No ways, bra. I'm tired, but I will see you at training tomorrow morning. It was good to meet you, TJ. Good luck for the rest of your trial."

"Thanks, was good to meet you too, Bongs."

TJ finishes his lunch, waits two hours for his food to settle and then goes to the gym on his own, not wanting to waste a single moment to improve. He walks into the gym situated on the clubs premises and notices only half the team have stayed behind; they are all doing some form of leg exercises.

He does the leg press machine, pushing as much weight as he can before squatting and lunging with weights. He is not used to the extra load, but he can feel his legs definitely hurt more when using the extra weight. The physiotherapist has been watching him for a while and decides to offer TJ some encouragement.

"Focus on repetition and form when doing the exercises," she says, as she demonstrates lunging with a light weight. "If you do the exercises wrong, you will hurt yourself, so it is more important to do the exercise correctly than the amount of weight you pick up or lift. You don't need to bulk up to play this sport, but you do need to be strong."

"Thank you very much," he replies and he does as he is told, making sure he is doing the exercises correctly rather than pushing too hard. The physiotherapist nods her head in approval and then moves on to another player. Once again, TJ is pleasantly surprised at how helpful everybody is at the club.

He finishes the gym session, stretches and pours himself the ice cold water available at the gym.

He walks out, gets into a taxi outside the training complex and, as the taxi pulls off, he notices Impi's training ground becoming smaller in the rear-view mirror of the taxi; slowly disappearing in the distance.

No matter what happens, I'm going to make the most of this experience, he thinks as the training ground drifts out of sight.

Thursday

TJ warms up with the team and they then begin doing a rondo before moving on to a one-touch passing drill. After the passing they move onto 1v1 situations.

The wingers are taking on the full backs, the strikers are taking on the centre backs and the central midfielders are playing 1v1s against each other. TJ copes well in these difficult situations. His time spent doing skills at the petrol station, running at the mechanic or a rock he placed in the mud, have helped him immensely with this drill.

The teams then get split between attack and defence and they begin paying 2v1, 3v2 and 4v3 games against one another. They are learning to deal with situations where the team or the opposition has more numbers and an overload. Sometimes the attack has more players and sometimes the defence has more players and each player needs to learn how to cope in these situations. If the attack has a man advantage they need to make sure they make diagonal, cross over runs and use the extra man. The attacker needs to draw the defender in before making a pass. If the defence has fewer players, they need to stay tight to one another to close the gaps for the attackers to get through. Defending narrow and forcing them wide, using the touch line as an extra defender. TJ is enjoying himself and trying his utmost to make the right decisions.

The coaches are constantly emphasizing the importance of being quick in transition, defensively and offensively. TJ has learned all about transition and he makes sure he is switched on when his team needs to counter and, if they lose the ball, he is ready to press immediately. It is about the players making the right decision, timing the decision correctly and using combination plays to open up the opposition. Each player needs to be on the same wavelength, using the right combinations and moving into the right channels on the field.

The players are constantly on the ball. There is no time for them to switch off with something always happening.

After the small sided games, the attackers set themselves up on the halfway line with the goalkeeper and defence setting up in front of the goals. It is a 7v5 half-field game of attack versus defence. The players not playing the game this weekend sit out and watch the starting line up compete against one another.

The half field game kicks off with the focus on transition and the head coach, assistant coach and sports scientist spend the entire hour explaining to each individual player what their role is on the field. They notice the tiniest of details and TJ listens intently to what the coaches say to each player and what roles each position needs to fulfil on the field. The head coach is also seen constantly writing in his large 'Training Notes' book.

Throughout the half-field game. TJ learns that the team uses a 4-2-3-1 system. Fullbacks need to get high up the pitch, put in dangerous crosses, block crosses from opposition wingers and create width for the team. The wingers are required to either hug the touchline or cut in from wide positions. They are encouraged to use their trickery and they are allowed to express themselves with the ball. Both wingers in this team cut in on their stronger foot to shoot at goal while the fullbacks are required to hug the touchline, create width and put in dangerous crosses for the strikers and midfielders running into the box. Every wide player needs to provide width.

He learns that the central defenders are required to win headers, read the game, be aggressive in the tackle and be able to play out from defence. One defender is right footed and is a very hard and commanding defender. The other central defender is left footed and is far more calm and composed than his defensive compatriot.

He sees the two central midfielders are the brain of the team, always passing and moving. One word the head coach likes to use is industry; they need to work harder than anybody else on the field. They need to keep switching the play and look for forward passes that unlock the opposition defence. They are encouraged to get into the box when they are in the opposition's final third to get goals for the team, taking the goal-scoring burden off the attackers. One central midfielder is a box to box midfielder, who works tirelessly up and down the pitch. The other central midfielder always sits deep, to protect the back four and win important tackles for the team. He is known as 'The General' in midfield and he dictates the tempo of the team, breaks up the opposition's attacks and distributes the ball from right to left.

TJ has enjoyed watching the attacking midfielder behind the striker the most. He has got license to roam all over the field and be creative with the ball. He is the link between the midfield and the attack and he is arguably the team's best player. He has wonderful vision and is a genius when manipulating the ball with his feet. TJ feels he improvises well.

Hearing the coaches talk, he learns that the striker is the main outlet for the team and is required to move into important channels, giving the team as many options as possible in attack. The striker's movement needs to be excellent and his link up play needs to be valuable. Most importantly, the head coach begs the striker to score goals.

The coaches call an end to the half-field game and each player jogs in to hear the post session team talk. The coaching team again emphasize the importance of keeping the ball and being quick in transition.

TJ listens intently, trying to gather as much knowledge as he can. He is still becoming accustomed to team and grass field training again.

Friday

It is the middle of an afternoon training session. The sun is setting on a late Friday afternoon. An extremely hot day has left the players with sweat pouring off their bodies. The coaches are trying to prepare them for the league game being played against Tshwane Tigers tomorrow.

The session is not as intense as the sessions earlier in the week and it is more of a tactical session, with a few set pieces being worked on as well. The players who are not involved in the game tomorrow had done a morning session with the coaches.

TJ did the morning session: possession drills in which he performed averagely but still keeping the same consistency he has had in the week thus far. He has come to watch the afternoon tactical session, hoping to learn something new. He wonders why the team don't do double sessions every day. He feels he has the energy to do double sessions.

This current training the players are doing is set piece training, attacking corners and free kicks, as well as defending corners and free kicks. The head coach says his most intelligent player must be at the front post when defending set pieces and he encourages a man marking system, not a zonal marking system with defending set pieces. They use a mixed marking system during game play. He also encourages the free-kick takers, corner takers and penalty takers to always stay thirty minutes after every training session to work on that part of their game. If they do not want to work on the set pieces after training, then they will not be the penalty taker, corner taker or free kick taker anymore. TJ wants to join the penalty takers after training.

The head coach has been doing a lot more talking in this training session, trying to motivate each player and talking tactically about tomorrow's game.

TJ has noticed a few trends so far this week. He has noticed the head coach does not talk to players who arrive late and he does not allow them to train with the team either. They have to do their own individual training. He does not talk to players who are injured, as he feels it is their own fault for being injured and not taking care of their bodies. It is the same for players who wear the wrong kit. Players are also forced to run laps for a long period of time if they are late or incorrectly dressed. Each player is warned that if they drink alcohol or smoke, they run the risk of being dropped to the bench. The head coach also has a lot of rules about working as a team and being there for one another.

After the set piece training, the team moves on to doing a practice match of attack versus defence. The entire match day squad is involved.

TJ watches from the side lines with the rest of the reserve team's second choice players. The game continues as the first choice striker passes the ball out wide to the left winger who dribbles past the right back with ease. He put in a half-hearted tackle, possibly not wanting to be too aggressive in a practice match.

The head coach stops the game immediately and looks sternly at the right back.

"What have I told you before?" he shouts. "There are no friends on the training field! You need to be better than the player next to you! You have to walk off this field today and say you were the best player on it. That is the attitude you need to have at training every day. So never take it easy on a team mate! You think the opponent is going to care if he is a good guy or not? You need to be hard on one another, not to hurt each other but to prepare each other. Training needs to be just as intense as matches are. You can all be friends after training again, but during the training session there are no friends or enemies. Push one another to improve! You all need one another, so push each other!"

One of the players then blatantly criticizes the right back for not making the tackle.

"Hey! That's my job! I get paid to find mistakes and improve the team, not you. It is not your job" shouts the head coach.

"But coach, I just wanted to..."

"Do you see that badge on your chest?" he interrupts.

"Yes, coach."

"It is the same badge as the guy next to you. Whether you like him or not, as soon as you step onto this field you are all brothers. You need to be helping each other and protecting each other when the coach screams at you. You need one another, so stick together, no matter what. You need to help your team mate if he has made a mistake, not criticize him. That is my job. If you have a problem with someone, sort it out off this field. On this field we are all one. We are a team. One player suffers and we all suffer. One player triumphs and we all triumph. This is a team sport. If you want to be an individual, go swim or play golf. You need your team mates to support you and be there with you."

The guilty player looks to the ground and nods his head.

"On the field each week this team needs to be one single and un-movable unit, with players willing to do anything for the guy next to them," says the assistant coach. "Fight for your team mates, move for your team mates and protect each other. I also want to add that just before that missed tackle there was a terrible pass."

The assistant coach finds the central midfielder and points his finger at him. "You, if your team mates are not in an open space, you do not pass! It is not your fault if you can't pass to them. It is their fault for not being open. So if you cannot pass, protect the ball and wait for someone to open up for you, never just kick the ball away! No more sloppy mistakes. We need to get the basics right!"

The head coach nods his head in agreement.

"You are grown men now," says the head coach. "You need to be able to solve your own problems on the field. You should not be rely-ing on us coaches to give you all the solutions to your problems. We cannot play for you. We cannot go onto the field and kick the ball for you. You need to be able to communicate with one another and solve your own problems on the field together. As coaches, we can only guide you and show you the right way in training. You are the ones who need to do it on the field."

"Yes, you all need to be on the same wavelength as one another," says the sports scientist. "You need to know what your team mate wants to do and he needs to know what you want to do at the exact same time. It is all about timing. That is what we do in training. We try finding the solutions together. We need to know each other well enough to have the same ideas at the same time on the field."

TJ is amazed to see the united front of the coaching team, each member sharing the same football philosophy and knowing exactly what they want from the team.

The players continue with the session and TJ is beginning to understand the repetition Bongani had warned him about.

After the light training session is complete, the starting eleven for the home game tomorrow is announced as the head coach wants the players who start tomorrow to be mentally prepared for it. The match day squad will travel on a bus together. TJ will be watching the game from the stands.

He has learned that the entire match day squad are required to sleep at the club the night before the game. Each room is built for two players and players share a room based on their positions on the field. The two goalkeepers stay together, the right back and right winger, the left back and left winger, the two central defenders, the two central midfielders, the attacking midfielder and striker all share rooms together.

The head coach believes that players who play in the same areas on the field need to share a room to understand one another better and improve the team's patterns of play. They need to know one another as people to create a bond and understanding on the field together.

Once the coaching team has finished their pre-match de-briefing with the match day squad, they all head to the canteen to eat dinner together.

TJ joins the rest of the players not selected for the game in the dressing room. He changes into casual clothes, preparing to spend an evening with Marley.

"What is that book the coach carries around with him? He's always writing in it," he asks Bongani, who is not involved in the match day squad either.

Bongani is putting on deodorant and looks like he is preparing for a night out.

"The coach writes everything in that book. He apparently writes down every single detail of every single training session, every single day. It has injury information, what the weather is like for the day, how each player has trained, our strengths and weaknesses. I am told it has every detail."

Much like my own training diary, TJ immediately thinks. He looks at the way his team mate is dressed.

"Where are you going tonight, Bongs?"

"Taking my girlfriend on a date. Hopefully I get lucky tonight!' he replies with a mischievous smile.

TJ laughs. "Well good luck then, my boy!"

"When you look as good as me, there is nothing to worry about. See you tomorrow, TJ. Enjoy your evening."

TJ packs his bag and then walks out the dressing room, the fresh air of the night blowing onto his face. There are a few lights guiding him and as he turns around the corner of the dressing room he sees the assistant coach walking towards him.

"Rustenburg, is that you?"

"It is sir."

"Forgive me, but I would only properly recognize you with your football kit on. How are you finding your trial so far?"

"I'm really enjoying it, thank you, sir. But I've been meaning to ask you why the training has not changed much this week? I also thought we would be training double sessions, but we have only been doing one session every day."

"I haven't had a player ask me those questions before," says the assistant coach. "Well, repetition is important. The more we train in a certain way, the more the way we play becomes a routine, it becomes second nature. Then we only do single sessions because it is all about the quality of work we do, not the quantity of minutes we spend out on the field; quality over quantity. We could spend five hours on the field and learn the same amount as a team who might spend one hour on the field. It is about the quality of work we do, not the quantity of time we spend working. Do you understand?"

"I do, thank you, sir."

"No problem. Keep pushing yourself in training."

"I will."

TJ remembers the mechanic teaching him about the importance of repetition. He gets into a taxi and travels to his cousin's home in Soweto. There have been many times in the training sessions the coaches have reiterated things the mechanic has taught him.

When he arrives home, he finds Marley playing FIFA on his PlayStation. TJ greets him.

"How was training, superstar?" asks Marley.

"It was good. I really dig the head coach."

"That's cool. Why's that?"

"It's only been four days but I just like the way he sees football and like all his rules and stuff. I think the rules help get the best out of the team. He told us that he and his coaching team have been training young men and players their entire coaching careers; he used to play for Impi Football Club himself. I can tell he has the respect and trust of the players. Everyone is willing to run and work their hardest for him. I've seen he even takes the time to get to know everyone as individuals. It's like he understands all the player's moods and who they are as human beings, not just as footballers. He keeps his distance from us and stuff, he lets us know he is the boss and not our friend, but he seems very approachable. So, like, we are scared of him on the field but off the field it feels like we can approach him to talk about anything happening in our lives."

"Sounds great, a hard but fair kind of coach. What about the way he likes to play? Like what's you guys' style of play?"

"I'm not too sure about that yet, but the training is fun and intense at the same time. From what I've seen so far I guess it would be keeping things simple on the field. Keeping possession, doing the basic things effectively and then we will be an effective player for the team. He emphasizes the importance of communication in the team as well. The team members need to get to know one another and create a bond. Even if you don't like a certain person in the team, you have to work together on the field."

"That's pretty cool. My style of play would be possession football too, just keeping the ball and stuff like my created team on FIFA. I guess that's what you mean by keeping it simple?"

"Yeah, I suppose so."

"It's so awesome that you're training at Impi, TJ. I wish I had your talent to work with this coach too."

"It's not talent, Bob. If you want something, then work for it. Instead of playing video games, you could be kicking a ball outside for real with me, improving yourself."

"Na, I'm chilled thanks. The couch is a great place to play football."

TJ laughs. "Suit yourself, Bobby. By the way, we are playing a game tomorrow. I'm not playing but it will be cool if you come and watch the team with me."

"I'm keen! We can go together. Hopefully this time the taxis don't ditch us."

"Let's hope not."

TJ puts his temporary training kit and boots in the corner of the room and watches Bob play his PlayStation game as they talk about football and share a few jokes together throughout the evening. They talk for hours and at one point in the conversation TJ smiles widely, feeling grateful to be sharing this time with his cousin who loves football just as much as he does.

Before he goes to bed, he takes out his training diary and writes down everything he has learned at Impi throughout the week. He also adjusts what he has written about his strengths and weaknesses as a player.

This thing has quite a few important lessons in it now, he thinks as he finishes writing. He closes the book and falls asleep next to his snoring cousin.

Saturday

Marley and TJ arrive at the game, joining the supporters in the stands who are singing and dancing, eagerly anticipating the reserve league football match.

Impi Football Club reserves are playing against Tshwane Tigers reserve team in the Micron Diski Challenge, the national reserve league in South Africa. There are thousands of supporters who have come to watch and support the teams. Each game is also broadcast live on television.

Marley and TJ are sitting right behind both teams' benches, close enough to hear each team's coaches shouting from the bench. They have a front row seat to watch the football.

The game kicks off to the excitement of the crowd. TJ will find out if he has the ability to play at this level. His temporary team are playing against tough opposition and it is not going to be an easy game. He watches on, trying to learn and understand as much as he can. The game is being played aggressively, with each player on the field fighting to prove they are capable and worthy of playing in the first team.

"Impi are playing the game at a very high tempo; it looks like they want to get to Tshwane Tigers's box as quickly as possible," says Marley.

"Good spot, Bob. That's exactly what the coach wants the team to do. It's because there are more rewards in the opposition half and more risks playing football close to our own goals. We need to be taking risks in the final third. The coaches also encourage us to pass forward as often as possible. If we have the option to play forward then we should."

The game is intense but the Impi Football Club head coach is calmly giving out instructions to the team. The team is keeping the ball well, but they are only playing football in their own half and not playing in the opposition half.

"Forward! Positive! We need momentum!" shouts the assistant coach.

"Your team is also playing with a high defensive line, TJ."

"It's to put as much pressure on Tshwane Tigers as we can. There is space for them to get in behind our defence, but our centre backs are quick and capable of handling any possible danger. We also like playing the offside trap."

"I see."

"When our team loses the ball, we immediately press and try to win it back. We have to win the fifty-fifty challenges and the second balls. After our defender wins a header, a team mate needs to immediately react to win the second ball."

Twenty-five minutes into the game and it is still 0-0.

"*Eish*, Impi are dominating the ball, TJ! You guys are playing lots of short passes, always trying to build the play out from the back."

"Yeah, like I said last night, we play simple, possession football and the coach always instructs us about the importance of keeping the ball. We need to draw the Tshwane Tigers players out of their positions by keeping possession. Then we need to look for the space behind them when they become frustrated with not having the ball. We are dragging their players out of their positions, and do you see how we are always switching the play? It is to keep Tshwane Tigers moving. Playing diagonal passes helps open spaces for our attack."

Bob is fascinated as he replies, "I've been looking and I've seen, when Tshwane Tigers gets the ball, your team presses hard to try and delay their attack so that everybody in your team can get into their correct defensive position."

"Yes, we do try winning the ball back as quickly as possible but, if we don't, then we sit back and wait for the opposition to make a mistake. We also don't delay any of our own attacks. Everything is done at an intense speed with no players taking any unnecessary extra touches on the ball."

"That's good."

"The philosophy of the coach is that the longer we have the ball, the more chance we have of scoring and the less chance the opposition has of putting the ball past our own goalkeeper. It is how my coach at the petrol station said to play football. Just pass to a player with the same colour shirt and then move into open space, keeping it simple and making sure you do the small things extraordinarily well."

Bob nods his head, astonished by how much his older cousin knows. Impi are dominating the ball, playing scintillating football and creating easy goal-scoring opportunities, but they haven't taken their chances. It is the forty-third minute and the Impi holding midfielder misplaces a pass.

"Not there!" TJ shouts nervously, as Tshwane Tigers intercept the ball and hit Impi Football Club on a fast counter attack. It is quick, one-touch football as the unorganized Impi defence struggles to stop them. The ball gets played to the Tshwane Tigers striker, one on one with the goalkeeper, and he scores the opening goal, capitalizing on the holding midfielder's poor error. Their fans and players celebrate as the holding midfielder drops his head. Team mates pat him on the back and they walk back to the halfway line.

Shortly after the goal, the referee blows the half time whistle. Impi end the half 1-0 down.

"Yoh, your team missed such easy chances, TJ! They need a striker like you in this team!" Marley shouts with passion.

TJ would love the opportunity to play in the reserve league and in this Impi team. The team are currently sitting in fourth place on the log and he feels he can contribute to a team that seems desperate for goals. They defend very well and they defend as a compact unit, but they don't take their opportunities whenever they are in front of goal. They are going to need to take their chances today or they will most likely lose this game.

The second half begins and Tshwane Tigers immediately begin defending deep.

"Why are they doing that, TJ?"

"They are parking the bus, allowing us to have the ball. By sitting deep they are making it more difficult for us to create chances because there is limited space for us in the final third. Tshwane Tigers will rely on the counter attack to create chances for themselves now."

It is a tough second half for Impi Football Club. They are keeping the ball with ease and it is boring to watch. The Impi fans have quietened in the stands as the talented attacking midfielder of the team produces a wonderful piece of skill on the edge of the box. He gets past the man, creates space for himself and shoots inches wide of the goals. The wonderful piece of skill livens up the stands.

"Did you see that skill? They hit him with a snake bite!" shouts Marley.

"A snake bite? You mean an elastico?" replies TJ.

"Yeah. Whatever it was, it was cool!"

TJ smiles at his younger cousin.

The game continues in a similar fashion until the eighty-seventh minute; wonderful football being played on the edge of the box by Impi Football Club which creates space for the right winger to run into the box. He crosses the ball low for one of the central midfielders, who taps the ball in, equalizing for Impi. The supporters go wild, but the team does not celebrate as the central midfielder picks the ball out of the goals and sprints back to the halfway line, trying not to waste any time so they can maybe grab a winning goal.

They apply plenty of pressure on the Tshwane Tigers defence in the dying minutes of the match, but the game ends as a draw; a scalp for Tshwane Tigers. There is disappointment on the Impi players' faces when the referee blows the final whistle. It is a game in which they dominated and should have won, had they taken their chances and not conceded a sloppy goal. However they showed good fighting spirit to equalize so late in the game.

TJ loved every moment of the experience with Marley and he is even more motivated than before to earn himself a place in this team. He wants to feel the experience of the supporters shouting his name and his team mates hugging him after scoring a winning goal. There is an opportunity for him to become the striker of this team; they are very one-dimensional and he just needs to prove that he has something more to offer than the current striker.

"I can do this, Bob. I can play in this team," he says to his younger cousin as they exit the stadium with the rest of the crowd in the stands.

Five days later

It is the end of the Friday afternoon training session as the head coach calls the players in after finishing their cool down. There is no league game tomorrow.

TJ has been doing all he can in each training session, and he does not feel out of place in training. He feels as though he has found exactly where he wants to be. However, it is not up to him to decide whether he stays or leaves. He knows it will take something special from him to get the head coach to register him midway through the season. He has learned many things in these past two weeks and he has given all he can, handling every drill the coaching team has given to him and the team. Having trained and passed on mud for three months, the grass has been easier and smoother to pass and take a first touch on. He has worked exceptionally hard in each session, never standing still, always moving and doing whatever he was told to do. He has given his absolute best.

"We are playing a friendly match against Soweto Giants reserve team tomorrow," says the head coach, gathering the team together. "We are going to give some of the players who have not been playing matches a chance to keep fit and to push for a starting spot in the team. Soweto Giants will be doing the same thing. We will be kicking off at ten, so make sure you are here on time."

The head coach then tells each player who will be involved in the exhibition match tomorrow. It will be the final day of TJ's trial and he is desperately hoping he has done enough to earn a spot in the team tomorrow. The coaches have not given him any indication of what they think of him.

"Rustenburg," says the head coach, looking at TJ, "you will be on the bench tomorrow. Depending on how the game is going, you might be given a chance to show what you've got. We are still allowed to register players for the remainder of the season, but I need to see your ID book tomorrow as we have a few twenty-one year olds who come here but their ten-year-old child is here to watch them and their thirtieth birthday is next month."

The entire team laughs as TJ smiles, nodding his head, feeling incredibly thrilled to be given a chance in the squad. He joins the team who will be involved in the game tomorrow at dinner.

After dinner he stays in a room with Bongani, who will also be sitting on the bench with him tomorrow. He plays on the left wing, a naturally talented player but very lazy. He is also eighteen years old.

Lying in separate beds, TJ visualizes what he will do if given a chance during the match tomorrow.

"I hope I get to play, Bongs, to show the coaches what I'm really capable of."

"I hope you do too, brother. But listen: even if you don't play tomorrow you've done really well in training. The guys in the team are impressed with you. Let's just hope the coaches are as impressed as the rest of us."

"So how does the coach treat players on the bench? Does he give each player a chance?"

"You might come on and you might not," he says. "The coach says we need to be angry that we are on the bench, but we must still be confident and prepared to come on. He says he needs to do what is best for the team and not what is best for each individual. I suppose we need to respect his decisions. The badge on our chest is what matters most, not the individual player. The coach will do what he thinks is best for the team."

"I understand. Are you angry you are on the bench?"

"Very, but what can I do? Hopefully I also get a chance tomorrow to show what I'm capable of as well. The strikers in this team are average, so you have an opportunity; the left winger is insanely good, so I haven't got much chance of playing. The coaches love him more, anyways."

"Don't say that, brother. I've learned you should never make excuses or blame anyone else for what is happening to you. You have the power to change your circumstances. Just be more confident in your abilities, Bongs. I rate you could be better than him if you worked harder."

"You really think so?"

"I do. Don't you have a contract here?"

"I don't. I'm hoping to earn one. I was registered in the team at the beginning of the year, but they say only players they believe have the ability to play in the first team are offered contracts. I'm still young so I guess I'm not too worried yet."

TJ looks up at the ceiling, realizing the opportunity he has to completely change his life tomorrow. Getting asked to stay isn't enough for him. He needs a contract.

"Let's get some sleep and make sure we are ready for tomorrow, TJ. It's derby day! Even though it's a friendly there will still be lots of supporters at the ground tomorrow and I can't wait!"

TJ feels the fire in his belly as he closes his eyes feeling ready for possibly one of the biggest days in his life tomorrow.

Saturday

The supporter's of both teams flock into the neutral venue in Soweto as the ground begins to fill up with people. Marley is one of them. There are many die-hard supporters, friends and family who have come to watch their loved ones perform. Those who were fortunate enough to hear about the exhibition match want to see the reserve teams in action. These players are nowhere near the starting line up of the first team, but this is the biggest rivalry in the country and the people who have heard about the match still want to find out who wins the game for a few bragging rights.

TJ puts on the Impi Football Club shirt with the rest of the team in the dressing room as the head coach walks in and scans the room.

"I want to make it crystal clear that the focus for all of us is to win the very next game we are about to play. Don't think about what has happened or what will happen in two months' time. Just focus on the game we have to play right now. Trying to win the next game we play is the only expectation we have as coaches, even in friendly matches. Many of you haven't been playing enough football. Today is your chance. Prove you have what it takes to wear the Impi Football Club badge today!"

The players listen intently and then head out to warm up. Rain falls softly onto the slightly damp and muddy field. The warm up routines require lots of dancing and movement as the philosophy of the Impi coaching team is that football is all about rhythm. It is keeping with a South African tradition that the warm ups include dancing routines while stretching as, without rhythm in a football team, there is no balance and flow. It has been explained to TJ that a footballer needs rhythm too; a footballer without rhythm in his game will most likely struggle. A player needs momentum.

After the warm up, TJ puts on a purple bib and takes a seat on the bench with another eight players sitting next to him. He has noticed a good camaraderie between all the players in this team. He hasn't said much to any of them, still keeping his distance and his focus.

The teams huddle up for their final words of motivation from the captains. They set up in the formations, the referee checks the goalkeepers are ready and he blows his whistle as the game kicks off to the roar of the crowd.

TJ immediately begins watching, trying to identify any weaknesses the opposition may have individually or as a team. He also watches to analyse what his own team is doing. He focuses specifically on what the strikers of his team are doing, what spaces they are moving into and what decisions they are making. He looks to see if the opposition goalkeeper is confident with shots in the air or on the ground and what the field conditions are like.

Ten minutes pass by as the temporary captain of the Impi team attains the ball five metres outside the opposition box. He looks up and does not see any options. He then drives past the approaching centre back and shoots the ball with power. The ball takes flight and cannons past the hopeless Soweto Giants goalkeeper and into the back of the net. Noise erupts in the small stadium as Impi Football

Club's supporters jump and hug one another. The players jump and hug their captain.

The game kicks off again and maintains its high intensity, both teams not giving each other a moment to catch their breath. The rain is beginning to fall harder, water dripping off each player's face and the mud dirtying their clothes as they all compete aggressively for the ball, tackles flying in from all angles and players swearing at one another.

The game is a friendly, but it is being played at full throttle with both teams wanting and needing to win.

Thirty minutes in and it is still 1-0 to Impi. The ball gets played out right. The Impi fullback takes a touch, looks up and puts in a wonderful cross; the tall, strong Impi Football Club striker sprints into the box, makes contact with the ball and misses a volley just four metres from the goals. The supporters moan, the Impi coaching staff have disappointed looks on their faces and the players on the bench click their tongues with disapproval. That is the second clear cut chance the striker has missed in the game.

"He wouldn't find the goals today even if they hit him in the face. You definitely coming on brother. Be ready," Bongani whispers to TJ.

The game continues. Both teams desperately want to beat each other as the supporters of each team in the neutral venue scream and shout at each exciting incident, demanding nothing but the best from their respective teams. The players in both teams need to prove their worth to their coaches.

Throughout the first half TJ notices that the assistant coach does most of the screaming on the side line; the head coach sits calmly and silently. He does not react emotionally, only occasionally screaming out instructions.

Thirty-nine minutes gone as the Impi Football Club centre back plays the ball back to his goalkeeper and the Soweto Giants striker puts pressure on the nervous second choice keeper. The goalkeeper takes a poor first touch and passes it straight to the onrushing striker's feet. The striker cushions the ball, takes a touch past the helpless goalkeeper and slides the ball into the empty net. Their supporters scream and their players celebrate wildly as they equalize. They have capitalized on a calamitous goalkeeping error to draw level. The Impi players' heads drop as they walk to the halfway line to take kick off.

The rest of the half continues in the same intense manner and, after five more minutes of chances, robust tackling and emotional shouting, the referee ends the first half, the score at 1-1.

It has not been a game that has entertained with quality football but it has entertained with pure grit and determination from both teams.

The players and the coaches enter the dressing room and not a single player criticizes the goalkeeper for his dreadful mistake. TJ looks around and notices the team's heads are down, upset with conceding the goal. The room is dead silent and the energy levels low as the head coach analyses his players.

"Lift your heads, gentlemen. It's just a goal. It is not the end of the world. If you do not believe we can still win this, then tell me now and I will substitute you," says the head coach in an assertive tone.

The entire team remains silent lifting their heads to look at their authoritative head coach.

He looks at the goalkeeper. "You learn as a child, never pass across your goals like that!"

The goalkeeper looks to the floor, disappointed with himself. The head coach then says, "But it's okay, you are allowed to make mistakes. But understand they will be punished. An honest mistake is fine but the team and you will be punished for it. It's gone now, so don't let it affect the rest of your game."

He then looks around at the entire team. "We are keeping the ball well but our movement and decision making has been poor. We need to be switching the play more and stretching their defence. When the ball comes from the left, then switch it to the right. Then, when we are defending we are not shifting when they are switching the ball. We need to shift. Another thing, their keeper is poor in the air, so let's put some more crosses in to test him and can we please put the ball into the net! We have had five decent half chances and haven't taken any of them. Stay composed in those situations!"

The entire team nods their heads and you can feel the atmosphere in the room changing.

"We need to be moving off the ball a lot better and looking for better spaces to move into," says the assistant coach. "We need to ask ourselves 'where is the best place for me to be on the field right now?' And that will help us with our movement. And please, if there is no one open, do not pass the ball! Keep it and wait for someone to open up. Let's play to feet more often, rather than passing into the space. We are rushing our passes in the final third. Don't force it! Be patient! Wait and look for the right opportunities to score. Create better angles for ourselves and put them inside a triangle when we have the ball. Let's communicate where you want the ball to be passed."

"We need the momentum to shift in our favour and all we need for that to happen is one moment of magic," says the sports scientist, giving his analysis of what he has seen so far. "So keep pushing and fighting for each other and, when the moment arises, take the chance! We're fitter than they are and we need to fight to the end of the ninety minutes!"

TJ notices that while each coach speaks he uses the terms 'we' or 'us'.

"We are definitely unlucky to be drawing, but you get what you deserve in football!" shouts the head coach. "So don't complain about it. We can't change it now. We can only go out and try doing things better in the second half! Give it everything you have, gentlemen! We can do this!"

The players clap loudly and sprint out of the dressing room, full of determined energy.

TJ take his seat on the bench again, feeling fresh and ready to come on if he is needed.

The players set themselves up, the referee blows his whistle and the second half begins. The players continue giving their utmost, unwavering in their efforts as the crowd's excitement increases but, just four minutes into the second half, Soweto Giants are awarded a free kick just outside the area.

A player from their team steps up. He runs towards the ball and curls in a wonderfully executed free kick. It goes over the wall, beats the goalkeeper and, just like that, the score line becomes 2-1. Their supporters and players go wild, but their coaching staff and the Impi coaching staff remain calm. The Impi players do not drop their heads, kicking off and continuing to give everything they have.

Everybody involved in the game can sense that the momentum is shifting and the game is turning in Soweto Giants's favour. They continue to put pressure on Impi Football Club; the Impi backline putting their bodies on the line trying to stop each wave of attack coming at them.

They eventually escape the constant pressure and the game settles down once again.

Fifty-eight minutes gone and the striker for Impi Football Club misses yet another golden opportunity. The head coach shakes his head. "Rustenburg!" he shouts, calling TJ, who is warming up on the side line.

TJ runs towards the head coach.

"Your old coach told me you play striker. Is that true?"

"My favourite position is striker, but I can play anywhere you need me, sir."

"Okay, take off your bib. You are going up front. This is your chance, boy. Sink or swim."

TJ nods his head, not showing any signs of nervousness, feeling the football gods are on his side giving him the opportunity to play in his preferred position.

"Show them your killer instinct, brother!" shouts Bongani as TJ takes off his bib. He has thirty minutes to show what he is capable of. Thirty minutes that could possibly change his entire life.

The ball goes out for a throw in and the head coach calls his disappointed striker off the field to be replaced. TJ tucks in his shirt and sprints onto field. The supporters are unsure of who he is.

He breathes out heavily and focuses. They take the throw in and he immediately presses the Soweto Giants back four as they pass it amongst themselves.

They then kick it long and Impi regain possession.

TJ stays aware of what is happening around him, moving into any open spaces he sees, constantly moving and staying on his toes, trying his best to open the space and move into the correct channels, but the team is struggling to get the ball to his feet. He wants it played to his feet so the team can build their attack and not rush forward.

The ball eventually gets to him by chance and he is hit instantly by a hard slide tackle from behind.

"Play on!" shouts the referee; the Impi fans boo and jeer the contentious decision.

The tackle has grazed the skin off the back of his calf. He pulls up his sock and stands up immediately off the wet floor, not allowing the opponent to think he has gotten the better of him.

"You are not getting past me today, boy! Try dribbling me and I will break your legs!" says the opponent aggressively.

TJ simply looks him in the eye and takes a deep breath, controlling the anger inside of him. He keeps going without feeling the least bit intimidated.

It is gruelling, but TJ keeps the ball close to him on the odd occasions he receives it. The opposition are biting at his ankles every time he receives the ball. He does not seem rattled that they are trying to hurt him.

He is passed the ball on the halfway line. Managing to find space to turn, as he sees his left back out wide, he decides against the long ball and passes it simply to the midfielder near him, helping the team to simplify their game. He is keeping his cool and doing what the situation requires in each passing minute.

Ten minutes left, and time running out for Impi to salvage something from the game.

The captain receives the ball in the middle of the pitch. TJ immediately sprints into the left hand channel of the oppositions half, into open space. The captain passes a through ball for him; he times his run to perfection and beats the defender in a sprint race to the ball. TJ controls the ball and shields it away from the aggressive right back; the right back is hassling him but he stays strong on the ball.

TJ passes to his left back who is making an overlapping run and he spins off the opponent. The left back passes the ball back to TJ on the edge of the box, a wonderful one-two, and he chops the ball with his right foot, giving him enough space to cross.

TJ looks up and crosses the ball with his left foot towards the back post.

The Soweto Giants goalkeeper flaps at the ball, misreading the cross. The Impi right wing jumps up above the centre back at the far post, heading the ball across the goals. It bounces in the middle of the area and the Impi attacking midfielder sprints towards the ball. A Soweto Giants player pulls frantically on his shirt. He sticks his toe out and just manages to punt the ball over the goal line.

The supporters go wild. The Impi players on the bench jump up and celebrate as the attacking midfielder takes the ball out the goals and sprints back to the halfway line with the rest of the team: 2-2.

The game kicks off and continues in an intense manner. Emotions are running high, both sets of players lunging hard into challenges and tempers flaring. Not many chances being created, rushed football being played, neither team wanting to make a mistake or give each other an opportunity.

Both sets of supporters are singing and both coaching teams are barking out instructions. The heat of the moment has taken hold of everybody involved.

Time is running out for either team to win the game; it is almost over and the scores are still level.

"Three minutes left!" shouts the referee as the ball goes out for a corner to Soweto Giants. The Impi players organize themselves at the back.

TJ realizes this is not a normal situation; he is going to have to do something special if he is going to be remembered. He needs to prove he is not just some player that has walked off the street but that he deserves to be on this field. He is just hoping he gets the chance to do that.

He positions himself in between the half way line and his team's box. He anticipates the ball will be headed here if his team wins the header defending the corner.

The rain has stopped as the corner is taken; the Impi centre back jumps high and firmly heads the ball out of the danger in the box.

"Get out! Get out, boys!" shouts the commanding centre back.

TJ reads the situation perfectly as the ball bounces directly towards his feet. Normally he would hold up the ball and wait for one of his quicker team mates to start a counter attack.

He looks up and sees his own winger shouting for the ball but he immediately decides to turn and run with the ball instead. He will either be told to never return if he gets tackled, or he will beat the opposition defender and show what he is really capable of doing. The risk is worth the reward, he feels.

Turning sharply, he gets his head up and runs at speed towards the opposition defender, approaching him from the half way line. He continuously shifts his body, trying to put the defender off balance. The same defender who tackled him earlier in the match is trying his best to jockey TJ.

TJ is driving with the ball, keeping it close to his boot as the tired opponent tracks back on his heels.

He runs the ball all the way into the Soweto Giants half. The defender now has no other choice but to make a tackle to stop the ball from making its way any closer to his team's box.

He slides in hard.

TJ executes two perfectly timed step overs and adds a burst of speed that takes him past the desperate lunge of the opponent.

The noise grows louder on the stands. The Impi bench begin standing up.

The Soweto Giants full back covering his team mate now shifts, needing to try and stop the marauding TJ.

As the fullback approaches and lunges in, TJ does a 360 degree turn, spectacularly going past the defender and accelerating as fast as he can towards the box.

"Yoh, yoh, yoh, they hit him with a three-sixty, bra!" shouts one of the players on the bench.

The excitement grows even more on the Impi bench and amongst the supporters as that skill takes TJ into the Soweto Giants box, unmarked and left with nothing but the opposition goalkeeper to beat.

It is a one on one situation. He quickly decides he is going to shoot across the onrushing keeper, who is widening his arms to narrow the angle.

TJ pulls his leg back and suddenly feels the wrath of another player's studs grazing down the back of his leg yet again.

He stretches out his arms as he falls firmly on the muddy ground with no way of staying on his feet. An opposition defender has just made a last ditch attempt to stop him from scoring.

The Impi players protest for a penalty as the Soweto Giants players plead their team mate's innocence.

TJ stands up, rubs the back of his leg and begins walking uncomfortably, feeling the after effects of the tackle. He suddenly notices the referee pointing to the penalty spot and then gives the opposition defender a straight red card for a professional foul.

The captain of the team pats TJ on the back and picks up the ball lying on the ground to take the penalty.

TJ immediately snatches the ball out of his older team mate's hands without thinking.

"I won the penalty, I will take it," he says adamantly.

The captain pushes him and tries to grab the ball out of his hands but TJ refuses to give it to him.

"Leave him! Let him take it!" shouts the Impi head coach with pure rage in his voice.

The captain does as he is told, allowing TJ to have the ball.

He then walks past bumping his shoulder against TJ's, looking at him with disgust in his eyes.

TJ knows what he just did was wrong but he feels it is the wrong choice for the right reason. He will take responsibility for his actions and accept any consequences that come from them, but he needs to prove himself.

He puts the ball on the white muddy spot and then takes a few steps backwards.

He feels he has earned the right to take the penalty with the run he made, but now the pressure suddenly takes hold of him as he realizes what he is doing. The opposition goalkeeper is clapping and shouting loudly, trying his best to put TJ off. Mental doubts creep into the forefront of TJ's mind.

What if I miss, he thinks. *I have never scored a penalty in a game before, how am I going to score a winning goal? If I miss this I will definitely be told to leave. I'm not good enough; I must just accept it. I'm going to have to go back to Rustenburg when I miss.*

He shakes his head, suddenly realizing where he is as he takes a look around him, stopping his thoughts with a deep breath.

He remembers the three Cs the mechanic taught him when taking penalties.

The referee blows the whistle for TJ to take the penalty.

There is dead silence around the ground. The crowd is holding its breath, the players readying themselves to pounce on the rebound as he looks the energetic goalkeeper in the eyes.

He blows the air out of his lungs and then trots purposefully towards the ball.

He strikes the ball with venom, using the laces of his right boot. It takes flight.

The Soweto Giants goalkeeper dives towards the ball, stretching out his finger tips.

The ball beats the keeper and flies straight into the top right hand corner of the goals. The sound of the wet ball thrashing against the white net can be heard for the briefest moment.

There is then an eruption of noise as the Impi supporters scream and jump uncontrollably. Their bench celebrates wildly, running onto the field, joining the players on the pitch sprinting towards TJ.

Every player bombards him, screaming loudly. He smiles widely at his team mates in pure ecstasy.

They eventually let him go and he immediately looks towards the crowd. There are smiles on every Impi supporters face. He fist pumps passionately towards Marley and the rest of the fans going wild in the stands.

"Come on!" he shouts proudly towards them. A moment he will never forget. He then jogs back to the halfway line with the rest of his team to wait for the opposition to take their kick off.

Soweto Giants kick off and the referee immediately blows his whistle to signal the end of the game.

TJ smiles and celebrates putting his hands in the air; closing his eyes in gratitude of the moment.

The Impi Football Club reserve team has just won the friendly game against their bitter rivals.

There are smiles on each of the young Impi player's and supporter's faces. TJ immediately looks for his captain. "Sorry I did that. I never meant to show any disrespect, I just really needed to show what I can do," he says after finding him in the crowd of players.

"Don't worry. I understand why you did it. Just be happy you scored because if you'd missed there would be problems."

TJ nods his head as they embrace each other with a hand shake before going to shake the hands of the opposition.

The sports scientist instructs them to take a jog to cool down and the players run to applaud and thank their fans for their support as the few Impi fans that came to the game clap in return and then begin exiting the facility singing and dancing.

After stretching and cooling down they return to the dressing room together, each player rubbing TJ's head or tapping his leg passionately to congratulate him.

"You did it, brother!" shouts Bongani sitting next to him, tapping TJ's leg ecstatically.

The Impi head coach walks in and looks around at his upbeat team; an entirely different atmosphere to half time.

"That was a good work out for most of you. Well done on the result but I am not happy with the performance. You showed good hunger and fighting spirit, however there are things we need to fix in training this week. Some of you showed me you are ready for more minutes on the pitch while others showed me they are not. Everybody must be back here at training tomorrow for a light recovery and video analysis session."

The players drink water, say thank you to their coaches and most of them head to the showers to wash off the mud and freshen up.

TJ waits for every player and coaching staff member to move away from the head coach before approaching him to find out what will happen to him from here.

The head coach shakes the last player's hand and then looks at TJ who is standing alone.

The sun is beginning to creep through the grey clouds as it shines through the large dressing room window.

The head coach stares at him in silence and TJ looks back, not knowing what to expect.

"I hope you realize you had three team mates open the entire time you ran with the ball. We share the ball in this team, boy," says the head coach.

"I know, sir."

"Then you disrespected a team mate who has been at the club for over three years when you have only been on the pitch wearing our shirt for less than thirty minutes!"

TJ looks to the ground anticipating that he might not have made the right choices on the field according to the head coach. However, he knows if he could rewind time and play the match all over again, he would make the exact same choices, so he will have no regrets.

"However, I do understand why you did what you did, but if you ever do it again you will never step foot onto a field with an Impi Football Club shirt on again. Do you understand me?" says the head coach assertively.

What did he just say, TJ thinks as a sudden wave of excitement moves through his body.

"I understand, sir," he replies, trying his best to seem calm.

"Good. Meet me in my office after training tomorrow."

"Okay, sir."

"Tomorrow you find out if you will be staying at this club or moving on."

Sunday

It is the final day of TJ's trial at Impi Football Club.

He is getting to know each of the players in the team but he hasn't got too comfortable as he knows he might need to go on a trial elsewhere if Impi feel they do not need him.

The players who played the match do a recovery session involving lots of light jogging and stretching. After the light session, a few players go for massages or ice baths and then go through to a video analysis session. It is TJ's first ever video analysis session and he enjoys watching himself on the field, especially reliving the match winning penalty on the projector screen.

The game is analysed from the team's perspective and each individual player's perspective. Players are then told what they should be working on in training this coming week. It is about identifying strengths and weaknesses in the team as well as each individual player.

After the video analysis session is complete, the players leave to most likely go spend time with their friends or families.

TJ's two week trial has officially ended as he walks towards the head coach's office, not feeling any form of nervousness. He has done all he can and there will be no regrets if he does not get told he is wanted by the club.

He enters into the head coach's small and quaint office. There is a small, dark brown desk with a laptop and the name Mr Sifiso Amandla written on a golden steel rectangular plaque.

Mr Amandla is staring intensely at the laptop, sitting comfortably in his chair. There is a chair opposite him. Also on the desk are photos of his family and on the walls there are team photographs and posters with inspirational sayings on them.

The one poster looks hand written and it says:

If you are playing football for yourself, stop playing

Another poster TJ notices says:

FORM IS TEMPORARY, CLASS IS PERMANENT

Mr Amandla notices TJ looking at the poster.

"You like that one?" he asks.

"Yes, sir."

"There is nothing more potent and exciting than a footballer in form but as the quote says, 'form is temporary'. Class is that something special in a player that never changes. As a coach I need to know the difference between class and form. I need to put an in form player in the team at the right time. A classy player can be relied upon all year long but, if you like quotes, have a look at my favourite one."

Mr Amandla pulls a wooden plaque out of a drawer from underneath his table and it says:

If you want to go fast, go alone.
If you want to go far then go together

"I like them all, sir," says TJ, also noticing a few organized pieces of paper and the famous 'Training Notes' book on the desk. Mr Amandla puts the plaque back into his drawer.

"Take a seat, Rustenburg. You're making me uncomfortable."

TJ sits down as Mr Amandla looks at his computer again.

"I just want to tell you how grateful I am for the opportunity you have given me to train over these past two weeks, sir. I have learned so much and, whether you keep me or not, I am very grateful you gave me a chance to show what I am capable of."

Mr Amandla looks away from his computer screen and takes his reading glasses off, putting them on the pile of papers lying on his desk. He then looks directly at TJ.

"We need balance in our lives," he begins saying. "Getting good school marks or working hard at your job, spending time with friends, spending time with family, doing what you love, trying to do everything in moderation every single day. Football is the same. Just like you need balance in your life, our team needs balance. It needs to have an equal balance of youth, players in their prime and experienced players. It needs to be balanced in attack, defence and transition. It needs to be balanced left, right and centrally. I do not want a player who is going to upset this balance. I would rather have my best eleven that work well together than my eleven best players all trying to make things work. Do you understand what I am trying to say?"

"Yes, sir. You would rather have a team that works well together than the best players in the country all playing in one team."

Mr Amandla nods his head as TJ anticipates his temporary head coach is about to tell him that he does not want him to unbalance his reserve team.

"I need eleven players on the field who are willing to run for ninety minutes and work until they cannot run or work anymore. Players need to be hungry for success; hungry to be the best. Eleven players working as a unit is far more valuable than eleven players who are world class individuals. It is like a metal chain. If one part of the chain is weak, then the entire chain is weak. A football team is the same: it is only as strong as its weakest link."

TJ is already beginning to accept that he needs to find another club to trial at. He takes a deep breath to stay calm as the head coach looks him in the eyes now.

TJ looks back with conviction and strength.

"When I look at you, I see a young man who is willing to sweat blood and tears for the badge on the front of his chest and that is what it is all about. About having pride and passion when you put on that shirt and knowing the privilege you have of playing for that badge. It is about doing whatever you can for the guy next to you wearing the same badge on his heart."

TJ feels a sudden surge of extraordinary emotions flowing into the pit his stomach.

Is this really happening? It sounds like he might actually want to keep me, he thinks.

The head coach pulls out a small pile of pages in his drawer and puts them firmly on the dark brown desk.

"I want you to lead my attack for the rest of the season, Thulani. I need a leader from the front and a player that puts the ball into the back of the net! I know you are a young man but age is just a number. If you are good enough, you are old enough. Potential and experience need to work together."

TJ can barely believe what he has just heard. "You want me to lead your attack?" he asks, somewhat stunned.

Mr Amandla smiles noticing the shock on his face.

"I knew from the moment you told me you were different from other players that you have what it takes. I have been involved in this game for a long time and there are very few players who have the confidence to run through those gates and refuse to take no for an answer. It is not just that inner steel and resilience that I like about you. Technically, you are very gifted too. You keep the game simple and you do all the basics of the game correctly. There is a special art to keeping things simple. You make quick, intelligent decisions, you're fast, you're strong and you have some wonderful skill. There are still many things for you to work on, but you are definitely ready for this level and we would love to have you as a part of our team for the remainder of the season. The window is still open to register players. So my final question to you Thulani... is this a team you see a bright future with?"

TJ does not have to think twice. "Yes, sir!" he answers immediately.

Mr Amandla then hands the pile of papers to him.

It is a contract offer.

He gives TJ a pen. "Here is our contract offer, just sign in the designated areas. It is a two-year contract whereby you will be given free boots each season and you will be earning ten thousand Rand a month. Not a terrible salary for an eighteen year old doing what he loves, is it?"

TJ smiles. "No, it's not, sir."

He scans through the contract, pretending to read it, as all he wants to do is get to the end of it and sign on the dotted line. This is a moment he has been dreaming about his entire life.

He signs on the pages he needs to without hesitation, stands up to shake Mr Amandla's hand and says, "Thanks again, sir. I will do everything I can to repay the faith you have shown in me. I won't let you down."

"You've earned it, but don't thank me yet. The hard work begins now. It is easy to get a contract, but it is harder to keep it. I'm looking forward to working with you."

TJ nods his head. "I understand," he says as he walks out of the office feeling as if he is a hundred feet tall.

He waits until he is far enough from the office.

"Yessssssssss! Come on!" suddenly bellows out from his voice.

He has done it.

There is an incredible sense of joy surging through his entire body. His heart is beating out of his chest and he cannot contain the wide smile right across his face.

All the months and years of hard work, sacrifice, self doubt and perseverance have led me to this incredible moment, he thinks. *My first professional contract: I can't believe it. I worked an entire year to buy new boots and now I will be getting new boots for free each year. Mama and the mechanic would be so proud.*

He begins thinking about all those days he spent focusing on the large grey rock, the hard, torturous physical training he needed to push through and how hard he had to work in the technical training sessions at the petrol station.

He thinks about the mechanic.

"I owe him everything. None of this would have been possible without him," he says, not caring who hears.

The life lessons and football lessons he learned at the petrol station have served him well.

He takes a deep breath; reminding himself to live in the present moment as he walks towards a white taxi feeling incredibly proud of what he has achieved.

"It's time for me to show the football world what I am really made of."

EPILOGUE

Four weeks since signing on the dotted line, TJ has found his own small place to rent in Soweto. He clothes and feeds himself with his very own money each month.

Many people do jobs every day of their lives that they do not love, it takes a courageous soul to persevere when things get hard and I am very grateful to be earning money doing something I love every day.

TJ writes this in his diary before leaving his bedroom at the Impi Football Club training complex.

He has shown great form in the number 27 jersey over the past few weeks and his presence has brought more goals to a goal-shy team. He has scored three goals for his new club already and the club's supporters are beginning to enjoy watching their new number 27 leading their reserve team attack each week. His goals have been made up of a variety; one header, one volley and one tap in.

His team mates are impressed with his intelligent movement and the new options he is giving the team in attack. His team mates are getting to know him better, talking to him more and showing him respect. TJ has earned their trust. He was even asked to dance and sing in front of the entire team after he signed his contract as an initiation. He is luckily not the worst dancer in the world with some dancing rhythm inherited from his mother.

The opposition they have played in the past few weeks were in the middle of the table but next on the calendar is a trip back to Rustenburg for TJ, to face his old club, Rustenburg Rovers.

Rustenburg Rovers are first on the reserve team log and Impi are now in second place, breathing down their necks.

There are three games left in the season and Impi Football Club need to win this game if they have any chance of catching Rustenburg Rovers for the reserve league title. The winners of the reserve league are given a free trip to Holland to play in an international tournament, which gives the players some much needed exposure on the international stage.

The team have breakfast together and then leave the training complex together, travelling by bus to Rustenburg. Their kick off time is 13:00.

TJ sits in the middle of the bus with Bongani, looking out the window at the same terrain he drove past in the blue and white bus just over two months ago; remembering how he felt travelling to Gauteng with hope in his heart.

He thinks about his mother, desperately hoping she is doing well. He does not know if she has bought herself a cell phone yet so he has been sending her letters to inform her of his progress. He hasn't received any letters in return but he let her know that he would be playing in Rustenburg today.

He is hoping he will have time to see the mechanic. He spoke to the old man on the phone and asked him if he would attend the match. The mechanic said he would try his best to be there.

His nostalgic thoughts do not remain long in his head as he starts preparing himself mentally for the upcoming match. He clears his mind and simply watches how each of his team mates are behaving on the bus. He then looks down and smiles proudly, enjoying the fact that he has an Impi Football Club badge perched on his chest. There are millions of children around the country who all dream of being in his position and he feels very privileged and honoured to be wearing it.

He will most likely be playing against some of his old team mates today and he is looking forward to seeing their faces again as well as exchanging stories of how things have been going in each of their lives.

Neo, the creative attacking midfielder who is regarded as genius by the team, looks over from the seat just across from Bongani. Neo stays in the same room as TJ before games, as requested by the head coach because of their positions on the field.

"So, how do you feel about facing your old team today TJ? Do you have any tips for us?"

"Not really, and I feel chilled, Neo. It's just another game and I'll try my best to help the team win the three points. I have no idea what to expect but if they are ahead of us on the log they can't be too bad. It will be cool seeing some of my old team mates today."

"Might be cool for you to see them but I'm hoping we give your old team mates a proper beating!"

"Let's hope so! It's a good thing you are at the peak of your powers at the moment. It's going to help."

Neo smiles at TJ and then continues his conversation with the team mate next to him.

"So, you're not nervous to face your old team then?" asks Bongani.

"Of course not! I can't wait to show them how much I've improved."

TJ has not seen Katlego or Zavi since the day he got cut from the Rustenburg Rovers team. He does not hold any resentment towards the academy as it was probably justified that they did not choose him based on the footballer he was all those months ago.

There have been many things that have changed since then and he is certain his old friends will not recognize the person and the footballer he has become.

He never changed as a person. His football ability and potential never changed either, it was just unlocked and shown to him by the mechanic.

There are red leaves on the driveway at the Phokeng sports campus as the bus pulls up at the front gate. The bus then parks by the field and TJ notices the grass is beginning to turn yellow again as the summer months begin to surrender themselves to autumn. It is almost a year ago since he was on this same field as a Rustenburg Rovers player scoring goals for their team.

The players get off the bus and, as TJ steps down onto the ground, he is suddenly hit by a whirlwind of emotions.

He sees the mechanic waiting at the entrance of the field looking out at the dying grass.

"Coach!" shouts TJ with pure excitement. The mechanic turns around and smiles widely at his former football student.

"TJ!" he shouts with gusto.

"I can't believe you've already gotten older and uglier, sir!"

"It must be all the stress you put me through those six months you were with me!"

They laugh as TJ hugs him, incredibly happy to see the old man again.

"You did it son, you did it!" says the mechanic, patting TJ's back passionately.

"I couldn't have done it without you, coach!"

The mechanic lets go and smiles proudly at TJ.

"I don't think I've been this excited for a football match in years champ."

"Well let's hope we can entertain you then today!"

"Let's hope so. Enjoy yourself, TJ. I will come see you after the final whistle."

"Sounds good," says TJ, shaking the mechanic's hand firmly. He then walks to the dressing room with a spring in his step.

"Who was that?" asks Bongani as TJ sits down next to him.

"My secret weapon," he replies with a smile.

TJ changes into his kit with the rest of the players and then puts his shin pads and Copa Mundial boots on. There is local music being played by one of the players as they all get dressed. Each player has their own superstitions and pre-match routines before a game. TJ does not have any superstitions.

As soon as everyone is ready, the players exit the dressing room and begin warming up together. Mr Amandla has already told the players who is in the starting line up and TJ is starting up front for the fourth game in a row.

They do their rhythmic dancing routine to get their blood pumping and their bodies moving.

TJ looks over to the opposition warm up and recognizes some of his old team mates. He sees Zavi and Katlego, but they do not see him. He also looks to analyse the opposition, to find out the height of their defenders and goalkeeper as well as identify which players look slow or fast in the warm up.

There is a small crowd gathered around the field as the 13:00 kick off looms. TJ looks over to the stands and is suddenly stunned and shocked by what he sees.

He stops what he is doing.

He sees his mother entering into the venue. Tears immediately form in his eyes. He has missed her more than he knew.

She puts her handbag down and sees her son in the beaming bright Orange and Black Impi Football Club kit. She waves at him with tears in her eyes.

TJ waves back and smiles. "I will come to you after the game!" he shouts loudly with joyful emotion and she nods her head.

TJ feels incredibly motivated, as if he needed any added motivation for today's fixture.

After the warm up is complete, both teams head to their respective dressing rooms before kick-off.

None of TJ's former team mates have seen him. He does not have any expectations for the game other than simply enjoying himself, hoping he can create memories and bring joy to everyone watching today.

He sits down on the bench in the dressing room and breathes deeply a few times to focus himself. He has seen the mechanic, his old team mates and his mother, but still manages to keep calm as he tightens his boot laces, waiting for the pre-match team talk from Mr Amandla.

The assistant coach explains to each player their individual responsibilities on the field. He walks around the dressing room giving each player a short tactical talk to remind them of what their duties are when attacking and defending on the field. The sports scientist checks for any issues and asks how each player is feeling physically.

Mr Amandla walks in and a complete silence falls upon the dressing room. Each player's eyes are fixed entirely on him as they await his team talk for a very important fixture.

Mr Amandla takes off his Impi cap, rubs his hairless scalp calmly with his right hand and looks at the players intensely.

"You all deserve to be here today. Every one of you has something special. If you did not deserve to be wearing this shirt, you wouldn't be," he says with conviction.

He then reminds his team about the opposition's strengths and weaknesses and how they can use their own strengths to expose their weaknesses.

"Now I want you all to focus," he says sharply.

The dressing room is silent.

"When you step onto a football field, nothing else matters. You focus on football and football only. No matter what problems you have in the world, when your boot makes contact with that field today, football is the only thing that matters. The first ten minutes are vital. Let them know immediately who they are up against. We keep that ball today! I want the opposition to be on their hands and knees, begging and pleading for that ball! Begging to touch it just for a few minutes! We must not let them touch it! When they come off that field today they must say that it was the longest ninety minutes of their entire lives! Three years from now they will remember the day they played against this Impi Football Club team and they are never going to want to experience it ever again! If by some miracle they do get the ball today, you hunt! You hunt them down and you press! You press together! I want you hungry for that ball. They do not get a second to breathe or think when they get that ball! Do your hear me? We fight for each other out there today!"

TJ feels his blood pumping as the energy in the dressing room rises frantically.

"Good luck, gentlemen!" he then shouts, ending his team talk. The team begin clapping their hands thunderously, shouting and screaming excitedly.

"Come on, boys!" is a loud shout from one of the players.

The atmosphere in the dressing room is electric. The entire team is fired up and raring to go, like a pack of hungry wolves wanting to be let out to hunt.

The coaching team leaves the room and the captain, Alpheus, huddles the team together.

"Talk to each other out there, help each other, gents. We are all brothers on that field today, a team of brothers all fighting for the same badge. The man who sheds his sweat and puts his body on the line for the team mates next to him out there today will forever be my brother."

The team nod their heads excitedly at the captain's words and then all go down on one knee to pray. The captain prays and after the prayer a large amount of excitement and energy is produced once more as the entire team begins jumping and chanting in the dressing room.

They then storm out into the roar of the crowd and the bright sunshine. Goose bumps settle onto TJ's skin.

The shirt with the number 27 and Sibeko on the back of it is hit by the sunlight as TJ runs onto the field.

Both sets of supporters are extremely noisy as the Impi captain wins the toss and chooses to take the kick off.

TJ jogs to the centre circle to start the game seeing Katlego and Zavi out the corner of his eye; they recognize him in return. There is total surprise on their faces.

He looks to his mother and the mechanic in the stands. Their eyes are focused entirely on him.

He blows the air out of his lungs and a gentle smile then appears on his face.

"One touch, one pass and one moment at a time," he says, looking up at the referee and waiting for the whistle to blow.

ABOUT THE AUTHOR

KEAGAN RAY HERTZ

Named after Liverpool players playing on the day of my birth, it is no secret that football has been in my blood since that rainy day in December 1994. The beautiful game has been on my mind every single day from the earliest times I can remember.

I began coaching young children at the ripe age of fifteen, falling in love with helping them improve their football ability and their lives. Nine years later and I have worked at some superb amateur clubs, some great academies and have run a successful soccer school. I have been extremely blessed to work with some wonderful minds, some fantastic players and some incredible people who are uncompromisingly driven and determined to enhance the game in this country. If it were not for the faith and trust placed in me by these people, this book would never have been written. The lessons taught by them and learned through personal experience have been well received.

Dreaming of one day managing a top club, I began my relentless pursuit of gaining knowledge, experience and expertise in the game of football. I observed, wrote, listened, studied, examined and sacrificed much to the desire of becoming the greatest football coach or manager on the planet. Little did I know that life was preparing me for the privileged task of writing this book. I never felt coaching was enough for me: I've always felt there was more I could be doing for the game and the people involved in it.

I want to give back to this extraordinary game; a game that has brought me so much joy and happiness throughout my life thus far. I truly hope you enjoy reading the book as much as I enjoyed writing it.

My true hope, however, is that you find peace in this beautiful journey we call 'life'.

All my love.

Keagan Ray Hertz, author of A ball in the mud